My eyes looked past all the conventional hardware to a curious device beyond them, directly in front of Butler Library and nearly hidden by overgrown hedges. I couldn't have named it—it looked like an octopus making love to a console stereo—but it obviously didn't come with the landscaping. Carlson was using Butler for his base of operations. God knew what the device was for, but a man without his adenoids in a city full of Muskies and hungry German shepherds would not have built it further from home than could be helped. This was the place.

I drew in a great chest- and belly-full of air, and my grin hurt my cheeks. I held up my rifle and watched my hands. Rock steady.

Carlson, you murdering bastard, I thought, *this is it. The human race has found you, and its Hand is near. A few more breaths and you die violently, old man, like a harmless cat in a smokeshop window, like an eight-year-old boy on a Harlem sidewalk, like a planetwide civilization you thought you could improve on. Get you ready.*

I moved forward.

—From "By Any Other Name"

BAEN BOOKS by Spider Robinson

By Any Other Name
The Star Dancers (with Jeanne Robinson)
Starmind (with Jeanne Robinson) (forthcoming)
Deathkiller
Lifehouse
User Friendly
Telempath (forthcoming)

BY ANY OTHER NAME

SPIDER ROBINSON

BY ANY OTHER NAME

This is a work of fiction. All the characters and events portrayed in this book are fictional, and any resemblance to real people or incidents is purely coincidental.

A Baen Books Original

Baen Publishing Enterprises
P.O. Box 1403
Riverdale, NY 10471
www.baen.com

ISBN: 0-671-31974-4

Cover art by Richard Martin
Interior art by Rocky Coffin

First printing, February 2001

Distributed by Simon & Schuster
1230 Avenue of the Americas
New York, NY 10020

Production by Windhaven Press, Auburn, NH
Printed in the United States of America

CONTENTS

Foreword 1

Melancholy Elephants 7

Half an Oaf 29

Antinomy 61

Satan's Children 101

Apogee 147

No Renewal 153

Tin Ear 161

In the Olden Days 171

Silly Weapons 179

Nobody Likes to Be Lonely 183

"If This Goes On—" 231

True Minds 233

Common Sense 255

Chronic Offender.. 263

High Infidelity 291

Rubber Soul 305

The Crazy Years 315

By Any Other Name 351

For my friends Ted and Diana Powell
—and for Ben Bova,
without whom all this would not have
been necessary . . .

FOREWORD

Perhaps a story collection should be allowed to speak for itself.

That was my original intention; I submitted this book to Toni Weisskopf without a foreword. The basic plan was simple: to gather all the short stories I've written that aren't already collected in *User Friendly* (Baen 1998), with a little bit of nonfiction for lagniappe. So the assembly process was not onerous. Basically I pulled manuscripts from the trunk, glanced at their titles, nodded nostalgically, and added them to the pile. Deciding their order was a no-brainer: begin and end with a Hugo-winner, and in between those, alternate humorous and serious stories. Writing a foreword seemed superfluous.

Then a few days ago the galley proofs arrived, and I sat down and read them through, and here I am writing a foreword after all.

1

I have not written short fiction for some time now. Novels pay *so* much better that, without consciously planning to, I just stopped getting short story ideas a few years back. So I hadn't read any of those stories particularly recently. Some I had not read in twenty years or more. As I rediscovered them now, unexpected patterns emerged.

I'd begun the galleys firmly resolved to do nothing but correct typos. I was determined to make no retroactive improvements to these stories—to let them stand as they first came into the world, flaws and all. But I found I kept wanting to push dates forward. I was rather startled to realize how many of these stories are now chronologically outdated. Written, in some cases, in the early 1970s, they tended to be set in the "distant future" of twenty or thirty years later. I'm most comfortable in that range: the further ahead into the future I speculate, the less confident I am about my own guesses—and if I'm dubious, how am I to convince a reader? But history has begun to overtake me.

I was not dismayed—or even surprised—at how often my guesses about the future had turned out to be dead wrong. I've never claimed or wished to be a prophet; I write about possible futures, and strive for plausible ones.

But I *was* somewhat surprised at just *how* my speculations were wrong: over and over, it seems, I was too optimistic. I don't mean that all the stories you're about to read are upbeat, by any means. But most of the futures I imagined were, in retrospect, at least a little better than the one we actually got. At least more technologically advanced.

I find I'm proud of that.

I only pray I can manage to sustain that attitude

of positive expectation, that tendency toward benign delusion, through the *next* quarter-century of tumult and shenanigans. And infect as many other people with it as possible.

Because unconscious expectations are *so* important. We need all the Placebo we can get. It's been shown again and again: if you introduce a new teacher to a perfectly average class of kids, and tell him they're the Advanced group, by the end of the year *they will be*. This real year 2000 may not be quite as advanced as some of the ones I envisioned for entertainment purposes . . . but it is, I think, a far nicer one than most average citizens living in the 1970s or 1980s would have believed possible. (Just for a start: no Cold War.) Optimistic science fiction may just have had something to do with that. As my friend Stephen Gaskin once said, "What you put your attention on prospers."

Case in point: the title story of this book.

It was, if memory serves, the third story I ever tried to write for money. I'd sent my first one to the most popular magazine in the field, *Analog*—talk about irrational optimism—and miraculously, it sold. But the second, set in the same tavern, had not sold there . . . or anywhere else. Then from somewhere came "By Any Other Name," and I just *knew* this one was going to sell. Perhaps it's weird to call it an optimistic story, since it posits the total collapse of technological civilization—but it also suggests that humanity will ultimately survive just about any collapse. In any event, it was a much more complex and ambitious story than anything I'd ever tried before, and I certainly sent it off with high hopes.

It was bounced by every market in science fiction.

More than a dozen rejections, beginning with *Analog* and ending underneath the bottom of the barrel. The last editor on the list lost the damn thing for several months . . . then rejected it . . . then lost it again. (I was so green, the only other copy in existence was the handwritten first draft.)

By the time I finally got it back, I had written several other stories, and not one of *them* had sold, either. I suspect the only reason I even took the manuscript out of the envelope was so it would burn better in the fireplace. But my own opening sentence caught me. I ended up reading the damn thing all the way through one more time—

—and by God, I still liked it. All thirteen of those editors, I decided on the spot, were *wrong*.

So I rejected the rejections. I mailed the story, unchanged, to Ben Bova at *Analog* a second time. It was a perfect act of irrational optimism, of benign delusion.

You guessed it: he bought it this time.

But it wasn't just a sale. "By Any Other Name" was my first Analog cover story. (Jack Gaughan's splendid painting for that cover hangs in my home today; God rest his generous soul.) It won my first AnLab, the monthly *Analog* reader's poll. A year later it won me my first Hugo Award from readers worldwide. It was a career-maker. It became the nucleus of my first novel, *Telempath*. Most important of all, it was one of a pair of stories which persuaded a young woman named Jeanne, in spite of her better judgment, to let me court her . . .

So maybe that's one reason why I'm optimistic by policy. It seems to be working for me.

(Epilogue I can't resist: over a decade later, I got up the nerve to ask Ben if he realized he'd rejected a Hugo-winning story the first time he saw it. Oh sure, he said, I had to—no choice. How come? I asked.

(He gave me a pitying look. "Spider, that was an election year—remember? And then you expect me to buy a story where the alien villains are basically giant killer farts, named 'Musky'?" He shook his head emphatically. "Nixon that.")

In that spirit of reckless optimism, I've adulterated this collection of short fiction with a pinch of non-fiction.

One evening in 1996 Jeanne and I were strolling through town with our friend Shannon Rupp, then the dance critic for Vancouver's alternative weekly *The Georgia Straight*, and as is my custom, I was shooting my mouth off. An airliner had just fallen into the sea, and all the media believed it had either been terrorist sabotage, or just possibly a covered-up accidental missile launch from a U.S. Navy destroyer. I was pontificating on why both theories had to be hogwash . . . and Shannon interrupted. "Write that all down," she said. And do what with it, I asked. "Send it to *The Globe and Mail*," she said. "I'll bet they buy it."

Well, that was just silly. *The Globe and Mail* was Canada's national newspaper, its journal of record, the Grey Lady of the North. What would they want with the unsolicited opinions of an American-born science fiction writer who lived about as far from Toronto as a Canadian resident can get, and whose most recent journalistic credentials—lame ones—were almost thirty years old?

But Shannon finally bullied me into trying it. And Warren Clements bought the piece, and asked for more, and that's how I became an Op-Ed columnist—like nearly everything else I've accomplished in my life so far: by accident.

I've provided herein some samples of the column that ran in *The Globe and Mail* every three weeks from 1996–99 under the running title, "The Crazy Years." If you don't care for fact—or at least, for opinions about facts—with your fiction, by all means skip over them. If they do catch your interest, as of this writing I'm still producing a column a month for *The Globe and Mail*, and two columns a month for David Gerrold and Ben Bova's new cybersite *Galaxy Online* (www.galaxyonline.com).

And now on to the fiction. After all this talk of optimism, naturally the first story in line, which won the 1983 Hugo for Short Story, is one of the gloomier prognostications I've ever made. Oh well. The year "Melancholy Elephants" is set in has *not* arrived yet— maybe this time the real future will turn out brighter than the one I dreamed.

One can hope . . .

—*British Columbia*
18 September, 2000

MELANCHOLY ELEPHANTS

This story is dedicated to
Virginia Heinlein

She sat zazen, concentrating on not concentrating, until it was time to prepare for the appointment. Sitting *seemed* to produce the usual serenity, put everything in perspective. Her hand did not tremble as she applied her make-up; tranquil features looked back at her from the mirror. She was mildly surprised, in fact, at just how calm she was, until she got out of the hotel elevator at the garage level and the mugger made his play. She killed him instead of disabling him. Which was obviously not a measured, balanced action—the official fuss and paperwork could

7

make her late. Annoyed at herself, she stuffed the
corpse under a shiny new Westinghouse roadable
whose owner she knew to be in Luna, and continued on to her own car. This would have to be squared
later, and it would cost. No help for it—she fought
to regain at least the semblance of tranquility as her
car emerged from the garage and turned north.

Nothing must interfere with this meeting, or with
her role in it.

*Dozens of man-years and God knows how many
dollars,* she thought, *funnelling down to perhaps a
half hour of conversation. All the effort, all the hope.
Insignificant on the scale of the Great Wheel, of
course . . . but when you balance it all on a half hour
of talk, it's like balancing a stereo cartridge on a
needlepoint: It only takes a gram or so of weight to
wear out a piece of diamond. I must be harder than
diamond.*

Rather than clear a window and watch Washington,
D.C. roll by beneath her car, she turned on the television. She absorbed and integrated the news, on the
chance that there might be some late-breaking item
she could turn to her advantage in the conversation
to come; none developed. Shortly the car addressed
her: "Grounding, ma'am. I.D. eyeball request." When
the car landed she cleared and then opened her window, presented her pass and I.D. to a Marine in dress
blues, and was cleared at once. At the Marine's direction she re-opaqued the window and surrendered
control of her car to the house computer, and when
the car parked itself and powered down she got out
without haste. A man she knew was waiting to meet
her, smiling.

"Dorothy, it's good to see you again."

"Hello, Phillip. Good of you to meet me."

"You look lovely this evening."

"You're too kind."

She did not chafe at the meaningless pleasantries. She needed Phil's support, or she might. But she did reflect on how many, many sentences have been worn smooth with use, rendered meaningless by centuries of repetition. It was by no means a new thought.

"If you'll come with me, he'll see you at once."

"Thank you, Phillip." She wanted to ask what the old man's mood was, but knew it would put Phil in an impossible position.

"I rather think your luck is good; the old man seems to be in excellent spirits tonight."

She smiled her thanks, and decided that if and when Phil got around to making his pass she would accept him.

The corridors through which he led her then were broad and high and long; the building dated back to a time of cheap power. Even in Washington, few others would have dared to live in such an energy-wasteful environment. The extremely spare decor reinforced the impression created by the place's dimensions: bare space from carpet to ceiling, broken approximately every forty meters by some exquisitely simple object d'art of at least a megabuck's value, appropriately displayed. An unadorned, perfect, white porcelain bowl, over a thousand years old, on a rough cherrywood pedestal. An arresting color photograph of a snow-covered country road, silk-screened onto stretched silver foil; the time of day changed as one walked past it. A crystal globe, a meter in diameter, within which danced a hologram of the immortal Shara Drummond; since she had ceased performing before the advent of holo technology, this had to be an expensive computer reconstruction. A small sealed glassite chamber containing the first vacuum-sculpture ever made, Nakagawa's legendary Starstone. A visitor in no hurry could study an object at leisure, then walk quite a distance in undistracted contemplation before encountering another. A visitor in a hurry, like Dorothy, would not *quite* encounter peripherally astonishing stimuli often enough to get the trick of filtering them out. Each tugged at her attention, intruded on her thoughts; they were distracting both intrinsically and as a reminder of the measure of their owner's wealth. To approach this man in his own home, whether at leisure or in haste, was to be humbled. She knew the effect was intentional, and could not transcend it; this irritated her, which irritated her. She struggled for detachment.

At the end of the seemingly endless corridors was an elevator. Phillip handed her into it, punched a floor button, without giving her a chance to see which one, and stepped back into the doorway. "Good luck, Dorothy."

"Thank you, Phillip. Any topics to be sure and avoid?"

"Well . . . don't bring up hemorrhoids."

"I didn't know one could."

He smiled. "Are we still on for lunch Thursday?"

"Unless you'd rather make it dinner."

One eyebrow lifted. "And breakfast?"

She appeared to consider it. "Brunch," she decided. He half-bowed and stepped back.

The elevator door closed and she forgot Phillip's existence.

Sentient beings are innumerable; I vow to save them all. The deluding passions are limitless; I vow to extinguish them all. The truth is limitless; I—

The elevator door opened again, truncating the

Vow of the Bodhisattva. She had not felt the elevator stop—yet she knew that she must have descended at least a hundred meters. She left the elevator.

The room was larger than she had expected; nonetheless the big powered chair dominated it easily. The chair also seemed to dominate—at least visually—its occupant. A misleading impression, as he dominated all this massive home, everything in it and, to a great degree, the country in which it stood. But he did not look like much.

A scent symphony was in progress, the cinnamon passage of Bulachevski's "Childhood." It happened to be one of her personal favorites, and this encouraged her.

"Hello, Senator."

"Hello, Mrs. Martin. Welcome to my home. Forgive me for not rising."

"Of course. It was most gracious of you to receive me."

"It is my pleasure and privilege. A man my age appreciates a chance to spend time with a woman as beautiful and intelligent as yourself."

"Senator, how soon do we start talking to each other?"

He raised that part of his face which had once held an eyebrow.

"We haven't *said* anything yet that is true. You do not stand because you cannot. Your gracious reception cost me three carefully hoarded favors and a good deal of folding cash. More than the going rate; you are seeing me reluctantly. You have at least eight mistresses that I know of, each of whom makes me look like a dull matron. I concealed a warm corpse on the way here because I dared not be late; my time is short and my business urgent. Can we begin?"

She held her breath and prayed silently. Everything she had been able to learn about the Senator told her that this was the correct way to approach him. But was it?

The mummy-like face fissured in a broad grin. "Right away. Mrs. Martin, I like you and that's the truth. My time is short, too. What do you want of me?"

"Don't you know?"

"I can make an excellent guess. I hate guessing."

"I am heavily and publicly committed to the defeat of S.4217896."

"Yes, but for all I know you might have come here to sell out."

"Oh." She tried not to show her surprise. "What makes you think that possible?"

"Your organization is large and well-financed and fairly efficient, Mrs. Martin, and there's something about it I don't understand."

"What is that?"

"Your objective. Your arguments are weak and implausible, and whenever this is pointed out to one of you, you simply keep on pushing. Many times I have seen people take a position without apparent logic to it—but I've always been able to see the logic if I kept on looking hard enough. But as I see it, S.'896 would work to the clear and lasting advantage of the group you claim to represent, the artists. There's too much intelligence in your organization to square with your goals. So I have to wonder what you *are* working for, and why. One possibility is that you're willing to roll over on this copyright thing in exchange for whatever it is that you *really* want. Follow me?"

"Senator, I *am* working on behalf of all artists— and in a broader sense—"

He looked pained, or rather, more pained. ". . . 'for all mankind,' oh my *God*, Mrs. Martin, really now."

"I *know* you have heard that countless times, and probably said it as often." He grinned evilly. "This is one of those rare times when it happens to be true. I believe that if S.'896 does pass, our species will suffer significant trauma."

He raised a skeletal hand, tugged at his lower lip. "Now that I have ascertained where you stand, I believe I can save you a good deal of money. By concluding this audience, and seeing that the squeeze you paid for half an hour of my time is refunded pro rata."

Her heart sank, but she kept her voice even. "Without even hearing the hidden logic behind our arguments?"

"It would be pointless and cruel to make you go into your spiel, ma'am. You see, I cannot help you."

She wanted to cry out, and savagely refused herself permission. *Control*, whispered a part of her mind, while another part shouted that a man such as this did not lightly use the words, "I cannot." But he *had* to be wrong. Perhaps the sentence was only a bargaining gambit. . . .

No sign of the internal conflict showed; her voice was calm and measured. "Sir, I have not come here to lobby. I simply wanted to inform you personally that our organization intends to make a no-strings campaign donation in the amount of—"

"Mrs. Martin, please! Before you commit yourself, I repeat, I cannot help you. Regardless of the sum offered."

"Sir, it is substantial."

"I'm sure. Nonetheless it is insufficient."

She knew she should not ask. "Senator, *why*?"

He frowned, a frightening sight.

"Look," she said, the desperation almost showing through now, "keep the pro rata if it buys me an answer! Until I'm convinced that my mission is utterly hopeless, I must not abandon it: answering me is the quickest way to get me out of your office. Your scanners have watched me quite thoroughly, you know that I'm not abscamming you."

Still frowning, he nodded. "Very well. I cannot accept your campaign donation because I have already accepted one from another source."

Her very worst secret fear was realized. He had already taken money from the other side. The one thing any politician must do, no matter how powerful, is stay bought. It was all over.

All her panic and tension vanished, to be replaced by a sadness so great and so pervasive that for a moment she thought it might literally stop her heart.

Too late! Oh my darling, I was too late!

She realized bleakly that there were too many people in her life, too many responsibilities and entanglements. It would be at least a month before she could honorably suicide.

"—you all right, Mrs. Martin?" the old man was saying, sharp concern in his voice.

She gathered discipline around her like a familiar cloak. "Yes, sir, thank you. Thank you for speaking plainly." She stood up and smoothed her skirt. "And for your—"

"Mrs. Martin."

"—gracious hos—Yes?"

"Will you tell me your arguments? Why shouldn't I support '896?"

She blinked sharply. "You just said it would be pointless and cruel."

"If I held out the slightest hope, yes, it would be. If you'd rather not waste your time, I will not compel you. But I am curious."

"Intellectual curiosity?"

He seemed to sit up a little straighter—surely an illusion, for a prosthetic spine is not motile. "Mrs. Martin, I happen to be committed to a course of action. That does not mean I don't care whether the action is good or bad."

"Oh." She thought for a moment. "If I convince you, you will not thank me."

"I know. I saw the look on your face a moment ago, and . . . it reminded me of a night many years ago. Night my mother died. If you've got a sadness that big, and I can take on a part of it, I should try. Sit down."

She sat.

"Now tell me: what's so damned awful about extending copyright to meet the realities of modern life? Customarily I try to listen to both sides before accepting a campaign donation—but this seemed so open and shut, so straightforward . . ."

"Senator, that bill is a short-term boon, to some artists—and a long-term disaster for all artists, on Earth and off."

"'In the long run, Mr. President,'" he began quoting Keynes.

"—we are some of us still alive," she finished softly and pointedly. "Aren't we? You've put your finger on part of the problem."

"What is this disaster you speak of?" he asked.

"The worst psychic trauma the race has yet suffered."

He studied her carefully and frowned again. "Such a possibility is not even hinted at in your literature or materials."

"To do so would precipitate the trauma. At present only a handful of people know, even in my organization. I'm telling *you* because you asked, and because I am certain that you are the only person recording this conversation. I'm betting that you will wipe the tape."

He blinked, and sucked at the memory of his teeth. "My, my," he said mildly. "Let me get comfortable." He had the chair recline sharply and massage his lower limbs; she saw that he could still watch her by overhead mirror if he chose. His eyes were closed. "All right, go ahead."

She needed no time to chose her words. "Do you know how old art is, Senator?"

"As old as man, I suppose. In fact, it may be part of the definition."

"Good answer," she said. "Remember that. But for all present-day intents and purposes, you might as well say that art is a little over 15,600 years old. That's the age of the oldest surviving artwork, the cave paintings at Lascaux. Doubtless the cave-painters sang, and danced, and even told stories—but these arts left no record more durable than the memory of a man. Perhaps it was the story tellers who next learned how to preserve their art. Countless more generations would pass before a workable method of musical notation was devised and standardized. Dancers only learned in the last few centuries how to leave even the most rudimentary record of their art.

"The racial memory of our species has been getting longer since Lascaux. The biggest single improvement came with the invention of writing: our memory-span went from a few generations to as many as the Bible has been around. But it took a massive effort to sustain a memory that long: it was difficult to hand-copy manuscripts faster than barbarians, plagues, or other natural disasters could destroy them. The obvious solution was the printing press: to make and disseminate so many copies of a manuscript or art work that *some* would survive any catastrophe.

"But with the printing press a new idea was born. Art was suddenly mass-marketable, and there was money in it. Writers decided that they should own the right to copy their work. The notion of copyright was waiting to be born.

"Then in the last hundred and fifty years came the largest quantum jumps in human racial memory. Recording technologies. Visual: photography, film, video, Xerox, holo. Audio: low-fi, hi-fi, stereo, and digital. Then computers, the ultimate in information storage. Each of these technologies generated new art forms, and new ways of preserving the ancient art forms. And each required a reassessment of the idea of copyright.

"You know the system we have now, unchanged since the mid-twentieth-century. Copyright ceases to exist fifty years after the death of the copyright holder. But the size of the human race has increased drastically since the 1900s—and so has the average human lifespan. Most people in developed nations now expect to live to be a hundred and twenty; you yourself are considerably older. And so, naturally, S. '896 now seeks to extend copyright into perpetuity."

"Well," the senator interrupted, "what is *wrong* with that? Should a man's work cease to be his simply because he has neglected to keep on breathing? Mrs. Martin, you yourself will be wealthy all your life if

that bill passes. Do you truly wish to give away your
late husband's genius?"

She winced in spite of herself.

"Forgive my bluntness, but that is what I understand *least* about your position."

"Senator, if I try to hoard the fruits of my husband's
genius, I may cripple my race. Don't you see what
perpetual copyright implies? It is perpetual racial
memory! That bill will give the human race an
elephant's memory. *Have you ever seen a cheerful
elephant?*"

He was silent for a time. Then: "I'm still not sure
I understand the problem."

"Don't feel bad, sir. The problem has been directly
under the nose of all of us for at *least* eighty years,
and hardly anyone has noticed."

"Why is that?"

"I think it comes down to a kind of innate failure of mathematical intuition, common to most
humans. We tend to confuse any sufficiently high
number with infinity."

"Well, anything above ten to the eighty-fifth might
as well be infinity."

"Beg pardon?"

"Sorry—I should not have interrupted. That is the
current best-guess for the number of atoms in the
Universe. Go on."

She struggled to get back on the rails. "Well, it
takes a lot less than that to equal 'infinity' in most
minds. For millions of years we looked at the
ocean and said, 'That is infinite. It will accept our
garbage and waste forever.' We looked at the sky
and said, 'That is infinite: it will hold an infinite
amount of smoke.' We *like* the idea of infinity. A
problem with infinity in it is easily solved. How

long can you pollute a planet infinitely large? Easy: forever. Stop thinking.

"Then one day there are so many of us that the planet no longer seems infinitely large.

"So we go elsewhere. There are infinite resources in the *rest* of the solar system, aren't there? I think you are one of the few people alive wise enough to realize that there are *not* infinite resources in the solar system, and sophisticated enough to have included that awareness in your plans."

The senator now looked troubled. He sipped something from a straw. "Relate all this to your problem."

"Do you remember a case from about eighty years ago, involving the song 'My Sweet Lord' by George Harrison?"

"Remember it? I did research on it. My firm won."

"Your firm convinced the court that Harrison had gotten the tune for that song from a song called 'He's So Fine,' written over ten years earlier. Shortly thereafter Yoko Ono was accused of stealing 'You're My Angel' from the classic 'Makin' Whoopee,' written more than thirty years earlier. Chuck Berry's estate eventually took John Lennon's estate to court over 'Come Together.' Then in the late '80s the great Plagiarism Plague *really* got started in the courts. From then on it was open season on popular composers, and still is. But it really hit the fan at the turn of the century, when Brindle's *Ringsong* was shown to be 'substantially similar' to one of Corelli's concertos.

"There are eighty-eight notes. One hundred and seventy-six, if your ear is good enough to pick out quarter tones. Add in rests and so forth, different time signatures. Pick a figure for maximum number of notes a melody can contain. I do not know the figure

for the maximum possible number of melodies—too
many variables—but I am sure it is quite high.

"*I am certain that it is not infinity.*

"For one thing, a great many of those possible
arrays of eighty-eight notes will not be perceived as
music, as melody, by the human ear. Perhaps more
than half. They will not be hummable, whistleable,
listenable—some will be actively unpleasant to hear.
Another large fraction will be so similar to each other
as to be effectively identical: if you change three notes
of the Moonlight Sonata, you have not created something new.

"I do not know the figure for the maximum number of discretely appreciable melodies, and again I'm
certain it is quite high, and again I am certain that
it is not infinity. There are sixteen billion of us alive,
Senator, more than all the people that have ever lived.
Thanks to our technology, better than half of us have
no meaningful work to do; fifty-four percent of our
population is entered on the tax rolls as artists.
Because the synthesizer is so cheap and versatile, a
majority of those artists are musicians, and a great
many are composers. Do you know what it is like to
be a composer these days, Senator?"

"I know a few composers."

"Who are still working?"

"Well . . . three of 'em."

"How often do they bring out a new piece?"

Pause. "I would say once every five years on average. Hmmm. Never thought of it before, but—"

"Did you know that at present two out of every
five copyright submissions to the Music Division are
rejected on the first computer search?"

The old man's face had stopped registering surprise, other than for histrionic purposes, more than

a century before; nonetheless, she knew she had rocked him. "No, I did not."

"Why would you know? Who would talk about it? But it is a fact nonetheless. Another fact is that, when the increase in number of working composers is taken into account, the *rate* of submissions to the Copyright Office is decreasing significantly. There are more composers than ever, but their individual productivity is declining. Who is the most popular composer alive?"

"Uh . . . I suppose that Vachandra fellow,"

"Correct. He has been working for a little over fifty years. If you began now to play every note he ever wrote, in succession, you would be done in twelve hours. Wagner wrote well over sixty hours of music— the Ring alone runs twenty-one hours. The Beatles— essentially two composers—produced over twelve hours of original music in *less than ten years*. Why were the greats of yesteryear so much more prolific?

"There were more enjoyable permutations of eighty-eight notes for them to find."

"Oh my," the senator whispered.

"Now go back to the 1970s again. Remember the *Roots* plagiarism case? And the dozens like it that followed? Around the same time a writer named van Vogt sued the makers of a successful film called *Alien*, for plagiarism of a story forty years later. Two other writers named Bova and Ellison sued a television studio for stealing a series idea. All three collected.

"That ended the legal principle that one does not copyright *ideas* but *arrangements of words*. The number of word-arrangements is finite, but the number of *ideas* is *much* smaller. Certainly, they can be retold in endless ways—*West Side Story* is a brilliant reworking of *Romeo and Juliet*. But it was only possible because *Romeo and Juliet* was in the public domain. Remember too that of the finite number of stories that can be told, a certain number will be *bad stories*.

"As for visual artists—well, once a man demonstrated in the laboratory an ability to distinguish between eighty-one distinct shades of color accurately. I think that's an upper limit. There is a maximum amount of information that the eye is capable of absorbing, and much of that will be the equivalent of noise—"

"But . . . but . . ." This man was reputed never to have hesitated in any way under any circumstances. "But there'll always be change . . . there'll always be new discoveries, new horizons, new social attitudes, to infuse art with new—"

"Not as fast as artists breed. Do you know about the great split in literature at the beginning of the twentieth century? The mainstream essentially abandoned the Novel of Ideas after Henry James, and turned its collective attention to the Novel of Character. They had sucked that dry by mid-century, and they're still chewing on the pulp today. Meanwhile a small group of writers, desperate for something new to write about, for a new story to tell, invented a new genre called science fiction. They mined the future for ideas. The infinite future—like the infinite coal and oil and copper they had then too. In less than a century they had mined it out; there hasn't been a genuinely original idea in science fiction in over fifty years. Fantasy has always been touted as the 'literature of infinite possibility'—but there is even a theoretical upper limit to the 'meaningfully impossible,' and we are fast reaching it."

"We can create new art forms," he said.

"People have been trying to create new art forms for a long time, sir. Almost all fell by the wayside. People just didn't like them."

"We'll *learn* to like them. Damn it, we'll have to."

"And they'll help, for a while. More new art forms have been born in the last two centuries than in the previous million years—though none in the last fifteen years. Scent-symphonies, tactile sculpture, kinetic sculpture, zero-gravity dance—they're all rich new fields, and they are generating mountains of new copyrights. Mountains of finite size. The ultimate bottleneck is this: that *we have only five senses with which to apprehend art, and that is a finite number.* Can I have some water, please?"

"Of course." The old man appeared to have regained his usual control, but the glass which emerged from the arm of her chair contained apple juice. She ignored this and continued.

"But that's not what I'm afraid of, Senator. The theoretical heat-death of artistic expression is something we may never really approach in fact. Long before that point, the game will collapse."

She paused to gather her thoughts, sipped her juice. A part of her mind noted that it harmonized with the recurrent cinnamon motif of Bulachevski's scent-symphony, which was still in progress.

"Artists have been deluding themselves for centuries with the notion that they create. In fact they do nothing of the sort. They discover. Inherent in the nature of reality are a number of combinations of musical tones that will be perceived as pleasing by a human central nervous system. For millennia we have been discovering them, implicit in the universe—and telling ourselves that we 'created' them. To create implies infinite possibility, to discover implies finite

possibility. As a species I think we will react poorly
to having our noses rubbed in the fact that we are
discoverers and not creators."

She stopped speaking and sat very straight. Unaccountably her feet hurt. She closed her eyes, and
continued speaking.

"My husband wrote a song for me, on the occa-
sion of our fortieth wedding anniversary. It was our
love in music, unique and special and intimate, the
most beautiful melody I ever heard in my live. It
made him so happy to have written it. Of his last ten
compositions he had burned five for being derivative,
and the others had all failed copyright clearance. But
this was fresh, special—he joked that my love for him
had inspired him. The next day he submitted it for
clearance, and learned that it had been a popular air
during his early childhood, and had already been
unsuccessfully submitted fourteen times since its
original registration. A week later he burned all his
manuscripts and working tapes and killed himself."

She was silent for a long time, and the senator did
not speak.

"'*Ars longa, vita brevis est,*'" she said at last.
"There's been comfort of a kind in that for thousands of years. But art is long, not infinite. 'The
Magic goes away.' One day we will *use it up*—unless
we can learn to recycle it like any other finite
resource." Her voice gained strength. "Senator, that
bill has to fail, if I have to take you on to do it.
Perhaps I can't win—but I'm going to fight you! A
copyright must not be allowed to last more than fifty
years—after which it should be flushed from the
memory banks of the Copyright Office. We need
selective voluntary amnesia if Discoverers of Art are
to continue to work without psychic damage. Fact

should be remembered—but dreams?" She shivered.
". . . Dreams should be forgotten when we wake.
Or one day we will find ourselves unable to sleep.
Given eight billion artists with effective working
lifetimes in excess of a century, we can no longer
allow individuals to own their discoveries in perpetuity. We must do it the way the human race did
it for a million years—by forgetting, and rediscov-
ering. Because one day the infinite number of
monkeys will have nothing else to write *except* the
complete works of Shakespeare. And they would
probably rather not *know* that when it happens."

Now she was finished, nothing more to say. So was
the scent-symphony, whose last motif was fading
slowly from the air. No clock ticked, no artifact
hummed. The stillness was complete, for perhaps half
a minute.

"If you live long enough," the senator said slowly
at last, "there is nothing new under the sun." He
shifted in his great chair. "If you're lucky, you die
sooner that that. I haven't heard a new dirty joke in
fifty years." He seemed to sit up straight in his chair.
"I will kill S.4217896."

She stiffened in shock. After a time, she slumped
slightly and resumed breathing. So many emotions
fought for ascendancy that she barely had time to
recognize them as they went by. She could not
speak.

"Furthermore," he went on, "I will not tell anyone why I'm doing it. It will begin the end of my
career in public life, which I did not ever plan to
leave, but you have convinced me that I must. I am
both . . . glad, and—" His face tightened with pain—
"and *bitterly* sorry that you told me why I must."

"So am I, sir," she said softly, almost inaudibly.

He looked at her sharply. "Some kinds of fight, you can't feel good even if you win them. Only two kinds of people take on fights like that: fools, and remarkable people. I think you are a remarkable person, Mrs. Martin."

She stood, knocking over her juice. "I wish to God I were a fool," she cried, feeling her control begin to crack at last.

"Dorothy!" he thundered.

She flinched as if he had struck her. "Sir?" she said automatically.

"Do *not* go to pieces! That is an order. You're wound up too tight; the pieces might not go back together again."

"So what?" she asked bitterly.

He was using the full power of his voice now, the voice which had stopped at least one war. "So how many friends do you think a man my age has *got*, damn it? Do you think minds like yours are common? We *share* this business now, and that makes us friends. You are the first person to come out of that elevator and really surprise me in a quarter of a century. And soon, when the word gets around that I've broken faith, people will stop coming out of the elevator. You think like me, and I can't afford to lose you." He smiled, and the smile seemed to melt decades from his face. "Hang on, Dorothy," he said, "and we will comfort each other in our terrible knowledge. All right?"

For several moments she concentrated exclusively on her breathing, slowing and regularizing it. Then, tentatively, she probed at her emotions.

"Why," she said wonderingly, "It *is* better . . . shared."

"Anything is."

She looked at him then, and tried to smile and finally succeeded. "Thank you, Senator."

He returned her smile as he wiped all recordings of their conversation. "Call me Bob."

"Yes, Robert."

HALF AN OAF

When the upper half of an extremely fat man
materialized before him over the pool table in the
living room, Spud nearly swallowed his Adam's apple.
But then he saw that the man was a stranger, and
relaxed.

Spud wasn't allowed to use the pool table when
his mother was home. Mrs. Flynn had been raised
on a steady diet of B-movies, and firmly believed that
a widow woman who raised a boy by herself in
Brooklyn stood a better than even chance of watching her son grow into Jimmy Cagney. Such prophe-
cies, of course, are virtually always self-fulfilling. She
could not get the damned pool table out of the living room door—God knew how the apartment's previous tenant had gotten it in—but she was determined
not to allow her son to develop an interest in a game
that could only lead him to the pool hall, the saloon,

29

the getaway car, the insufficiently fortified hideout and the morgue, more or less in that order. So she flatly forbade him to go near the pool table even before they moved in. Clearly, playing pool must be a lot of fun, and so at age twelve Spud was regularly losing his lunch money in a neighborhood pool hall whose savoriness can be inferred from the fact that they let him in.

But whenever his mother went out to get loaded, which was frequently these days, Spud always took his personal cue and bag of balls from their hiding place and set 'em up in the living room. He didn't intend to keep getting hustled for lunch money *all* his life, and his piano teacher, a nun with a literally incredible goiter, had succeeded in convincing him that practice was the only way to master anything. (She had not, unfortunately, succeeded in convincing him to practice the piano.) He was working on a hopelessly impractical triple-cushion shot when the fat man—or rather, half of the fat man—appeared before him, rattling him so much that he sank the shot.

He failed to notice. For a heart-stopping moment he had thought it was his mother, reeling up the fire escape in some new apotheosis of intoxication, hours off schedule. When he saw that it was not, he let out a relieved breath and waited to see if the truncated stranger would die.

The $\frac{\text{fatman}}{2}$ did not die. Neither did he drop the four inches to the surface of the pool table. What he did was stare vacantly around him, scratching his ribs and nodding. He appeared satisfied with something, and he patted the red plastic belt which formed his lower perimeter contentedly, adjusting a derby with his other hand. His face was round, bland and stupid, and he wore a shirt of particularly villainous green.

After a time Spud got tired of being ignored—twelve-year-olds in Brooklyn are nowhere near as respectful of their elders as they are where you come from—and spoke up.

"Transporter malfunction, huh?" he asked with a hint of derision.

"Eh?" said the fat man, noticing Spud for the first time. "Whassat, kid?"

"You're from the *Enterprise*, right?"

"Never heard of it. I'm from Canarsie. What's this about a malfunction?"

Spud pointed.

"So my fly's open, big deal . . ." the $\frac{fatman}{2}$ let go of his derby and reached down absently to adjust matters, and his thick muscles rebounded from the green felt tabletop, sinking the seven-ball. He glanced down in surprise, uttered an exclamation, and began cursing with a fluency that inspired Spud's admiration. His pudgy face reddened, taking on the appearance of an enormously swollen cherry pepper, and he struck at the plastic belt with the air of a man who, having petted the nice kitty, has been enthusiastically clawed.

". . . slut-ruttin' gimp-frimpin' turtle-tuppin' clone of a week-old dog turd," he finished, and paused for breath. "I shoulda had my head examined. I shoulda never listened ta that hag-shagger, I *knew* it. 'Practically new,' he says. 'A steal,' he says. Well, it's still got a week left on the warranty, and I'll . . ."

Spud rapped the butt-end of his cue on the floor, and the stranger broke off, noticing him again. "If you're not from the *Enterprise*," Spud asked reasonably, "where are you from? I mean, how did you get here?"

"Time machine," scowled the fat man, gesturing angrily at the belt. "I'm from the future."

"Looks like half of you is still there." Spud grinned.

"Who ast you? What am I, blind? Go on, laugh— I'll kick you in . . . I mean, I'll punch ya face. Bug-huggin' salesman with his big discount, I'll sue his socks off."

The pool hall had taught Spud how to placate enraged elders, and somehow he was beginning to like his hemispheric visitor. "Look, it won't do you any good to get mad at me. *I* didn't sell you a Jap time machine."

"Jap? I wish it was. This duck-fucker's made in Hoboken. Look, get me offa this pool table, will ya? I mean, it feels screwy to look down and see three balls." He held out his hand.

Spud transferred the cue to his left hand, grabbed the pudgy fingers, and tugged. When nothing happened, he tugged harder. The $\frac{fatman}{2}$ moved slightly. Spud sighed, circled the pool table, climbed onto its surface on his knees, braced his feet against the cushion, and heaved from behind. The half-torso moved forward reluctantly, like a piano on ancient casters. Eventually it was clear of the table, still the same distance from the floor.

"Thanks, kid . . . look, what's your name?"

"Spud Flynn."

"Pleased to meetcha, Spud. I'm Joe Koziack. Listen, are your parents home?"

"My mother's out. I got no father."

"Oh, a clone, huh? Well, that's a break anyway. I'd hate to try and talk my way out of this one with a grownup. No offense. Look, are we in Brooklyn? I gotta get to Manhattan right away."

"Yeah, we're in Brooklyn. But I can't push you to Manhattan—you weigh a ton."

Joe's face fell as he considered this. "How the hell am I gonna get there, then?"

"Beats me. Why don't you walk?"

Joe snorted. "With no legs?"

"You got legs," Spud said. "They just ain't here."

Joe began to reply, then shut up and looked thoughtful. "Might work at that," he decided at last. "I sure an' hell don't understand how this time-travel stuff works, and it *feels* like I still got legs. I'll try it." He squared his shoulders, looked down and then quickly backed up, and tried a step.

His upper torso moved forward two feet.

"I'll be damned," he said happily. "It works."

He took a few more steps, said, "OUCH, DAMMIT," and grabbed at the empty air below him, leaning forward. "Bashed my cop-toppin' knee," he snarled.

"On what?"

Joe looked puzzled. "I guess on the wall back home in 2007," he decided. "I can't seem to go forward any farther."

Spud got behind him and pushed again, and Joe moved forward a few feet more. "Jesus, that feels weird," Joe exclaimed. "My legs're still against the wall, but I still feel attached to them.

"That's as far as I go," Spud panted. "You're too heavy."

"How come? There's only half as much of me."

"So what's that—a hundred and fifty pounds?"

"Huh. I guess you're right. But I got to think of *something*. I *gotta* get to Manhattan."

"Why?" Spud asked.

"To get to a garage," Joe explained impatiently. "The guys that make these time-belts, they got repair stations set up all the way down the temporal line in case one gets wrecked up or you kill the batteries. The nearest dealership's in Manhattan, and the repairs're free till the warranty runs out. But how am I gonna get there?"

"Why don't you use the belt to go back home?" asked Spud, scratching his curly head.

"Sure, and find out I left my lungs and one kidney back here? I could maybe leave my heart in San Francisco, but my kidney in Brooklyn? Nuts—this belt stays switched off till I get to the complaint department." He frowned mightily. "But how?"

"I got it," Spud cried. "Close your eyes. Now try to remember the room you started in, and which way you were facing. Now, where's the door?"

"Uh . . . that way," said Joe, pointing. He shuffled sideways, swore as he felt an invisible doorknob catch him in the groin, and stopped. "Now how the hell do I open the door with no hands?" he grumbled. "Oh, crap." His torso dropped suddenly, ending up on its back on the floor, propped up on splayed elbows. The derby remained fixed on his head. His face contorted and sweat sprang out on his forehead. "Shoes . . . too slop-toppin' . . . slippery," he gasped. "Can't get . . . a decent grip." He relaxed slightly, gritted his teeth, and said, "There. One shoe. Oh Christ, the second one's always the hardest. Unnh. Got it. Now I gotcha, you son of a foreman." After a bit more exertion he spread his fingers on the floor, slid himself backward, and appeared to push his torso from the floor with one hand. Spud watched with interest.

"That was pretty neat," the boy remarked. "From underneath you look like a cross-section of a person."

"Go on."

"You had lasagna for supper."

Joe paled a little. "Christ, I hope I don't start leaking. Well, anyhow, thanks for everything, kid— I'll be seein' ya."

"Say, hold on," Spud called as Joe's upper body began to float from the living room. "How're you gonna keep from bumping into things all the way to Manhattan? I mean, it's ten miles, easy, from here to the bridge. You could get run over or something. *Either* half."

Joe froze, and thought that one over. He was silent for a long time.

"Maybe I got an angle," he said at last. He backed up slightly. "There. I feel the doorway with my heels. Now you move me a couple of feet, okay?" Spud complied.

"Terrific! I can feel the doorway. When I walk, my legs back home move too. When I stand still and you move me, the legs stay put. So we can do it after all."

" 'We' my foot," Spud objected. "You haven't been paying attention. I told you—I can't push you to New York."

"Look, Spud," Joe said, a sudden look of cunning on his pudding face, "how'd you like to be rich?"

Spud looked skeptical. "Hey, Joe, I watch TV— I read sf—I've heard this one before. I don't know anything about the stock market thirty years ago, I couldn't even tell you who was president then, and you don't look like a historian to me. What could you tell me to make me rich?"

"I'm a sports nut," Joe said triumphantly. "Tell me

what year it is, I'll tell you who's gonna win the World Series, the Rose Bowl, the Stanley Cup. You could clean up."

Spud thought it over. He shot pool with one of the best bookies in the neighborhood, a gentleman named "Odds" Evenwright. On the other hand, Mom would be home in a couple of hours.

"I'll give you all the help I can," Joe promised. "Just give me a hand now and then."

"Okay," Spud said reluctantly. "But we gotta hurry."

"Fine, Spud, fine. I knew I could count on you. All right, let's give it a try." The $\frac{\text{fatman}}{2}$ closed his eyes, turned right and began to move forward gingerly. "Lemme see if I can remember."

"Wait a minute," said Spud with a touch of contempt. Joe, he decided, was not very bright. "You've gotta get out of *this* room first. You're gonna hit that wall in a minute."

Joe opened his eyes, blinked. "Yeah."

"Hold on. Where your legs are—is that this building, thirty-two years from now? I mean, if it is, how come the doors are in different places and stuff?"

"Nah—I started in a ten-year-old building."

Spud sneered. "Cripes, you're lucky you didn't pop out in midair! Or inside somebody's fireplace. That was dumb—you should have started on the ground out in the open someplace."

Joe reddened. "What makes you think there *is* anyplace out in the open in Brooklyn in 2007, smartmouth? I checked the Hall of Records and found out there was a building here in 1976, and the floor heights matched. So I took a chance. Now stop needlin' me and help me figure this out."

"I guess," Spud said reluctantly, "I'll have to push you out into the hall, and then you can take it from there, I hope." He dug in his heels and pushed. "Hey, squat a little, will you? Your center of gravity's too high." Koziack complied, and was gradually boyhandled out into the hall. It was empty.

"Okay," Spud panted at last. "Try walking." Joe moved forward tentatively, then grinned and began to move faster, swinging his heavy arms.

"Say," he said, "this is all right."

"Well, let's get going before somebody comes along and sees you," Spud urged.

"Sure thing," Koziack agreed, quickening his pace. "Wouldn't want aaaaaaAAAAAARGH!!!" His eyes widened for a moment, his arms flailed, and suddenly he dropped to the floor and began to bounce violently up and down, spinning rapidly. Spud jumped away, wondering if Joe had gone mad or epileptic. At last the $\frac{fatman}{2}$ came to rest on his back, cursing feebly, the derby still on his head but quite flattened.

"You okay?" Spud asked tentatively.

Joe lurched upright and began rubbing the back of his head vigorously. "Fell down the mug-pluggin' stairs," he said petulantly.

"Why don't you watch where you're going?"

"How the hell am I supposed to do that?" Joe barked.

"Well, be more careful," Spud said angrily. "You keep makin' noise and somebody's gonna come investigate."

"In *Brooklyn?* Come on! Jesus, my ass hurts."

"Lucky you didn't break a leg," Spud told him. "Let's get going."

"Yeah." Groaning, Joe began to move forward again. The pair reached the elevator without further incident, and Joe pushed the DOWN button. "Wish my own building had elevators," he complained bitterly, still trying to rub the place that hurt. *Migod,* thought Spud, *he literally can't find it with both hands!* He giggled, stopped when he saw Joe glare.

The elevator slid back. A bearded young man with very long hair emerged, shouldered past the two, started down the hall and then did a triple-take in slow motion. Trembling, he took a plastic baggie of some green substance from his pocket, looked from it to Koziack and back again. "I guess it *is* worth two hundred an ounce," he said to himself, and continued on his way.

Oblivious, Spud was waving Joe to follow him into the elevator. The $\frac{fatman}{2}$ attempted to comply, bounced off empty air in the doorway.

"Shit," he said.

"Come on, come on," Spud said impatiently.

"I *can't.* My own hallway isn't wide enough. You'll have to push me in."

Spud raised his eyes heavenward. He set the "emergency stop" switch. Immediately alarm bells began to yammer, reverberating through the entire building. Swearing furiously, Spud scrambled past Joe into the hallway and pushed him into the elevator as fast as he could, scurrying in after him. He slapped the controls, the clamour ceased, and the car began to descend.

At once Joe rose to the ceiling, banging his head and flattening the derby entirely. The car's descent slowed. He roared with pain and did a sort of reverse-pushup, lowering his head a few inches. He glared down at Spud. "How . . . many . . . floors?" he grunted, teeth gritting with effort.

Spud glanced at the indicator behind Joe. "Three more," he announced.

"Jesus."

The elevator descended at about three-quarter-normal speed, but eventually it reached the ground floor, and the doors opened on a miraculously empty lobby. Joe dropped his hands with a sigh of relief—and remained a few inches below the ceiling, too high to get out the door.

"Oh, for the luvva—what do I do now?" he groaned. Spud shrugged helplessly. As they pondered, the doors slid closed and the car, in answer to some distant summons, began to rise rapidly. Joe dropped like an anvil, let out a howl as he struck the floor. "I'll sue," he gibbered, "I'll sue the bastard! Oh my kidneys! Oh my gut!"

"Oh my achin' back," Spud finished. "Now someone'll see us—I mean, you. Supposed they aren't stoned?" Joe was too involved in the novel sensation of internal bruising; it was up to Spud to think of something. He frowned—then smiled. Snatching the mashed derby from Joe's head, he pushed the crown back out and placed the hat, upsidedown, on the floor in front of Joe.

The door slid back at the third floor: a rotund matron with a face like an overripe avocado stepped into the car and then stopped short, wide-eyed. She went white, and then suddenly red with embarrassment.

"Oh, you poor man," she said sympathetically, averting her eyes, and dropped a five-dollar bill in the derby. "I never supported that war myself." She turned around and faced forward, pushing the button marked "L."

Barely in time, Spud leaped onto Joe's shoulders and threw up his hands. They hit the ceiling together with a muffled thud, clamping their teeth to avoid exclaiming. The stout lady kept up a running monologue about a cousin of hers who had also left in Vietnam some parts of his anatomy which she was reluctant to name, muffling the sounds the two did make, and she left the elevator at the ground floor without looking back. "Good luck," she called over a brawny shoulder, and was gone.

Spud made a convulsive effort, heaved Joe a few feet down from the ceiling, and leaped from his shoulders toward the closing door. He landed on his belly, and the door closed on his hand, springing open again at once. It closed on his hand twice more before he had enough breath back to scream at Joe, who shook off his stupor and left the elevator, snatching up his derby and holding the door for Spud to emerge. The boy exited on his knees, cradling his hand and swearing.

Joe helped him up. "Sorry," he said apologetically. "I was afraid I'd step on ya."

"With WHAT?" Spud hollered.

"I *said* I was sorry, Spud. I just got shook up. Thanks for helping me out there. Look, I'll split this finnif with you . . ." A murderous glare from Spud cut him off. The boy held out his hand.

"Fork it over," he said darkly.

"Whaddya mean? She give it to me, didn't she?"

"I'll give it to you," Spud barked. "You say you're gonna make me rich, but all I've got so far is a stiff neck and a mashed hand. Come on, give—you haven't got a pocket to put it in anyway."

"I guess you're right, Spud," Joe decided. "I owe ya for the help. If a grownup saw me and found out about the belt, it'd probably cause a paradox or something, and I'd end upon a one-way trip to the Pleistocene. The temporal cops're pretty tough about that kind of stuff." He handed over the money, and

Spud, mollified now, stuffed it into his pants and considered his next move. The lobby was still empty, but that could change at any moment.

"Look," he said finally, ticking off his options on his fingers, "we can't take the subway—we'd cause a riot. Likewise the bus, and besides, we haven't got exact change. A Brooklyn cabbie *can't* be startled, but five bucks won't get us to the bridge. And we can't walk. So there's only one thing to do."

"What's that?"

"I'll have to clout a car."

Joe brightened. "I knew you'd think of something, kid. Hey, what do I do in the meantime?"

Spud considered. Between them and the curtained lobby-door, some interior decorator's horribly botched bonsai caught (or, more accurately, bushwacked) his eye; it rose repulsively from a kind of enormous marble wastebasket filled with vermiculite, a good three feet high.

"Squat behind that," he said, pointing. "If anybody comes in, make out like you're tying your shoelace. If you hear the elevator behind you, go around the other side of it."

Joe nodded. "You know," he said, replacing his derby on his balding pink head, "I just thought. While we was upstairs at your place I shoulda grabbed something to wear that went down to the floor. Dumb. Well, I sure ain't goin' back."

"It wouldn't do you any good anyway," Spud told him. "The only clothes we got like that are Mom's— you couldn't wear them."

Joe looked puzzled, and then light slowly dawned. "Oh, yeah, I remember from my history class. This is a tight-ass era. Men couldn't wear dresses and women couldn't wear pants."

"Women can wear pants," Spud said, confused.

"That's right—I remember now. 'The Twilight of Sexual Inequality,' my teacher called it, the last days when women still oppressed men."

"I think you've got that backwards," Spud corrected.

"I don't *think* so," Joe said dubiously.

"I hope you're better at sports. Look, this is wasting time. Get down behind that cactus and keep your eyes open. I'll be back as soon as I can."

"Okay, Spud. Look, uh . . . Spud?" Joe looked sheepish. "Listen, I really appreciate this. I really do know about sports history. I mean, I'll see that you make out on this."

Spud smiled suddenly. "That's okay, Joe. You're too fat, and you're not very bright, but for some reason I like you. I'll see that you get fixed up." Joe blushed and stammered, and Spud left the lobby.

He pondered on what he had said, as with a small part of his attention, he set about stealing a car. It was funny, he thought as he pushed open an unlocked vent-window and snaked his slender arm inside to open the door—Joe was pretty dumb, all right, and he complained a lot, and he was heavier than a garbage can full of cement—but something about him appealed to Spud. *He's got guts,* the boy decided as he smashed the ignition and shorted the wires. *If I found myself in a strange place with no legs, I bet I'd freak out.* He gunned the engine to warm it up fast and tried to imagine what it must be like for Joe to walk around without being able to see where he was going—or rather, seeing where only part of him was going. The notion unsettled him; he decided that in Joe's place he'd be too terrified to move an inch. *And yet,* he reflected as he eased the car—a battered

'59 Buick—from its parking space, *that big goon is going to try and make it all the way to Manhattan. Yeah, he's got guts.*

Or perhaps, it occurred to him as he double-parked in front of the door of his building, Joe simply didn't have the imagination to be afraid. *Well, in that case* somebody's *got to help him,* Spud decided, and headed for the opaquely-curtained front door, leaving the engine running. He had never read *Of Mice and Men,* but he had an intuitive conviction that it was the duty of the bright ones to keep the dumb ones from getting into scrapes. His mother had often said as much of her late husband.

As he pushed open the door he saw Joe—or rather, what there was to see of Joe—bending over a prostrate young woman, tugging her dress off over her head.

"What the *hell* are you doing, you moron!" he screamed, leaping in through the door and slamming it behind him. "You trying to get us busted?"

Joe straightened, embarrassment on his round face. Since he retained his grip on the long dress, the girl's head and arms rose into the air and then fell with a thud as the dress came free. Joe winced. "I'm sorry, Spud," he pleaded. "I couldn't help it."

"What happened?"

"I couldn't help it. I tried to get behind the thing like you said, but there was a wall in the way—of my legs, I mean. So while I was tryin' ta think what to do this fem come in an' seen me an' just fainted. So I look at her for a while an' I look at her dress an' I think: Joe, would you rather people look at you funny, or would you rather be in the Pleistocene? So I take the dress." He held it up; its hem brushed the floor.

Spud looked down at the girl. She was in her late twenties, with long blond hair and a green headband. She wore only extremely small and extremely loud floral print panties and a pair of sandals. Her breasts were enormous, rising and falling as she breathed. She was out cold. Spud stared for a long time.

"Hey," Joe said sharply. "You're only a kid. What're you lookin' at?"

"I'm not sure," Spud said slowly, "but I got a feeling I'll figure it out in a couple of years, and I'll want to remember."

Joe roared with sudden laughter. "You'll do, kid." He glanced down. "Kinda wish I had my other half along myself." He shook his head sadly. "Well, let's get going."

"Wait a minute, stupid," Spud snapped. "You can't just leave her there. This is a rough neighborhood."

"Well, what am I sposta do?" Joe demanded. "I don't know which apartment is hers."

Spud's forehead wrinkled in thought. The laundry room? No, old Mrs. Cadwallader always ripped off any clothes left here. Leave the two of them here and go grab one of Mom's housecoats? No good: either the girl would awaken while he was gone or, with Joe's luck, a cop would walk in. Probably a platoon of cops.

"Look," Joe said happily, "it fits. I thought it would—she's almost as big on top as I am, an' it looked loose." The $\frac{\text{fatman}}{2}$ had seemingly become an integer, albeit in drag. Draped in paisley, he looked like a psychedelic priest and something like Henry the Eighth dressed for bed, As Anne Boleyn might have done, Spud shuddered.

"Well," he said ironically, "at least you're not so conspicuous now."

"Yeah, that's what I thought," Joe agreed cheerfully. Spud opened his mouth, then closed it again. Time was short—someone might come in at any second. The girl still snored; apparently the bang on the head had combined with her faint to put her deep under. They simply couldn't leave her here.

"We'll have to take her with us," Spud decided.

"Hey," Joe said reproachfully.

"You got a better idea? Come on, we'll put her in the trunk." Grumbling, but unable to come up with a better idea, Joe picked the girl up in his beefy arms, headed for the door—and bounced off thin air, dropping her again.

Failing to find an obscenity he hadn't used yet, Spud sighed. He bent over the girl, got a grip on her, hesitated, got a different grip on her, and hoisted her over his shoulder. Panting and staggering, he got the front door open, peered up and down the street, and reeled awkwardly out to the waiting Buick. It took only a few seconds to smash open the trunk lock, but Spud hadn't realized they made seconds that long. He dumped the girl into the musty trunk with a sigh of relief, folding her like a cot, and looked about for something with which to tie the trunk closed. There was nothing useful in the trunk, nor the car itself, nor in his pockets. He thought of weighing the lid down with the spare tire and fetching something from inside the building, but she was lying on the spare, his arms were weary, and he was still conscious of the urgent need for haste.

Then he did a double-take, looked down at her again. He couldn't use the *sandals*, but . . .

As soon as he had fashioned the floral-print trunk latch (which took him a bit longer than it should have), he hurried back inside and pushed Joe to the car with the last of his strength. "I hope you can drive, Spud," Joe said brightly as they reached the curb. "*I* sure as hell can't."

Instead of replying, Spud got in. Joe lowered himself and sidled into the car, where he floated an eerie few inches from the seat. Spud put it in drive, and pulled away slowly. Joe sank deep in the seat-back, and the car behaved as if it had a wood stove tied to the rear-bumper, but it moved.

Automobiles turned out to be something with which Joe was familiar in the same sense that Spud was familiar with biplanes, and he was about as comfortable with the reality as Spud would have been in the rear cockpit of a Spad (had Spud's Spad sped). A little bit of the Brooklyn-Queens Expressway was enough to lighten his complexion about two shades past albino. But he adapted quickly enough, and by the time the fifth homicidal psychopath had tried his level best to kill them (that is, within the first mile) he found his voice and said, with a fair imitation of diffidence, "I didn't think they'd decriminalized murder this early."

Spud gaped at him.

"Yeah," Joe said, seeing the boys puzzlement. "Got to be too many people, an' they just couldn't seem to get a war going. That's why I put my life savings into this here cut-rate time-belt, to escape. I lost my job, so I became . . . eligible. Just my luck I gotta get a lemon. Last time *I'll* ever buy hot merchandise."

Spud stared in astonishment, glanced back barely in time to foil the sixth potential assassin. "Won't the cops be after you for escaping?"

"Oh, you're welcome to escape, if you can. And if you can afford time-travel, you can become a previous administration's problem, so they're glad to see you go. You can only go backward into the past or return to when you started, you know—the future's impossible to get to."

"How's that?" Spud asked curiously. Time-travel always worked both ways on television.

"Damfino. Somethin' about the machine can recycle reality but it can't create it—whatever that means."

Spud thought awhile, absently dodging a junkie in a panel truck. "So it's sort of open season on your legs back in 2007, huh?"

"I guess," said Joe uneasily. "Be difficult to iden- tify 'em as mine, though. The pictures they print in the daily Eligibles column are always head shots, and they sure can't fingerprint me. I guess I'm okay."

"Hey," Spud said, slapping his forehead and the horn in a single smooth motion (scaring onto the shoulder a little old lady in a new Lincoln Continental who had just pulled onto the highway in front of them at five miles per hour), "it just dawned on me: what the hell *is* going on back in your time? I mean, there's a pair of legs wandering around in crazy circles, falling down stairs, right now they're probably standing still on a sidewalk or something . . ."

"Sitting," Joe interrupted.

". . . sitting on a sidewalk. So what's going on? Are you causing a riot back there or what?"

"I don't think so," Joe said, scratching his chin. "I left about three in the morning."

"Why then?"

"Well, I . . . I didn't want my wife to know I was goin'. I didn't tell her about the belt."

Spud started to nod—he wouldn't have told his mother. Then he frowned sharply. "You mean you left your wife back there to get killed? You . . ."

"No, kid, no!" Joe flung up his hands. "It ain't like you think. I was gonna come back here into the past and make a bundle on the Series, and then go back to the same moment I left and buy another belt for Alice. Honest, I love my wife, dammit!"

Spud thought. "How much to you need?"

"For a good belt, made in Japan? Twenty grand, your money. Which is the same in ours, in numbers, only we call 'em Rockefellers instead of dollars."

Spud whistled a descending arpeggio. "How'd you expect to win that kind of money? That takes a big stake, and you said you sunk your savings in the belt."

"Yeah," Koziack smiled, "but they terminate your life-insurance when you go Eligible, and I got five thousand Rockies from that. I even remembered to change it to dollars," he added proudly. "It's right . . ." His face darkened.

". . . here in your pocket," Spud finished. "Terrific." His eyes widened. "Hey, wait—you're in trouble!"

"Huh?"

"Your legs are back in 2007, sitting on the sidewalk, right? So they're *creating reality*. Get it? They're making future—you *can't* go back to the moment you left 'cause time is going on after it already. So if you don't get back soon, the sun'll come up and some blood-thirsty nut'll kill your wife."

Joe blanched. "Oh Jesus God," he breathed. "I think you're right." He glanced at a passing sign, which read, MANHATTAN—10 MILES. "Does this thing go any . . . ulp . . . faster?"

The car leaped forward.

To his credit, Joe kept his eyes bravely open as Spud yanked the car in and out of high-speed traffic, snaking through holes that hadn't appeared to be there and doing unspeakable things to the Buick's transmission. But Joe was almost—almost—grateful when the sound of an ululating siren became audible over the snarling horns and screaming brakes.

Spud glanced in the mirror, located the whirling gumball machine in the rear-view mirror, and groaned aloud. "Just our luck! The cops—and us with only five bucks between us. Twelve years old, no license, a stolen car, a half a fat guy in a dress—cripes, even fifty bucks'd be cutting it close." Thinking furiously, he pulled over and parked on the grass, beneath a hellishly bright highway light. "Maybe I can go back and talk to them before they see you," he said to Joe, and began to get out.

"Wait, Spud!" Joe said urgently. He snatched a handful of cigarette butts from the ashtray, smeared black grime on Spud's upper lip. "There. Now you look maybe sixteen."

Spud grinned. "You're okay, Joe." He got out.

Twenty feet behind them, Patrolman Vitelli turned to his partner. "Freaks," he said happily. "Kids. Probably clouted the car, no license. Let me have it."

"Don't take a cent less than seventy-five," Patrolman Duffy advised.

"I dunno, Pat. They don't look like they got more than fifty to me."

"Well, all right," Duffy grumbled. "But I want an ounce of whatever they're smokin'. We're running low."

Vitelli nodded and got out of the black and white, one hand on his pistol. Spud met him halfway, and a certain lengthy ritual dialogue was held.

"Five bucks!" Vitelli roared. "You must be outa your mind."

"I wish I was," Spud said fervently. "Honest to God, it's all I got."

"How about your friend?" Vitelli said, and started for the Buick, which sat clearly illuminated in the pool of light beneath the arc light.

"He's stone broke," Spud said hastily. "I'm takin' him to Bellevue—he thinks he may have leprosy."

Vitelli pulled up short with one hand on the truck. "You got a license and registration?" he growled.

Spud's heart sank. "I . . ."

Vitelli nodded. "All right, buddy. Let's open the trunk."

Spud's heart bounced off his shoes and rocketed back up, lodging behind his palate. Seeing his reaction, Vitelli looked down at the trunk, noticing for the first time the odd nature of its fastening. He tugged experimentally, flimsy fabric parted, and the trunk lid rose.

Blinking at the light, the blond girl sat up stiffly, a muddy treadprint on her . . . person.

The air filled with the sound of screeching brakes.

Vitelli staggered back as if he'd been slapped with a sandbag. He looked from the girl to Spud to the girl to Spud, and his eyes narrowed.

"Oh, boy," he said softly. "Oh boy." He unholstered his gun.

"Look, officer, I can explain," Spud said without the least shred of conviction.

"Hey," said the blond girl, clearly dazed.

"Holy shit," said Duffy in the squad car.

"Excuse me," said Joe, getting out of the Buick.

Both cops gasped as they caught sight of him, and Vitelli began to shake his head slowly. Seeing their expressions, the girl raised up onto her knees and peered around the trunk lid, completing the task of converting what had been three lanes of rushing traffic into a goggle-eyed parking lot.

"My dress," she yelped.

Koziack stood beside the Buick a little uncertainly, searching for words in all the likely places. "Oh shit," he said at last, and began to pull the dress over his head, removing the derby. "Pleistocene, here I come."

Vitelli froze. The gun dropped from his nerveless fingers; the hand stayed before him, index finger crooked.

"Tony," came a shaky voice from the squad car, "forget the ounce."

Spud examined the glaze in Vitelli's eyes and bolted for the car. "Come on," he screamed at Joe. The girl barely (I'm sorry, really) managed to jump from the trunk before the car sprang forward like a plane trying to outrun a bullet, lurching off the shoulder in front of a ten-mile traffic pileup that showed no slightest sign of beginning to start up again.

Behind them Vitelli still stood like a statue, imaginary gun still pointing at where Joe had been standing. Tears leaked from his unblinking eyes.

As the girl stared around her with widening eyes, car doors began to open.

Spud was thoroughly spooked, but he relaxed a good deal when the toll-booth attendant at the Brooklyn Bridge failed to show any interest in a twelve-year-old driving a car with the trunk wide open. Joe had the dress folded over where his lap should have been, and the attendant only changed the five and went back to his egg salad sandwich without comment.

"Where are we going?" Spud asked, speaking for the first time since they had left the two policemen and the girl behind.

Joe named a midtown address in the forties.

"Great. How're we gonna get you from the car into the place?"

Joe chuckled. "Hey, Spud—this may be 1976, but Manhattan is Manhattan. Nobody'll notice a thing."

"Yeah, I guess you're right. What do you figure to do?"

Joe's grin atrophied. "Jeez, I dunno. Get the belt fixed first—I ain't thought about after that."

Spud snorted. "Joe, I think you're a good guy and I'm your pal, but if you didn't have a roof on your mouth, you'd blow your derby off every time you hiccuped. Look, it's simple: you get the belt fixed, you get both halves of you back together, and it's maybe ten o'clock, right?"

"If those goniffs at the dealership don't take too long fixin' the belt," Joe agreed.

"So you give me the insurance money, and use the belt to go a few months ahead. By the time, with the Series and the Bowl games and maybe a little Olympics action, we can split, say, fifty grand. You take your half and take the time-belt back to the moment your legs left 2007, at 10:01. You buy your wife a time-belt first thing in the morning and you're both safe."

"Sounds great," Joe said a little slowly, "but . . . uh . . ."

Spud glanced at him irritably. "What's wrong with it?" he demanded.

"I don't want you should be offended, Spud. I mean, you're obviously a tough, smart little guy, but . . ."

"Spit it out!"

"Spud, there is no way in the world a twelve-year-old kid is gonna take fifty grand from the bookies and keep it." Joe shrugged apologetically. "I'm sorry, but you know I'm right."

Spud grimaced and banged the wheel with his fist. "I'll go to a *lot* of bookies," he began.

"Spud, Spud, you get into that bracket, at your age, the word has just gotta spread. You *know* that."

The boy jammed on the brakes for a traffic light and swore. "Dammit, you're right."

Joe slumped sadly in his seat. "And I can't do it myself. If I get caught bettin' on sports events of the past myself, it's the Pleistocene for me."

Spud stared, astounded. "Then how did you figure to accomplish *anything*?"

"Well . . ." Joe looked embarrassed. "I guess I thought I'd find some guy I could trust. I didn't think he'd be . . . so young."

"A grownup you can *trust*? Joe, you really are a moron."

"Well. I didn't have no choice, fragit. Besides, it might still work. How much do you think you *could* score, say, on one big event like the Series, if you hustled all the books you could get to?"

Twenty thousand, Spud thought, but he said nothing.

Joe had been right: the sight of half a fat man being dragged across the sidewalk by a twelve-year-old with ashes on his upper lip aroused no reaction at all in midtown Manhattan on a Friday night. One out-of-towner on his way to the theater blinked a few times, but his attention was distracted almost immediately by a midget in a gorilla suit, wearing a sandwich sign advertising an off-off-off-Broadway play about bestiality. Spud and Joe reached their destination without commotion, a glass door in a group of six by

which one entered various sections of a single building, like a thief seeking the correct route to the
Sarcophagus Room of Tut's Tomb. The one they chose
was labeled, "Breadbody & McTwee, Importers," and
opened on a tall stairway. Spud left Joe at the foot
of the stairs and went to fetch assistance. Shortly he
came back down with a moronic-looking pimply teen-
ager in dirty green coveralls, "Dinny" written in red
lace on his breast pocket.

"Be goddamn," Dinny said with what Joe felt was
excessive amusement. "Never seen anything like it.
I thought this kid was nuts. Come on, let's go."
Chuckling to himself, he helped Spud haul Joe
upstairs to the shop. They brought him into a smallish
room filled with oscilloscopes, signal generators,
computer terminals, assorted unidentifiable hardware,
tools, spare parts, beer cans, as-yet unpublished issues
of *Playboy* and *Analog*, overflowing ashtrays, a muted
radio, and a cheap desk piled with carbon copies of
God only knew what. Dinny sat on a cigarette-scarred
stool, still chuckling, and pulled down a reference
book from an overhead shelf. He chewed gum and
picked at his pimples as he thumbed through it, as
though to demonstrate that he could do all three at
once. It was clearly his showpiece. At last he looked
up, shreds of gum decorating his grin, and nodded
to Joe.

"If it's what I t'ink it is," he pronounced, "I c'n
fix it. Got yer warranty papers?"

Joe nodded briefly, retrieved them from a
compartment in the time-belt and handed them over.
"How long will it take?"

"Take it easy," Dinny said unresponsively, and began
studying the papers like an orangutan inspecting the
Magna Carta. Joe curbed his impatience with a visible

effort and rummaged in a nearby ashtray, selecting the longest butt he could find.

"Joe," Spud whispered, "how come that goof is the only one here?"

"Whaddya expect at nine thirty on a Friday night, the regional manager?" Joe whispered back savagely.

"I hope he knows what he's doing."

"Me too, but I can't wait for somebody better, dammit. Alice is in danger, and my legs've been using up my time for me back there. Besides, I've had to piss for the last hour-and-a-half."

Spud nodded grimly and selected a butt of his own. They smoked for what seemed like an interminable time in silence broken only by the rustling of paper and the sound of Dinny's pimples popping.

"Awright," the mechanic said at last, "the warranty's still good. Lucky you didn't come ta me a week from now."

"The speed you're goin', maybe I have," Joe snapped. "Come on, come on, will ya? Get me my legs back—I ain't got all night."

"Take it easy," Dinny said with infuriating glee. "You'll get your legs back. Just relax. Come on over inna light." Moving with sadistic slowness, he acquired a device that seemed something like a hand-held fluoroscope with a six-inch screen, and began running it around the belt. He stopped, gazed at the screen for a full ten seconds, and sucked his teeth.

"Sorry, mister," he drawled, straightening up and grinning. "I can't help you."

"What the hell are you talkin' about?" Joe roared.

"Somebody tampered with this belt, tried to jinx the override cutout so they could visit some Interdicted Period—probably wanted to see the Crucifixion or some other event that a vested-interest group got declared Off-Limits. I bet that's why it don't work right. It takes a specialist to work on one of these, you know." He smiled proudly, pleased with the last sentence.

"So you can't fix it?" Koziack groaned.

"Maybe yes, maybe no, but I ain't gonna try 'less I see some cash. That belt's been tampered with," Dinny said, relishing the moment. "The warranty's void."

Joe howled like a gutshot buffalo, and stepped forward. His meaty right fist traveled six inches from his shoulder, caught Dinny full in the mouth and dropped him in his tracks, popping the mechanic's upper lip and three pimples. "I'd stomp on ya if I could, ya smart-ass mugger-hugger," Joe roared down at the unconscious Dinny. "Think you're funny!"

"Easy, Joe," Spud yelled. "Don't get excited. We gotta *do* something."

"What the hell *can* we do?" Joe cried despairingly. "That crumb is the only mechanic in a hundred miles—we'll never get to the next one in time, and we haven't got a prayer anyway with four dollars and change. Crummy pap-lapper, I oughta . . . oh *damn* it." He began to cry.

"Hey, Joe," Spud protested, flustered beyond measure at seeing a sober grownup cry, "come on, take it easy. Come on now, cut it out." Joe, his face in his hands, shook his head and kept on sobbing.

Spud thought furiously, and suddenly a light dawned and was filled with a strange prescience, a déjà vu kind of certainty that startled him with its intensity. He wasted no time examining it. Stepping close to Joe, he bent at the waist, swung from the hip, and kicked the belt as hard as he could, squarely on the spot Dinny had last examined. A sob became a startled yell—and Joe's fat legs appeared beneath him, growing downward from the belt like tubers.

"What the hell did you kick me for?" Joe demanded, glaring indignantly at Spud. "What'd I do to you?"

Spud pointed.

Joe looked down. "Wa-HOO!!" he shouted gleefully. "You *did* it, Spud, I got my legs back! Oh, Spud, baby, you're beautiful, *I got my legs back!*" He began to caper around the room in a spontaneous improvised goat-dance, knocking equipment crashing in all directions, and Spud danced with him, laughing and whooping and for the first time in this story looking his age. Together they careened like an improbable vaudeville team, the big fat man and the mustached midget, howling like fools.

At last they subsided, and Joe sat down to catch his breath. "Woo-ee," he panted, "what a break. Hey, Spud, I really gotta thank you, honest to God. Look, I been thinkin'—you can't make enough from the bookies for both of us without stickin' your neck way out. So the hell with that, see? I'll give you the Series winner like I promised, but you keep all the dough. I'll figure out some other way to get the scratch— with the belt workin' again it shouldn't be too hard."

Spud laughed and shook his head. "Thanks, Joe," he said. "That's really nice of you, and I appreciate it—but 'figuring out' isn't exactly your strong suit. Besides, I've been doing some thinking too. If I won fifty bucks shooting pool, that'd make me happy— I'd be proud, I'd've earned it. But to make twenty-thousand on a fixed game with no gamble at all—that's no kick. You need the money—you take it, just like we planned. I'll see the bookies tonight."

"But you earned it, kid," Joe said in bewilderment.

"You went through a lotta work to get me here, and you fixed the belt."

"That's all right," Spud insisted. "I don't want money—but there's one thing you *can* do for me."

"Anything," Joe agreed. "As soon as I take a piss."

Three hours later, having ditched the car and visited the home of "Odds" Evenwright, where he placed a large bet on a certain ball club, Spud arrived home to find precisely what he had expected:

His mother, awesomely drunk and madder than hell, sitting next to the pool table on which his personal cue and balls still rested, waiting for him to come home.

"Hi, Mom," he said cheerfully as he entered the living room, and braced himself. With a cry of alcoholic fury, Mrs. Flynn lurched from her chair and began to close on him.

Then she pulled up short, realizing belatedly that her son was accompanied by a stranger. For a moment, old reflex manners nearly took hold, but the drink was upon her and her Irish was up. "Are you the tramp who's been teachin' my Clarence to shoot pool, you tramp?" she screeched, shaking her fist and very nearly capsizing with the effort. "You fat bum, are the one'sh been corrupting my boy?"

"Not me," Joe said politely, and disappeared.

"They ran out of pink elephants," he explained earnestly, reappearing three feet to the left and vanishing again.

"So I came instead," he went on from six feet to the right.

"Which is anyway novel," he finished from behind her, disappeared one last time and reappeared with his nose an inch from hers. Her eyes crossed, kept on crossing, and she went down like a felled tree, landing with the boneless grace of the totally stoned.

Spud giggled, and it was not an unsympathetic giggle. "Thanks, Joe," he said, slapping the fat man on the back. "You've done me a big favor."

"Glad I could help, kid," Joe said, putting his own arm around the boy. "It must be tough to have a juicer for an old lady."

"Don't worry, Joe," Spud said, feeling that the same unexplainable certainty he had felt at the time-belt repair shop. "Somehow I've got a feeling Mom has taken her last drink."

Joe nodded happily. "I'll be back after the Series," he said, "and we can always try a second treatment."

"Okay, but we won't have to. Now get out of here and get back to your wife—it's late."

Joe nodded again. "Sure thing, Spud." He stuck out his hand. "Thanks for everything, pal—I couldn't have made it without you. See you in a couple o' weeks and then, who knows—Alice an' I might just decide this era's the one we want to settle down in."

"Not if you're smart," Spud said wryly.

"Well, in that case, maybe I'll be seein' ya again sometime," Joe pointed out. He reached down, making an adjustment on the time-belt, waved good-bye and vanished.

Or nearly. A pair of fat legs still stood in the living room, topped by the time-belt. As Spud stared, one of the legs stamped its foot in frustration and fury.

Sighing, Spud moved forward to kick the damned thing again.

ANTINOMY

The first awakening was just awful.

She was naked and terribly cold. She appeared to be in a plastic coffin, from whose walls grew wrinkled plastic arms with plastic hands that did things to her. Most of the things hurt dreadfully *But I don't have nightmares like this,* she thought wildly. She tried to say it aloud and it came out "A."

Even allowing for the sound-deadening coffin walls, the voice sounded distant. "Christ, she's awake already."

Eyes appeared over hers, through a transparent panel she had failed to see since it had showed only a ceiling the same color as the coffin's interior. The face was masked and capped in white, the eyes pouched in wrinkles. *Marcus Welby. Now it makes enough sense. Now I'll believe it. I don't have nightmares like this.*

"I believe you're right." The voice was profession-
ally detached. A plastic hand selected something that
lay by her side, pressed it to her arm. "There."

*Thank you, Doctor. If my brain doesn't want to
remember what you're operating on me for, I don't
much suppose it'll want to record the operation itself.
Bye.*

She slept.

The second awakening was better.

She was astonished not to hurt. She had expected
to hurt, somewhere, although she had also expected
to be too dopey to pay it any mind. Neither condition obtained.

She was definitely in a hospital, although some of
the gadgetry seemed absurdly ultramodern. *This
certainly isn't Bellevue*, she mused. *I must have contracted something fancy. How long has it been since
I went to bed "last night"?*

Her hands were folded across her belly; her right
hand held something hard. It turned out to be a
traditional nurse-call buzzer—save that it was
cordless. Lifting her arm to examine it had told her
how terribly weak she was, but she thumbed the
button easily—it was not spring loaded. "*Nice* hospital," she said aloud, and her voice sounded too
high. *Something with my throat? Or my ears? Or
my . . . brain?*

The buzzer might be improved, but the other end
of the process had not changed appreciably; no one
appeared for a while. She awarded her attention to
the window beside her, no contest in a hospital room,
and what she saw through it startled her profoundly.

She *was* in Bellevue, after all, rather high up in
the new tower; the rooftops below her across the
street and the river beyond them told her that. But

she absorbed the datum almost unconsciously, much more startled by the policeman who was flying above those rooftops, a few hundred feet away, in an over-size garbage can.

Yep, my brain. The operation was a failure, but the patient lived.

For a ghastly moment there was great a abyss within her, into which she must surely fall. But her mind had more strength than her body. She willed the abyss to disappear, and it did. *I may be insane, but I'm not going to go nuts over it,* she thought, and giggled. She decided the giggle was a healthy sign, and did it again, realizing her error when she found she could not stop.

It was mercifully shorter than such episodes usu-ally are; she simply lost the strength to giggle. The room swam for a while, then, but lucidity returned rather rapidly.

Let's see. Time travel, huh? That means . . .

The door opened to admit—not a nurse—but a young man of about twenty-five, five years her jun-ior. He was tall and somehow self-effacing. His clothes and appearance did not strike her as conservative, but she decided they probably were—for this era. He did not look like a man who would preen more than convention required. He wore a sidearm, but his hand was nowhere near the grip.

"What year is this, anyway?" she asked as he opened his mouth, and he closed it. He began to look elated and opened his mouth again, and she said, "And what did I die of?" and he closed it again. He was silent then for a moment, and when he had worked it out she could see that the elation was gone.

But in its place was a subtler, more personal plea-sure. "I congratulate you on the speed of your uptake," he said pleasantly. "You've just saved me most of twenty minutes of hard work."

"The hell you say. I can deduce what *happened,* all right, but that saves you twenty seconds, max. 'How' and 'why' are going to take just as long as you expected. And don't forget 'when.'" Her voice still seemed too high, though less so.

"How about 'who'? I'm Bill McLaughlin."

"I'm Marie Antoinette, *what the hell year is it?*" The italics cost her the last of her energy; as he replied "1995," his voice faded and the phosphor dots of her vision began to enlarge and drift apart. She was too bemused by his answer to be annoyed.

Something happened to her arm again, and picture and sound returned with even greater clarity. "Forgive me, Ms. Harding. The first thing I'm supposed to do is give you the stimulant. But then the first thing you're supposed to do is be semiconscious."

"And we've dispensed with the second thing," she said, her voice normal again now, "which is telling me that I've been a corpsicle for ten years. So tell me why, and why I don't *remember* any of it. As far as I know I went to sleep last night and woke up here, with a brief interlude inside something that must have been a defroster."

"I thought you *had* remembered, from your first question. I hoped you had, Ms. Harding. You'd have been the first . . . never mind—your next question made it plain that you don't. Very briefly, ten years ago you discovered that you had leukemia . . ."

"Myelocytic or lymphocytic?"

"Neither. Acute."

She paled. "No wonder I've suppressed the memory."

"You haven't. Let me finish. Acute Luke was the

diagnosis, a new rogue variant with a bitch's bastard of a prognosis. In a little under sixteen weeks they tried corticosteroids, L-aspiraginase, cytosine arabinoside, massive irradiation, and mercrystate crystals, with no more success than they'd expected, which was none and negatory. They told you that the new bone-marrow transplant idea showed great promise, but it might be a few years. And so you elected to become a corpsicle. You took another few weeks arranging your affairs and then went to a Cold Sleep Center and had yourself frozen."

"*Alive?*"

"They had just announced the big breakthrough. A week of drugs and a high-helium atmosphere and you can defrost a living person instead of preserved meat. You got in on the ground floor."

"And the catch?"

"The process scrubs the top six months to a year off your memory."

"Why?"

"I've been throwing around terminology to demonstrate how thoroughly I've read your file. But I'm not a doctor. I don't understand the alleged 'explanation' they gave me, and I dare say you won't either."

"Okay." She forgot the matter, instantly and forever. "If you're not a doctor, who are you, Mr. McLaughlin?"

"Bill. I'm an Orientator. The phrase won't be familiar to you—"

"—but I can figure it out, Bill. Unless things have slowed down considerably since I was alive, ten years is a hell of a jump. You're going to teach me how to dress and speak and recognize the ladies' room."

"And hopefully to stay alive."

"For how long? Did they fix it?"

"Yes. A spinal implant, right after you were thawed. It releases a white-cell antagonist into your bloodstream, and it's triggered by a white-cell surplus. The antagonist favors rogue cells."

"Slick. I always liked feedback control. Is it foolproof?"

"Is anything? Oh, you'll need a new implant every five years, and you'll have to take a week of chemotherapy here to make sure the implant isn't rejected before we can let you go. But the worst side-effect we know of is partial hair-loss. You're fixed, Ms. Harding."

She relaxed all over, for the first time since the start of the conversation. With the relaxation came a dreamy feeling, and she knew she had been subtly drugged, and was pleased that she had resisted it, quite unconsciously, for as long as had been necessary. She disliked don't-worry drugs; she preferred to worry if she had a mind to.

"Virginia. Not Ms. Harding. And I'm pleased with the Orientator I drew, Bill. It will take you awhile to get to the nut, but you haven't said a single inane thing yet, which under the circumstances makes you a remarkable person."

"I like to think so, Virginia. By the way, you'll doubtless be pleased to know that your fortune has come through the last ten years intact. In fact, it's actually grown considerably."

"There goes your no-hitter."

"Beg pardon?"

"Two stupid statements in one breath. First, of *course* my fortune has grown. A fortune the size of mine can't *help* but grow—which is one of the major faults of our economic system. What could be sillier than a goose that insists on burying you in golden eggs? Which leads to number two: I'm anything but pleased. I was hoping against hope that I was broke."

His face worked briefly, ending in a puzzled frown. "You're probably right on the first count, but I think the second is ignorance rather than stupidity. I've never been rich." His tone was almost wistful.

"Count your blessings. And be grateful you can count that high."

He looked dubious. "I suppose I'll have to take your word for it."

"When do I start getting hungry?"

"Tomorrow. You can walk now, if you don't overdo it, and in about an hour you'll be required to sleep."

"Well, let's go."

"Where to?"

"Eh? *Outside*, Bill. Or the nearest balcony or solarium. I haven't had a breath of fresh air in ten years."

"The solarium it is."

As he was helping her into a robe and slippers the door chimed and opened again, admitting a man in the time-honored white garb of a medical man on duty, save that the stethoscope around his neck was cordless as the call-buzzer had been. The pickup was doubtless in his breast pocket, and she was willing to bet that it was warm to the skin.

The newcomer appeared to be a few years older than she, a pleasant-looking man with grey-ribbed temples and plain features. She recognized the wrinkled eyes and knew he was the doctor who had peered into her plastic coffin.

McLaughlin said, "Hello, Dr. Higgins. Virginia Harding, Dr. Thomas Higgins, Bellevue's Director of Cryonics."

Higgins met her eyes squarely and bowed. "Ms. Harding. I'm pleased to see you up and about."

Still has the same detached voice. Stuffy man. "You did a good job on me, Dr. Higgins."

"Except for the moment of premature consciousness, yes, I did. But the machines say you weren't harmed psychologically, and I'm inclined to believe them."

"They're right. I'm some tough."

"I know. That's why I brought you up to Level One Awareness in a half-day instead of a week. I knew your subconscious would fret less."

Discriminating machines, she thought. *I don't know that I like that.*

"Doctor," McLaughlin cut in, "I hate to cut you off, but Ms. Harding has asked for fresh air, and—"

"—and has less than an hour of consciousness left today. I understand. Don't let me keep you."

"Thank you, Doctor," Virginia Harding said. "I'd like to speak further with you tomorrow, if you're free."

He almost frowned, caught himself. "Later in the week, perhaps. Enjoy your walk."

"I shall. Oh, how I shall. Thank you again."

"Thank Hoskins and Parvati. They did the implant."

"I will, tomorrow. Good-bye, Doctor."

She left with McLaughlin, and as soon as the door had closed behind them, Higgins went to the window and slammed his fist into it squarely, shattering the shatterproof glass and two knuckles. Shards dropped thirty long stories, and he did not hear them land.

McLaughlin entered the office and closed the door. Higgins's office was not spare or austere. The furnishings were many and comfortable, and in fact the entire room had a lived-in air which hinted that Higgins's apartment might well be spare and austere. Shelves of books covered two walls; most looked medical and all looked used. The predominant color of the room was black—not at all a fashionable color—but in no single instance was the black morbid, any more than is the night sky. It gave a special vividness to the flowers on the desk, which were the red of rubies, and to the profusion of hand-tended plants which sat beneath the broad cast window (now opaqued) in a riotous splash of many colors for which our language has only the single word "green." It put crisper outlines on anything that moved in the office, brought both visitors and owner into sharper relief.

But the owner was not making use of this sharpening of perception at the moment. He was staring fixedly down at his desk; precisely, in fact, at the empty place where a man will put a picture of his wife and family if he has them. He could not have seen McLaughlin if he tried; his eyes were blinded with tears. Had McLaughlin not seen them, he might have thought the other to be in an autohypnotic trance or a warm creative fog, neither of which states were unusual enough to call for comment.

Since he did see the tears, he did not back silently out of the office. "Tom." There was no response. "Tom," he said again, a little louder, and then "TOM!"

"Yes?" Higgins said evenly, sounding like a man talking on an intercom. His gaze remained fixed, but the deep-set wrinkles around it relaxed a bit.

"She's asleep."

Higgins nodded. He took a bottle from an open drawer and swallowed long. He didn't have to uncap

it first, and there weren't many swallows that size left.
He set it, clumsily, on the desk.

"For God's sake, Tom," McLaughlin said half-
angrily. "You remind me of Monsieur Rick in
Casablanca. Want me to play 'As Time goes By' now?"

Higgins looked up for the first time, and smiled
beatifically. "You might," he said, voice steady. " 'You
must remember this . . . as time goes by.'" He smiled
again. "I often wonder." He looked down again,
obviously forgetting McLaughlin's existence.

Self-pity in this man shocked McLaughlin, and
cheerful self-pity disturbed him profoundly. "Jesus,"
he said harshly. "That bad?" Higgins did not hear. He
saw Higgins's hand then, with its half-glove of bandage, and sucked air through his teeth. He called
Higgins's name again, elicited no reaction at all.

He sighed, drew his gun and put a slug into the
ceiling. The roar filled the office, trapped by sound-
proofing. Higgins started violently, becoming fully
aware just as his own gun cleared the holster. He
seemed quite sober.

"Now that I've got your attention," McLaughlin said
dryly, "would you care to tell me about it?"

"No." Higgins grimaced. "Yes and no. I don't
suppose I have much choice. She didn't remember
a thing." His voice changed for the last sentence; it
was very nearly a question.

"No, she didn't."

"None of them have yet. Almost a hundred awak-
enings, and not one remembers anything that happened more than ten to twelve months before they
were put to sleep. And still somehow I hoped . . . I
had hope . . ."

McLaughlin's voice was firm. "When you gave me
her file, you said 'used to know her,' and that you

didn't want to go near her 'to avoid upsetting her.' You asked me to give her special attention, to take the best possible care of her, and you threw in some flattery about me being your best Orientator. Then you come barging into her room on no pretext at all, chat aimlessly, break your hand and get drunk. So you loved her. And you loved her in the last year."

"I diagnosed her leukemia," Higgins said emotionlessly. "It's hard to miss upper abdomen swelling and lymph node swelling in the groin when you're making love, but I managed for weeks. It was after she had the tooth pulled and it wouldn't stop bleeding that . . ." He trailed off.

"She loved you too."

"Yes." Higgins's voice was bleak, hollow.

"Bleeding Christ, Tom," McLaughlin burst out. "Couldn't you have waited to . . ." He broke off, thinking bitterly that Virginia Harding had given him too much credit.

"We tried to. We knew that every day we waited decreased her chances of surviving cryology, but we tried. She insisted that we try. Then the crisis came . . . oh damn it, Bill, *damn* it."

McLaughlin was glad to hear the profanity—it was the first sign of steam blowing off. "Well, she's alive and healthy now."

"Yes. I've been thanking God for that for three months now, ever since Hoskins and Parvati announced the unequivocal success of spinal implants. I've thanked God over ten thousand times, and I don't think He believed me once. I don't think *I* believed me once. Now doesn't that make me a selfish son of a bitch?"

McLaughlin grinned. "Head of Department and

you live like a monk, because you're selfish. For years,
every dime you make disappears down a hole somewhere, and everybody wonders why you're so friendly
with Hoskins and Parvati, who aren't even in your own
department, and only now, as I'm figuring out where
the money's been going, do I realize what a truly
selfish son of a bitch you are, Higgins."

Higgins smiled horribly. "We talked about it a lot,
that last month. I wanted to be frozen too, for as long
as they had to freeze her."

"What would that have accomplished? Then neither of you would have remembered."

"But we'd have entered and left freeze at the *same
time*, and come out of it with sets of memories that
ran nearly to the day we met. We'd effectively be
precisely the people who fell in love once before; we
could have left notes for ourselves and the rest
would've been inevitable. But she wouldn't hear of
it. She pointed out that the period in question could
be any fraction of forever, with no warranty. I insisted,
and got quite histrionic about it. Finally she brought
up our age difference."

"I wondered about the chronology."

"She was thirty, I was twenty-five. Your age. It was
something we kidded about, but it stung a bit when
we did. So she asked me to wait five years, and then
if I still wanted to be frozen, fine. In those five years
I clawed my way up to head of section here, because
I wanted to do everything I could to ensure her
survival. And in the fifth year they thought her type
of leukemia might be curable with marrow transplants,
so I hung around for the two years it took to be sure
they were wrong. And in the eighth year Hoskins
started looking for a safe white-cell antagonist, and
again I had to stay room temperature to finance him,

because nobody else could smell that he was a genius. When he met Parvati, I knew they'd lick it, and I told myself that if they needed me, that meant she needed me. I wasn't wealthy like her—I had to keep working to keep them both funded properly. So I stayed."

Higgins rubbed his eyes, then made his hands lie very still before him, left on right. "Now there's a ten-year span between us, the more pronounced because she hasn't experienced a single minute of it. Will she love me again or won't she?" The bandaged right hand escaped from the left, began to tap on the desk. "For ten years I told myself I could stand to know the answer to that question. For ten years it was the last thing I thought before I fell asleep and the first thing I thought when I woke up. *Will she love me or won't she?*

"She made me promise that I'd tell her everything when she was awakened, that I'd tell her how our love had been. She swore that she'd love me again. I promised, and she must have known I lied, or suspected it, because she left a ten-page letter to herself in her file. The day I became Department Head I burned the fucking thing. I don't want her to love me because she thinks she should.

"Will she love me or won't she? For ten years I believed I could face the answer. Then it came time to wake her up, and I lost my nerve. I couldn't stand to know the answer. I gave her file to you.

"And then I saw her on the monitor, heard her voice coming out of my desk, and I knew I couldn't stand *not* to know."

He reached clumsily for the bottle, and knocked it clear off the desk. Incredibly, it contrived to shatter on the thick black carpet, staining it a deeper black.

He considered this, while the autovac cleaned up the glass, clacking in disapproval.

"Do you know a liquor store that delivers?"

"In *this* day and age?" McLaughlin exclaimed, but Higgins was not listening. "Jesus Christ," he said suddenly. "Here." He produced a flask and passed it across the desk.

Higgins looked him in the eye. "Thanks, Bill." He drank.

McLaughlin took a long swallow himself and passed it back. They sat in silence for a while, in a communion and a comradeship as ancient as alcohol, as pain itself. Synthetic leather creaked convincingly as they passed the flask. Their breathing slowed.

If a clock whirs on a deskface and no one is listening, is there really a sound? In a soundproof office with opaqued windows, is it not always night? The two men shared the long night of the present, forsaking past and future, for nearly half an hour, while all around them hundreds upon hundreds worked, wept, smiled, dozed, watched television, screamed, were visited by relatives and friends, smoked, ate, died.

At last McLaughlin sighed and studied his hands. "When I was a grad student," he said to them, "I did a hitch on an Amerind reservation in New Mexico. Got friendly with an old man named Wanoma, face like a map of the desert. Grandfather-grandson relationship—close in that culture. He let me see his own grandfather's bones. He taught me how to pray. One night the son of a nephew, a boy he'd had hopes for, got alone-drunk and fell off a motorcycle. Broke his neck. I heard about it and went to see Wanoma that night. We sat under the moon—it was a harvest moon—and watched a fire until it was ashes. Just after the last coal went dark, Wanoma lifted his head and cried out in Zuni. He cried out, 'Ai-yah, my heart is full of sorrow.' "

McLaughlin glanced up at his boss and took a swallow. "You know, it's impossible for a white man to say those words and not sound silly. Or theatrical. It's a simple statement of a genuine universal, and there's no way for a white man to say it. I've tried two or three times since. You can't say it in English."

Higgins smiled painfully and nodded.

"I cried out too," McLaughlin went on, "after Wanoma did. The English of it was, 'Ai-yah, my brother's heart is full of sorrow. His heart is my heart.' Happens I haven't ever tried to say that since, but you can see it sounds hokey too."

Higgins's smile became less pained, and his eyes lost some of their squint. "Thanks, Bill."

"What'll you do?"

The smile remained. "Whatever I must. I believe I'll take the tour with you day after tomorrow. You can use the extra gun."

The Orientator went poker faced. "Are you up to it, Tom? You've got to be fair to her, you know."

"I know. Today's world is pretty crazy. She's got a right to integrate herself back into it without tripping over past karma. She'll never know. I'll have control on Thursday, Bill. Partly thanks to you. But you do know why I selected you for her Orientator, don't you?"

"No. I don't think I do."

"I thought you'd at least have suspected. Personality Profiles are a delightful magic. Perhaps if we ever develop a science of psychology we'll understand why we get results out of them. According to the computer, your PP matches almost precisely to my own—of ten years ago. Probably why we get along so well."

"I don't follow."

"Is love a matter of happy accident or a matter of psychological inevitability? Was what 'Ginia and I had fated in the stars, or was it a chance of jigsawing of personality traits? Will the woman she was ten years ago love the man I've become? Or the kind of man I was then? Or some third kind?"

"Oh, fine," McLaughlin said, getting angry. "So I'm your competition."

"Aha," Higgins pounced. "You do feel something for her."

"I . . ." McLaughlin got red.

"You're my competition," Higgins said steadily. "And, as you have said, you are my brother. Would you like another drink?"

McLaughlin opened his mouth, then closed it. He rose and left in great haste, and when he had gained the hallway he cannoned into a young nurse with red hair and improbably grey eyes. He mumbled apology and continued on his way, failing to notice her. He did not know Deborah Manning.

Behind him, Higgins passed out.

Throughout the intervening next day Higgins was conscious of eyes on him. He was conscious of little enough else as he sleep-walked through his duties. The immense hospital complex seemed to have been packed full of grey Jell-O, very near to setting. He ploughed doggedly through it, making noises with his mouth, making decisions, making marks on pieces of paper, discharging his responsibilities with the least part of his mind. But he was conscious of the eyes.

A hospital grapevine is like no other on earth. If

you want a message heard by every employee, it is quicker to tell two nurses and an intern than it would be to assemble the staff and make an announcement. Certainly McLaughlin had said nothing, even to his hypothetical closest friend; he knew that any closest friend has at least one *other* closest friend. But at least three OR personnel knew that the Old Man had wakened one personally the other day. And a janitor knew that the Old Man was in the habit of dropping by the vaults once a week or so just after the start of the graveyard shift, to check on the nonexistent progress of a corpsicle named Harding. And the OR team and the janitor worked within the same (admittedly huge) wing, albeit on different floors. So did the clerk-typist in whose purview were Virginia Harding's files, and she was engaged to the anesthetist. Within twenty-four hours, the entire hospital staff and a majority of the patients had added two and two.

(Virginia Harding, of course, heard nary a word, got not so much as a hint. A hospital staff may spill Mercurochrome. It often spills blood. But it never spills beans.)

Eyes watched Higgins all day. And so perhaps it was natural that eyes watched him in his dreams that night. But they did not make him afraid or uneasy. Eyes that watch oneself continuously become, after a time, like a second ego, freeing the first from the burden of introspection. They almost comforted him. They helped.

I have been many places, touched many lives since I touched her, he thought as he shaved the next morning, *and been changed by them. Will she love me or won't she?*

There were an endless three more hours of work to be taken care of that morning, and then at last the Jell-O dispersed, his vision cleared and she was before him, dressed for the street, chatting with McLaughlin. There were greetings, explanations of some sort were made for his presence in the party, and they left the room, to solve the mouse's maze of corridors that led to the street and the city outside.

It was a warm fall day. The streets were unusually crowded, with people and cars, but he knew they would not seem so to Virginia. The sky seemed unusually overcast, the air particularly muggy, but he knew it would seem otherwise to her. The faces of the pedestrians they passed seemed to him markedly cheerful and optimistic, and he felt that this was a judgement with which she *would* agree. This was not a new pattern of thought for him. For over five years now, since the world she knew had changed enough for him to perceive, he had been accustomed to observe that world in the light of what she would think of it. Having an unconscious standard of comparison, he had marked the changes of the last decade more acutely than his contemporaries, more acutely perhaps than even McLaughlin, whose interest was only professional.

Too, knowing her better than McLaughlin, he was better able to anticipate the questions she would ask. A policeman went overhead in a floater bucket, and McLaughlin began to describe the effects that force-fields were beginning to exert on her transportation holdings and other financial interests. Higgins cut him off before she could, and described the effects single-person flight was having on social and sexual customs, winning a smile from her and a thoughtful look from the Orientator. When McLaughlin began listing some of the unfamiliar gadgetry she could expect to see,

Higgins interrupted with a brief sketch of the current state of America's spiritual renaissance. When McLaughlin gave her a personal wrist-phone, Higgins showed her how to set it to refuse calls.

McLaughlin had, of course, already told her a good deal about Civil War Two and the virtual annihilation of the American black, and had been surprised at how little surprised she was. But when, now, he made a passing reference to the unparalleled savagery of the conflict, Higgins saw a chance to make points by partly explaining that bloodiness with a paraphrase of a speech Virginia herself had made ten years before, on the folly of an urban-renewal package concept which had sited low-income housing immediately around urban and suburban transportation hubs. "Built in disaster," she agreed approvingly, and did not feel obliged to mention that the same thought had occurred to her a decade ago. Higgins permitted himself to be encouraged.

But about that time, as they were approaching one of the new downtown parks, Higgins noticed the expression on McLaughlin's face, and somehow recognized it as one he had seen before—from the inside.

At once he was ashamed of the fatuous pleasure he had been taking in outmaneuvering the younger man. It was a cheap triumph, achieved through unfair advantage. Higgins decided sourly that he would never have forced this "duel with his younger self" unless he had been just this smugly sure of the outcome, and his self-esteem dropped sharply. He shut his mouth and resolved to let McLaughlin lead the conversation.

It immediately took a turning he could not have followed if he tried.

As the trio entered the park, they passed a group of teenagers. Higgins paid them no mind—he had long since reached the age when adolescents, especially in groups, regarded him as an alien life form, and he was nearly ready to agree with them. But he noticed Virginia Harding noticing them, and followed her gaze.

The group was talking in loud voices, the incomprehensible gibberish of the young. There was nothing Higgins could see about them that Harding ought to find striking. They were dressed no differently than any one of a hundred teenagers she had passed on the walk so far, were quite nondescript. Well, now that he looked closer, he saw rather higher-than-average intelligence in most of the faces. Honor-student types, down to the carefully cultivated look of aged cynicism. That *was* rather at variance with the raucousness of their voices, but Higgins still failed to see what held Harding's interest.

"What on earth are they saying?" she asked, watching them over her shoulder as they passed.

Higgins strained, heard only nonsense. He saw McLaughlin grinning.

"They're Goofing," the Orientator said.

"Beg pardon?"

"Goofing. The very latest in sophisticated humor." Harding still looked curious.

"It sort of grew out of the old Firesign Theater of the seventies. Their kind of comedy laid the ground-work for the immortal Spiwack, and he created Goofing, or as he called it, speaking with spooned tongue. It's a kind of double-talk, except that it's designed to actually convey information, more or less in spite of itself. The idea is to *almost* make sense, to get across as much of your point as possible without ever saying anything comprehensible."

Higgins snorted, afraid.

"I'm not sure I understand," Harding said.

"Well, for instance, if Spiwack wanted to publicly libel, say, the president, he'd Goof. Uh . . ." McLaughlin twisted his voice into a fair imitation of a broken-down prizefighter striving to sound authoritative. "That guy there, see, in my youth we would of referred to him as a man with a tissue paper asshole. What you call a kinda guy that sucks blueberries through a straw, see? A guy like what would whistle at a doorknob, you know what I mean? He ain't got all his toes."

Harding began to giggle. Higgins began sweating, all over.

"I'm tellin' ya, the biggest plum *he's* got is the one under his ear, see what I'm sayin'? If whiskers was pickles, he'd have a goat. First sign of saddlebags an' he'll be under his pants. If I was you I'd keep my finger out of *his* nose, an' you can forget I said so. Good night."

Harding was laughing out loud now. "That's marvellous!" A spasm shook her. "That's the most . . . *conspicuous* thing I've ever baked." McLaughlin began to laugh. "I've never been so identified in all my shoes." They were both laughing together now, and Higgins had about four seconds in which to grab his wrist-phone behind his back and dial his own code, before they could notice him standing there and realize they had left him behind and become politely apologetic, and he just made it, but even so he had time in which to reflect that a shared belly-laugh can be as intimate as making love. *It may even be a prerequisite,* he thought, and then his phone was humming its A-major chord.

The business of unclipping the earphone and fiddling with the gain gave him all the time he needed to devise an emergency that would require his return, and he marvelled at his lightning cleverness that balked at producing a joke. He really tried, as he spoke with his nonexistent caller, prolonging the conversation with grunts to give himself time. When he was ready he switched off, and in his best W.C. Fields voice said, "It appears that one of my clients had contracted farfalonis of the blowhole," and to his absolute horror they both said "Huh?" together and then got it, and in that moment he hated McLaughlin more than he had ever hated anything, even the cancer that had come sipping her blood a decade before. *Keep your face straight,* he commanded himself savagely. *She's looking at you.*

And McLaughlin rescued the moment, in that split second before Higgins's control would have cracked, doing his prizefighter imitation. "Aw Jeez, Tom, that hard cider. If it ain't one thing, it's two things. Go ahead; we'll keep your shoes warm."

Higgins nodded. "Hello, Virginia."

"Gesundheit, Doctor," she said regarding him oddly.

He turned on his heel to go, and saw the tallest of the group of teenagers fold at the waist, take four rapid steps backward and fall with the boneless sprawl of the totally drunk. *But drunks don't spurt red from their bellies*, Higgins thought dizzily, just as the flat *crack* reached his ears.

Mucker!!

Eyes report: a middle-aged black man with three days' growth of beard, a hundred meters away and twenty meters up in a stolen floater bucket with blood on its surface. Firing a police rifle of extremely heavy caliber with snipersights. Clearly crazed with grief or stoned out of control, he is not making use of the sights, but firing from the hip. His forehead and cheek are bloody and one eye is ruined: some policeman sold his floater dearly.

Memory reports: It has been sixteen weeks since the Treaty of Philadelphia officially "ended" CW II. Nevertheless, known-dead statistics are still filtering slowly back to next-of-kin; the envelope in his breast pocket looks like a government form letter.

Ears report: Two more shots have been fired. Despite eyes' report, his accuracy is hellish—each shot hit someone. Neither of them is Virginia.

Nose reports: all three(?) wounded have blown all sphincters. Death, too, has its own smell, as does blood. The other one: is that fear?

Hand reports: Gun located, clearing holster ... now. Safety off, barrel coming up fast.

WHITE OUT!

The slug smashed into Higgins's side and spun him completely around twice before slamming him to earth beside the path. His brain continued to record all sensory reports, so in a sense he was conscious; but he would not audit these memories for days, so in a sense he was unconscious too. His head was placed so that he could see Virginia Harding, in a sideways crouch, extend her gun and fire with extreme care. McLaughlin stood tall before her, firing rapidly from the hip, and her shot took his right earlobe off. He screamed and dropped to one knee.

She ignored him and raced to Higgins's side. "It looks all right, Tom," she lied convincingly. She was efficiently taking his pulse as she fumbled with his clothing. "Get an ambulance," she barked at someone out of vision. Whoever it was apparently failed to understand the archaism, for she amended it to "A doctor, dammit. *Now*," and the whip of command was in her voice. As she turned back to Higgins, McLaughlin came up with a handkerchief pressed to his ear.

"You got him," he said weakly.

"I know," she said, and finished unbuttoning Higgins's shirt. Then, *"What the hell did you get in my way for?"*

"I . . . I," he stammered, taken aback. "I was trying to protect *you*."

"From a rifle like *that*?" she blazed. "If you got between one of those slugs and me all you'd do is tumble it for me. Blasting away from the hip like a cowboy . . ."

"I was trying to spoil his aim," McLaughlin said stiffly.

"You bloody idiot, you can't scare a kamikaze! The only thing to do was drop him, fast."

"I'm sorry."

"I nearly blew your damn head off."

McLaughlin began an angry retort, but about then even Higgins's delayed action consciousness faded. The last sensation he retained was that of her hands gently touching his face. That made it a fine memory-sequence, all in all, and when he reviewed it later on he only regretted not having been there at the time.

All things considered, McLaughlin was rather lucky. It took him only three days of rather classical confusion to face his problem, conceive of several solutions, select the least drastic, and persuade a pretty nurse to help him put it into effect. But it was after they had gone to his apartment and gone to bed that he really got lucky; his penis flatly refused to erect.

He of course did not, at that time, think of this as a stroke of luck. He did not know Deborah Manning. He in fact literally did not know her last name. She had simply walked past at the right moment, a vaguely-remembered face framed in red hair, grey eyes improbable enough to stick in the mind. In a mood of go-to-hell desperation he had baldly propositioned her, as though this were still the promiscuous seventies, and he had been surprised when she accepted. He did not know Debbie Manning.

In normal circumstances he would have considered his disfunction trivial, done the gentlemanly thing and tried again in the morning. In the shape he was in it nearly cracked him. Even so, he tried to be chivalrous, but she pulled him up next to her with a gentle firmness and looked closely at him. He had the odd, inexplicable feeling that she had been . . . *prepared* for this eventuality.

He seldom watched peoples' eyes closely—popular opinion and literary convention to the contrary, he found peoples' mouths much more expressive of the spirit within. But something about her eyes held his. Perhaps it was that they were not trying to. They were staring only for information, for a deeper understanding . . . he realized with a start that they were looking at his mouth. For a moment he started to *look* back, took in clean high cheeks and soft lips, was beginning to genuinely notice her for the first time when she said "Does she know?" with just the right mixture of tenderness and distance to open him up like a clam.

"No," he blurted, his pain once again demanding his attention.

"Well, you'll just have to tell her then," she said earnestly, and he began to cry.

"I can't," he sobbed, "I *can't.*"

She took the word at face value. Her face saddened. She hugged him closer, and her shoulder blades were warm under his hands. "That *is* terrible. What is her name, and how did it come about?"

It no more occurred to him to question the ethics of telling her than it had occurred to him to wonder by what sorcery she had identified his brand of pain in the first place, or to wonder why she chose to involve herself in it. Head tucked in the hollow between her neck and shoulder, legs wrapped in hers, he told her everything in his heart. She spoke only to prompt him, keeping her *self* from his attention, and yet somehow what he told her held more honesty and truth than what he had been telling himself.

"He's been in the hospital for three days," he concluded, "and she's been to visit him twice a day— and she's begged off our Orientation Walks every damn day. She leaves word with the charge nurse."

"You've tried to see her anyway? After work?"

"No. I can read print."

"Can't you read the print on your own heart? You don't seem like a quitter to me, Bill."

"Dammit," he raged, "I don't *want* to love her, I've tried *not* to love her, and I can't get her out of my head."

She made the softest of snorting sounds. "You will be given a billion dollars if in the next ten seconds you do *not* think of a green horse." Pause. "You know better than that."

"Well, how do you get someone out of your head, then?"

"Why do you want to?"

"Why? Because . . . " he stumbled. "Well, this sounds silly in words, but . . . I haven't got the right to her. I mean, Tom has put literally his whole life into her for ten years now. He's not just my boss—he's my friend, and if he wants her that bad he ought to have her."

"She's an object, then? A prize? He shot more tin ducks, he wins her?"

"Of course not. I mean he ought to have his *chance* with her, a fair chance, without tripping over the image of himself as a young stud. He's *earned* it. Dammit, I . . . this sounds like ego, but I'm unfair competition. What man can compete with his younger self?"

"Any man who has grown as he aged," she said with certainty.

He pulled back—just far enough to be able to see her face. "What do you mean?" He sounded almost petulant.

She brushed hair from her face, freed some that was trapped between their bodies. "Why did Dr. Higgins rope you into this in the first place?"

He opened his mouth and nothing came out.

"He may not know," she said, "but his subconscious does. Yours does too, or you wouldn't be so damfool guilty."

"What are you talking about?"

"If you *are* unfair competition, he does not deserve her, and I don't care how many years he's dedicated to her sacred memory. Make up your mind: are you crying because you can't have her or because you could?" Her voice softened suddenly—took on a tone which only his subconscious associated with that of a father confessor from his Catholic youth. "Do you honestly believe in your heart of hearts that you could take her away from him if you tried?"

Those words could certainly have held sting, but they did not somehow. The silence stretched, and her face and gaze held a boundless compassion that told him that he must give her an answer, and that it must be the truth.

"I don't know," he cried, and began to scramble from the bed. But her soft hands had a grip like iron—and there was nowhere for him to go. He sat on the side of the bed, and she moved to sit beside him. With the same phenomenal strength, she took his chin and turned his face to see hers. At the sight of it he was thunderstruck. Her face seemed to glow with a light of its own, to be somehow *larger* than it was, and with softer edges than flesh can have. Her neck muscles were bars of tension and her face and lips were utterly slack; her eyes were twin tractor beams of incredible strength locked on his soul, on his attention.

"Then you have to find out, don't you?" she said in the most natural voice in the world.

And she sat and watched his face go through several distinct changes, and after a time she said "Don't you?" again very softly.

"Tom is my friend," he whispered bleakly.

She released his eyes, got up and started getting dressed. He felt vaguely that he should stop her, but he could not assemble the volition. As she dressed, she spoke for the first time of herself. "All my life people have brought problems to me," she said distantly. "I don't know why. Sometimes I think I attract pain. They tell me their story as though I had some wisdom to give them, and along about the time they're restating the problem for the third time they tell me what they want to hear; and I always wait a few more paragraphs and then repeat it back to them. And they light right up and go away praising my name. I've gotten used to it."

What do I want to hear? he asked himself, and honestly did not know.

"One man, though . . . once a man came to me who had been engaged to a woman for six years, all through school. They had gotten as far as selecting the wallpaper for the house. And one day she told him she felt a Vocation. God had called her to be a nun." Debbie pulled red hair out from under her collar and swept it back with both hands, glancing at the mirror over a nearby bureau. "He was a devout Catholic himself. By his own rules, *he couldn't even be sad*. He was supposed to rejoice." She rubbed at a lipstick smear near the base of her throat. "There's a word for that, and I'm amazed at how few people know it, because it's the word for the sharpest tragedy a human can feel. 'Antinomy.' It means, 'contradiction between two propositions which seem equally urgent and necessary.'" She retrieved her purse, took out a pack of Reefer and selected one. "I didn't know what in hell's name to tell that man," she said reflectively, and put the joint back in the pack.

Suddenly she turned and confronted him. "I still don't, Bill. *I* don't know which one of you Virginia would pick in a fair contest, and I don't know what it would do to Dr. Higgins if he *were* to lose her to you. A torch that burns for ten years must be awfully hot." She shuddered. "It might just have burned him to a crisp already.

"But you, on the other hand: I would say that you could get over her, more or less completely, in six months. Eight at the outside. If that's what you decide, I'll come back for you in . . . oh, a few weeks. You'll be ready for me then." She smiled gently, and reached out to touch his cheek. "Of course . . . if you do that . . . you'll never know, will you?" And she was gone.

Five minutes later he jumped up and said, "Hey wait!" and then felt very foolish indeed.

Virginia Harding took off her headphones, switched off the stereo, and sighed irritably. Ponty's bow had just been starting to really smoke, but the flood of visual imagery it evoked had been so intolerably rich that involuntarily she had opened her eyes—and seen the clock on the far wall. The relaxation period she had allowed herself was over.

Here I sit, she thought, *a major medical miracle, not a week out of the icebox and I'm buried in work. God, I hate money.*

She could, of course, have done almost literally anything she chose; had she requested it, the president of the hospital's board of directors would happily have dropped whatever he was doing and come to stand by her bedside and turn pages for her. But such freedom was too crushing for her to be anything but responsible with it.

Only the poor can afford to goof off. I can't even spare the time for a walk with Bill. Dammit, I still owe him an apology too. She would have enjoyed nothing more than to spend a pleasant hour with the handsome young Orientator, learning how to get along in polite society. But business traditionally came before pleasure, and she had more pressing duties. A fortune such as hers represented the life energy of many many people; as long as it persisted in *being* hers, she meant to take personal responsibility for it.

It had been out of her direct control for over a decade, and the very world of finance in which its power inhered had changed markedly in the interim. She was trying to absorb a decade at once—and determined to waste no time. A powered desk with computer-bank inputs had been installed in her hospital room, and the table to the left of it held literally hundreds of microfloppy discs, arranged by general heading in eight cartons and chronologically within them. The table on the right held the half-carton she had managed to review over the last five days. She had required three one-hour lectures by an earnest, aged specialist-synthesist to understand even that much. She had *expected* to encounter startling degrees and kinds of change, but this was incredible.

Another hour and a half on the Delanier-Garcia Act, she decided, *half an hour of exercise, lunch and those damnable pills, snatch ten minutes to visit Tom and then let the damned medicos poke and prod and test me for the rest of the afternoon. Supper if I've the stomach for any, see Tom again, then back to work. With any luck I'll have 1987 down by the time I fall asleep. God's teeth.*

She was already on her feet, her robe belted and slippers on. She activated the intercom and ordered coffee, crossed the room and sat down at the desk, which began to hum slightly. She lit its monitor screen, put the Silent Steno on standby and was rummaging in the nearest carton for her next disc when a happy thought struck her. Perhaps the last disc in the box would turn out to be a summary. She pulled it out and fed it to the desk, and by God it was—it appeared to be an excellent and thorough summary at that. *Do you suppose,* she asked herself,

that the last disc in the last box would be a complete
*overview? Would Charlesworthy & Cavanaugh be that
thoughtful? Worth a try. God, I need some shortcuts.*
She selected that disc and popped the other, setting
it aside for later.

The door chimed and opened, admitting one of her
nurses—the one whose taste in eyeshadow was abominable. He held a glass that appeared to contain milk
and lemon juice half and half with rust flakes stirred
in. From across the room it smelled bad.

"I'm sorry," she said gravely. "Even in a hospital
you can't tell me that's a cup of coffee."

"Corpuscle paint, Ms. Harding," he said cheerfully.
"Doctor's orders."

"Kindly tell the doctor that I would be obliged if
he would insert his thumb, rectally, to the extent of
the first joint, pick himself up and hold himself at
arm's length until I drink that stuff. Advise him to
put on an overcoat first, because hell's going to freeze
over in the meantime. And speaking of hell, where
in it is my coffee?"

"I'm sorry, Ms. Harding. No coffee. Stains the
paint—you don't want tacky corpuscles."

"*Dammit . . .*"

"Come on, drink it. It doesn't taste as bad as it
smells. Quite."

"Couldn't I take it intravenously or something? Oh
Christ, give it to me." She drained it in a single gulp
and shivered, beating her fists on her desk in revulsion. "God. God. God. Damn. Can't I just have my
leukemia back?"

His face sobered. "Ms. Harding—look, it's none of
my business, but if I was you, I'd be a little more
grateful. You give those lab boys a hard time. You've
come back literally from death's door. Why don't you

be patient while we make sure it's locked behind you?"

She sat perfectly still for five seconds, and then saw from his face that he thought he had just booted his job out the window. "Oh Manuel, I'm sorry. I'm not angry. I'm ... astounded. You're right, I haven't been very gracious about it all. It's just that, from my point of view, as far as *I* remember, I never *had* leukemia. I guess I resent the doctors for trying to tell me that I ever was that close to dying. I'll try and be a better patient." She made a face. "But God, that stuff tastes ghastly."

He smiled and turned to go, but she called him back. "Would you leave word for Bill McLaughlin that I won't be able to see him until tomorrow after all?"

"He didn't come in today," the nurse said. "But I'll leave word." He left, holding the glass between thumb and forefinger.

She turned back to her desk and inserted the new disc, but did not start it. Instead she chewed her lip and fretted. *I wonder if I was as blasé last time. When they told me I had it. Are those memories gone because I want them to be?*

She knew perfectly well that they were not. But anything that reminded her of those missing six months upset her. She could not reasonably regret the bargain she had made, but almost she did. Theft of her memories struck her as the most damnable invasion of privacy, made her very flesh crawl, and it did not help to reflect that it had been done with her knowledge and consent. From her point of view it had *not*; it had been authorized by another person who had once occupied this body, now deceased, by suicide. A life shackled to great wealth had taught her that her memories were the *only* things uniquely hers, and she mourned them, good, bad, or indifferent. Mourned them more than she missed the ten years spent in freeze: she had not *experienced* those.

She had tried repeatedly to pin down exactly what was the last thing she could remember before waking up in the plastic coffin, and had found the task maddeningly difficult. There were half a dozen candidates for last-remembered-day in her memory, none of them conveniently cross-referenced with time and date, and at least one or two of those appeared to be false memories, cryonic dreams. She had the feeling that if she had tried immediately upon awakening, she would have remembered, as you can sometimes remember last night's dream if you try at once. But she had been her usual efficient self, throwing all her energies into adapting to the new situation.

Dammit, I want those memories back! I know I swapped six months for a lifetime, but at that rate it'll be five months and twenty-five days before I'm even breaking even. I think I'd even settle for a record of some kind—if only I'd had the sense to start a diary!

She grimaced in disgust at the lack of foresight of the dead Virginia Harding, and activated the datadisc with an angry gesture. And then she dropped her jaw and said, "Jesus Christ in a floater bucket!"

The first frame read, "PERSONAL DIARY OF VIRGINIA HARDING."

If you have never experienced major surgery, you are probably unfamiliar with the effects of three days of morphine followed by a day of Demerol. Rather similar results might be obtained by taking a massive dose of LSD-25 while hopelessly drunk. Part of the consciousness is fragmented . . . and part expanded.

Time-sense and durational perception go all to hell, as
do coordination, motor skills, and concentration—and
yet often the patient, turning inward, makes a quantum leap toward a new plateau of self-understanding
and insight. Everything seems suddenly clear: struc-
tures of lies crumble, hypocrisies are stripped naked,
and years' worth of comfortable rationalizations collapse
like cardboard kettles, splashing boiling water everywhere. Perhaps the mind reacts to major shock by
reassessing, with ruthless honesty, everything that has
brought it there. Even Saint Paul must have been close
to something when he found himself on the ground
beside his horse, and Higgins had the advantage of
being colossally stoned.

While someone ran an absurd stop-start, variable-
speed movie in front of his eyes, comprised of doctors and nurses and IV bottles and bedpans and
blessed pricks on the arm, his mind's eye looked upon
himself and pronounced him a fool. His stupidity
seemed so massive, so transparent in retrospect that
he was filled with neither dismay nor despair, but only
wonder.

*My God, it's so obvious! How could I have had my
eyes so tightly shut? Choking up like that when they
started to Goof, for Christ's sake—do I need a neon
sign? I used to have a sense of humor—if there was
anything Ginny and I had in common it was a gift
for repartee—and after ten years of "selfless dedica-
tion" to Ginny and leukemia and keeping the money
coming that's exactly what I haven't got anymore and
I damned well know it. I've shriveled up like a rai-
sin, an ingrown man.*

*I've been a zombie for ten mortal years, telling
myself that neurotic monomania was a Great And
Tragic Love, trying to cry loud enough to get what*

I wanted. The only friend I made in those whole ten years was Bill, and I didn't hesitate to use him when I found out our PPs matched. I knew bloody well that I'd grown smaller instead of bigger since she loved me, and he was the perfect excuse for my ego. Play games with his head to avoid overhauling my own. I was going to lose, I knew I was going to lose, and then I was going to accidentally "let slip" the truth to her, and spend the next ten years bathing in some- one else's pity than my own. What an incredible, impossible, histrionic fool I've been, like a neurotic child saying, "Well, if you won't give me the candy I'll just smash my hand with a hammer."

If only I hadn't needed her so much when I met her. Oh. I must find some way to set this right, as quickly as possible!

His eyes clicked into focus, and Virginia Harding was sitting by his bedside in a soft brown robe, smiling warmly. He felt his eyes widen.

"Dilated to see you," he blurted and giggled.

Her smile disappeared. "Eh?"

"Pardon me. Demerol was first synthesized to wean Hitler off morphine; consequently, I'm Germanic- depressive these days." *See? The ability is still there. Dormant, atrophied, but still there.*

The smile returned. "I see you're feeling better."

"How would you know?"

It vanished again. "What are you talking about?"

"I know you're probably quite busy, but I expected a visit before this." *Light, jovial—keep it up, boy.*

"Tom Higgins, I have been here twice a day ever since you got out of OR."

"What?"

"You have conversed with me, lucidly and at length, told me funny stories and discussed contemporary politics with great insight, as far as I can tell. You don't remember."

"Not a bit of it." He shook his head groggily. *What did I say? What did I tell her?* "That's incredible. That's just incredible. You've been here . . ."

"Six times. This is the seventh."

"My God. I wonder where *I* was. This is appalling."

"Tom, you may not understand me, but I know precisely how you feel."

"Eh?" *That made you jump.* "Oh yes, your missing six months." *Suppose sometime in my lost three days we had agreed to love each other forever—would that still be binding now?* "God, what an odd sensation."

"Yes, it is," she agreed, and something in her voice made him glance sharply at her. She flushed and got up from her bedside chair, began to pace around the room. "It might not be so bad if the memories just stayed *completely* gone . . ."

"What do you mean?"

She appeared not to hear the urgency in his voice. "Well, it's nothing I can pin down. I . . . I just started wondering. Wondering why I kept visiting you so regularly. I mean, I like you—but I've been so damned busy I haven't had time to scratch, I've been missing sleep and missing meals, and every time visiting hours opened up I stole ten minutes to come and see you. At first I chalked it off to a not unreasonable feeling that I was in your debt—not just because you defrosted me without spoiling anything, but because you got shot trying to protect me too. There was a rock outcropping right next to you that would have made peachy cover."

"I . . . I . . ." he sputtered.

"That felt right," she went on doggedly, "but not entirely. I felt . . . I *feel* something else for you, something I don't understand. Sometimes when I look at you, there's . . . there's a feeling something like déjà vu, a vague feeling that there's something between us that I don't know. I know it's crazy—you'd surely have told me by now—but did I ever know you? Before?"

There it is, tied up in a pink ribbon on a silver salver. You're a damned fool if you don't reach out and take it. In a few days she'll be out of this mausoleum and back with her friends and acquaintances. Some meddling bastard will tell her sooner or later— do it now, while there's still a chance. You can pull it off: you've seen your error—now that you've got her down off the damn pedestal you can give her a mature love, you can grow tall enough to be a good man for her, you can do it right this time.

All you've got to do is grow ten years' worth overnight.

"Ms. Harding, to the best of my knowledge I never saw you before this week." *And that's the damn truth.*

She stopped pacing, and her shoulders squared. "I told you it was crazy. I guess I didn't want to admit that all those memories were completely gone. I'll just have to get used to it I suppose."

"I imagine so." *We both will.* "Ms. Harding?"

"Yes?"

"Whatever the reasons, I do appreciate your coming to see me, and I'm sorry I don't recall the other visits, but right at the moment my wound is giving me merry hell. Could you come back again, another time? And ask them to send in someone with another shot?"

He failed to notice the eagerness with which she

agreed. When she had gone and the door had closed behind her, he lowered his face into his hands and wept.

Her desk possessed a destruct unit for the incineration of confidential reports, and she found that it accepted unerasable discs. She was just closing the lid when the door chimed and McLaughlin came in, looking a bit haggard. "I hope I'm not intruding," he said.

"Not at all, come in," she said automatically. She pushed the *burn* button, felt the brief burst of heat, and took her hand away. "Come on in, Bill, I'm glad you came."

"They gave me your message, but I . . ." He appeared to be searching for words.

"No, really, I changed my plans. Are you on call tonight, Bill? Or otherwise occupied?"

He looked startled. "No."

"I intended to spend the night reading these damned reports, but all of a sudden I feel an overwhelming urge to get stinking drunk with someone— no." She caught herself and looked closely at him, seemed to see him as though for the first time. "No, by God, to get stinking drunk with *you*. Are you willing?"

He hesitated for a long time.

"I'll go out and get a bottle," he said at last.

"There's one in the closet. Bourbon okay?"

Higgins was about cried out when his own door chimed. Even so, he nearly decided to feign sleep, but at the last moment he sighed, wiped his face with his sleeves, and called out, "Come in."

The door opened to admit a young nurse with high cheeks, soft lips, vivid red hair, and improbably grey eyes.

"Hello, nurse," he said. He did not know her either. "I'm afraid I need something for pain."

"I know," she said softly, and moved closer.

SATAN'S CHILDREN

A beginning is the end of something, always.

Zaccur Bishop saw the murder clearly, watched it happen—although he was not to realize it for over an hour.

He might not have noticed it at all, had it happened anywhere but at the Scorpio. The victim himself did not realize that he had been murdered for nearly ten minutes, and when he did he made no outcry. It would have been pointless: there was no way to demonstrate that he was dead, let alone that he had been killed, nor anything whatever to be done about it. If the police had been informed—and somehow convinced—of all the facts, they would have done their level best to forget them. The killer was perhaps as far from the compulsive-confessor type as it is possible to be: indeed, that was precisely his motive. It is difficult to imagine another crime at once so

public and so clandestine. In any other club in the
world it would have been perfect. But since it happened at the Scorpio, it brought the world down like
a house of cards.

The Scorpio was one of those clubs that God sends
every once in a while to sustain the faithful. Benched
from the folkie-circuit for reasons he refused to discuss, a musician named Ed Finnegan somehow convinced the owners of a Chinese restaurant near
Dalhousie University to let him have their basement
and an unreasonable sum of money. (Finnegan used
to claim that when he vacationed in Ireland, the
Blarney Stone tried to kiss him.) He found that the
basement comprised two large windowless rooms.
The one just inside the front door he made into a
rather conventional bar—save that it was not conven-
tionally overdecorated. The second room, a much
larger one which had once held the oil furnace (the
building predated solar heat), he painted jet black and
ceilinged with acoustic tile. He went then to the
University, and to other universities in Halifax, prowl-
ing halls and coffeehouses, bars, and dormitories,
listening to every musician he heard. To a selected
few he introduced himself, and explained that he was
opening a club called Scorpio. It would include, he
said, a large music room with a proper stage and
spotlight. Within this music room, normal human
speech would be forbidden to all save the performers. Anyone wishing food or drink could raise their
hand and, when the waitress responded, point to their
order on the menu silk-screened into the tablecloth.
The door to this room, Finnegan added, would be
unlocked only between songs. The PA system was his
own: six Shure mikes with boomstands, two Teac
mixers, a pair of 600-watt Toyota amps, two speaker

columns, four wall speakers, and a dependable stage
monitor. Wednesday and Thursday were Open Mike
Nights, with a thirty-minute-per-act limit, and all other
nights were paying gigs. Finnegan apologized for the
meagerness of the pay: little more than the traditional
all-you-can-drink and hat privileges. The house piano,
he added, was in tune.

Within a month the Scorpio was legend, and the
Chinese restaurant upstairs had to close at sunset—
for lack of parking. There have always been more
good serious musicians than there were places for
them to play; not a vein for the tapping but an artery.
Any serious musician will sell his or her soul for an
intelligent, sensitive, *listening* audience. No other kind
would put up with Finnegan's house rules, and any
other kind was ejected—at least as far as the bar,
which featured a free juke box, Irish coffee, and
Löwenbräu draft.

It was only because the house rules were so rig-
idly enforced that Zack happened to notice even that
most inconspicuous of murders.

It happened in the spring of his twenty-fourth year.
He was about to do the last song in his midevening
solo set; Jill sat at a stageside table nursing a plain
orange juice and helping him with her wide brown
eyes. The set had gone well so far, his guitar playing less sloppy than usual, his voice doing what he
wanted it to, his audience responding well. But they
were getting restive: time to bottle it up and bring
Jill back onstage. While his subconscious searched its
files for the right song, he kept the patter flowing.

"No, really, it's true, genties and ladlemen of the
audio radiance, I nearly had a contract with Chess
Records once. Fella named King came to see me from
Chess, but I could see he just wanted old Zack Bishop

for his pawn. He was a screaming queen, and he
spent a whole knight tryin' to rook me, but finally I
says, 'Come back when you can show me a check,
mate.'" The crowd groaned dutifully, and Jill held her
nose. Lifting her chin to do so exposed the delicate
beauty of her throat, the soft grace of the place where
it joined her shoulders, and his closing song was
chosen.

"No, but frivolously, folks," he said soberly, "it's
nearly time to bring Jill on back up here and have her
sing a few—but I've got one last spasm in me first. I
guess you could say that this song was the proximate
cause of Jill and me getting together in the first place.
See, I met this lady and all of a sudden it seemed like
there was a whole lot of things we wanted to say to
each other, and the only ones I could get out of my
mouth had to do with, like, meaningful relationships,
and emotional commitments, and how our personalities
complemented each other and like that." He began to
pick a simple C-Em-Am-G cycle in medium slow
tempo, the ancient Gibson ringing richly, and Jill
smiled. "But I knew that the main thing I wanted to
say had nothing to do with that stuff. I knew I wasn't
being totally honest. And so I had to write this song."
And he sang:

> *Come to my bedside and let there be sharing*
> *Uncounterfeitable sign of your caring*
> *Take off the clothes of your body and mind*
> *Bring me your nakedness ... help me in mine ...*
>
> *Help me believe that I'm worthy of trust*
> *Bring me a love that includes honest lust*
> *Warmth is for fire; fire is for burning . . .*
> *Love is for bringing an ending . . . to yearning*

For I love you in a hundred ways
And not for this alone
But your lovin' is the sweetest lovin'
I have ever known

He was singing directly to Jill, he always sang this song directly to Jill, and although in any other bar or coffeehouse in the world an open fistfight would not have distracted his attention from her, his eye was caught now by a tall, massively bearded man in black leather who was insensitive enough to pick this moment to change seats. The man picked a stageside table at which one other man was already seated, and in the split second glance that Zack gave him, the bearded man met his eyes with a bold, almost challenging manner.

Back to Jill.

Come to my bedside and let there be giving
Licking and laughing and loving and living
Sing me a song that has never been sung
Dance at the end of my fingers and tongue

Take me inside you and bring up your knees.
Wrap me up tight in your thighs and then
        squeeze
Or if you feel like it you get on top
Love me however you please, but please . . .
        don't stop

For I love you in a hundred ways
And not for this alone
But your lovin' is the sweetest lovin'
I have ever known

The obnoxious man was now trying to talk to the man he had joined, a rather elderly gentleman with shaggy white hair and ferocious mustaches. It was apparent that they were acquainted. Zack could see the old man try to shush his new tablemate, and he could see that the bearded man was unwilling to be shushed. Others in the audience were also having their attention distracted, and resenting it. Mentally gritting his teeth, Zack forced his eyes away and threw himself into the bridge of the song.

I know just what you're thinking of
There's more to love than making love
There's much more to the flower than the bloom
But every time we meet in bed
I find myself inside your head
Even as I'm entering your womb

The Shadow appeared as if by magic, and the Shadow was large and wide and dark black and he plainly had sand. None too gently he kicked the bearded man's chair and, when the latter turned, held a finger to his lips. They glared at each other for a few seconds, and then the bearded man turned around again. He gave up trying to talk to the white-haired man, but Zack had the funny idea that his look of disappointment was counterfeit—he seemed underneath it to be somehow *satisfied* at being silenced. Taking the old man's left hand in his own, he produced a felt-tip pen and began writing on the other's palm. Quite angry now, Zack yanked his attention back to his song, wishing fiercely that he and Jill were alone.

So come to my bedside and let there be
     loving

Twisting and moaning and thrusting and
    shoving
I will be gentle—you know that I can
For you I will be quite a singular man . . .

Here's my identity, stamped on my genes
Take this my offering, know what it means
Let us become what we started to be
On that long ago night when you first came
    with me

Oh lady, I love you in a hundred ways
And not for this alone
But your lovin' is the sweetest lovin'
I have ever known

The applause was louder than usual, sympathy for a delicate song shamefully treated. Zack smiled half-ruefully at Jill, took a deep draught from the Löwenbräu on the empty chair beside him, and turned to deliver a stinging rebuke to the bearded man. But he was gone, must have left the instant the song ended—Shadow was just closing the door behind him. The old man with the absurd mustaches sat alone, staring at the writing on his palm with a look of total puzzlement. Neither of them knew that he was dead. The old man too rose and left the room as the applause trailed away.

To hell with him, Zack decided. He put the beer down at his feet and waved Jill up onto the stage. "Thank you folks, now we'll bring Jill back up here so she and I can do a medley of our hit . . ."

The set went on.

❖   ❖   ❖

The reason so many musicians seem to go a little nutty when they achieve success, demanding absurd luxuries and royal treatment, is that prior to that time they have been customarily treated like pigs. In no other branch of the arts is the artist permitted so little dignity by his merchandisers and his audience, given so little respect or courtesy. Ed Finnegan was a musician himself, and he understood. He knew, for instance, that a soundproof dressing room is a pearl without price to a musician, and so he figured out a cheap way to provide one. He simply erected a single soundproof wall, parallel to the music room's east wall and about five feet from it. The resulting corridor was wide enough to allow two men with guitars to pass each other safely, long enough to pace nervously, and silent enough to tune up or rehearse in.

And it was peaceful enough to be an ideal place to linger after the last set, to recover from the enormous expenditure of energy, to enjoy the first *tasted* drink of the night, to hide from those dozens of eyes half-seen through the spotlight glare, to take off the sweat-soaked image and lounge around in one's psychic underwear. The north door led to the parking lot and was always locked to the outside; the south door opened onto stage right, and had a large sign on its other side that said clearly, "If the performers wish to chat, sign autographs, accept drinks or tokes or negotiate for your daughter's wedding gig, they will have left this door open and you won't be reading this. PLEASE DO NOT ENTER. DON'T KNOCK IF YOU CAN HELP IT. RESPECT US AND WE'LL MAKE BETTER MUSIC. Thank you—Finnegan."

It was sanctuary.

Zack customarily came offstage utterly exhausted,

while Jill always finished a gig boiling over with
nervous energy. Happily, this could be counterbal-
anced by their differing metabolic reactions to marijuana: it always gave Zack energy and mellowed Jill.
The after-gig toke was becoming a ritual with them,
one they looked forward to unconsciously. Tonight's
toke was a little unusual. They were smoking a lit-
eral cigar of grass, GMI's newest marketing innovation, and assessing the validity of the product's
advertising slogan: "It doesn't get you any higher—
but it's more fun!"

Zack lay on his back on the rug, watching excess
smoke drift lazily up from his mouth toward the high
ceiling. An internal timer went off and he exhaled,
considered his head. "Let me see that pack," he said,
raising up on one elbow. Jill, just finishing her own
toke, nodded and passed over both cigar and pack.

Zack turned the pack over, scanned it and nodded.
"Brilliant," he said. He was beginning to come out
of his postperformance torpor. He toked, and croaked
"Fucking brilliant," again.

Jill managed to look a question while suppressing
a cough.

He exhaled. "Look," he said. " 'Guaranteed one
hundred percent pure marijuana.' See what that
means?"

"It means I'm not crazy, I really *am* stoned."

"No, no, the whole cigar business. Remember the
weather we had last spring? Half the GMI dope fields
got pasted with like thirty-two straight days of rain,
which is terrific for growing rope and rotten for
growing smoke. Stalks like bamboo, leaves like tiny
and worth squat, dope so pisspoor you'd have to
smoke a cigar-full of it to get off. So what did they
do?" He grinned wolfishly. "*They made cigars*. They

bluffed it out, just made like they planned it and made cigars. They're pure grass, all right—but you'd have to be an idiot to smoke a whole cigar of *good* grass. And by Christ I'll bet they pick up a big share of the market. These things *are* more fun."

"What do you think that is?" Jill asked. "*Why* is it more fun? Is it just the exaggerated oral trip?"

"Partly that," he admitted. "Oh hell, back when I smoked tobacco I knew that cigars were stronger, cooler, and tastier—I just couldn't afford 'em. But these aren't much more expensive than joints. Breaks down to about a dime a hit. Why, don't you like 'em?"

She took another long toke, her expression going blank while she considered. Suddenly her eyes focused, on him. "Does it turn you on to watch me smoke it?" she asked suddenly.

He blushed to his hairline and stammered.

"Honesty, remember? Like you said when you sang our song tonight. Trust me enough to be honest."

"Well," he equivocated, "I hadn't thought about . . ." He trailed off, and they both said "bullshit" simultaneously and broke up. "Yeah, it turns me on," he admitted.

She regarded the cigar carefully, took a most sensuous toke. "Then I shall chain smoke 'em all the way home," she said. "Here." She handed him the stogie, then began changing out of her stage clothes, making a small production out of it for him.

Eight months we've been living together, Zack thought, *and she hasn't lost that mischievous enthusiasm for making me horny. What a lady!* He put the cigar in his teeth, waggled it and rolled his eyes. "Why wait 'til we get home?" he leered.

"I predict another Groucho Marx revival if those things catch on." Her bra landed on top of the blouse.

"I like a gal with a strong will," he quoted, "Or at least a weak won't." He rose and headed for her. She did not shrink away—but neither did she come alive in his arms.

"Not here, Zack."

"Why not? It was fun in that elevator, wasn't it?"

"That was different. Someone could come in."

"Come on, the place is closed, Finnegan and the Shadow are mopping up beer and counting the take, nobody's gonna *fuck a duck.*"

Startled, she pulled away and followed his gaze. A shining figure stood in the open doorway.

She was by now wearing only ankle-length skirt and panties, and Zack had the skirt halfway down her hips, but she, and he, stood quite still, staring at the apparition. It was several moments after they began wishing for the power of motion that they recalled that they possessed it; moments more before they used it.

"It was true," the old man said.

He seemed to shine. He shimmered, he crackled with an energy only barely visible, only just intangible. His skin and clothes gave the impression of being on the verge of bursting spontaneously into flame. He shone as the Christ must have shone, as the Buddha must have shone, and a Kirlian photograph of him at that moment would have been a nova-blur.

Zack had a sudden, inexplicable and quite vivid recollection of the afternoon of his mother's funeral, five years past. He remembered suddenly the way friends and relatives had regarded him as strangers, a little awed, as though he possessed some terrible new power. He remembered feeling at the time that they were correct—that by virtue of his grief and loss he was somehow charged with a strange kind of energy. Intuitively he had *known* that on this day of all days he could simply scream at the most determined and desperate mugger and frighten him away, on this day he could violate traffic laws with impunity, on this day he could stare down any man or woman alive. Coming in close personal contact with death had made him, for a time, a kind of temporary shaman.

And the old man was quite dead, and knew it.

"Your song, I mean. It was true. I was half afraid I'd find you two bickering, that all that affection was just a part of the act. Oh thank *God.*"

Zack had never seen anyone quite so utterly relieved. The old man was of medium height and appeared to be in robust health. Even his huge ungainly mustaches could not completely hide the lines of over half a century of laughter and smiles. His complexion was ruddy, his features weatherbeaten, and his eyes were infinitely kindly. His clothes were of a style which had not even been revived in years: bell-bottom jeans, multicolored paisley shirt with purple predominating, a double strand of beads and an Acadian scarf-cap sloppily tied. He wore no jewelry other than the beads and no make-up.

A kind of Hippie Gepetto, Zack decided. *So why am I paralyzed?*

"Come in," Jill said, and Zack glanced sharply at her, then quickly back. The old man stepped into the room, leaving the door ajar. He stared from Zack to Jill, and back again, from one pair of eyes to the other, and his own kindly eyes seemed to peel away onion-layers of self until he gazed at their naked hearts. Zack suddenly wanted to cry, and that made him angry enough to throw off his trance.

"It is the custom of the profession," he said coldly, "to knock and shout, 'Are you decent?' Or didn't you see the sign there on the door?"

"Both of you are decent," the old man said positively. Then he seemed to snap out of a trance of his own: his eyes widened and he saw Jill's half-nakedness for the first time. *"Oh,"* he said explosively, and then his smile returned. "Now I'm supposed to apologize," he twinkled, "but it wouldn't be true. Oh, I'm sorry if I've upset you—but that's the last look I'll ever get, and you're lovely." He stared at Jill's bare breasts for a long moment, watched their nipples harden, and Zack marvelled at his own inability to muster outrage. Jill just stood there . . .

The old man pulled his eyes away. "Thank you both. Please sit down, now, I have to say some preposterous things and I haven't much time. Please hear me out before you ask questions, and please—please!—believe me."

Jill put on the new blouse and jeans, while Zack seated himself from long habit on the camel-saddle edge of his guitar case. He was startled to discover the cigar still burning in his hand, stunned to see only a quarter-inch of ash on the end. He started to offer it to the old man; changed his mind; started to offer it to Jill; changed his mind; dropped the thing on the carpet and stepped on it.

"My name is Wesley George," the old man began.

"Right," Zack said automatically.

The old man sighed deeply. "I haven't much time," he repeated.

"What" *the hell would Wesley George be doing in Halifax?* Zack started to say, but Jill cut him off sharply with "He's Wesley George and he doesn't have much time" and before the intensity in her voice he subsided.

"Thank you," George said to Jill. "You *perceive* very well. I wonder how much you know already."

"Almost nothing," Jill said flatly, "but I know what I know."

He nodded. "Obviously you've both heard of me; Christ knows I'm notorious enough. But how much of it stuck? Given my name, how much do you know of me?"

"You're the last great dope wizard," Zack said, "and you were one of the first. You used to work for one of the 'ethical' drug outfits and you split. You synthesized DMT, and didn't get credit for it. You developed Mellow Yellow. You made STP safe and dependable. You develop new psychedelics and sell 'em cheap, sometimes you give 'em away, and some say you're stone nuts and some say you're the Holy Goof himself. You followed in the footsteps of Owsley Stanley, and you've never been successfully busted, and you're supposed to be richer than hell. A dealer friend of mine says you make molecules talk."

"You helped buy the first federal decrim bill on grass," Jill said, "and blocked the cocaine bill—both from behind the scenes. You founded the Continent Continent movement and gave away five million TM pills in a single day in New York."

"Some people say you don't exist," Zack added.

"As of now, they're right," George said. "I've been murdered."

Jill gasped; Zack just stared.

"In fact, you may have noticed it done," Wesley said to Zack. "You remember Sziller, the bearded man who spoiled your last solo? Did you see him write this?"

George held his left hand up, palm out. A black

felt-tip pen had written a telephone number there, precisely along his lifeline.

"Yeah," Zack agreed. "So what?"

"I dialed it a half hour ago. David Steinberg answered. He said that once he had a skull injury, and the hospital was so cheap they put a *paper* plate in his head. He said the only side effect was that every sunny day he *had* to go on a picnic. I hung up the phone and I knew I was dead."

"Dial-a-Joke," Jill said wonderingly.

"I don't get it," said Zack.

"I was supposed to meet Sziller here tonight—in the bar, after your set. I couldn't understand why he came into the music room and tried to talk to me there. He knew better. He *wanted* to be shushed, so he'd have to write his urgent message on my hand. And the urgent message was literally a joke. So what he really wanted was to write on my hand with a felt-tip pen."

"Jesus," Zack breathed, and Jill's face went featureless.

"In the next ten or fifteen minutes," George said conversationally, "I will have a fatal heart attack. It's an old CIA trick. A really first-rate autopsy might pick up some traces of a phosphoric acid ester—but I imagine Sziller and his people will be able to prevent that easily enough. They've got the building surrounded; I can't get as far as my car. You two are my last hope."

Zack's brain throbbed, and his eyelids felt packed with sand. George's utter detachment was scary. It said that Wesley George was possessed by something that made his own death unimportant—and it might be catching. His words implied that it was, and that he proposed to infect Zack and Jill. Zack had seen *North*

By Northwest, and had no intention of letting other people's realities hang him out on Mount Rushmore if there were any even dishonorable way to dodge.

But he could *perceive* pretty well himself, and he knew that whatever the old man had was a burden, a burden that would crush him even in death unless he could discharge it. Everything that was good in Zack yearned to answer the call in those kindly eyes; and the internal conflict—almost entirely subconscious—nearly tore him apart.

There was an alternative. It would be easy to simply disbelieve the old man's every word. Was it plausible that this glowing, healthy man could spontaneously die, killed by a bad joke? Zack told himself that Hitler and Rasputin had used just such charisma to sell the most palpable idiocies, that this shining old man with the presence of a Buddha was only a compelling madman with paranoid delusions. Zack had never seen a picture of Wesley George. He remembered the fake Abby Hoffman who had snarled up the feds for so long. He pulled scepticism around himself like a scaly cloak, and he looked at those eyes again, and louder and more insistent even than Jill's voice had been, they said that the old man was Wesley George and that he didn't have much time.

Zack swallowed something foul. "Tell us," he said, and was proud that his voice came out firm.

"You understand that I may get you both dipped in soft shit, maybe killed?"

Zack and Jill said, "Yes," together, and glanced at each other. This was a big step for both of them: there is all the difference in the world between agreeing to live together and agreeing to die together. Zack knew that whatever came afterward, they were married as of now, and he desperately wanted to think that through, but there was no time, no time. *What's more important than death and marriage?* he thought, and saw the same question on Jill's face, and then they turned back as one to Wesley George.

"Answer me a question first," the old man said. Both nodded. "Does the end justify the means?"

Zack thought hard and answered honestly. Much, he was sure, depended on this.

"I don't know," he said.

"Depends on the end," Jill said. "And the means."

George nodded, content. "People with a knee-jerk answer *either* way make me nervous," he said. "All right, children, into your hands I place the fate of modern civilization. I bring you Truth, and I think that the truth shall make you flee."

He glanced at his watch, displayed no visible reaction. But he took a pack of tobacco cigarettes from his shirt, lit one, and plainly gave his full attention to savoring the first toke. Then he spoke, and for the first time Zack noticed that the old man's voice was a pipe organ with a double bass register, a great resonant baritone that Disraeli or Geronimo might have been proud to own.

"I am a chemist. I have devoted my life to studying chemical aspects of consciousness and perception. My primary motivation has been the advancement of knowledge; my secondary motive has been to get people high—as many people, as many ways as possible. I think the biggest single problem in the world, for almost the last two decades, has been morale. Despairing people solve no problems. So I have pursued better living through chemistry, and I've made my share of mistakes, but in the main I think the world has profited from my existence as much as I have from its. And now I find that I am become

Prometheus, and that my friends want me dead just as badly as my enemies.

"I have synthesized truth.

"I have synthesized truth in my laboratory. I have distilled it into chemical substance. I have measured it in micrograms, prepared a dozen vectors for its use. It is not that hard to make. And I believe that if its seeds are once sown on this planet, the changes it will make will be the biggest in human history.

"Everything in the world that is founded on lies may die."

Zack groped for words, came up empty. He became aware that Jill's hand was clutching his tightly.

" 'What is truth?' asked jesting Pilate, and would not stay for answer. Neither will I, I'm afraid—but I ought to at least clarify the question. I cannot claim to have objective truth. I have no assurance that there is such a thing. But I *have* subjective truth, and I *know* that exists. I knew a preacher once who got remarkable results by looking people square in the eye and saying, 'You do *too* know what I mean.' "

A spasm crossed the old man's face and his glowing aura flickered. Zack and Jill moved toward him as one, and he waved them away impatiently.

"Even those of us who pay only lip service to the truth know what it is, deep down in our hearts. And we all believe in it, and know it when we see it. Even the best rationalization can fool only the surface mind that manufactures it; there is something beneath, call it the heart or the conscience, that knows better. It tenses up like a stiff neck muscle when you lie, in proportion to the size of the lie, and if it stiffens enough it can kill you for revenge. Ask Richard Corey. Most people seem to me, in my cynical moments, to keep things stabilized at about the discomfort of a dislocated shoulder or a tooth about to abscess. They trade honesty off in small chunks for pleasure, and wonder that their lives hold so little *joy*. Joy is incompatible with tensed shoulders and a stiff neck. You become uneasy with people in direct proportion to how many lies you have to keep track of in their presence.

"I have stumbled across a psychic muscle relaxant."

"Truth serum's been around a long time," Zack said.

"This is no more Pentothal than acid is grass!" George thundered, an Old Testament prophet enraged. He caught himself at once—in a single frantic instant he seemed to extrude his anger, stare at it critically, tie it off, and amputate it, in deliberate steps. "Sorry—rushed. Look: Pentothal will—sometimes get you a truthful answer to a direct question. *My* drug imbues you with a strong desire to get straight with all the people you've been lying to regardless of the consequences. Side effects include the usual accompaniments of confession—cathartic relief, euphoria to the point of exaltation and a tendency to babble—and a new one: visual color effects extremely reminiscent of organic mescaline."

He winced again, clamped his jaw for a moment, then continued.

"That alone might have been enough to stand the world on its ear—but the gods are jollier than that. The stuff is water-soluble—damn near anything-soluble—and skin-permeable and as concentrated as hell. Worse than acid for dosage, and it can be taken into the body just about every way there is. For Pentothal you have to actually shoot up the subject, and you have to hit the vein. My stuff—Christ, you could let a drop of candle wax harden on your palm, put a pinpoint's worth on the wax, shake hands with

a man and dose him six or seven hours' worth. You
could put it on a spitball and shoot it through a straw.
You could add it to nail polish or inject it into a
toothpaste tube or roll it up in a joint or simply spray
it from an atomizer. Put enough of it into a joint, in
a small room, and even the nonsmokers will get off.
The method Sziller has used to assassinate me would
work splendidly. There may be some kind of way to
guard against it—some antidote or immunization—
but I haven't found it yet. You see the implications,
of course."

At some point during George's speech Zack had
reached the subconscious decision to believe him
implicitly. With doubt had gone the last of his paral-
ysis, and now his mind was racing faster than usual
to catch up. "Give me a week and a barrel of hot
coffee and I think I could reason out most of the
major implications. All I get now is that you can make
people be truthful against their will." His expression
was dark.

"Zack, I know this sounds like sophistry, but that's
a matter of definition. Whoa!" He held up his hands.
"I know, son, I know. The Second Commandment of
Leary: 'Thou shalt not alter thy brother's consciousness without his consent.' So how about retroactive
consent?"

"Say again."

"The aftereffects. I've administered the drug to blind
volunteers. They knew only that they were sampling
a new psychedelic of unknown effect. In each case I
gave a preliminary 'attitude survey' questionnaire with
a few buried questions. In fourteen cases I satisfied
myself that the subject would probably *not* have taken
the drug if he or she had known its effect. In about
three-quarters of them I damn well knew it.

"The effects were the same for all but one. All fourteen of them experienced major life upheaval—usually irreversible and quite against their will—while under the effects of the drug. They all became violently angry at me after they came down. Then all fourteen stormed off to try and put their lives back together. Thirteen of them were back within a week, asking me to lay another hit on them."

Zack's eyes widened. "Addictive on a single hit. Jesus."

"No, *no!*" George said exasperatedly. "It's not the drug that's addictive, dammit. *It's the truth that's addictive.* Every one of those people came back for, like, three-four hits, and then they stopped coming by. I checked up on the ones I was in a position to. They had just simply rearranged their lives on solid principles of truth and honesty and begun to live that way all the time. *They didn't need the drug anymore.* Every damn one of them thanked me. One of them fucked me, sweetly and lovingly—at my age.

"I was worried myself that the damned stuff might be addictive. So I had at least as many subjects who *would* probably have taken the drug knowingly, and *all* of them asked for more and I told them no. Better than three-fourths of them have made similar life adjustments on their own, without any further chemical aid.

"Zack, living in truth *feels good.* And it sticks in your memory. Like, it's a truism with acid heads that you can never *truly* remember what tripping feels like. You *think* you do, but every time you trip it's like waking up all over again, you recognize the head coming on and you dig that your memories of it were shadows. *But this stuff you remember!* You're left with a vivid set of memories of just exactly how good it

felt to not have any psychic muscles bunched up for
the first time since you were two years old. You
remember joy; and you realize that you can recre-
ate it just by not ever lying any more. That's goddamn
hard, so you look for any help you can get, and if
you can't get any you just take your best shot.

"Those people ended up happier, Zack.

"Zack, Jill . . . a long long time ago a doctor named
Watt slapped me on the ass and forced me to live.
It was very much against my will; I cried like hell
and family legend says I tried to bite him. Now my
days are ended, and taking it all together I'm very
glad he went to the trouble. He had my retroactive
consent. It wasn't his fault anyhow: my parents had
already forced me to exist, before I had a will for it
to be against—and they have my retroactive consent.
Many times in my life, good friends and even strangers have kicked my ass where it needed kicking; at
least twice women have gently and compassionately
kicked me out—all against my will, and they all have
my retroactive consent, God bless 'em. Can it be
immoral to dose folks if you get no complaints?"

"What about the fourteenth person?" Jill asked.

George grimaced. "Touché."

"Beg pardon?"

"Nothing's perfect. The fourteenth man killed me."

"Oh."

The temperature in the room was moderate, but
George was drenched with sweat; his ruddy complexion was paling rapidly.

"Look, you two make up your own minds. You can
help them haul me out to the ambulance in a few
minutes and then walk away and forget you ever met
me, if that's what you want. But I have to ask you:
please, *take over this karma for me*. Someone has to,

one way or the other: I seriously doubt that the drug will ever be found again."

"Is there like a set of instructions for the stuff?" Zack asked. *Involved,* his head told him. "Notes, molecule diagrams—" *Somebody's getting infuckingvolved . . .*

"Complete instructions for synthesis, and about ten liters of the goods, in various forms. That's about enough to give everything on earth with two legs a couple of hits apiece. I tell you, it's easy to make. And it's *fucking* hard to stumble across. If I die, it dies with me, maybe forever. Blind luck *I* found it, just blind—"

"Where?" Zack and Jill interrupted simultaneously.

"Wait a minute, you've got to understand. It's in a *very* public place—I thought that was a good idea at the time, but . . . never mind. The point is, from the moment you pick up the stuff, you must be very very careful. They don't have to physically touch you—try not to let anyone come near you if you can help it, anyone at all—"

"I'll know a fed when I see one," Zack said grimly, "north *or* south."

"No, NO, not feds, not *any* kind of feds! Think that way and you're dead. It wasn't feds that killed me."

"Who then?" Jill asked.

"In my line of work, I customarily do business with a loosely affiliated organization of non-Syndicate drug dealers. It has no name. It is international in scope, and if it ever held a meeting, a substantial fraction of the world's wealth would sit in one room. I offered them this drug for distribution, before I really understood what I had. Sziller is one of the principals of the group."

"Jesus God," Zack breathed. *"Dealers* had *Wesley George* snuffed? That's like the apostles offing Jesus."

"One of them did," George pointed out sadly. "Think it through, son: dope dealers can't afford honesty."

"But—"

"Suppose the feds did get hold of the stuff," Jill suggested.

"Oh."

"Or the Syndicate," George agreed. "Or their own customers, or—"

"What's the drug called?" Jill asked.

"The chemical name wouldn't mean a thing to some of the brightest chemists in the world, and I never planned to market it under that. Up until I knew what it was I called it The New Batch, and since then I've taken to calling it TWT. The Whole Truth." Suddenly urgency overtook him and he was angry again. "Listen, fuck this," he blazed, "I mean fuck all this garbage. OK? I haven't got time to waste on trivia. Will you do it is the important thing; will you take on the karma I've brought you? Will you turn Truth loose on the world for me? Please, you aaaAAAAAAHHH-EE shit." He clutched at his right arm, screamed again in awful pain and fell to the floor.

"We promise, we promise," Jill was screaming, and Zack was thundering "Where, *where?* Where, dammit?" and Jill had George's head on her lap and Zack had his hands and they clutched like steel and *"Where?"* he shouted again, and George was bucking in agony, breathing in with great whooping gargles and breathing out with sprays of saliva, jaw muscles like bulging biceps on his face, and "Hitch" he managed through his teeth, and Zack tried, "Hitch.

Hitchhike, *a locker at the hitching depot*" very fast and then added "Key in your pocket?" and George borrowed energy from his death struggle to nod twice, "Okay, right Wesley, it's covered, man," and George relaxed all over at once and shat his pants. They thought he was dead, then, but the blue-grey eyelids rolled heavily up one last time and he saw Jill's face over his, raining tears. "Nice tits . . ." he said ". . . Thanks . . . children . . . thanks . . . sorry," and in the middle of the last word he did die, and his glowing aura died with him.

The Shadow was standing in the doorway, filling it full, breathing hard. "I heard the sound, man, what—oh holy *shit*, man. What the fuck *happenin'* here?"

Zack's voice was perfect, his delivery impeccable, startled but not involved. "What can I tell ya, Shadow? The old guy comes back to talk blues and like that and his pump quits. Call the croaker, will ya? And pour me a triple."

"Shee-it," the Shadow rumbled. "Nev' a dull night aroun' this fuckin' joint. Hey, *Finnegan*! Finnegan, God damn it." The big black bouncer left to find his boss.

Zack found a numbered key in George's pants, and turned to Jill. Their eyes met and locked. "Yes," Jill said finally, and they both nodded. And then together they pried Zack's right hand from the clutching fingers of the dead dope wizard, and together they made him comfortable on the floor, and then they began packing up their instruments and gear.

Zack and Jill held a hasty war council in the flimsy balcony of their second-floor apartment. It overlooked a yard so small it would have been hard put not to,

as Zack loved to say, and offered a splendid view of
the enormous oil refining facility across the street.
The view of Halifax Harbour which the architect had
planned was forever hidden now behind it, but the
cooling breezes still came at night, salt-scented and
rich. Even at two A.M. the city was noisy, like a
dormitory after lights out, but all the houses on this
block were dark and still.

"I think we should pack our bags," Zack said,
sipping coffee.

"And do what?"

"The dealers must know that Wesley brought a
large amount of Truth with him—he intended to turn
it over to them for distribution. They don't know
where it's stashed, and they must be shitting a brick
wondering who else does. We're suspect because
we're known to have spoken with him, and a hitching depot is a natural stash—so we don't go near the
stuff."

"But we've *got* to—"

"We will. Look, tomorrow we're *supposed* to go on
tour, right?"

"Screw the tour."

"No, hon, look! This is the smart way. We do just
exactly what we would have done if we'd never met
Wesley George. We act natural, do the tour as
planned—we pack our bags and *go down to the
hitching depot* and take off. But some friend of ours—
say, John—goes in just ahead of us and scores the
bag. Then we show up and ignore him, and by and
by the three of us make up a full car for somebody,
and after we're out of the terminal and about to
board, out of the public eye, John changes his mind
and fades and we take over the bag. Zippo bang, off
on tour."

"I'll say it again. Screw the tour. We've got more important things to do."

"Like what?"

"?"

"What do *you* wanna do with the stuff? Call the reporters? Stand on Barrington Street and give away samples? Call the heat? Look. We're proposing to unleash truth on the world. I'm willing to take a crack at that, but I'd like to live to see what happens. So I don't want to be connected with it publicly in any way if I can help it. We keep our cover and do our tour—and we sprinkle fairy dust as we go."

"Dose people, you mean?"

"Dose the most visible people we can find, and make damn sure we don't get caught at it. We're supposed to hit nineteen cities in twenty-eight days, in a random pattern that even a computer couldn't figure out. I intend to leave behind us the God-damnedest trail of headlines in history."

"Zack, I don't follow your thinking."

"Okay." He paused, took a deep breath, slowed himself visibly. "Okay . . . considering what we've got here, it behooves me to be honest. I have doubts about this. Heavy doubts. The decision we're making is incredibly arrogant. We're talking about destroying the world, as we know it."

"To hell with the world as we know it, Zack, it stinks. A world of truth *has* to be better."

"Okay, in my gut something agrees with you. But I'm still not sure. A world of truth may be better— but the period of turmoil while the old world collapses is sure going to squash a lot of people. Nice people. Good people. Jill, something *else* in my gut suspects that *maybe even good people need lies sometimes.*

"So I want to hedge my bets. I want to experiment first and see what happens. To do that I have to make another arrogant decision: to dose selected individuals, cold-bloodedly and without giving them a chance, let alone a vote. Wesley experimented himself, with a lab and volunteers and procedure and tests, until he proved to his satisfaction that it was okay to turn this stuff loose. Well, I haven't got any of that—but I have to establish to *my* satisfaction that it's cool."

"Do you doubt his results?" Jill asked indignantly.

"To *my* satisfaction. Not Wesley's, or even yours, my darling, or anyone else's. And yes, frankly, I have some doubts about his results."

Jill clouded up. "How can you—?"

"Baby, *listen to me.* I believe that every word Wesley George said to us was the absolute unbiased truth as he knew it. But *he himself had taken the drug.* That makes him suspect."

Jill dropped her eyes. "That retroactive consent business bothered me a little too."

Zack nodded. "Yeah. If everybody comes out of prefrontal lobotomy with a smile on his face, what does that prove? If you kidnapped somebody and put a droud in their head, made 'em a wirehead, they'd thank you on their way out—but so what? Things like that are like scooping out somebody's *self* and replacing it with a new one. The new one says thanks—but the old one was *murdered.* I want to make *sure* that *Homo veritas* is a good thing—*in the opinion of Homo sapiens.*

"So I propose that neither of us take the drug. I propose that we abstain, and take careful precautions not to accidentally contaminate ourselves while we're using it. We'll dose others but not ourselves, and then when the tour is over—or sooner if it feels right—

we'll sit down and look over what we've done and how it turned out. Then if we're still agreed, we'll take a couple of hits together and call CBC News. By then there'll be so much evidence they'll have to believe us, and then . . . then the word will be out. Too far out for the dealers to have it squashed or discredited. Or the government."

"And then the world will end."

"And a new one will begin . . . but first we've got to *know*. Am I crazy or does that make sense to you?"

Jill was silent a long time. Her face got the blank look that meant she was thinking hard. After a few minutes she got up and began pacing the apartment. "It's risky, Zack. Once the headlines start coming they'll figure out what happened and come after us."

"And the only people who know our schedule are Fat Jack and the Agency. We'll tell 'em there's a skip tracer after us and they'll both keep shut—"

"But—"

"Jill, this ain't the feds after us—it's a bunch of dealers who dasn't let anybody know they exist. They *can't* have the resources they'd need to trace us, even if they did know what city we were in."

"They might. A dealers' union'd have to be international. That's a lot of weight, Zack, a lot of money."

"Darlin'—if all you got is pisspoor dope . . ." He broke off and shrugged.

Jill grinned suddenly. "You make cigars. Let's get packed. More coffee?"

They took little time in packing and preparing their apartment for a long absence. This would be their third tour together; by now it was routine. At last everything that needed doing was done, the lights were out save for the bedside lamp, and they were ready for bed. They undressed quickly and silently, with no flirting byplay, and slid under the covers. They snuggled together spoon fashion for a few silent minutes, and then Zack began rubbing her neck and shoulders with his free hand, kneading with guitarist's fingers and lover's knowledge. They had not yet spoken a word of the change that the events of the evening had brought to their relationship, and both knew it, and the tension in the room was thick enough to smell. Zack thought of a hundred things to say, and each one sounded stupider than the last.

"Zack?"

"Yeah?"

"We're probably going to die, aren't we?"

"We're positively going to die." She stiffened almost imperceptibly under his fingers. "But I could have told you that yesterday, or last week." She relaxed again. "Difference is, yesterday I couldn't have told you positively that we'd die *together*."

Zack would have sworn they were inextricably entwined, but somehow she rolled round into his arms in one fluid motion, then pulled him on top of her with another. Their embrace was eight-legged and whole-hearted and completely nonsexual, and about a minute of it was all their muscles would tolerate. Then they drew apart just far enough to meet each other's eyes. They shared that, too, for a long minute, and then Zack smiled.

"Have you ever noticed that there is no position or combination of positions in which we do *not* fit together like nesting cups?"

She giggled, and in the middle of the giggle tears leaked from her laughing eyes. "Oh, Zack," she cried, and hugged him again. "I love you so much."

"I know, baby, I know," he murmured in her ear, stroking her hair. "It's not every day that you find something worth dying for—*and* something worth living for. Both at the same time. Christ, I love you."

They both discovered his rigid erection at the same instant, and an instant later they discovered her sopping wetness, and for the first time in their relationship their loins joined without manual aid from either of them. Together they sucked air slowly through their teeth, and then he began to pull his head back to meet her eyes and she stopped him, grabbing his head with her hands and pushing her tongue into his ear. His hips arched reflexively, his hands clutched her shoulders, her legs locked round his, and the oldest dance began again. It was eleven A.M. before they finally slept, and by that time they were in someone else's car, heading, ironically enough, north by northwest.

It's the best way out of Halifax.

The reader wishing a detailed account of Zack and Jill's activities over the next month can find it at any library with a good newstape and newspaper morgue. The reader is advised to bring a lunch. At any time of the year the individual stories that the two folksingers sowed behind them like depth charges would have been hot copy—but God had ordained that Wesley George drop dead in August, smack in the middle of Silly Season. The news media of the entire North American Confederation went into grateful orgasmic convulsions.

Not all the stories made the news. The events involving the Rev. Schwartz in Montreal, for instance, were entirely suppressed at the time, by the husbands involved, and have only recently come to light. When militant radical leader Mtu Zanje, the notorious "White Mau Mau," was found in Harlem with bullets from sixteen different unregistered guns in him, there was at that time nothing to connect it with the other stories, and it got three inches on page forty-three.

Indeed, the most incredible thing in retrospect is that no one, at the time, connected *any* of the stories. Though each new uproar was dutifully covered in detail, not one journalist, commentator or observer divined any common denominator in them until the month was nearly up. Confronted with the naked truth, the people of North America did not recognize it.

But certainly every one of them saw it or heard about it, in living color stereo and thirty-six point type and four-channel FM, in weekly news magazines and on documentary shows, in gossip columns and radio talk shows, in political cartoons and in comedians' routines. Zack and Jill strongly preferred to examine their results from a distance, and so they tended to be splashy.

In St. John, New Brunswick, they hit an elderly and prominent judge who had more wrinkles than a William Goldman novel, while he was sitting in open court on a controversial treason case. After an astonishing twenty-seven-minute monologue, the aged barrister died in a successful attempt to cover, with the sidearm he had snatched from his bailiff, the defendant's escape. Zack and Jill, sitting in the audience, were considerably startled, but they had to agree that only once had they seen a man die happier: the judge's dead face was as smooth as a baby's.

In Montreal (in addition to the Rev. Schwartz), they managed to catch a Conservative MP on his way into a TV studio and shake his hand. The program's producer turned out to have seen the old movie *Network*—he kept the politician on the air, physically

knocking down the programming director when that
became necessary. The MP had been—er—liberally
dosed; after forty-five minutes of emotional confession he began specifically outlining the secret dreams
he had had ever since he first took office, the really
good programs he had constructed in his imagination
but never dared speak aloud, knowing they could
never be implemented in the real world of power
blocs and interest groups. He went home that night
a broken but resigned man, and woke up the next
morning to confront a landslide of favorable response,
an overwhelming mandate to implement his dreams.
To be sure, very very few of the people who had
voted for him in the last election ever did so again.
But in the *next* election (and every subsequent election involving him) the ninety percent of the electorate who traditionally never vote turned out almost
to a person. The producer is now his chief aide.

In Ottawa they tried for the Prime Minister, but
they could not get near him or near anything that
could get near him. But they did get the aging Peter
Gzowski on *90 Minutes Live.* He too chanced to have
seen *Network,* and he had much more survival instinct
than its protagonist: the first thing he did upon leaving
the studio was to make an extensive tape recording
and mail several dubs thereof to friends with instructions for their disposal in the event of his sudden
death. Accordingly he is still alive and broadcasting
today, and there are very few lids left for him to tear
off these days.

Outside Toronto Zack and Jill made their most
spectacular single raid, at the Universal Light and
Truth Convocation. It was a kind of week-long spiritual olympics: over a dozen famous gurus, swamis,
reverends, Zen masters, Sufis, priests, priestesses and

assorted spiritual teachers had gathered with thousands of their followers on a donated hundred-acre
pasture to debate theology and sell each other
incense, with full media coverage. Zack and Jill
walked through the Showdown of the Shamen and
between them missed not a one. One committed
suicide. One went mad. Four denounced themselves
to their followers and fled. Seven denounced themselves to their followers and stayed. Four wept too
hard to speak, the one the others called The Fat Boy
(although he was middle-aged) bit off his tongue, and
exactly one teacher—the old man who had brought
few followers and nothing for sale—exhibited no
change whatsoever in his manner or behavior but
went home very thoughtfully to Tennessee. It is now
known that he could have blown the story then and
there, for he was a telepath, but he chose not to. The
single suicide bothered Jill deeply; but only because
she happened to know of and blackly despise that particular holy man, and was dismayed by the pleasure
she felt at his death. But Zack challenged her to name
one way in which his demise either diminished the
world or personally benefited her, and she came tentatively to accept that her pleasure might be legiti-
mate.

They happened to arrive in Detroit just before the
annual meeting of the Board of Directors of General
Motors. Madame President absentmindedly pocketed
the cigar she found on the back seat of her Rolls that
morning, though it was not her brand, and it had
been saturated with enough odorless, tasteless TWT
to dose Madison Square Garden. It is of course
impossible to ever know exactly what transpired that
day in that most sacrosanct and guarded and unpublic
of rooms—but we have the text of the press release

that ensued, and we do know that all GM products subsequent to 1994 burn alcohol instead of gasoline, and exhibit a sharp upward curve in safety and reliability.

In Chicago Zack and Jill got a prominent and wealthy realtor-developer and all his tame engineers, ecologists, lawyers and other promotion experts in the middle of a public debate over a massive rezoning proposal. There are no more slums in Chicago, and the developer is, of course, its present mayor.

In Cleveland they got a used car salesman, a TV repairman, a plumber, an auto mechanic, and a Doctor of Philosophy in one glorious afternoon.

In New York they got Mtu Zanje, quite by accident. The renegade white led a force of sixteen New Black Panthers in a smash-and-grab raid on the downtown club where Zack and Jill were playing. Mtu Zanje personally took Jill's purse, and smoked a cigar which he found therein on his way back uptown. Zack and Jill never learned of his death or their role in it, but it is doubtful that they would have mourned.

In Boston they concentrated on policemen, as many as they could reach in two mornings and afternoons, and by the time they left that town it was rocking on its metaphorical foundations. Interesting things came boiling up out of the cracks, and most of them have since decomposed in the presence of air and sunlight.

In Portland, Maine, Zack figured a way to plant a timed-release canister in the air-conditioning system of that city's largest Welfare Center. A great many people voluntarily left the welfare roll over the ensuing month, and none have yet returned—or starved. There are, of course, a lot of unemployed caseworkers . . .

And then they were on their way home to Halifax.

But this is a listing only of the headlines that Zack and Jill left behind them—not of everything that happened on that trip. Not even of everything important; at least, not to Zack and Jill.

In Quebec a laundry van just missed killing them both, then roared away.

In Ottawa they went out for a late night walk just before a tremendous explosion partially destroyed their motel. It had apparently originated in the room next to theirs, which was unoccupied.

In Toronto they were attacked on the streets by what might have been a pair of honest muggers, but by then they were going armed and they got one apiece.

In Detroit the driver of the cab they had taken (at ruinous expense) to eliminate a suspected tail apparently went mad and deliberately jumped a divider into high-speed oncoming traffic. In any car crash, the Law of Chaos prevails, and in this instance it killed the driver and left Zack and Jill bruised and shaken but otherwise unharmed.

They knew enemy action when they saw it, and so they did the most confusing thing they could think of: stopped showing up for their scheduled gigs, but kept on following the itinerary. They also adopted reasonably ingenious disguises and, with some trepidation, stopped travelling together. Apparently the combination worked; they were not molested again until they showed up for the New York gig to break the pattern, and then only by Mtu Zanje, which they agreed was coincidence. But it made them thoughtful, and they rented several hours of complete privacy in a videotape studio before leaving town.

And on the road to Boston they each combed their

memory for friends remembered as One Of The Nice Ones, people they could trust, and in that city they met in the Tremont Street Post Office and spent an hour addressing and mailing VidCaset Mailer packs. Each pack contained within it, in addition to its program material, a twenty-second trailer holding five hundred hits of TWT in blotter form—a smuggling innovation of which Zack was sinfully proud.

They had not yet taken TWT themselves, but their decision was made. They agreed at the end of that day to take it together when they got back to Halifax. They would do it in the Scorpio, alone together, in the dressing room where Wesley George had died.

They waited until well after closing, after Finnegan and the Shadow had locked up behind them and driven away the last two cars in the parking lot. Then they waited another hour to be sure.

The night was chill and still, save for the occasional distant street sounds from more active parts of town. There was no moon and the sky was lightly overcast; darkness was total. They waited in the black together, waiting not for any particular event or signal but only until it felt right, and they both knew that time without words. They were more married already than most couples get to be in a lifetime, and they were no longer in any hurry at all.

When it was time they rose from their cramped positions behind the building's trash compactor and walked stealthily around to the front of the building to the descending stairway that led to the outer door of the dressing room. Like all of Finnegan's regulars they knew how to slip its lock, and did so with minimal noise.

As soon as the door clicked shut behind them, Jill heaved a great sigh, compounded of relief and fatigue and déjà vu. "This is where it all started," she breathed. "The tour is over. Full circle."

Zack looked around at pitch blackness. "From the smell in here, I would guess that it was Starship Earth played here tonight."

Jill giggled. "Still living on soybeans, too. Zack, can we put the light on, do you think?"

"Hmmm. No windows, but this door isn't really tight. I don't think it'd be smart, hon."

"How about a candle?"

"Sold. Let me see—ouch!—if the Starship left the—yeah, here's a couple." He struck the light, and started both candles. The room sprang into being around them, as though painted at once in broad strokes of butter and chocolate. It was, after a solid month of perpetually new surroundings, breathtakingly familiar and comfortable. It lifted their hearts, even though both found their eyes going at once to the spot on which Wesley George had fallen.

"If your ghost is here, Wesley, rest easy, man," Zack said quietly. "It got covered. And we're both back to do truth ourselves. They killed you, man, but they didn't stop you."

After a pause, Jill said, "Thank you, Wesley," just as quietly. Then she turned to Zack. "You know, I don't even feel like we *need* to take the stuff, in a place."

"I know, hon, I know. We've been more and more honest with each other, opened up more every day, like the truth was gonna come sooner or later so we might as well get straight now. I guess I know you better than I've ever known any human, let alone any woman. But if fair is fair and right is right we've *got* to take the stuff. I wouldn't have the balls not to."

"Sure. Come on—Wesley's waiting."

Together they walked hand in hand, past the cigar-
burn in the rug, to Wesley's dying place. The whisper of their boots on the rug echoed oddly in the
soundproof room, then faded to silence.

"The door was open that night," Jill whispered.

"Yeah," Zack agreed. He turned the knob, eased
the door open and yelped in surprise and fright. A
bulky figure sat on the stage ten feet away, half-
propped against an amp, ankles crossed before it. It
was in deep shadow, but Zack would have known that
silhouette in a coal cellar. He pushed the door open
wider, and the candlelight fell on the figure, confirm-
ing his guess.

"Finnegan!" he cried in relief and astonishment.
"Jesus Christ, man, you scared me. I swear I saw you
leave an hour ago."

"Nope," said the barkeep. He was of medium
height and stocky, bald as a grape but with fuzzy
brown hair all over his face and neck. It was the kind
of face within which the unbroken nose was incongruous. He scratched his crinkly chin with a left hand
multiply callused from twenty years of guitar and
dobro and mandolin and fiddle, and grinned what his
dentist referred to as the Thousand Dollar Grin. "You
just thought you did."

"Well shit, yeah, so it seems. Look, we're just sort
of into a little head thing here if that's cool, meant
to tell you later . . ."

"Sure."

A noise came from behind Zack, and he turned
quickly to Jill. "Look, baby, it's Finn—"

Jill had not made the noise, nor did she make one
now. Sziller had made the noise as he slipped the lock
on the outside door, and he made another one as he
snapped the hammer back on the silenced Colt. It

echoed in the dressing room. Zack spun back to Finnegan, and the barkeep's right hand was up out of his lap now and there was a .357 Magnum in it.

Too tired, Zack thought wearily, *too frigging tired. I wasn't cautious enough and so it ends here.*

"I'm sorry, Jill," he said aloud, still facing Finnegan.

"I," Finnegan said clearly and precisely, "am a bi-federal agent, authorized to act in either the American or the Canadian sector. Narcotics has been my main turf for years now."

"Sure," Zack agreed. "What better cover for a narc than a musician?"

"This one," Finnegan said complacently. "I always hated being on the road. Halifax has always been a smuggler's port—why not just sit here and let the stuff come to me? All the beer I can drink—"

Sziller was going through the knapsack Jill had left by the door, without taking his eyes or his gun off them for an instant.

"So how come you're in bed with Sziller?" Zack demanded. Sziller looked up and grinned, arraying his massive beard like a peacock's tail.

"George blew my cover," Finnegan said cheerfully. "He knew me from back when and spilled the soybeans. If he'd known you two were regulars here he'd likely have warned you. So after Sziller did him in and then . . . found out he had not adequately secured the goods . . . he naturally came straight to me."

"Finnegan's got a better organization than we do," Sziller chuckled. His voice was like a lizard's would sound if lizards could talk. "More manpower, more resources, more protection."

"And Sziller knew that TWT would mean the end of me too if it got out. He figured that our interest coincided for once—in a world of truth, what use is a narc? How can he work?"

Much too goddam tired, Zack told himself. *I'm hallucinating.* Finnegan appeared to be winking at him. Zack glanced to see if Jill were reacting to it, but her eyes were locked on Sziller, whose eyes were locked on her. Zack glanced swiftly back, and Finnegan still appeared to be winking, and now he was waving Zack toward him. Zack stood still; he preferred to die in the dressing room.

"He took a gamble," Finnegan went on, "a gamble that I would go just as far as he would to see that drug destroyed. Well, we missed you in Quebec and Ottawa and Toronto, and you fooled us when you went to Portland instead of your gig in Bangor, but I guess we've got you now."

"You're wrong," Jill said, turning to glare at Finnegan. "It's too late. You're both too late. You can kill us, but you can never recall the truth now."

"People forget headlines," Sziller sneered confidently. "Even a month of headlines. Nothing."

"You're still wrong," Zack said, staring in confusion from Sziller to Jill to the gesticulating Finnegan. "We put about thirty tapes and TWT samples in the mail—"

"Jerks," Sziller said, shaking his head. "Outthought every step of the way. Look, sonny, if you want to move a lot of dope with minimum risk, where do you get a job?" He paused and grinned again. "The Post Office, dummy."

"No," Zack and Jill said together, and Finnegan barked *"Yes,"* quite sharply. They both turned to look at him.

"You can bug any room with a window in it, children," he said wearily. "And that dressing room, of course, has always been bugged. Oh, *look*, dammit."

He held up a VidCaset Mailer pack with broken seals, and at *last* they both started forward involuntarily toward it, and as he cleared the dressing room doorway Zack finally caught on, and he reached behind him and an incredible thing happened.

It must be borne in mind that both Zack and Jill had, as they had earlier recognized, been steadily raising the truth level between them for over a month, unconsciously attempting to soften the blow of their first TWT experience. The Tennessee preacher earlier noted had once said publicly that all people are born potentially telepathic—but that if we're ever going to get any message-traffic capacity, we must first shovel the shit out of the Communications Room. This room, he said, was called by some the subconscious mind. Zack and Jill had almost certainly been exposed to at least threshold contamination with TWT, and they were, as it happens, the first subjects to be a couple and very much in love. They had lived together through a month that could have killed them at any time, and they were already beginning to display minor telepathic rapport.

Whatever the reasons, for one fractionated instant their hands touched, glancingly, and—Jill who had seen none of Finnegan's winking and almost nothing of his urgent gestures—knew all at once exactly what was about to happen and what to do, and Zack *knew* that she knew and that he didn't have to worry about her. Sziller was close behind them; there was no time even for one last flickerglance at each other. They grinned and winked together at Finnegan and Zack dove left and Jill dove right and Sziller came into the doorway with the Colt extended, wondering why

Finnegan hadn't fired already, and there was just time for his face to register *of course, he has no silencer* before Finnegan shot him.

A .357 Magnum throwing a 120-grain Supervel hollow-point can kill you if it hits you in the foot, from hydrostatic shock to the brain. Sziller took it in the solar plexus and slammed back into the dressing room to land with a wet, meaty thud.

The echoes roared and crackled away like the treble thunder that comes sometimes with heat lightning.

"I'm kind of more than your garden variety narc," Finnegan said calmly. "Maybe you guessed."

"Yes," Jill said for both of them. "A few seconds ago. To arrange that many convincingly bungled hits, you've got to be *big*. But you took a big chance with that cab driver."

"Hell, he wasn't mine. The guy just happened to flip—happens all the time."

"I believe you," she said, again for the two of them.

"People will have heard that shot," Zack suggested diffidently.

"Nobody who wasn't expecting it, son," Finnegan said, and sighed. "Nobody who wasn't expecting it."

Zack nodded. "Question?"

"Sure."

"How come you're still holding that gun out?"

"Because both of you still have yours," the government man said softly.

No one moved for a long frozen moment. Zack was caught with his right hand under him; in attempting to conceal the gun he had lost the use of it. Jill's was behind a crouching leg, but she left it there.

"We don't figure you, Ed," she said softly. "That's all. You see that, don't you?"

"Of course," he said. "So lighten up on the iron and by and by we'll all go get ham and eggs at my place. I'll teach you that song about Bad-Eye Bill and the Eskimo gal."

"You're not relaxing us worth a shit, Finnegan," Zack grated. "Talk. How big *are* you?"

Finnegan pursed his lips, blew a tiny bubble between them. "Big. Bigger than narcotics. Bifederality leaves a lot of gaps. I guess you could say I'm The Man, Zaccur old son. For our purposes, anyway. Oh, I have superiors, including the President *and* the Prime Minister. I'm so clever and nimble none of them is even afraid of me. I think the PM rather likes me. It's important that you know how heavy I am—it'll help you believe the rest."

He paused there, and Zack said "Try us," in a gentler tone of voice.

Finnegan looked around him at the darkened music room, at shadowy formica-toadstool tables bristling with chair legs, at the great hovering-buzzard blot that was the high spotlight, at a stage full of amplifiers and a piano like stolid dwarves and a troll come to sit in judgment on him, at the mocking red glow of the sign over the door that claimed it was an exit. He took a deep breath, and spoke very carefully.

"Did you ever wonder why a man takes on a job like mine?" He wet his lips. "He takes it on because it's a job that someone has to do, and he sees that the man doing it is a bloody bungling butcher playing James Bond with the fate of the world. Can you see that? I hated his job as much as I hated him, but I understood that in a world like this one, *some*body *has* to do that job. Somebody just plain *has* to do that job, and I decided that no one in sight could do a better job than me. So I forced him to retire and I took his job. It is a filthy pig fucker of a job, and it has damaged me to do it—but *somebody had to*. Look, I have done things that horrify me, things that diminish me, but I did good things, too, and I have been striving every minute toward a world in which my job didn't exist, in which nobody had to shoulder that load. I've been working to put myself out of a job, without the faintest shred of hope, for over ten years—and now it's Christmas and I'm free, I'm fucking *FREE*. That makes me so happy that I could go down to the cemetery and dig up Wes and kiss him on the mouldy lips, so happy I'll feel just *terrible* if I can't talk you two out of killing me.

"My job is finished, now—nobody knows it but you and me, but it's all over but the shouting. And in gratitude to you and Wes I intend to use my last gasp of power and influence to try and keep you two alive when the shit hits the fan."

"Huh?"

"I kind of liked your idea, so I let your VidCaset packs go through. But first I erased 'em and rerecorded. Audio only, voice out of a voder, nothing identifying you two. That won't fool a computer for long, they're all friends of yours, but it buys us time."

"For what?" Jill asked.

"Time to get you two underground, of course. How would you like to be, oh, say, a writer and her husband in Colorado for six months or so? You'd look good as a blond."

"Finnegan," Zack said with great weariness, "this all has a certain compelling inner consistency to it, but you surely understand our position. Unless you can prove any of this, we're going to have to shoot it out."

"Why you damned fools," Finnegan blazed,

"what're you wasting time for? You've got some of
the stuff with you—*give me a taste.*"

There was a pause while the pair thought that over.
"How do we do this?" Jill asked at last.

"Put your guns on me," Finnegan said.

They stared.

"Come on, dammit. For now that's the only way
we can trust each other. Just like the world out
there—guns at each other's heads because we fear lies
and treachery, the sneak attack. Put your fucking guns
on me, and in an hour that world will be on its way
out. *Come on!*" he roared.

Hesitantly, the two brought up their guns, until all
three weapons threatened life. Jill's other hand
brought a tiny stoppered vial from her pants. Slowly,
carefully, she advanced toward Finnegan, holding out
the truth, and when she was three feet away she saw
Finnegan grin and heard Zack chuckle, and then she
was giggling helplessly at the thought of three solemn faces above pistol sights, and all at once all three
of them were convulsed with great racking whoops
of laughter at themselves, and they threw away their
guns as one. They held their sides and roared and
roared with laughter until all three had fallen to the
floor, and then they pounded weakly on the floor and
laughed some more.

There was a pause for panting and catching of
breath and a few tapering giggles, and then Jill
unstoppered the vial and upended it against each
proffered fingertip and her own. Each licked their
finger eagerly, and from about that time on everything began to be all right. Literally.

An ending is the beginning of something, always.

APOGEE

He sat on plush leather in the finest, most opulent office in town, surveying a desk on which even a careless pilot could have landed a helicopter. Flicking an entirely imaginary speck of lint from the lapel of his newest four-hundred-dollar suit, he yawned for perhaps the twentieth time since his secretaries had gone home for the day, and stifled the yawn with an exquisitely manicured hand. His countenance was that of a man with perfect health, job security, much money, and considerable prestige—with a paradoxical frown overlaid.

"Hell," he said succinctly and most uncharacteristically.

"Yeah?" said the demon which appeared flaming beyond the desk.

The temprature in the room rose sharply, but the seated man did not (as a matter of fact, could not) sweat. He squainted at the blazing horned creature and automatically moved his Moroccan leather cigar box away from it. "You want to tone that down a bit?" he said, scowling.

"Listen," it told him, "with the price of a watt these days, you should turn out the lights and put a mirror behind me." But its fiery brilliance moderated to a cheery glow, and the carpet stopped smelling bad. It sat down on thin air, tail coiled, and blew a perfect smoke ring. "Now, what's on your mind?"

He hesitated; took the plunge. "I'm not satisfied."

The demon sneered. "A beef, huh? You guys gimme a pain. You want the Moon for a soul like yours?"

"Now wait a minute," he said indignantly, with just a touch of fear. "We've got a contract."

"Yeah, yeah," it sighed. "And you want to talk fine print. You guys read too many stories. All right, let's haul out the contract and get this over with."

A large piece of foolscap appeared between them on the desk, smouldering around the edges. It was covered with minuscule type, and one of the signatures glistened red.

"Standard issue contract, with bonus provisions contingent on your promise to deliver a large consignment of souls other than your own, as described in appended schedule A-2 . . ." The appendix materialized beside the contract, and the demon looked it over. "Seems to be in order. What's the beef?"

"I'm not satisfied," he repeated, and glared uncomfortably at the demon.

"Oh, for cryin' out loud," it burst out, "what do you want from my life? You got everything you asked for. I honor my service contracts, I supplied everything requested, and I mean everything. I *worked* for you, baby."

"I don't care," he said petulantly. "I'm not happy. It's right there in the appendix, the Lifetime Approval Option. I've got to *enjoy* all that you give me. And I don't."

"Look," the demon said angrily, "I did my best for you pal—you've got all I can give you. Unbelievable riches, total health, raw power, the job you always wanted and complete autonomy. You can say any dumb thing that comes into your head—and believe me, you've said some lulus—and people agree with you. You can make the wildest bonehead decisions and they work out okay. You couldn't louse up if you tried, and believe you me it's taken some doing. So what's not to enjoy?"

He glared at it, his jowls quivering. "I'm bored, dammit. There's nothing left to achieve."

"It's your own fault," said the demon. "You insisted on having everything right away, and so you ran out of dreams too fast." It sneered at him. "Greedy."

"I don't care," he snapped. "You made a deal and I want satisfaction. Literally."

The demon stood and began pacing the floor, trailing wisps of blue smoke. "Look," it said irritably, "there's nothing more I can *do*. You've got the whole works."

"It's not enough. I'm bored."

The demon looked harassed, then thoughtful. "Maybe there's a way," it said slowly.

"Yes," he prodded eagerly.

"It's a way-out idea, but it just might work. The only thing you haven't tried. I'll turn you into a woman, and . . ."

"No," he said firmly.

It grimaced. "Worth a try. Well, I guess there's only one possibility, then."

"Well, come on, come on. Out with it."

"I'll turn you into a masochist, and let the whole job come down around your ears." The demon smiled. "Take a big bite out of my work load."

"Are you out of your mind?" he exploded.

"Think about it," it said reasonably. "There's nowhere to go from here but back downhill, and you could enjoy that as much as the ride up. Don't you understand? You'd be a *masochist*. You'll lose everything I've ever given you with just as much joy as you experienced in receiving it, only this time you'll be *doing it all yourself*, through your own natural ineptitude. All I'll do is help you appreciate it."

He started to say that it was the craziest thing he'd ever heard, and paused. He was silent for a long time, rubbing his five o'clock shadow, and the demon waited. At last he cleared his throat.

"Do you really think it's feasible?" he asked.

"*Thought* so," said the demon with sly satisfaction. "You've been kidding yourself all these years; this is what you really wanted all along." He began an angry retort, but paused. All at once he experienced a flash of nostalgia for his ulcer. It *might* be nice to whimper again . . .

"All right," he said suddenly. "Do it."

"It's done."

The demon disappeared, leaving behind it the traditional smell of brimstone (with added petroleum derivatives) and a scorched carpet.

He discovered that his feet hurt, and realized with what was now the closest thing to glee that he could experience that he was sweating profusely. The demon was right—*this* was what he had really craved all along, this was what he had been born for. The fall would be more spectacular than the rise. His head began to ache dully.

Picking up the special phone, he made two calls, then dialed his unlisted home number. "Hello, Pat? Dick. Sorry I'm late, dear. I'll be sleeping here tonight. I have to meet early tomorrow with Ron and Gordon about some plumbers. Yes, I'll see you tomorrow night. What? No, dear, nothing's wrong. Everything is fine. Everything is just fine. Good night, dear."

He hung up and looked across the room at the presidential seal over the door. He began to laugh, and then he cried, and continued to cry for months thereafter.

NO RENEWAL

Douglas Bent Jr. sits in his kitchen, waiting for his tea to heat. It is May twelfth, his birthday, and he has prepared wintergreen tea. Douglas allows himself this extravagance because he knows he will receive no birthday present from anyone but himself. By a trick of Time and timing, he has outlived all his friends, all his relatives. The concept of neighborliness, too, has predeceased him; not because he has none, but because he has too many.

His may be, for all he knows, the last small farm in Nova Scotia, and it is bordered on three sides by vast mined-out clay pits, gaping concentric cavities whose insides were scraped out and eaten long ago, their husk thrown away to rot. On the remaining perimeter is an apartment-hive, packed with antlike swarms of people. Douglas knows none of them as individuals; at times, he doubts the trick is possible.

Once Douglas's family owned hundreds of acres along what was then called simply the Shore Road; once the Bent spread ran from the Bay of Fundy itself back over the peak of the great North Mountain, included a sawmill, rushing streams, hundreds of thousands of trees, and acre after acre of pasture and hay and rich farmland; once the Bents were one of the best-known families from Annapolis Royal to Bridgetown, their livestock the envy of the entire Annapolis Valley.

Then the petrochemical industry died of thirst. With it, of course, went the plastics industry. Clay suddenly became an essential substitute—and the Annapolis Valley is mostly clay.

Now the Shore Road is the Fundy Trail, six lanes of high-speed traffic; the Bent spread is fourteen acres on the most inaccessible part of the Mountain; the sawmill has been replaced by the industrial park that ate the clay; the pasture and the streams and the farmland have been disemboweled or paved over; all the Bents save Douglas Jr. are dead or moved to the cities; and perhaps no one now living in the Valley has ever seen a live cow, pig, duck, goat or chicken, let alone eaten them. Agribusiness has destroyed agriculture, and stynthoprotein feeds (some of) the world. Douglas grows only what crops replenish themselves, feeds only himself.

He sits waiting for the water to boil, curses for the millionth time the solar-powered electric stove that supplanted the family's woodburner when firewood became impossible to obtain. Electric stoves take too long to heat, call for no tending, perform their task with impersonal callousness. They do not warm a room.

Douglas's gnarled fingers idly sort through the

wintergreen he picked this morning, spurn the jar of sugar that stands nearby. All his life Douglas has made wintergreen tea from fresh maple sap, which requires no sweetening. But this spring he journeyed with drill and hammer and tap and bucket to his only remaining maple tree, and found it dead. He has bought maple-flavored sugar for his birthday tea, but he knows it will not be the same. Then again, next spring he may find no wintergreen.

So *many* old familiar friends have failed to reappear in their season lately—the deer moss has gone wherever the hell the deer went to, crows no longer raid the compost heap, even the lupens have decreased in number and brilliance. The soil, perhaps made self-conscious by its conspicuous isolation, no longer bursts with life.

Douglas realizes that his own sap no longer runs in the spring, that the walls of his house ring with no voice save his own. If a farm surrounded by wasteland cannot survive, how then shall a man? *It is my birthday,* he thinks, *how old am I today?*

He cannot remember.

He looks up at the goddamelectricclock (the family's two-hundred-year-old-cuckoo clock, being wood, did not survive the Panic Winter of '94), reads the date from its face (there are no longer trees to spare for fripperies like paper calendars), sits back with a grunt. *2049, like I thought, but when was I born?*

So many things have changed in Douglas's lifetime, so many of Life's familiar immutable aspects gone forever. The Danielses to the east died childless: their land now holds a sewage treatment plant. On the west the creeping border of Annapolis Royal has eaten the land up, excreting concrete and steel and far too many people as it went: Annapolis is now as choked as New York City was in Douglas's father's day. Economic helplessness has driven Douglas back up the North Mountain, step by inexorable step, and the profits (he winces at the word) that he reaped from selling off his land parcel by parcel (as, in his youth, he bought it from his ancestors) have been eaten away by the rising cost of living. Here, on his last fourteen acres, in the two-story house he built with his own hands and by Jesus *wood*, Douglas Bent Jr. has made his last stand.

He questions his body as his father taught him to do, is told in reply that he has at least ten or twenty more years of life left. *How old am I?* he wonders again, *forty-five? Fifty? More?* He has simply lost track, for the years do not mean what they did. It matters little; though he may have vitality for twenty years more, he has money for no more than five. Less, if the new tax laws penalizing old age are pushed through in Halifax.

The water has begun to boil. Douglas places wintergreen and sugar in the earthenware mug his mother made (back when clay was dug out of the backyard with a shovel), moves the pot from the stove, and pours. His nostrils test the aroma: to his dismay, the fake smells genuine. Sighing from his belly, he moves to the rocking chair by the kitchen window, places the mug on the sill, and sits down to watch another sunset. From here Douglas can see the Bay, when the wind is right and the smoke from the industrial park does not come between. Even then he can no longer see the far shores of New Brunswick, for the air is thicker than when Douglas was a child.

The goddamclock hums, the mug steams. The

winds are from the north—a cold night is coming, and tomorrow may be one of the improbable "bay-streamer" days with which Nova Scotia salts its spring. It does not matter to Douglas: his solar heating is far too efficient. His gaze wanders down the access road which leads to the highway; it curves downhill and left and disappears behind the birch and alders and pine that line it for a half mile from the house. If Douglas looks at the road right, he can sometimes convince himself that around the bend are not strip-mining shells and brick apartment-hives but arable land, waving grain and the world he once knew. Fields and yaller dogs and grazing goats and spring mud and tractors and barns and goat berries like stockpiles of B-B shot . . .

Douglas's mind wanders a lot these days. It has been a long time since he enjoyed thinking, and so he has lost the habit. It has been a long time since he had anyone with whom to share his thoughts, and so he has lost the inclination. It has been a long time since he understood the world well enough to think about it, and so he has lost the ability.

Douglas sits and rocks and sips his tea, spilling it down the front of his beard and failing to notice. *How old am I?* he thinks for the third time, and summons enough will to try and find out. Rising from the rocker with an effort, he walks on weary wiry legs to the living room, climbs the stairs to the attic, pausing halfway to rest.

My father was sixty-one he recalls as he sits, wheezing, on the stair *when he accepted euthanasia. Surely I'm not that old. What keeps me alive?*

He has no answer.

When he reaches the attic, Douglas spends fifteen minutes in locating the ancient trunk in which Bent

family records are kept. They are minutes well spent:
Douglas is cheered by many of the antiques he must
shift to get at the trunk. Here is the potter's wheel
his mother worked; there the head of the axe with
which he once took off his right big toe; over in the
corner a battered peavey from the long-gone sawmill
days. They remind him of a childhood when life still
made sense, and bring a smile to his grizzled features.
It does not stay long.

Opening the trunk presents difficulties—it is locked
and Douglas cannot remember where he put the key.
He has not seen it for many years, or the trunk for
that matter. Finally he gives up, smashes the old lock
with the peavey, and levers up the lid (the Bents have
always learned leverage as they got old, working
efficiently long after strength has gone). It opens with
a shriek, hinges protesting their shattered sleep.

The past leaps out at him like the woes of the
world from Pandora's Box. On top of the pile is a
picture of Douglas's parents, Douglas Sr. and Sarah,
smiling on their wedding day, Grandfather Lester
behind them near an enormous barn, grazing cattle
visible in the background.

Beneath the picture he finds a collection of receipts
for paid grain bills, remembers the days when food
was cheap enough to feed animals, and there were
animals to be fed. Digging deeper, he comes across
canceled checks, insurance policies, tax records, a
collection of report cards and letters wrapped in
ribbon. Douglas pulls up short at the hand-made
rosary he gave his mother for her fifteenth anniversary, and wonders if either of them still believed in
God even then. Again, it is hard to remember.

At last he locates his birth certificate. He stands,
groaning with the ache in his calves and knees, and

threads his way through the crowded attic to the west window, where the light from the setting sun is sufficient to read the fading document. He seats himself on the shell of a television that has not worked since he was a boy, holds the paper close to his face and squints.

"May twelfth, 1989," reads the date on the top.

Why, I'm sixty years old he tells himself in wonderment. *Sixty. I'll be damned.*

There is something about that number that rings a bell in Douglas's tired old mind, something he can't quite recall about what it means to be sixty years old. He squints at the birth certificate again.

And there on the last line, he sees it, sees what he had almost forgotten, and realizes that he was wrong—he will be getting a birthday present today after all.

For the bottom line of his birth certificate says, simply and blessedly, ". . . Expiry Date: May twelfth, 2049."

Downstairs, for the first time in years, there is a knock at the door.

TIN EAR

Call them Stargates if you want to. The term was firmly engraved in the public's mind, by science fiction writers with a weakness for grandiose jargon, fully fifty years before the first Spatial Anomaly was discovered and the War started. If you do call them Stargates, you probably call us Stargate Keepers, or Keepers for short.

But we call 'em 'Holes, for short, and we call ourselves Wipers.

It's all in how you look at it, of course. If we ever got to enter one, instead of just watching them and mopping up what comes out, we might have a different name for them—or if not, at least a different name for ourselves. ". . . and cheap ones, too," as the joke goes.

But the Enemy's drones keep popping out at irregular intervals, robot-destroyer planetoids with

simple but straightforward programs written somewhere on the far side of hyperspace. So, in addition
to the heroes who get to go after the source—and
keep failing to return—somebody has to mount guard
over every known 'Hole, to sound the alarm when
a drone comes through, and hopefully to neutralize
it (before it neutralizes *us*). The War is still, after
twenty years, at the stage where intact prizes are more
valuable than confirmed kills. Data outworth debris,
and will for decades to come.

For the Enemy, apparently, as much as for us, or
I wouldn't be here. The first Enemy drone I ever saw
could certainly have killed us both, if it had wanted
to.

It was well that Walter and I inhabited separate
Pods. We didn't get along at all. The only things we
had in common were (*a*) an abiding hatred for the
government which had drafted us into this sillyass
suicidal employ (". . . before we had a chance to
volunteer like gentlemen," we always added) and (*b*)
a deep enjoyment of music.

But all Wipers share these two things. One of the
few compensations our cramped and claustrophobic
Pods feature are their microtape libraries and excellent
playback systems (you can't read properly on combat status). And so it was possible for Walter and me
to spend endless hours within the same general volume of space, listening to separate masterpieces over
our headphones and arguing only occasionally. Walter
had no sense of humor whatsoever, despised anyone
who did, loathed any music of satirical, parodying or
punning nature, and therefore was impossible to discuss music with. Or anything much.

But you can listen to a lot of good music if you
have nothing else to do.

I was seventeen hours into Wagner's *Ring Des Nie-belungen,* thoroughly exhausted but with the end in sight, when Walter's commlaser overrode my head-phones. "George."

"Wha?" I yelled, but there was too much cacoph-ony. We both had to kill our tapes. Damned if he didn't have *Siegfried* on himself, which annoyed me— I was certain, without asking, that he liked Wagner for all the wrong reasons.

"Alert status," he said, yanking me from music back to reality.

"Right." I slapped switches and reached out to touch my imitation rabbit's foot. So the 'Hole was puckering up, eh? A noble death might lie seconds away. With all possible speed I joined Walter in train-ing all the considerable firepower we possessed on the 'Hole.

And the bastard popped out a couple thousand miles *to one side of* the 'Hole and bagged us both. Unheard of; still unexplained. Even Abacus Al, the computer you can count on, was caught flat-footed. Tractor beam grabs me, *clang!,* reels in fast, *CLANG!,* half a billion Rockies' worth of Terran hardware on alien flypaper, *slump,* body goes limp in shock-webbing, *ping!,* lights go out.

"George," Walter was saying in my headphones, "are you all right?"

"I'll see," I replied, but by then some sort of anti-laser device must've been interposed by the drone-planetoid which held us captive, for the headphones went dead. I sighed and checked my Pod. It was on its gyrostabilized tail, "upright." All my video screens were dead, except for the one that showed me about twenty degrees of starry space straight "overhead"— my location with reference to Walter was unknown.

This was serious if I intended to live, which I did. But before I tried the radio I inspected my weapons control systems (dead in all directions except "up"), main drive (alive, but insufficient to pry me loose), and my body (alive and apparently unharmed). *Then* I heated up the radio on standard emergency band.

"Down one freak, Cipher A," I said crisply and quickly, getting it all out before static jammed that frequency. Then I dialed 'er down to the next frequency on the "standard" list, instructed Abacus Al the AnaLogic to convert to Cipher A before transmitting. "Walter?"

"Here." Flat, mechanical voice—Als rendition of human speech, just like what Walter was hearing from me.

"Simpleton machine."

"Yah."

"Capture, not kill. Programmed to immobilize us, disarm us, blind us, and prevent meaningful communication between us. As soon as it dopes out Cipher A, it'll . . ."

A million pounds of frying bacon drowned me out. I dropped freak by the same interval again and shifted to Cipher B, allegedly a much tougher cipher to break. They call it "the best nonperfect cipher possible."

Walter was waiting on the new freak. "It's essential," he began at once, "that we determine whether this drone-planetoid is a Mark I or a Mark II."

"Damn right," I agreed. "If we can work out our relative positions we've at least got options."

And a roar of static threw Cipher B out the window.

Both types of Enemy planetoid have only the two

tractor beams—but the relative *positions* of them are one of the chief distinguishing features from the outside. If this was a Mark I, we could both throw full power to our drives—and while they wouldn't be sufficient to peel us loose, their energies should cross, like surgical paired-lasers, at the center of the planetoid, burning out its volitional hardware. If this were Mark the Second, the same maneuver would have our drives cross in the heart of the power-plant and distribute the component atoms of all three of us across an enormous spherical volume of space. But how could we compute our positions blind, on a sphere with no agreed-upon poles or meridians anyhow, and communicate them to each other's computers without tripping the damned planetoid's squelch-program? The cagey son of a bitch had cracked Cipher B too easily—apparently it was programmed to jam anything that it computed to be "exchange of meaningful information" whether it could decipher it or not. That suggested that Cipher C, the Perfect Cipher might be the only answer.

The perfect cipher (really a code-cipher) was devised way back in the 1900s, and has never been improved upon. You have a computer generate an *enormous* run of random numbers, in duplicate. You give a copy of the printout to each communicator, and down the column of random numbers they go, each writing out the alphabet, one letter to each number, over and over again. For each successive letter they want to encipher and send, they jump down to the next alphabet-group in line, select the random number adjacent to the desired letter, and transmit that number. A savvy AnaLogic deduces pauses, activates voder: communication. The cipher *cannot* be broken by any one not in possession of an identical list of random numbers, for it produces utterly no pattern. (We had a code by the way, a true code, in which prearranged four-letter groups stood for various prearranged phrases. But not a phrase on the list applied to our situation—I Love the Army— and using a series of exclusively four-letter groups would have tipped off the alien computer that a code was in use.)

But Cipher C had one flaw that I could see, and so I hesitated before dialing the frequency again. If we lost *this* chance we were effectively deaf and dumb as well as blind. *Oh God,* I prayed *give Walter just this once, and for no more than fifteen minutes, at least half a brain.* I dialed the new freak.

". . . got to take starsights," he was saying. "It's the only way to . . ."

"SHUT UP!"

"Eh?"

"No sound; Listen. *Heed.* Okay? *Carefully.* Yes, 'sights,' but do not under any circumstances repeat any phrase or word-group I use. *Comprende?*"

I breathed a silent prayer.

"Why shouldn't I repeat any phrase or word-group you use?" Walter asked, puzzlement plain even through voder.

"GODDAMMIT," I roared, but I was addressing only another roar of static. Groups with identical numbers of characters, in repeated sequence, were the only clue the Enemy computer had needed. It was "meaningful communication," so it was jammed.

One more standard band left on the list. If we had to hunt for each other on offbeat frequencies, it could take forever to establish contact.

I scratched a telemetry contact and consulted Abacus Al. "How," I programmed, "can I communicate meaningful information without communicating meaningful information?"

That's the kind of question that makes most computers self-destruct, like an audio amplfier with no output connected. But Al is built to return whimsy with whimsy, and his sense of humor is as subtle as my own. "WRITE A POEM," he replied, "OR SING A SONG."

I snorted.

"No good," I punched. "Can't use words."

"HUM," Al printed.

A nova went off in my skull.

I crosswired the microtape library in Al's belly to the radio in his rump, and had him activate the last standard frequency. It was live but silent: Walter had finally figured out his previous stupidity. He waited for me to come up with inspiration this time.

I keyed the opening bars of an ancient Beatles' song. "We Can Work It Out." In clear. And then killed it before the melody repeated.

A long silence, while Walter slowly worked it out in his thick head. *Come on, dummy,* I yelled in my head, *give me something to work with!*

And my headphones filled with the strains of the most poignant song from *Cabaret*: "Maybe This Time."

Thank God!

I keyed Al's starchart displays and thought hard. The chunk of sky *I* saw was useless unless I could learn what Walter was seeing over his *own* head— the two combined would give us a fix. I couldn't see the 'Hole, and I had to assume he couldn't either, or he'd have surely mentioned it already.

Or would he? Anyone with half a brain would have . . .

I keyed in the early twenty-first-century Revivalist dirge, "Is There a Hole in Your Bucket?" and hoped he wouldn't think I was requesting a damage report.

He responded with the late twenty-first-century anti-Revivalist ballad, "The Sky Ain't Holy No More."

Okay, then. Back to the Beatles. "Tell Me What You See."

Walter paused a long time, and at last gave up and sent the intro to Donald MacLean's Van Gogh song—the line that goes, "Starry, starry night . . ." He was plainly stymied.

Hmmm. I'd have to think for both of us.

Inspiration came. I punched for a late twenty-first-century drugging-song called—"Brother Have You Got Any Reds?" There were few prominent red stars in this galactic neighborhood—if any appeared in Walter's "window" it might help Al figure our positions.

His uptake was improving; the answer was immediate. Ellington's immortal: "I Ain't Got Nothin' But the Blues."

So much for that one.

I was stumped. I could think of no more leading questions to ask Walter with music. If he couldn't, for once, make his own mind start working in punny ways, we were both sunk. Any time now, real live Enemies might pop out of the 'Hole, and there was no way of telling what they were like, because no human had ever survived a meeting with them at that time. *Come on, Walter.*

And he floored me. The piece he selected almost eluded me, so obscure was it: an incredibly ancient children's jingle called, "The Bear Went Over the Mountain."

I studied the starcharts feverishly, trying to visualize the geometry ("cosmometry?")—I lacked enough skill to have Al do it for me. If Walter could see the Bear at all, it seemed to me . . .

I sent the chorus of "Smack Dab in the Middle," the legendary Charles's version, and hoped Walter could sense the question mark.

Again, his answer baffled me momentarily—another Beatles song. *He loves me?* I thought wildly, and then I got it. "Yeah yeah yeah!"

My fingers tickled Abacus Al's keys, a ruby light blinked agreement, and Al's tactical assessment appeared on the display.

MARK ONE, it read.

"Walter," I yelled in clear, "Main drive. *Now!*"

And so when the *live* Enemies came through the 'Hole, *we* had the drop on *them*, which is how man got his first alien corpses to study, which is why we're (according to the government) winning the War these days. But the part of the whole episode that I remember best is when we were waiting there dead in space—in ambush—our remaining weaponry aimed at the 'Hole, and Walter was saying dazedly, "The most amazing thing is that the damned thing just sat there listening to us plot its destruction, with no more sense of self-preservation than the foresight of its programmers allowed. It just sat there . . ."

He giggled—at least, from anyone else I'd have called that sound a giggle.

" . . . sat there the . . .the whole time . . ."

He was definitely giggling now, and it must be racial instinct because he was doing it right.

". . . the . . . the whole time just . . ."

He lost control and began laughing out loud.

"Just *taking notes*," he whooped, and I dissolved into shuddering laughter myself. Our mutual need for catharsis transformed his modest stinker into the grandest pun ever made, and we roared. Even Abacus Al blinked a few times.

"Walter," I said, "I've got a feeling the rest of this hitch is going to be okay."

And then alarms were going off and we went smoothly into action as a *unit*, and the Enemy never had a chance.

IN THE OLDEN DAYS

George Maugham returned home from work much later than usual, and in a sour frame of mind. He was tired and knew that he had missed an excellent home-cooked meal, and things had not gone well at work despite his extra hours of labor. His face, as he came through the door, held that expression that would cause his wife to become especially understanding.

"Light on in the kids' window," he said crankily as he hung his coat by the door and removed his boots. "It's late."

Luanna Maugham truly was an extraordinary woman. With only a minimal use of her face and the suggestion of a shrug and the single word "Grandpa," she managed to convey amusement and irony and compassion and tolerant acceptance, and thereby begin diffusing his potential grumpiness. He felt the last of it bleed from him as she put into his hands a cup of dark sweetness which he knew perfectly well would turn out to be precisely drinking temperature. He understood how much she did for him.

But he still felt that he should follow up the issue of their children's bedtime. "I wish he wouldn't keep them up so late," he said, pitching his voice to signal his altered motivation.

"Well," she said, "they can sleep in tomorrow morning—no school. And he does tell fairy tales *so* well, dear."

"It's not the fairy tales I mind," he said, faintly surprised to feel a little of his irritation returning. "I just hope he's not filling their heads with all that other garbage." He sipped from his cup, which was indeed the right temperature. "All those hairy old stories of his. About the Good Old Days When Men Were Men And Women Knew Their Place." He shook his head. Yes, he was losing his good humor again.

"Why do his stories bother you so?" she asked gently. "Honestly, they seem pretty harmless to me."

"I think all that old stuff depresses them. Nightmares and that sort of thing. Confuses them. Boring, too, the same old stuff over and over again."

Mrs. Maugham did *not* point out that their two children never had nightmares, or permitted themselves to be bored. She made, in fact no response at all, and after a sufficient pause, he shook his head and continued speaking, more hesitantly. "I mean . . . there's something about it I can't . . ." He glanced down at his cup, and perhaps he found there the words he wanted. He sipped them. "Here it is: if the Good Old Days were so good, then I and my generation were fools for allowing things to change— then the world that *we* made is inferior—and I don't think it is. I mean, every generation of kids grows up convinced that their parents are idiots who've buggered everything up, don't they, and I certainly don't want or need *my* father encouraging the kids to feel that way." He wiped his lip with the heel of his hand. "I've worked hard, all my life, to make this a better world than the one I was born into, and . . . and it is, Lu, it *is*."

She took his face in her hands, kissed him, and bathed him in her very best smile. "Of course it is," she lied.

"And that," Grandpa was saying just then, with the warm glow of the storyteller who knows he has wowed 'em again, "is the story of how Princess Julie rescued the young blacksmith Jason from the Dark Tower, and together they slew the King of the Dolts." He bowed his head and began rolling his final cigarette of the night.

The applause was, considering the size of the house, gratifying. "That was really neat, Grampa," Julie said enthusiastically, and little Jason clapped his hands and echoed, "Really neat!"

"Now, tomorrow night," he said, and paused to lick his cigarette paper, "I'll tell you what happened *next*."

"Oh God, yes," Julie said, smacking her forehead, "the Slime Monster, I forgot, he's still loose."

"The Slime Monster!" Jason cried. "But that's my favorite *part*! Grampa tell *now*."

"Oh yes, please, Grampa," Julie seconded. In point of fact, she was not really all that crazy about the Slime Monster—he was pretty yucky—but now he represented that most precious commodity any child can know: a few minutes more of after-bedtime awakeness.

But the old man had been braced for this. "Not a chance, munchkins. Way past your bedtimes, and your folks'll—"

A chorus of protests rained about his head.

"Can it," he said, in the tone that meant he was serious, and the storm chopped off short. He was mildly pleased by this small reflection of his authority, and he blinked, and when his eyes opened Julie was holding out the candle to light his cigarette for him, and little Jason was inexpertly but enthusiastically trying to massage the right knee which, he knew (and occasionally remembered), gave Grandpa trouble a lot, because of something that Jason understood was called "our fright us." How, the old man wondered mildly, do they manage an instant one-eighty without even shifting gears?

"You can tell us tomorrow, Grampa," Julie assured him, with the massive nonchalance that only a six-year old girl can lift, "I don't matter about it." She put down the candle and got him an ashtray.

"Yeah," Jason picked up his cue. "Who cares about a dumb old Slime Monster?" He then attempted to look as if that last sentence were sincere, and failed; Julie gave him a dirty look for overplaying his hand.

Little con artists, Grandpa thought fondly, there's hope for the race yet. He waited for the pitch, enjoying the knee-massage.

"I'll make you a deal, Grampa," Julie said.

"A deal?"

"If I can ask you a question you can't answer, you have to tell about the Olden Days for ten minutes."

He appeared to think about it while he smoked. "Seven minutes." There was no timepiece in the room.

"Nine," Julie said at once.

"Eight."

"Eight and a half."

"Done."

The old man did not expect to lose. He was expecting some kind of trick question, but he felt that he had heard most, perhaps all, of the classic conundrums over the course of his years, and he figured he could cobble up a trick answer to whatever Julie had up her sleeve. And she sideswiped him.

"You know that poem, 'Roses are red, violets are blue'?" she asked.

"Which one? There are hundreds."

"That's what I mean," she said, springing the trap. "I know a millyum of 'em. Roses are red, violets are blue—"

"—outhouse is smelly and so are you," Jason interrupted loudly, and broke up.

She glared at her younger brother and pursed her lips. "Don't be such a child," she said gravely, and nearly caught Grandpa smiling. "So that's my question."

"What?"

"Why do they always say that?"

"You mean, 'Roses are red, violets—?'"

"When they're *not*."

"Not what?"

She looked up at the ceiling as though inviting God to bear witness to the impossibility of communicating with grownups. "*Blue*," she said.

The old man's jaw dropped.

"Violets are *violet*," she amplified.

He was thunderstruck. She was absolutely right, and all at once he could not imagine why the question had not occurred to him decades earlier. "I'll be damned. You win, Princess. I have no idea how that one got started. You've got me dead to rights."

"Oh boy," Jason crowed, releasing Grandpa's knee at once and returning to his bed. "You kids nowadays," he prompted as Julie crawled in beside him.

Grandpa accepted the inevitable.

"You kids nowadays don't know nothing about nothing," he said. "Now in the Olden Days . . ."

Grinning triumphantly, Julie fluffed up her pillow and stretched out on the pallet, pulling her blanket delicately up over her small legs, just to the knees. Jason pulled his own blanket to his chin, uncaring that this bared his feet, and stared at the ceiling.

". . . in the Olden Days it wasn't like it is these days. Men were men in them days, and women knew their place in the world. This world has been going straight to hell since I was a boy, children, and you can dip me if it looks like getting any better. Things you kids take for granted nowadays, why, in the Olden Days we'd have laughed at the thought. Sometimes we did.

"F'rinstance, this business of gettin' up at six in the goddam morning and havin' a goddam potato pancake for breakfast, an' then walkin' twenty goddam kilometers to the goddam little red schoolhouse—in the Olden Days there wasn't *none* of that crap. We got up at eight like civilized children, and walked twenty goddam meters to where a *bus* come and hauled us the whole five klicks to a school the likes of which a child like you'll never see, more's the pity."

"Tell about the bus," Jason ordered.

"It was big enough for sixty kids to play in, and it was warm in the winter, sometimes *too* warm, and God Himself drove it, and it smelled wonderful and just the same every day. And when it took you home after school, there was none of this nonsense of grabbing some refried beans and goin' off to haul rock and brush for the goddam road crew for fifty cents a week, I'll tell you that. Why, if a feller had tried to hire me when I was your age, at a good salary, mind you, they'd have locked him up for *exploiting* me! No sir, we'd come home after a hard day of learning, and we'd play ball or watch TV or read a book, whatever we felt like—ah Christ, we lived like kings and we never even knew it!

"You, Julie, you'll have children before you're sixteen, and a good wife and mother you'll be—but in the Olden Days you might have been an executive, or a doctor, or a dancer. Jason, you'll grow up to be a good farmer—if they don't hang you—but if you'd been born when I was, you could have made movies in Thailand, or flown airliners to Paris, or picked rocks off the goddam face of the Moon and brought 'em home. And before any of that, you both could have had something you're never going to know—a mysterious, terrible, wonderful thing called adolescence.

"But my generation, and your father and mother's, we threw it all away, because it wasn't perfect. The best I can explain it is that they all voted themselves a free lunch, democratic as hell, and then tried to duck out when the check arrived. They spent every dime they had, and all of your money besides, and they *still* had to wash some dishes. There was two packs of idiots, you see. On one side you had rich sons of bitches, excuse my language, and they were arrogant. Couldn't be bothered to build a nuclear power plant to specs or a car that worked, couldn't be bothered to hide their contempt. Why, do you know that banks actually used to set out, for the use of their customers, pens that didn't work—and then chain them in place to prevent their theft? Worse than that, they were the dumbest aristocrats in the history of man. They couldn't be bothered to take care of their own peasants. I mean, if you want a horse to break his back for you, do you feed him, or take all his hay to make yourself pillows and mattresses?

"And then on the other side you had sincere, well-meanin' folks who were even dumber than the rich. Between the anti-teckers and the no-nukers and the stop-fusion jerks and the small-is-beautiful types and the appropriate-technology folks and the back-to-the-landers they managed to pull the plug, to throw away the whole goddam solar system. The car might have got us all to a gas station, running on fumes and momentum—but now that they shut the engine down there ain't enough gas left to get it started again . . ."

The old man's cigarette was too short to keep smoking. He pinched it out between two fingers, salvaged the unburnt tobacco, and began to take up his tale again. Then he saw that the children were both fast asleep. He let his breath out, covered them, and blew out the candle. He thought about going downstairs to ask his son-in-law how things had gone in the fields, whether the crop had been saved . . . but the stairs were hard on the old man's our fright us, and he really did not want to risk hearing bad news just now. Instead he went to the window and watched the moon, lonely now for several decades, and after a time he cried. For the children, who could never never hope that one day their grandchildren might have the stars . . .

SILLY WEAPONS
THROUGHOUT
HISTORY

People keep sending me their fanzines—amateur publications concerning sf and related subjects, and spanning the spectrum from mimeographs to four color offset. As with amateur efforts of any kind, some are just dreadful and some are sublime. One of the most piquant I have seen is a little 'zine out of Florida called the *Tabebuian*. It is the size of a pocket-calculator instruction pamphlet, much better printed, published by Mensa members Dave and Mardi Jenrette. I can attest to the fact that David's sense of humor is D. Jenrette. I wrote him a letter asking why, if Mensa people were so smart, they had named their organization after the Latin word for table (*mensa*) rather than mind (*mens*, an early example of unconscious sexism). He replied that the club's name is in fact derived from *menses*, and refers to their periodic meetings. (I gave this riposte a standing ovulation.)

Anyroad, one of the *Tab*'s running departments for a while was a feature called "Silly Weapons Throughout History." The first one I saw was the Jell-O Sword, a short-lived weapon rendered obsolete by the subsequent invention (a week later) of the bronze sword. Inspired, I retired to my Fantasy Workbench, and over the next few days I hammered out the following Silly Weapons:

The Swordbroad: Invented by a tribe of fanatical male chauvinists, the Prix, this armament consisted of a wife gripped by the ankles and whirled like a flail (Prix warriors made frequent jocular allusion to the sharp cutting edge of their wives' tongues). The weapon died out, along with the Prix, in a single generation—for tolerably obvious reasons.

The Rotator: A handgun in which the bullets are designed to rotate as well as revolve, presenting an approximately even chance of suicide with each use.

The Bullista: A weapon of admittedly limited range which attempted to sow confusion among the enemy by firing live cows into the midst, placing them upon a dilemma of the horns. (Also called the Cattling Gun.)

The Arbalust: A modification of the bullista, which sought to demoralize and distract the enemy by peppering their encampments with pornographic pictures and literature—yet another dilemma of the horns.

The Dogapult: Another modification of the bullista; self-explanatory.

The Cross'Bo: Yet another modification of the bullista, this weapon delivered a payload of enraged hobos. Thus gunnery officers had a choice between teats, tits, mastiffs, or bindlestiffs.

The Blunderbus: A hunter-seeker weapon which destroys the steering box in surface mass transit.

The Guided Missal: Originally developed as a specific deterrent to the Arbalust; as, however, it is hellishly more destructive, its use is now restricted by international convention to Sundays.

The Slingshit: self explanatory; still used in politics and in fandom.

And, of course, such obvious losers as the *foot ax, relish gas, studded mice,* and the effective but disgusting *snotgun.*

Ironically enough, since I wrote the above I have learned that the United States has recently been bombed several times by commercial airliners. Honest to God. True fact, documentation available. Airliner toilet holding tanks often leak, resulting in accumulations of blue ice on the fuselage during high-altitude flight. The blue ice is composed of roughly equal parts of urine; feces and blue liquid disinfectant. If the plane is required to make its landing descent rapidly enough, chunks of blue ice ranging to upwards of two hundred pounds can—and *do*—break loose and shell the countryside. I have seen a photograph of a roofless, floorless apartment that was demolished by a one-hundred-and-fifty-pound chunk of Blue Ice. It pulped an electric range in the apartment below. All the occupants escaped unscathed, but considerably unnerved.*

---

*Science fiction devotees beware: it's said to be exceptionally terrible if that stuff hits a Fan . . .

Now if *that* ain't a silly weapon, I don't know what is.

So it doesn't matter if you were cautious enough not to make your home near any strategic military targets. If you live anywhere near a commercial airport, you stand a chance of being attacked by an Icy B.M.

NOBODY LIKES TO
BE LONELY

The room looked quite comfortable when they brought McGinny in and left him alone. He had seen pictures, and knew what it was. But in his guts he could not believe that it was a cell.

It didn't look like a cell. It didn't taste like a cell, or feel like one, but most of all it didn't look like one. McGinny had been in jail once before, in this same county, and the cell then had borne all the classic hallmarks: bars, mildewed concrete walls, barred windows, an absurdly large lock, and miserably inadequate sanitary provisions consisting of a seatless toilet which stubbornly refused to flush and a badly cracked sink which exuded brown, rusty water.

But then, that had been so long ago that the charge for which McGinny had done time was possession of marijuana. That statute, while it still existed, had not been enforced in over ten years.

And in the meantime, prisons had changed. They had had to, of course. The Attica Uprising and the Tombs Rebellion, the Joliet Massacre and the Battle of New Alcatrz had been unmistakable signs that the traditional approach to penology was obsolete. A criminal population approaching thirty percent of the total simply could not be herded together and kept safely subjugated without the very sort of brutalization which an informed public would no longer tolerate.

But what if they were not herded together?

So it was that the room which met McGinny's eyes now was in appearance a pleasant, modestly appointed studio apartment—with a few anomalies. The convict seated himself in a remarkably comfortable, high-backed pseudo-leather armchair, padded with God alone knew what, and surveyed the unit which would be his universe until the time-lock on the room's only door ran out, ten years from now. *Lookit all the cubic,* he told himself wonderingly. Maybe this wouldn't be so bad after all.

The time-lock itself, not unnaturally, was the first thing that held his eye. It was set just below the apparently open window which was cut into the door of his cell. All that faced on his side of the door was an inverted triangular plate with rounded corners, small horizontal grooved slots in each corner. The overall effect was damnably like a skull.

"Pleased to meet ya," McGinny told it, returning its sour grin.

The window above the plate measured about three by three, and appeared empty of glass. So did the window on the opposite wall behind McGinny, but both were in fact enclosed with a synthetic material (trade-named "Nothing") which was so transparent as to appear invisible. It could not break, crack or get dirty. The second window looked out on a small courtyard, pleasantly landscaped with ferns and lush grasses, bordered by three fifteen-story wings just like the one which held McGinny's cell. The seven hundred and fifty windows of each were opaque from the outside. He sighed.

To his left was a bed, consisting of a mattress on top of a sealed box-spring which was clamped to the floor. Although the room's climate-control system made bedclothes superfluous, the penologists had been thoughtful enough to realize that a man (or woman) felt better with something over him as he slept. Hence they provided a sheet—made of paper. Above the bed were two horizontal slits, each about a half-meter wide. The upper one would dispense either paper sheets or paper clothes. It was activated by placing a used sheet or garment in the lower slot, which led to an incinerator somewhere in the bowels of the prison. Two pillows lay on the bed, each a featureless sponge.

Filling the space between the head of the bed and the corner of the room was a closet without a door. It had no transversing pole from which to suspend hangers, nor did it have hangers. Instead, suits of paper clothing—there were four of them—hung from small extrusions of plasteel high on the rear wall of the closet.

In the opposite corner, behind McGinny and to the right, was a spacious desk with voicewriter and drawing pencils. Above the desk was a reader which would display any book requested, page by page, so long as it was stored in the prison's central computer. Much of the fiction available was speculative, the authorities having decided that it would be all right to allow prisoners *some* form of escape. (McGinny knew that lately, the majority of science-fiction writers were ex-criminals, some of whose output was quite disturbing. Or perhaps that was not a new development.)

To the left of the desk was a quadio console, also computer-supplied, its four speakers represented by darker areas at four corners of the ceiling. Available tapes ranged from classical through rock to flash, with side trips into gregorian and neojazz. The console was nearly featureless: one spoke one's choice and selected tone and volume with simple slide switches. In appearance, therefore, the console resembled a washing machine with two small horns.

Directly adjacent to the quadio was the Automat: an equally large cube, with a serving platform let into its front and small slots on either side which dispensed rubber cutlery. It too was voice-activated, and was fed through the floor from a master unit which supplied the Automat with raw materials. Save for the absence of a slot into which to deposit one's quarters, it was identical to the Automats to be found on the average street corner—from McGinny's angle of vision at least. From the other end of the room one could have seen the unmistakable, time-honored shape of a toilet bowl, let into the Automat's left side. It drained to the prison's basement where paper and waste were filtered out and the remainder routed to the master food unit. This saved the taxpayers millions of dollars annually.

McGinny snorted, ceased his inventory of the room and rose from his chair. He went to the small sink on the right of the cell door and regarded himself in its "mirror," a glassless reflective surface.

As McGinny was one of many who had elected to inhibit their beards, there was no shaving unit next to the mirror; his hair would simply have to grow for the next ten years, or until he became sick enough to warrant the cutting open of the time-lock to permit a doctor to attend him. The doctor played a lot of golf.

Familiar, coarse features stared back at McGinny, restoring his confidence. His head was large, with a cap of wiry brown curls resting on elongated ears. His eyes were set close against a blunt nose, and his over-full lower lip gave him a pouting, petulant expression. As he saw again the room whose reflection surrounded his own, the pout became almost a sneer. These were the most spacious and luxurious quarters he had ever inhabited—few in the overcrowded world of 2007 had it so good.

Ten years? he thought, cheerfully. *I'll do it standing on my head. Elbow room, privacy, food cooked for me* . . . He frowned. *Sure will miss beer, though. And the fems.* His contentment beginning to fade, he returned to the armchair and dropped heavily into it. He found his gaze fixed on the window set in the cell door. It was strange—the window on the opposite wall looked out on open space, this one onto a plasteel corridor. And yet the exterior window gave a view of a false freedom, sculpted to make McGinny and other thousands feel better. In the corridor, men walked. Somehow, freedom was that way.

He shifted, scratched his crotch and considered the quadio. It seemed to him that his first choice in this cell was a significant event, demanding contemplation. He imagined himself ten years hence, narrating his prison saga to an enraptured fem with eyes like saucers, saying, "And do you know what the first thing I played in that taken place was?" This'd better be good; he'd hate to have to lie to her.

After a time he addressed the quadio. The room filled with the sound of a frenzied 4/4 piano solo from Leon Russell's legendary last album, *Live at Luna City*. Bass and moog came in together as the Master of Space and Time hurled his anthem:

"I'm just tryin' to stay 'live—and keep mah side- burns too."

Legs trembling, vaguely enjoying the play of cool air across his sweat-sheened, slender body, Solomon Orechal lay in the utter relaxation called afterglow and surveyed his bedroom. In so doing, he also surveyed his dining room, his living room, his kitchen, and his car—all at the same time.

He sighed, for perhaps the dozenth time that day; just as, in fact, he had sighed with an almost rhyth- mic regularity on every day since he had first moved into his own Mome, from the comparative spacious- ness of his parents' fish-and-see apartment. As the popular name indicated, a good efficiency was hard to find these days, but the Orechal ancestral apt (the building dated all the way back to 1957) had been in the family possession since before the Housing Riots—as the axe-scar and single bullet-hole in the door attested. Solomon had told himself often in the last two years that he had been a fool to strike out on his own. But the lure of adventure and the chal- lenge of living wherever he could find a parking space had been enough to pry him from the four-and-a-half- room home of his youth.

Besides, it was awkward, bringing your girlfriends into the bathroom to be alone.

Apropos of which:

It's very strange, thought Solomon. *I know just what she's going to say now . . .*

"Sol, why can't we do the Truth dope?"

. . . and yet there's nothing déjà vu about it.

Beside him on the narrow bed, Barbara raised on one elbow, half-leaned across him. Sleepily, earnestly, she brushed the hair out of his eyes and repeated, "Why won't you do Truth with me, lover?"

. . . even down to the soft but oh so insistent tone of voice, the way she lets her left breast brush me; and it's just nothing at all like déjà vu . . .

She was still talking, and there was that in her voice which acts directly on the glands, but he was miles ahead of her, his attention two levels removed, contemplating the frustration of Moebius's Band with what seemed a poignant bitterness. Vaguely, he monitored the persuasions and importunities, dropping a grunt here and there and looking impassive, until he heard the line he had been patiently waiting for.

". . . how," she was saying, timidly and inevitably, "can I help but think you're afraid of the Truth?"

His timing was magnificent.

"Afraid of the truth?" he asked quietly, paused. "What we just did . . . wasn't that the truth?" He brushed his fingertips along the underside of her belly, and she shivered. "Are you suggesting that that wasn't real? That we were just *fucking*? Because it sure seemed to *me* that we were making love. Maybe I was wrong."

He had her now, he knew it from the look on her face, but somehow he couldn't summon up the old elation, the sense of triumph. Mechanically, he moved for the coup-de-grace: now that you've stirred up the emotions, throw in a pseudologic and you're home free.

"You know why I don't do Truth Dope, man. I've told you a dozen times. I'm not afraid of the truth, I'm afraid of the *dope*."

She made one last try. "But Sol . . ."

"Now don't start, Barb. We've been through this, kark it. There's a mountain of evidence for each side, just like there always is when a new drug comes out. The law says it plays hob with your motivations, and the heads say it clears your vision. The law says it rots your body, and heads say it's a lie. You know what happened with pot." (It hadn't been until 1986 that it was proven that marijuana could cause tuberculosis. No real problem, as they had TB licked by that time—one shot at twelve and you couldn't get it if you tried—but it was too late for an awful lot of smokers who had thought that all the evidence was in by 1975.) "I lost my mother to TB, and I plan for the rest of my life to take the conservative opinion wherever possible. No thanks, Barb. I'll take my Truth the sloppy, human way, through inference and deduction. Maybe I'll be wrong a lot more often . . . but maybe I'll have a lot more often to be wrong in.

"Besides, I don't need any proof that you love me—even through you're trying to get me to do something I don't think is safe, to reassure *you*. Things like what just happened here a couple of minues ago are all the 'proof' I need."

There was, of course, nothing she could say to that, and she even apologized, but somehow even as he mounted her to prove again the depth of his love by the strength of his hips he knew that the subject was not closed, and that someday she would back him into a corner he couldn't talk his way out of, and on that day they would share the drug that made dissembly impossible, and she would leave him, just like all the others.

He moaned, but she misunderstood and held him tighter.

McGinny tried for the fifth time to cut the leathery soyburger with his rubber fork. This time the disposable plate danced on the serving platform and he nearly lost the meal entirely. He swore a hideous oath and flung the fork angrily from him, but with the blind malignance that inanimate objects display when a man is in a towering rage, it bounced from the plasteel wall and dropped with an absurdly loud, high splash into the toilet.

He rose quickly, cursing with a steady, monotonous rhythm. *Taken stuff tastes enough like rubber already,* he thought savagely, plunging his thick hand into the bowl. He was just too late to save the fork; the cell's designers had reasoned that a flushing mechanism could fail—a serious calamity in a time-locked room—and so that bowl simply emptied itself constantly, at a gentle speed which McGinny had not quite beaten.

Swearing louder now, he straightened and walked to the sink to wash his hands. He could not for the life of him understand why he felt that the water there would be any cleaner than that which laved the bowl, and it irritated him immensely.

Of course he burned his hands. But by that time the anger had reached the point from which one either tremblingly descends, or begins throwing things. He had few things to throw, and none he could spare. He counted to ten, then chanted Om Mani Padme Hum, and gradually the black rage subsided, at least to the point where he could see through the red haze.

Make the karkin' silverware rubber so we can't snuff ourselves, he thought, *and look how much good it does. I'm really filled with the joy of livin' now.*

Finally he walked back to the automat, sat down in the desk chair which stood before it, and picked the soyburger from the plate on the serving platform.

It was cold.

"GodDAMNit," he exploded. "Sunnabitchin' machine s'posta keep the taken stuff hot, just my *fuckin'* luck to get the one don't work for TEN TAKEN YEARS!"

There was nothing for it; the soyburger was all he would get until tomorrow morning. Growling, he raised it to his mouth and ripped off a piece with his teeth.

"Hi, there."

He whirled, his hand absurdly cocking the soyburger like a weapon. There in the window of the cell door, above the skull-like time-lock, was a face. A person!

McGinny ran to the door, flinging the soyburger into a corner. "Hello!" he shouted, and then pulled to a halt before the door, suddenly embarrassed. They looked at each other for a while, McGinny seeing the young kid, maybe twenty, with long blond hair and a Fu Manchu mustache, *looks like one o' them Trippies, oh, Jesus, I hope he likes to talk.*

"What are you in for?"

"Embezzlement," McGinny said automatically, a million questions that he could not form coherently enough to ask buzzing in his brain.

"Oh," said the youth, adjusting a uniform cap on his shaggy head. He seemed somehow just slightly disappointed. "I guess that must be pretty interesting stuff, embezzlement. I get to talk to all kinds of interesting people on this job. Once . . . once I talked to a rapist."

He almost seemed to be licking his lips, but McGinny was beyond noticing. He managed to stammer, "Hey, look, buddy . . . what . . . I mean, who are you? What are you doing here? How often do you come around? What . . . hey, how come I can even hear you in here?"

The kid chuckled. "They've got a two-way sound system on the door, man. Didn't you know? Listen, don't freak, I'm like, the guard. You didn't think they'd leave you alone with nobody to check on you, did you? Suppose you conked?"

"But," McGinny said, "I mean, do you come around a lot? *Can you stay awhile and talk?*"

"Oh, sure," the kid assured him. "That's why I took this job, man. I'm into people, where they're at, like. All I have to do is walk around and talk to interesting people, and I only gotta cover fifteen guys a day. See, if you want to know the truth, the job's welfare."

McGinny understood. The work-and-wage system as a means of distributing wealth was on its last legs— there simply wasn't enough work to go around, and the population continued to climb. As a last-ditch stopgap, the government had taken to making up idiot work so that there would be sufficient jobs available to keep the traditional economic system staggering on, but the farce was becoming more obvious every year. What more obvious example than this young Trippie, "guarding" men in sealed plasteel cells to earn his living.

But at this particular moment McGinny was overwhelmingly grateful for the continued sham. It was accidentally providing him with the means of maintaining his sanity.

"Listen," he said urgently, "listen, kid, if you'll come around and talk to me a lot, I'll . . ." He paused, baffled. He had nothing to offer. "I'll be grateful," he finished lamely, desperate with fear that he would be rejected.

"Sure, man," the kid grinned. "I like to talk. Mostly I like to listen. I'm interested in the criminal mind and all. I'll bet you've got some interesting stories to tell."

"Yeah, you bet, kid. I got the most *goddamned* interesting stories you ever heard in your life!" He paused again, embarrassed by his fervor.

"Hey, listen, man," the kid said softly. "I know how it is. Nobody likes to be lonely."

And he smiled.

The Mome ahead completed its business and gunned away noisily, and Sol pulled his own vehicle smoothly up alongside the Chase World Bank. Rolling down the forward driver's-side window, he addressed it.

"Solomon Orechal, 4763987IMHS967403888.453, license NY-45-83-299T."

The Bank, which bore a remarkable resemblance to a vacuum cleaner making love to a garbage can, asked San Francisco a question, received a reply, and answered without a millisecond's hesitation, "Sir?"

"Request additions and alterations allotment, three thousand dollars and zero cents; travel allotment, five hundred dollars and zero cents."

"Purpose?"

"A and A: Fortrex cooling unit. Travel: To Lesser Yuma."

"Justification?"

"Profession: entertainer."

"Type and Credit Number, please," the Bank said a bit more respectfully. Its voice was like a contralto kazoo.

"Folksinger. Number SWM-44557F, ASCAP. I'm my own agent."

This time the machine actually paused. Barbara squirmed on the seat next to Solomon, twisting her hair nervously. "Aren't you going to get it, lover?"

"Relax," he said easily. "The Bank's got to consult a human for this. Judgment decision required. It's bound to take a minute or so; they've got to decide if I'm worth shipping across the country."

"Oh, Sol . . ."

"Now don't worry, Barb, I told you. If the Bank says no, I'll use my own credit and we'll go just the same. Now relax, will you?"

The squat machine spoke up. "So ordered," it said emotionlessly, "and good luck to you, sir. Have a pleasant time in Lesser Yuma."

"You got it," she said excitedly as Solomon engaged gears and roared away from the Bank, "oh, baby, you got it! When can we go?"

"Get centered, mama," he answered as he slid the huge mobile home smoothly into the freeway traffic. "There's a lot of things we have to do first. We've got to get the cooling unit installed, gotta cop a big block of food, got to get the engine overhauled and tuned. Gotta say good bye to our parents. It'll be a couple of days, easy. Less if we bust ass."

Behind his practical words Solomon was immensely pleased with himself. Barbara had been difficult lately, carefully avoiding any mention of Truth Dope but finding more and more reasons to sulk. But he'd managed to find something to distract her. She'd never been out of New York State in her life, and travel held a fascination for her, as for so many. A similar feeling had been responsible for Solomon's decision to buy a Mome in the first place, and so he was somewhat excited about the trip himself.

And, too, his ego writhed with gratification that his performing record was in fact impressive enough to make the Bank invest in his relocation to an area where performers were scarce. Consciously he had never doubted the outcome, and he would never admit his subconscious doubts, but it felt good to *know*.

You had to be good to be a performer; it was one of the most sought-after jobs in the country. It wasn't only the tremendous prestige, nor even the almost orgasmic egoboo that applause brought. It was simply that the first time you saw drab, apathetic faces come alive during your set, the first time you made some of those thousands of crowded, useless people a little more content with their lot, somehow you never again felt that gut-ache of uselessness quite so sharply yourself.

"Sol," Barbara said softly, breaking into high reverie, "do we have to start . . . right away?" Her soft fingers traced a question mark on his thigh.

"Mama," he mock-growled, "I'll never be *that* busy!"

And no one was more surprised than he when, having found a place to park the Mome, he failed to achieve an erection.

"How did you ever come to be an embezzler, Mr. McGinny?"

"I embezzled."

"No, I mean why?"

"Because I wanted some money."

The kid was impervious to sarcasm. "What did you want the money for?" He adjusted the guard's cap that looked so incongruous atop his shaggy mane, his hand stroking his mustache on the way down in a mannerism that McGinny suspected he could learn to hate sometime in the next ten years. "I mean, it isn't like way back when people were hungry."

"Listen, what is this, a quiz show or something? I mean, what's it to you?"

"Oh, I'm just curious, is all. I mean, there's nothing much else to do on this job but talk with you fellows. Anyway, crime interests me, you know? Like the things that made you end up . . . in here."

"Well, it's none of your taken business, how do you like that?" McGinny snapped. The kid made as if to turn away, and suddenly McGinny almost panicked. The kid was a pain in the joints, but he was better than nothing, better than the tangled, tormenting company of McGinny's own thoughts, of his self-recrimination and his frustrated rage.

"No, wait, kid. Listen, I'm sorry, please wait. You . . . you don't want to lift off so soon. C'mon, look: a guy gets a little hot under the collar sometimes, you ask him personal questions. I didn't mean any offense."

The kid half-turned back to the door, stroking his mustache again.

"Look, it was like this, see? I'm an accountant, I was, I mean, and they pulled an audit at the wrong time. No big story—I just got caught with my hand in the cookie jar. Could have happened to a dozen other accountants, just happened to be me, that's all."

"Why'd you have your hand in the cookie jar?"

"I needed the money." There was a pause, and the kid turned to walk away again.

McGinny cracked. "It was a fem, dammit."

The kid turned back again, smiling now. A gentle smile. "Yeah?"

McGinny gave in. Maybe the kid was right—it might help to talk about it, straighten his thoughts. In any case it was certainly better than trying to think of something new to play on the quadio. Or something to dictate into the voicewriter, which stubbornly refused to do anything more than repeat his own thoughts back to him.

"It was like this: I had to get my hands on a whole lot of money at once to shut this fem up. She had something on me that could have ruined me, had me by the hairs, and she loved every minute of it, the little slot. She had it in for me, but she needed green more than she needed my scalp, and she didn't even care if I got burned getting it. 'You're an accountant,' she says. 'You can get it.' Sure. Easy. Ten years easy, and she walks away, laughing. I had a chance, I'd be in here for murder right now."

The kid was all ears now, face almost pressed up against the cell window like a child at a candy-store window. "What'd she have on you?" he breathed.

McGinny turned bright red. The kid didn't bother to pretend to leave again; he simply waited. After a time the prisoner answered him.

"See, she was . . . she was pregnant without a license, and she was far enough along she was going to start showing any day, and she said when they hauled her in she was going to name me in the affadavit. The pregnancy fine alone could have ruined me, let alone the Lifetime Child Support without even a welfare option. I mean every man's entitled to welfare, isn't he? You can see what a jam I was in. I just had to have the green—she said if I gave her enough money to keep her and the kid until she could leave him with a sitter and go to work, she'd tell the Man she didn't know who the father was."

"I don't get it," the kid said cheerfully. "What was the sweat? You'd have beat the heat easy. Kark, they couldn't pin an Elsie's on you—it's your word against hers. Unless there was a photographic record of the conception . . ." his voice trailed off with the faintest suggestion of a leer.

McGinny shrugged, made a face. "Well, maybe they couldn't have pinned an L.C.S. on me, if it came to that . . ." He seemed disinclined to continue.

"Then I don't understand why you took such a risk," the kid persisted.

"Well," McGinny said reluctantly, "I . . . I got a wife and kids."

"Oh," the kid said brightly. "Have you got a picture of them?"

"No I have not got a karkin' picture of them!"

"All right, all right, don't jump salty. I can take a hint. Sorry if I bothered you." The kid gave his mustache a final tug, turned, and walked out of view down the corridor. Suddenly terrified, not wanting to be alone with his memories, McGinny beat against the door with his fists.

"Wait, damn you, *wait!* Hold on a taken minute. I didn't mean to shout at you. Hey, listen, I'm sorry, wait, come back, please come back. Come back, you bastard you, don't leave me alone. You sonofabitch, I'll cut your heart out, COME BACK!"

Footsteps echoed faintly down the acoustically muffled hallway.

McGinny looked down at his hands stupidly. They

ached terribly, and the heels of them glowed an angry
red. He went to the mirror on shaky legs, tried a
sickly grin, then whirled and threw himself across the
bed, and very suddenly he was crying, the wild,
racking sobs of a child.

Sol looked around at the hundreds of prairie rats
who made up a cross-section of the population of this
particular sector of Lesser Yuma, brushed the guitar
strap out of the way of his wrist, and adjusted the
microphone with a feeling of growing desperation. He
wasn't reaching them, he just couldn't get it on for
this audience, and he felt a frustration which was
growing familiar of late.

It's the people, he told himself frantically, tuning
up to stall for time. There was plenty of parking space
left in the deserts, and hence a trouble-free existence
for Mome-owners who could afford cooling gear. But
the thousands who had flocked to the vast barren
expanses had learned quickly that boredom was the
price of ex-urban existence. They looked to entertain-
ers like Solomon to keep them going, but the wary
ennui they brought to a concert depressed him so
much (he told himself now) that he just couldn't seem
to get into his music tonight.

In desperation, he seized upon a song that summed
up his mood precisely, one of his own. For the first
time in his career he didn't care how the audience
liked it, whether it was what they wanted to hear. He
hurt, and so he sang.

This time next year . . .
I will have won or lost
This time next year . . .
my bridges all

will be crossed
I'll either be
in headlines
Or standin' in
the breadlines
It all depends
on how the dice are tossed

This time next year . . .
I will be up or down
Far away from here . . .
or still hung up in town
I'll either be in clover
Or barely turnin' over
It all depends on how
the deal goes down

I feel it comin' on—
it's O so close now
Wonder if it's
bad or good
Hope it isn't gonna be
an overdose now
Really wish I knew
where I stood

This time next year . . .
I'll either win or lose
This time I fear . . .
I'm on a short, short fuse
I'll either be together
Enjoyin' sunny weather
Or suckin' up
an awful lot of booze

He trailed off, fingers stinging from the harsh, emphatic runs. The catharsis of the blues left him literally exhausted, but the pain was reduced to an empty, fading ache.

The applause nearly frightened him out of his wits. From then on he had them, had them in the palm of his hand. Having made them cry, he could now make them laugh or clap or dance or anything he had a mind to. He had shown them that he shared something with them, and now they could empathize, let themselves be taken with him along whatever musical road he chose to pick.

It felt good.

It was on the way home, joyfully breaking the speed limit and humming snatches of his closing number, that he heard the news from Barbara.

"Sol?"

"Yeah, kitten? Here, have a toke."

"Later." She waved the joint away. "Sol, the clinic called while you were onstage. I came out to get my shawl and played back the message."

"Oh."

"There was a pause.

"Sol, they said . . . the results were negative."

A longer pause, long enough for humiliation to turn to anger.

"Well, what the hell is that supposed to mean? Why, they're full of shit. Negative! What is that supposed to signify, it's all in my karkin' mind? Is that it?"

She was silent, and his fury boiled over.

"ANSWER ME, GODDAMMIT! Is it all in my mind?"

"Sol, I don't *know*, baby, I don't know. Maybe they made a mistake." She was crying, soundless tears highlighted by oncoming headlights, and he flung the joint out the window in disgust.

"Don't make excuses for me, you taken slot! It's no big deal. So the results were negative, so there's a little something I got to work out in my head is all. You know I've got it. I just have to get it back."

He drove on furiously, concentrating on the road until his eyes ached from squinting. They left the Mome colony behind, took a seemingly abandoned side road up into the hills. The road swerved treacherously beside sheer precipices at some points, but Sol had his control back now, and his hands on the steering wheel were unnaturally steady. The ponderous Mome was like a live thing under his hands, and he drove it with a grim determination. Eventually they passed through a great shadow-filled crevice between two walls of granite, and came out upon a ridge overlooking a great valley, invisible in the darkness.

There were only seven or eight Momes parked here, clustered around the natural mountain spring which surfaced in this unlikely spot. It was sufficiently long that there was at least one acre for each of them. Solomon had been lucky to find this place; the few who had tended to keep their mouths shut. *We are all very happy here,* he thought savagely, wheeling the huge Mome to its parking space.

He parked, shut down the engine, extruded the watersucker and threw power to the house generator. Pushing the button that dropped the seat-back flat, he got up and walked to the back of the Mome, flinging himself down on the bed without a word.

Barbara got up and walked slowly back to the bed, sat down on the carpeted floor beside it.

"Sol, what do we do now?"

"What the kark can I do?" he said, voice muffled by the pillow.

"Well, as far as I can see, there's only two things left. Analysis, or . . ."

"Or the Truth Dope," he snarled, lifting his head to throw her a venomous glance. "Get my head candled or my chromosomes scrambled, that's the choice, huh?"

"Well, all I know is I'm pretty karkin' sick and tired of masturbating," she shot back, and then gasped.

He winced.

"I'm sorry, baby," she said pitifully. "You know I didn't meant that."

"Well, it's true, and there's nothing I can do about it," he barked. "I'll go to hell before I'll let some professional voyeur probe into my sex life. Analysis! No thanks, mama. If there's anything wrong with me, I'll fix it myself. I'm not about to have some fumble-fingered idiot 'adjusting' my personality for me."

"Then do some Truth, lover," she pleaded. "Just once, do Truth with me. Once we know what it is, we've got it licked. It'll never bother us again."

He tried to stall for time. "Ah, we'd never find a connection for Truth out here in the sticks. Forget it, mama. It'll pass."

She bit her lip. "Sol . . . I've got some here. I brought it with us from New York."

He stared at her, mouth dry, and knew that it was all over.

"Sol, please baby, take it with me. Honey, I don't want to live with a man who's . . . who's impotent."

It was the first time either of them had said the word, but he didn't explode as she had half expected him to. He only buried his head in the pillow for a long, long time, tasting defeat, accepting what was

to come. At last he raised himself upon his elbows
and regarded her levelly.

"Okay, Barbara," he said quietly. "We'll do Truth."

Shakin'!
Taken!
All forsaken!
I think I got to
Flash now, mama,
Believe I got to flash!

McGinny slumped in his chair, growling along with
the fuzzbass. The quadio's separation was improperly
adjusted, forcing him to hold his head at an uncomfortable angle. By now this had produced a permanent crick in his neck, which had a serious effect on
his peace of mind, not to mention his taste. The
snarling flash tune he had opted for was symptom-
atic of a growing unease (as, in startlingly close
analogy, it was with flash freaks outside the prison).
The ex-accountant was seething with frustrated rage,
and would not understand why.

The moog took a solo on the left front speaker,
began pouring on the watts. With a treble shriek, the
speaker went dead.

McGinny howled with rage, sprang from the chair,
and stood under the speaker, cursing fulminously.

He leaped upward and smashed his fist at the
darkened area behind which the dead speaker
crouched, accomplishing nothing whatever. "Ten
years," he gibbered, "Ten *years!*" He began slamming his fists against the near wall, flaying the limits
of his universe with a black hatred. His eye was
caught by the skull face of the time-lock, grinning
reminder of the unpaid balance of his sentence, and

he struck at it savagely, fracturing two knuckles on its hard surface.

His bellow of pain chopped off in the middle as he saw his jailer watching him from a foot away. The kid's face held a clinical interest; his cornflower-blue eyes gazed with infuriating calmness into McGinny's.

"Off," the prisoner snarled over his shoulder at the paraplegic quadio, which went completely silent at once. "What the hell are you staring at?" he demanded of the young guard.

"Why'd you hurt your hand?" the kid asked.

McGinny checked an angry retort. This kid was just too dumb to know any better, he decided. "Ah, the karkin' quadio blew a speaker," he grumbled.

"Looks okay from here," the kid said.

"Well, it doesn't sound okay from here," McGinny snapped. "Left front channel's gone."

"I didn't mean to rub it in, Mr. McGinny. I just thought you mighta thought . . ."

"Well-I-didn't-so-just-shut-up-about-it-all-right?" the prisoner said through grated teeth. Kark, this kid was dumb!

"Sure. Hey listen, wow, I meant to ask you. You never told me about how come you let that fem talk you into taking the green." The jailer tugged at his mustache and regarded McGinny expectantly.

McGinny turned, took a few steps from the window. Then he frowned and turned back resignedly. "It's like I told you: she was going to stick it to me."

"Yeah, but she couldn't prove a thing. Or could she?"

"She didn't have to prove it. I told you I got a wife and kids, didn't I? What do you think my wife'd do, I'm down in Paternity Court? What do you think my boss'd do? Bigshot Z.P.G. supporter, he'd toss me on the street in a minute. It ain't like if I sold illegal dope or run over somebody stoned. You can't get fired for criminal record anymore. But an unlicensed pregnancy? A third kid? Don't make me laugh. She didn't have to prove a thing to finish me off."

"Yeah, I guess I see . . ." said the kid. "But one thing I don't understand . . ."

"You don't understand nothing. You never been married. I'd have done anything to keep Alice from leaving me. Anything." His voice broke. "I . . . I loved her."

"That's what I don't understand," the kids said eagerly. "I mean, if you loved her so much, how come you topped this other fem? I mean, sure, everybody likes variety once in a while, but you must have a House in your neighborhood, you must have had the money."

"Hey, listen, I never paid for it in my life," McGinny said proudly. "I mean, half the thrill of love is in the conquest." He had read that somewhere.

"So, then, since your wife was already 'conquered' she didn't turn you on?"

"Of course she turned me on. I told you I loved her, didn't I? But there was this fem I met at the Automat, worked in the same building, and she looked like she never had it, you know? So I called her up that night, invited her out for a drive."

"Top her that night?" the kid exclaimed.

"Well, sure," McGinny said modestly. "You know, I kind of always had good luck with virgins."

"Plural? You mean there were others?"

"Not too karkin' many others. I told you I loved my wife," McGinny said suspiciously.

"But you said . . ."

"I know what I karkin' said," McGinny barked.

"Okay, take it easy. I was just asking. 'Cause I thought you meant . . ."

"Well, keep your thoughts to yourself. Jesus, you ask a lot of dopey questions. What's the matter, you got nothing better . . ." His voice trailed off as he caught himself. "I mean, what makes you so taken curious?"

"Oh, I just wonder a lot. You know, how come you're in there and I'm out here and all—I've always been kind of *philosophical*, you know? Into people, like I said. I mean, we all start out the same, and some of us do things others don't. I guess I'm just curious about what makes people tick. How come she got pregnant?"

"Huh?"

"I mean, don't you use anything?"

"Well, sure, but I mean, I didn't know. Hell, first date and all, I . . . I just figured she'd be using something. Nice piece like that . . ."

"But you said she looked like a virgin."

"Well, that's it, see? How was I supposed to know she'd spread right off like that?"

"But you just *said* you always had good luck with . . ."

"Get of my case, will you? I'm telling you, this fem was a slot. She . . . she told me it was all right, see, because she wanted to get me by the pills, pump me for green, get it?"

"Look, I don't know, you were there and I wasn't, but frankly that sounds like a load of used food to me," the kid said evenly. "You told me all she asked for was support until she could work again, didn't you? And just for that she was willing to take the rap and lose her own Welfare. Doesn't sound like a slot to me."

"Get out of here, you fuzz-faced stuffer! Who the hell asked for your opinion, anyway? Go on, get taken before I . . ."

"Before you what, bro?" the kid asked softly. "You can't get out of there, can you? You can't even snuff yourself to embarrass me. I'm not a captive audience, but you're sure a captive performer. I don't understand what you did, and you're going to explain it to me. Sooner or later."

"I'll see you in hell first," McGinny shouted, almost gibbering.

"Sooner or later," he repeated, tugging at his mustache.

McGinny's eyes widened, and he placed a hand on either side of the window. "You're enjoying this, aren't you? You little hark, you're really enjoying this!"

"Does that matter?" the kid asked softly. "Does it really make any difference whether I enjoy it or not? All I'm doing is asking you questions. The answers you already know yourself, right? Or you couldn't answer the questions. I'm not putting any words in your mouth—just asking questions so I can understand why you did what you did. All I want," he said simply, "is the truth."

"You want it, you clinical little bastard, but maybe I *don't*," McGinny snarled.

"Oh, well . . ." said the kid, shrugging. "There I can't help you, Mr. McGinny. I mean, even if I don't ask you another thing, you've got ten years to go, and there's no place to hide in there. How long you think you can duck the truth?"

"Forever, you lousy bastard," McGinny roared. "Get out of my life, go on, get the hell out of here." He turned away in dismissal, began pacing the room angrily. *I don't have to take this kind of sewage! I'll write to the Warden, to my Congressman, to . . .* he stopped suddenly, struck the obvious. Prisoners lost all their civil rights—including access to the postal computer network. His voicewriter lacked the familiar "Transmit" key. There was no way for him to get a letter to *anyone*, unless the kid agreed to take it down for him and deliver it.

Somebody else has got to come by, sooner or later, he thought frantically. *A maintenance man, somebody!*

No one had so far.

He was trapped, pure and simple, trapped with this shaggy punk kid with his words that twisted the truth into lies and made you feel like you'd done something wrong, like you deserved all this instead of merely being caught up in a web of circumstances that could have happened to anybody. *The little stuffer'll be back, to pick at me and twist everything all up. Enjoys it, like he was pulling the wings off flies, like . . .*

He spun around angrily, and the kid was still there, his face framed in the window over the skull-like time-lock.

"Spying on me, you . . ." McGinny groped for words.

"No," the kid murmured. "Just . . . just *observing* you."

McGinny howled.

The drug which Solomon Orechal's age knew as Truth Dope had been known to man for hundreds of years before a single word was ever written about it. Known, that is, to some men.

The first words written about Truth Dope appeared in the middle Twentieth Century. Author William Burroughs passed on a legend of unknown origin concerning a forgotten tribe in the trackless wilds of South America who used a drug he called "yage," which induced temporary mental telepathy between its users. The brief mention was too preposterous to be taken very seriously, of course, but there were many in those times who took preposterous things seriously. Rumors traveled the junkie grapevine, apocrypha rode the dealers' trail, and the A-heads spoke in whispers of yage.

In vain. Yage existed, and its ridiculous Lost Tribe as well. But they were not exactly lost.

They were hidden.

For the telepathy that its users experienced under the influence of yage was more than the ability to send and receive messages without material aid. It was rather a total dissolution of all the walls surrounding human consciousness, a complete opening of minds one to the other, providing the first and only escape from the solitary confinement of the human skull. It was a melding of personalities, a stripping away of all cover.

Two people who took yage simply had no secrets from one another. At all.

Secret thoughts, inner motivations, hopes, shames, dreams, pretenses, likes and dislikes and the true inner feelings of that part of the heart whose name is unpronounceable, all were laid bare to a partner in the yage experience.

That the drug should have remained so perfect a secret for so many hundreds of years was not in the least surprising. Realizing what they possessed, and its potential for good and evil, its discoverers—the Kundalu—adopted a policy of isolationism utterly simple in execution: anyone they did not recognize was apprehended, and yage stuffed down his throat.

Then they either killed him or married him.

This delightfully uncomplicated system lasted until 1984. Inevitably, the Kundalu were discovered, by a real estate developer looking for a place to put 2,650 condominiums. Over twelve hundred years of self-knowledge on a level unknown to mankind at large had made the Kandalu wise and canny indeed—175 of the condominiums had been built and fifty-three sold before the clearing crews stumbled across the Kandalu village.

The strange and humble Indians would not leave the land where holy yage grew, nor permit its razing.

They resisted the developer's half-hearted attempt to learn their vestigial spoken language, lest the secret of its growth be somehow wrested from them. He, in turn, was impatient—and out there in the bush, no sanctions could be applied to him—he was, after all, building *dwelling units*. He slaughtered the simple Kundalu to the last man.

It chanced that four of the crew assigned to demolish the primitively beautiful village of the Kandalu were welfare clients—counterculture types who recognized the ceremonial bowls of dried leaves they found for what they were: a communal drug. The foreman found them inside a structure like a decapitated dome, open to the skies but closed to the gaze of passersby, and he understood enough of the joyous babbling he overheard to shoot all four of them dead.

In six months he and the developer had a small but established corporate identity in the underworld of big-time drug traffic. In a year, the developer had him killed. Within four years, the developer was outselling the quasilegal giant, Speed Inc., and was giving even the mammoth completely legal International Marijuana Harvesters a pain in the balance sheet, despite the fact that Truth (as yage was brand-named) was still on the Illegal List.

The usual controversy flared in the news media, freighted with a larger than usual bulk of ignorance, for very little indeed was known about Truth Dope. In time the substance might completely overturn many time-honored concepts of personal privacy, many institutions of law and justice, many truisms of human psychology—but at present absolutely all that was known about it was that it was curiously resistant to chemical analysis, and that no more than three people could safely share the drug. The stress of mingling identities with a larger number was severely unhinging; the ego tended to *get lost*, and the secret of finding it again had died with the Kundalu. Before that had been proven to the counterculture's cynical satisfaction, many communes ended in gibbering insanity.

Nor did many triads flourish. By its nature truth became a couples' drug. Thus:

Solomon and Barbara sat naked in the rear of the Mome, facing each other in lotus. The windows were opaqued, the roof transparent; the mobile home was open to the skies but closed to the gaze of passersby.

"Should we smoke?"

Sol considered this at length, shrugged. "I don't see why not. The parts to be opened go deeper than pot can reach. Maybe it'll relax us. This is going to be a little scary."

Barbara caught his nervousness, mulled it over carefully. "Sol . . . you're really jumpy about this, aren't you?" A flash of insight: "You've done Truth before, haven't you?"

"Why ask? You'll know for yourself in a little while."

"Sol . . . Sol, maybe you're right. We don't have to rush into this. I don't . . ."

"You don't want to know?" Sol burst out. "After all the pleading and convincing you're scared of the Truth? Oh, no! Have a few tokes and then we'll get to it. I'm not going to call this off now, and then wait to see how long it is before you want to know again, before you start hinting and then urging and then demanding. No way, mama. We're doing Truth today."

Barbara lowered her eyes, and busied herself searching for the Grassmasters. She found a crumpled pack on the right-hand service shelf over the bed and passed them to him. Current social etiquette required the woman to wave the joint alight, but Solomon had chosen to smoke GMs specifically because they did not have ignotips, and had to be lit by hand. He enjoyed the archaic ritual of striking fire with his hands and placing it where it was needed, and spent a not insignificant portion of his income on the hard-to-find matches. Now more than ever, she sensed, he would want that feeling of control.

He accepted the marijuana impassively, producing a box of wooden matches from the pocket of the tunic which lay beside him on the bed. By his other side lay the ancient, handmade Gibson J-45 which was his comfort and sometimes his voice, and Solomon struck a match along the silk-and-steel A string with a quick snap of his wrist. Echoes of whispering giants overflowed the sounding-box, and Solomon sucked flame through the filtertip joint with a sharp urgency.

He passed the joint to Barbara, cupping it protectively in his hand. Reaching to take it, she was struck for the first time by how much in him was conservative, if not reactionary. His independent thinking had struck her until now only as an evidence of the creativity she admired and loved in him; all at once she realized how much of him yearned for an earlier age. He cupped the joint as if wary of detection—yet pot had been legalized long before his instincts were trained. He played an acoustic guitar in an electronic age—certainly it sounded mellower than contemporary instruments, but mostly it was *older*. In a dozen innocent mannerisms she detected for the first time an undercurrent of yearning for the uncomplicated past, when men still controlled their destiny. *If I keep pulling insights like this,* she thought, gulping smoke, *I won't need Truth.*

And it was true. Expecting imminent truth, her mind was revving up, extending the sensitivity threshold of its own built-in truth detectors, trying to approach both drug and experience as honestly and openly as possible.

She passed the joint back to Solomon, who took it impassively, emptying his lungs for a second hit. He would not meet her eyes.

She watched his bare chest fill as he drew on the smouldering cigarette, and became unaccountably aware of the weight of her own breasts. She looked down at them, and it was only when she observed that her nipple were swollen that she remembered that before the night was out, Solomon's impotence should be over at last. In a vivid flash of memory she saw again the look of his eyes when orgasm took him, and she shivered.

"Barb."

She looked up. He was holding out the joint, breath held tightly. Brushing hair from her eyes with a vague hand, she took the joint, which was burned down close to the filter.

She inhaled sharply.

Very suddenly, the air began to sparkle, and a gentle buzzing filled her head. "Whoops, I'm stoned," she said and giggled, taking another puff.

"Say, you must have been smoking some of that there merry-wanna," Solomon said gravely.

"Well, of course, ye damn fool," she crowed, spraying smoke. "How else would I get stoned?" They roared with laughter.

Sol retrieved the joint from her relaxing fingers and stubbed it out in an ashtray. Still giggling, he slid open a panel in the wall, removed an Oriental figurine: a carven dragon with sparkling eyes. He touched it under one wing, and it's mouth opened wide. Prisoned in its lower fangs was a blue capsule.

Solomon tilted the dragon. It spat the capsule onto his upturned palm.

Barbara stopped giggling. "Oh," she said. "Yes."

Solomon met her eyes. "Yes."

He made a long arm, pulled open the refrigerator, and removed a plastic flask, red with white logo. "Better take this with soda," he said judiciously. "Taken stuff tastes worse'n peyote."

He could have read that in a magazine, she thought.

He put the flask of coke on the bed between them, shifting his weight carefully to avoid spilling it. He dried his sweaty left hand on his thighs and broke the capsule open onto his palm. It made a powdery pile of gray veined with green, fine-grained and dry. He held out his hand.

Barbara reached, gingerly bisected the pile with her thumbnail, sweeping the two portions far apart.

Looking up at him one last time, she bent close, licked one of the two doses from his hand, and grabbed for the coke. She made a face. "Oooooh!"

He nodded gently as she gulped coke, then took the flask from her. Eyes on the remaining powder, he licked and gulped coke in almost the same motion. When he had swallowed, he put down the flask, wiped his hands on the bedspread, and took her hands in his.

"Okay, mama," he said with great tenderness, suddenly vulnerable. "Here we go."

McGinny came howling out of sleep, flailing wildly with leaden arms.

"Goddam skull-faced kid," he shouted, and then fell back exhausted, drenched in sour sweat. Coherence came slowly to his thoughts, and he was torn by an unbearable craving for a cigarette. He tried to masturbate, and could not.

He rolled finally from the bed, padded to the bookviewer, and selected a book at random, falling heavily into the chair. He stared at the displayed title page for a few moments, reached out to punch for the next page, and slapped the set off instead. He buried his face in his hands and wept.

Nerves stretched wire-tight, he shook with racking sobs. He dug his knuckles into his eyes, but could not banish the haunting palpebral vision of Annie beside him on her bed, naked and vulnerable, cringing under his wrath (his baby planted now in her belly). He ground the heels of his hands against his ears, but could not banish the sound of her tears as she begged him for emotional support ("You *said* you were going to divorce her. Mack, I need you with me on this—it's *our baby*.") He beat at his skull with his clenched fists, but he could not deny the memory of his decision to "borrow" enough money from his company to leave town, to go underground, and leave the whole impossible tangle of his life behind.

And above all, he could not shut out the voice of the blond kid with the incongruous hat, could not seal the holes that soft voice blasted through McGinny's carefully-wrought fortress of rationalization. When the mind refuses to face truth, it very often knows what it is doing: a high truth-level is only tolerable to saints and sinners who, loving themselves, have learned how to forgive themselves. But McGinny no longer had any choice.

For the kid never attacked in any overt way, never quite gave him a justification for his helpless rage. He just . . . asked questions, and McGinny could not keep the answers from leaping unbidden to his mind.

Nor could he forget them now. The jailer's soft voice, hideously amplified, seemed to fill the cell, as it had for days now.

"Well, I don't know, Mr. McGinny. You say that security and prestige were your goals, but doesn't it seem like you already had them both? And yet you weren't satisfied . . ."

"So then you're saying sex is a kind of like power trip for you, aren't you?"

"Well, why didn't your father divorce her then? I would have."

"Then Annie's probably having a pretty rough time of it now?"

"But isn't that just a fancy way of saying . . .?"

"But you just said . . ."

"But didn't you just . . .?"

"But I thought . . ."

"But . . ."

McGinny burst from the chair with an animal howl and swept the desk clean of paper with clawed hands, swinging his arms wide and scattering sheets in all directions. "I'll kill you," he shrieked, and tore at his hair.

He lurched around the cell, kicking and punching at the unyielding fixtures, slamming his shoulder into the wall with whimpered oaths. He beat on the surface of the quadio, snapping off both controls, and the machine roared into life. Shorted somewhere within, it picked its own tape, at peak volume. The selection was old, stereophonic, activating the rear speakers only—it balanced perfectly. The ear-splitting voice of Leon Russell plaintively asked:

Are we really happy
with this lonely
game we play?
Searching for
words to say
Searching but not finding
understanding anyway
We're lost
in this masquerade.

McGinny staggered, his hands over his ears. He could not shut out the song. He lay down on his back and smashed at the quadio with his bare heels, and it went dead with one last shriek.

As he lay panting on the floor, his ears still ringing, he opened his eyes to see the kid watching him from the door window.

McGinny began to sweat profusely. He struggled to his feet and looked wildly around the room. *Rubber silverware, paper sheets, no razor, GO AWAY, KID!*

"Say, did I hear noise just now? Kinda late to play the quadio, isn't it, Mr. McGinny? Oh, I bet I know. You got to missing Alice and the kids, didn't you, Mr. McGinny?

"Hey, Mr. McGinny! What are you . . . *hey!*

"Oh, holy shit."

"Oh, wow."

The kid's face pressed closer.

The drug came on very slowly at first.

For what seemed like hours, Barbara felt only a gradual numbing of her extremities, a slow falling-off of communication with the nerves and muscles of her limbs. She and Solomon gazed deep into each other's eyes, motionless in lotus. She yearned to let her gaze travel downward over his body, but she maintained eye contact tenaciously, as though afraid of opening a circuit that was being built between them.

Very suddenly she was blind. Almost immediately, all tactile sensation vanished from her body. Adrift in crackling black, she could no longer see or touch anything in any direction. Although she had learned enough from friends and media reports to be expecting this, it still took her by surprise. She yelped.

As from a great distance, she heard Solomon's voice reassuring her, needlessly explaining that they were only experiencing a repression of distractions, that it was only a drug which would wear off, the standard litany of calming things that are said to one who might be freaking out. The truly extraordinary thing was that the voice changed as it spoke from stereo to mon-aural, converging inside her skull, as though she had switched from speakers to headphones.

"It's okay, Sol, I'm all right," she assured him, and

then realized that she had not spoken aloud. She tried to and could not.

They drifted for a while in silence, then. And as they drifted, sparkling darkness everywhere, each became aware of a growing *presence*, for which no words or symbols existed, which their minds could not grasp but only see/feel/taste. Barbara concentrated as hard as she could on the complex abstract which was Solomon Orechal's identity in her mind; received no familiar echo.

Of course, she thought, *of course he sees himself differently than I do*. She waited patiently for her mind to construct a suitable analogy for the identity-waves she was beginning to receive, and wondered what *he* was seeing. *Soon I'll know*.

The darkness coalesced, lightened perceptibly. An image began to take form, seen simultaneously from all angles.

It was a smooth iridium sphere.

It gleamed before her in the swirling dark, self-contained and apparently impenetrable. Her heart began to beat faster, a bass drum miles below her.

As she watched, spellbound, she saw the polished surface of the sphere begin to discolor, to tarnish. Portions of its surface began to bubble and flake away, as thought the metallic sphere were immersed in a clear acid that was slowly oxidizing it away. A high, sharp whining became audible, a sound of reluctant disintegration.

The image disturbed and frightened Barbara. She sensed an uncontrollable power latent in the sphere, ready to burst it asunder when it was sufficiently weakened. Girlfriends had tried to tell her of their experiences with Truth, but the closest Barbara had heard to this was a woman who said she initially perceived her partner as a man in full medieval armor, visor down. Unsettled, Barbara found that she was employing a pressure she could not define, in a manner she could not describe, against the sphere she could not understand.

Whatever it is, she screamed silently, *let it end now. It's been too long already.*

Time stood still, and she slipped into a new plane of understanding, intuition refined into knowledge. She perceived all at once that the walls of the sphere drew strength in some way from the marijuana Solomon had smoked—and that he had known they would.

He lied, came the thought.

And at that, the sphere crumbled like a sugar Easter egg in a glass of boiling water.

Parts of that explosion of data she forgot as soon as she perceived them. Parts of it she would carry with her to the end of her days. Some things simply could not be forced into words, some translated as paragraphs, some as single words or impressions coded only to subvocalized grunts or wordless cries. Alone in the darkness that crackled and roared she recoiled, struggling to reduce the enormous input to something comprehensible, pursued by howling fragmentary echoes of forgotten thoughts and memories.

. . . thinks he's so smart, I'll break his . . . nobody knows but me . . . so alone like this, I . . . don't look . . . things on so I could squint in the mirror and see what a lady looked like in her . . . don't look in . . . I didn't mean to . . . won't let me, just bec . . . it wasn't cheating exactly, it was . . . don't I . . . so pretty, I wonder what her . . . don't . . . how could she do this to me after all we . . . holy shit, it squirted all over

*my . . . If only I . . . don't look insi . . . what's he doing
to Mother? . . . don't l . . . I . . .*

Shaken to her roots, she reeled but held on, too
terrified to let go. There was something beneath,
something hidden, something that made alarms go
off all over her subconscious. And as well as
something hidden, there was something missing,
and she knew intuitively that they were connected. *What's missing?* she screamed toward the
place where she had once supposed God to *be.*
What is wrong? The onslaught continued, keeping
her off-balance.

*Gawd you give a pain in the ass Janice, you
real . . . think I got away with it this ti . . . got to get
a B this term or Old Karkhead'll . . . don't loo . . . God
the Father Almighty Who . . . she suspects . . . other
kids get a bike so why can't . . . don't look insi . . . n't
you understand I've got to be the master in my
own . . . why   you . . . don't   look . . . seen
a . . . sunset . . . like . . . that before . . . hairy black
spider that . . . so alone and they . . . don't look
inside . . . DON'T LOOK INSIDE!*

Inside! With a sinking feeling of terror and despair
Barbara yanked her attention from the chaotic distracting turmoil that the sphere had held, and turned
it inward. She found only the confusion of her own
thoughts.

She was alone inside her skull.

Where was Solomon? Why was he not probing *her*
consciousness, as deep within her identity as she was
in his?

Frantic now, she reached back out to the welter
of tangled thoughts and forgotten memories emanating
from her lover, and . . . *swept* at it, in a manner
impossible to describe. The roar of swarming images

died as though she had struck a suppressor switch, and she saw several things very clearly.

She saw that Solomon had palmed most of his share of the drug.

She saw his consciousness, trembling, crouched, incoherent with terror.

She saw at last that which he had sought most to hide: that the feeling he professed to have for her was nonexistent, a cover for his real motivations.

She saw his true reason for clinging to her: a paralyzing fear of being, in history's most crowded era, intolerably alone.

She saw that her man had never confronted her identity as an individual, never allowed himself to perceive her as a person, as anything but a palliative for hideous loneliness. Nor anyone else in his life.

She saw that he was afraid to confront her identity, to accept the guilt he knew he bore for using another human being as a tool, a teddy-bear, a living fetish with which to ward off demons of solitude.

She saw the indifference with which he regarded her own hopes and needs and fears, saw the relentless guilt which made him despise himself for it.

She saw the desperation in which he had sought to hide the truth from them both by reducing his dosage of yage and distorting both their synaptic responses with pot.

Comprehension and compassion washed over her as a single wave, a wave of pity and love for this tormented man to whom she had given her heart, and she cried out in her mind: *it's all right, Sol, it's ALL RIGHT! Don't be afraid, please. I love you.*

Undrugged, he heard her not.

She saw swimming to the surface of his mind a

surreal cartoon figure of herself, choked with
revulsion, recoiling from the selfishness of his love,
face contorted with bitter rejection. *No!* she screamed
silently, but she knew that he could not hear, knew
she could not make him hear, and knew with astonished horror that he was snapping, could no longer
bear the crushing pain of the guilt he could not
forget; and she realized with a nauseating certainty
what he was going to do.

The throbbing undercurrent of fragmented voices
swelled to a shuddering roar in her skull, and now
each of those voices was only a throaty growl.

She screamed once, and then many times.

The hissing of the torch reverberated in the bare
corridor with an acoustic sibilance that was unpleasant
if you listened to it. Jerry and Vito had learned not
to listen to it.

"Ain't had this thing out of the shop in so long, I
feel like I oughta take it for a walk," Jerry said,
adjusting the oxy mix.

"Yeah," grunted Vito from behind his opaque mask.

"Naw, we sure don't have to do this very often."

Vito grunted again.

"Wonder what made him do it. You know? Whole
place like that to hisself, nobody to tell him when
to go to work, when to go to sleep. Just lie around
all day and think about fems, that's what I'd do."

"So get busted," Vito grumbled.

"Hey, bro. What's with you? You got a bellyache
or something?"

"Gimme the willies, that bird."

"Him? He ain't givin' nobody nothin'."

Vito grunted a third time, and Jerry shook his head,
returning to his cutting. *Welfare check's due tonight,*

he thought suddenly, and smiled behind the polarized mask that shielded his eyes from the arc of the torch.

Noises came from the distance, approaching. Hastily, Vito stubbed out a Gold and tucked the roach in his shirt pocket.

The warden came into view around the corner, followed by two long-haired guards. He swept past Vito and Jerry without a word, ignoring the torch, and peered into the window of the cell door.

"Mmmmm," he said. "Yes."

The two guards shifted their weight restlessly.

"All right," said the balding official. "All right. Obviously it's a suicide."

"Obviously," murmured one of the guards, a blond, mustached youth. The warden glared at him irritably.

"Why wasn't I notified at once?"

"You were, sir," the guard said evenly. "Union regs say you only have to check 'em twice on night shift unless otherwise ordered. That's how I found him an hour ago. It was already too late to help him."

"Oh, very well, very well," the warden grumbled. "Carry on, you two." He went away, trailing the two guards. The blond one was smiling faintly.

Jerry and Vito looked at each other, shrugged. Jerry realigned the still-snarling torch against the door, and Vito relit his joint.

"Sure is a good thing this old torch leaks so bad, or he'd have smelled that and taken your ass," Jerry grinned. Vito passed him the joint; he slid it behind his mask and toked quickly, before the smoke could accumulate and lace his eyes. After a time he left off tracing a nearly complete, foot-and-a-half circle in the plasteel door, and paused. Giggling, he began to inscribe eyes and a broadly smiling mouth within the circle. Vito watched and smoked silently.

Again echoes sounded distantly. "Jesus," said Jerry. Vito glared at him and swallowed the joint. Hastily, Jerry completed the circle and began hammering at the disc he had cut, frantic to unseat it before his artwork was seen.

He was barely in time; even as the plug fell into the cell with a crash, two fat men came into view at the end of the corridor. One wore black and one wore gray. Both wore the same expression.

Jerry and Vito scrambled to their feet and backed away from the door, striving to look straight. The fat men came near simultaneously, entirely ignoring the two workers.

The one in gray reached gingerly through the now hole in the cell door, pulled toward himself with a gloved hand. They both entered, walked a few paces inside, stopped.

"Not much either of us can do here, is there, Doctor?"

"It seems not, Father."

"Well, then . . ."

"Yes."

They emerged, began to walk away.

"Hey," Jerry yelped.

The physician turned. "Yes?"

"Wh . . . what do we do with . . . ?"

The fat gray man paused, thought for a moment. "Unlock the infirmary and put him in there somewhere. I'll have a vehicle sent." He and the priest left, talking about chess.

Jerry looked at Vito, who gave him a very black look. He knelt and extinguished the torch, and silence fell in the corridor.

They went inside.

"Jeez," Vito breathed softly. It sounded like a prayer.

The two-inch-thick plug was lying just inside the doorway, its imbecile smile upside down. Beyond it lay McGinny, on his back, a feral and bloody grin on his face. His wrists had been chewed open.

"Jeez," Vito said again, and began putting on his gloves.

Solomon Orechal sat in his chair and surveyed the room which was to be his home for the next twenty-to-life-depending. With a disgusted sigh he picked his J-45 from the bed, hit a G, tuned, hit an E, tuned, hit an E again. Satisfied, he modulated through D back into G, added a seventh.

"This time next year," he sang, and stopped.

After a while he sang "Pack Up Your Sorrows," and that was all right, but when he had finished he found himself wondering who he could give all *his* sorrows to, so he went right into Lightning's "Prison Blues," and managed to get off on that.

But before long, inevitably, he was playing the song he used to close every set, the one he hadn't wanted to play here, now. He was halfway into James Taylor's "Don't Let Me Be Lonely Tonight," when he saw the face at the cell window, blond mustache under a blue uniform hat. He leaped from the chair, tossing his pride-and-joy heedlessly toward the bed, and sprang to the window.

"HEY OUT THERE, can you hear me?" he shouted.

"Hey, man, be measured," came a soft voice, electronically muffled. "I can hear you heavy."

"Wow, listen," Solomon babbled, "you work here,

man? Or what? Hey listen, *you want to hear a song?* You got a minute?"

"Sure, bro, sure. Take it easy."

Solomon ran back to the bed, picked up his axe and threw the strap over his head. He began frantically patting his pockets for a flat-pick, discovered he held one in his hand.

"What are you in for?" the blond guard asked quietly.

"Huh? Me? Oh, uh . . . rape," Solomon said, gripping the pick. ". . . and murder," he added, and looked down, hitting a very intricate chord.

The blond jailer's eyes lit up, and he tugged at his mustache.

"IF THIS GOES ON—"

TRUE MINDS

Locating her was no trouble at all. He tried the first bar that he came to, and as he cleared the door the noise told him that he had found her.

Behind the bar, the proprietor glanced around and recognized Paul, and his expression changed radically. He had been in the midst of punching a phone number; now he cleared the screen and came over to Paul.

"Hi, Scotty."

"Another one, Mr. Curry?" He jerked a thumb over his shoulder toward the back of the bar. Just around a corner and out of sight, a small riot seemed to be in progress; as Scotty pointed, a large man sailed gracefully into view and landed so poorly that Paul decided he had been unconscious before he hit. The ruckus continued despite his absence.

"Afraid so, Scotty. I'm sorry."

"Jesus Christ. It's bad enough when they cry, but what the hell am I supposed to do with *this*? I dunno, I'm old fashioned, but I liked it back when ladies had to be ladylike."

A half-full quart of scotch emerged from the rear of the room at high speed and on a flat trajectory. It took out the mirror behind the bar and at least a dozen other bottles.

Paul almost smiled. "That is, and always has been, ladylike," he said, nodding toward the source of air-borne objects. "What you mean is, you liked it better when, if it came to it, you could beat them up."

"Is that what I mean? Maybe it is. Mr. Curry, why in hell don't he just *tell* them?"

"Think about it, Scotty," Paud advised. "If it were you . . . would *you* tell them?"

"Why—" the innkeeper began, and paused. He thought about it. "Why—" he began again, and again paused. "I guess," he said at last, "I wouldn't at that." The sound of breaking glass took him back from his thoughts. "But honest to God, Mr. Curry, you gotta *do* something. I'm ready to call the heat—and I *can't*. You know who she is. But what if I don't report it and somebody gets—"

A scream came from the back, a male voice, but so high and shrill that both men clenched their thigh muscles in empathy.

"—see?"

"You're covered," Paul told him. "From here on it's my problem," and he legged it for the source of the commotion.

As he rounded the corner she was just disposing of the last bouncer. The man had height, mass, and reach over her, but none of them seemed to be doing him any good. He was jackknifed forward, chin outthrust, in perfect position from her point of view; she was slapping him with big roundhouse swings, alternating left and right, slapping his unshaven face from side to side. Paul could not decide whether the bouncer was too preoccupied with his aching testicles to be aware of the slaps, or whether he welcomed them as an aid to losing consciousness. If the latter, his strategy worked—one last terrific left rolled up his eyes and put him down and out before Paul had time to intervene.

Paul Curry was, if the truth be known, terrified. He was slightly built, and lacked the skill, temperament, and training for combat which had not been enough to help the sleeping bouncer. Utensil, he thought wildly, where is there a utensil? Say, a morningstar. Nothing useful presented itself.

But love can involve one in strange and complex obligations, and so he moved forward emptyhanded.

She pivoted to face him, dropped into a crouch. He stopped short of engagement range and displayed the emptiness of his hands. "Miss Wingate," he began. He saw her eyes focus, watched her recognize him, and braced himself.

She left her crouch, straightened to her full height, and in the loudest voice he had ever heard coming from a woman she roared, *"He doesn't know ANYTHING about love!"*

And then—he would never forget it, it was one of the silliest and most terrible things he had ever seen—she clenched her right fist and cut loose, a short, vicious chop square on the button. Her own button. She went down harder than the bouncer had.

Scotty stuck his head gingerly around the corner. "Nice shot, Mr. Curry. I didn't know you could punch like that."

Paul thought, I am in a Hitchcock movie. Briefly he imagined himself trying to explain to the bartender that Anne Wingate had punched herself out. "Well," he said, "you've never pissed me off, Scotty. Give me a hand, will you?"

They got her onto a chair, checked pulse and pupils, failed to bring her around with smelling salts. "All right," Paul said at last, "I'll take her to my place and she can sleep it off." The bartender looked unhappy. "Don't worry, Scotty. I'm a gentleman."

"I know that, Mr. Curry," Scotty said, looked scandalized. "But what do I—"

"There'll be no beef to you," Paul said. "I'll see to it. She was never here, right?"

"I'll say it was a platoon of Marines."

"That'll work."

"Mr. Curry, honest to God, if Senator Wingate comes down on me, forty years of squeeze goes right down the—"

"The Senator will never hear a word about this, Scotty. Trust me."

Paul was painfully aware that his promise was backed by nothing at all. By the time the cab arrived he was feeling pessimistic—he insisted that the driver prove to him that his batteries held adequate charge. It is not necessarily a disaster to run out of juice, even in an Abandoned Area; one simply buttons up and waits for the transponder to fetch the police. But if one is in the company of the unconscious daughter of an extremely powerful man at the time, one can scarcely hope to stay out of the newstapes.

The batteries were indeed charged; the offended driver insisted that Paul prove he had the fare. As Paul and Scotty were loading her into the cab, she opened one eye, murmured, "not a single *thing*," and was out again. The trip was uneventful; even when the driver was forced to skirt Eagle turf, they drew only desultory small arms fire. She slept through it all.

Luck was with him; she did not begin vomiting until just as he was getting her out of the cab. Nonetheless he tipped the cabbie extra heavily, both by way of apology and to encourage amnesia. Mollified, the driver waited until Paul had gotten her safely indoors before pulling away.

She was half awake now. He managed to walk her most of the way to the bathroom. She sat docilely on the commode while he got her soiled clothes off. He knew she would return to full awareness very shortly after the first blast of cold shower hit her, and he was still determined not to be beaten up by her if he could avoid it. So he sat her down in the tub, made sure everything she would need was available, slapped the shower button and sprinted from the room while the water was still gurgling up the pipes. He was halfway to his laundry unit when the first scream sounded. It was the opening-gun of a great deal of cacophony, but he had thoughtfully locked the bathroom door behind him; the noise had ceased altogether by the time he had coffee and toast prepared.

He went down the hall, unlocked the bathroom door. "Miss Wingate," he said in a firm, clear voice, "the coffee is ready when you are."

The response was muttered.

"Beg pardon?"

"I said, Phillip Rose doesn't know one goddamned thing about love."

"The coffee will stay hot. Take your time." He went back to the kitchen and poured himself a cup. In about five minutes she came in. She wore the robe he had left for her. Her hair was in a towel. Very few people can manage the trick of being utterly formal and distant while dressed in robe and towel, but she had had expert training from an early age. She did not tell him how seldom she did this sort of thing, because she assumed he knew that.

"May I have some coffee, Mr. Curry?"

He watched the steadiness of her hand as she picked up the cup, and wondered if, given her money, he could buy himself physical resilience like that, or if a person just had to be born with it.

"Thank you for looking after me," she said. "I'm sorry I've been such a bother. I've put you to no end of expense and difficulty and I . . . not the *first* damned thing about it. This is very good coffee, Mister *how* can you work for a phoney like that?"

"I liked you better drunk."

"*I beg your pardon?*"

"And if you call Mr. Rose a phoney again, Miss Wingate, I will as politely as possible punch you in the mouth." Or die trying, he added to himself.

She took her time answering. "I apologize Mr. Curry. I am a guest under your roof. Forgive my bad manners." She looked suddenly sheepish. "This really is excellent coffee. Are my clothes salvageable?"

He was getting used to her Stengelese conversational style. "There was no difficulty and your apology is accepted and I'm pleased you like the coffee and he knows a great deal more about love than anyone alive and your clothes are in the laundry. Did I leave anything out?"

She looked stubborn and drank her coffee. He poured more, and passed her her purse so that she could have a cigarette.

"Don't worry," he said as she lit up. "The aspirins should take effect any minute."

She almost choked on smoke. "How do you know I took aspirins?" she asked sharply.

He raised an eyebrow. "Afraid I spied on you in my own bathroom? Miss Wingate, how do you think you got in the tub? I don't strip all my guests, but you were covered with vomit. Look, you got hurt and then drunk and then crazy, and then you passed out and woke up in a squall of icewater. If your head doesn't hurt, you're dead. There are aspirin in my medicine chest, clearly marked, and I assume you have an instinct for self-preservation."

She wore an odd expression, as if there were something extraordinary or dismaying about what he had said. "Oh," she said finally in a small voice. "Again I apologize."

"*De nada*, Miss Wingate."

"Anne."

"Paul."

"Paul, why do I get the impression that none of this is new to you?"

He poured himself another cup. "New to me?"

"You're too competent, too skilled at coping with troublesome drunken women. I'm not the first, am I?"

He laughed aloud, surprising himself. "Anne, you are not the twenty-first. I've been Mr. Rose's personal secretary for about ten years, and I would say that one of you manages to get past me every six or seven months, on the average." He frowned. "Too many." And thought, but you *looked* intelligent and stable.

"And you say he knows about love." She put down her cup, got up and paced. She came to his powered cookstool: the proper height for counter and cabinet work; a pedal for each wheel, heel for reverse, toe for forward. She sat on it and heel-and-toed it into rotating. It was a whole-body fidget, annoying to watch.

"Anne, love rides his back like a goblin. It lives in his belly like a cancer. He wears it like a spacesuit in a hostile environment. It wears him like a brake drum wears shoes. I can't tell whether he generates love or the other way around." His voice was rising; he was irritated by her continued rotation on the stool. "I think everybody knows that. Everybody who can read."

She stopped the stool suddenly, with her back to him. "Was there ever anything that 'everybody knew' that turned out to be so?"

His irritation increased. "I worry about anyone under eighteen who isn't a cynic—and anyone over eighteen who is. There are *thousands* of things that everybody knows that are true. Falling off a cliff will hurt you. It gets dark at night. Snow is cold. Philip Rose knows about love. Damn it, you've read his books."

"*Yes, I've read his fucking books!*" she yelled at his refrigerator.

Something told him that now was the time to shut up. He sat where he was, elbows on the table, pinching his lower lip between his thumbs, and looked at her back. It was some time before she spoke, but he did not mind the wait.

"When I was eight years old," she said at last, "my Aunt Claire gave me one of his juveniles. *Latchkey Kid.* It smacked me between the eyes."

He nodded uselessly.

"I'd always been loved. So thoroughly, so completely, so automatically that both I and the people who loved me took it for granted. The book made me understand what it *felt* like not to be loved. That would have been enough for most writers. But Rose went further. He made me love Cindy, even though she wasn't very likeable, and he made me see how even she could find love, even in a world like hers. He wasn't famous then, he only had a dozen or so books out.

"The next one I tried was *Tommy's Secret*. I don't suppose I could quote you more than a chapter or so at a time without referring to the text. For my tenth birthday I asked for a hardcover set of everything he had ever written. My father was scandalized—it wasn't expensive enough—so I let him buy me two sets. That way I had one copy to preserve, immaculate, and one I could mark up and underline and dog-ear. Soon I found I needed a third set. Some writers you want to keep, special and private, for yourself and a few close friends. Rose I gave away to anyone who didn't duck fast enough.

"There is a story he wrote, 'A Cup of Loneliness,' that is the only reason I didn't kill myself when I was sixteen."

Unseen, Paul nodded again.

"By then I was old enough to realize how much I owed Aunt Claire. Unfortunately I realized it at her funeral. After a while I decided that I was repaying her by giving Philip Rose to other people. I mailed copies of his books to every critic and reviewer I could find. In college I got three credits of independent study for a critical analysis of Rose's lifework to date that must have taken me forty-eight hours to put on paper. My professor got it published. I began to realize just how much weight my father's name carried, and I used it, to see that Philip Rose's career prospered. Eventually I had persuaded enough influential people to 'discover' him that public awareness of him started to grow.

"Part of that was selfish. He was obscure, next to nothing was known about him as a person in any references I could find. I wanted to know about him, about his life, about where he had been and what he had done and whether or not he had enough love in his own life."

Paul nodded a third time and lit one of her cigarettes.

"He didn't accept visitors and didn't give interviews and didn't return biographical questionnaires from Who's Who in Books and didn't put more than he could help in his 'About the Author' blurbs. All I knew was that it said in the back of *Broken Wings* that he was married, and then the PR for the next one, *A Country We Are Privileged to Visit*, mentioned that he lived alone in this city. It never occurred to me to actually approach him myself, any more than it would occur to most people to look up the President." (Curry happened to know that the President had been Anne Wingate's godfather.) "But I threw reporters and scholars at him until I realized I was wasting his time and mine. If *People* magazine can't get past you to him, no one can. I suppose I could have just put a good agency onto researching him, but the idea of setting detectives on Philip Rose is grotesque.

"I decided that I would make him famous, and sooner or later he would simply have to open up. Not that I claim to be responsible for his fame—even I'm not that arrogant. He was already certain to be a legend in his own lifetime—but I speeded up the process. And it didn't work worth a damn. Not since

Salinger has a writer been so famous, so loved, and so little known. You cover him well. I still don't know what went wrong with his marriage—or even what her name was.

"Finally I decided there was only one way to thank the man who had taught me everything I know about love. It's because of him that I studied lovemaking, so that I could give my lovers a gift that was something more than commonplace. It's because of him that I'm still involved in politics. It's because of him that I don't hate my father. It's because of him that I don't hate myself."

Paul interrupted for the first time. "You don't hate yourself, Anne, because he taught you how to forgive."

She banged her fist against the stool's flank. *"How can I forgive him for what he did?"*

He kept his own voice soft and low. "Don't you mean, How can I forgive him for what he didn't do?"

"Damn it, he didn't have to *do* anything. Just lay back and let me do the doing—"

"And that wouldn't be doing something? You say you've studied lovemaking: is there any such thing as a passive partner? Aside from necrophilia and rubber dolls? You wanted him to *do* you the favor of accepting pleasure from you. You're young and very beautiful: perhaps you've never met a man who wouldn't count that a privilege. You made your offer, and he declined politely—I'll bet my life it was politely—and so you decided to make him an offer he couldn't refuse. And learned the sad truth: that there is *no* offer a man cannot refuse if he must."

"Why 'must'? There was no obligation of any kind, expressed or implied—if he's half the telepath his books make him seem, he must have know that. All I wanted to do was say thanks."

"You *did* thank him. And then before he could say 'you're welcome,' you tried to ram your thanks down his throat, or down yours, or whatever, and made him throw you out. There's an old John Lennon song, 'Norwegian Wood.' I've always felt that he changed the title to avoid censorship. I think the song is about the nicest compliment a man can receive from a woman. Isn't it good?: *knowing she would.* But that message can be conveyed from twenty feet away, by body language. Only children need it confirmed by effort and sweat, that's what Lennon was trying to say. Damn it, Anne, haven't you ever been turned down?"

"Not like *that!*"

"You gave Mr. Rose exactly two choices: be raped or be rude. I wasn't there, but I *know*. Otherwise he would not have been rude."

"But—"

"Anne, I've been through this before, and I must say they usually take it better than you. But once every couple of years or so we get one so young and so blind with need that he has to be rude to turn her off. It always upsets him."

"Damn you," she yelled.

"Anne, the first step to forgiving yourself is facing up to what you've done wrong. Or did you think that your own upset was only hurt pride and frustration?"

"And how do you handle the dumb young insistent ones?" she asked bitterly, and spun the stool around to face him. He saw tear tracks. "Take the Master's sloppy seconds?"

"I lie to them, generally," he said evenly. "I talk to them until I get an idea of which excuse they're willing to be sold, and then I sell it to them. If it seems necessary, I figure out what sort of bribe or threat it will take to keep their mouths shut, and provide that. As for myself, I prefer bed partners who know as much about love as they do about lovemaking."

She flinched, but said nothing. She was studying his face.

"You say you've read all his books," he went on. "Do you recall reading in any of them a definition of 'love'? As opposed to lust or affection or need or any of a dozen other cousins?"

"No, I don't think he's ever defined it, in so many words."

"You're right. But there *is* a single, concise definition that runs through every thing he ever wrote. He never wrote it down because it had already been done, by another writer, about whom Mr. Rose feels much the same way you feel about him."

"The old man in free fall? The science fiction writer?"

"That's right. You *have* done your homework. He defined love as 'that condition in which the welfare and happiness of another are essential to your own.'"

She thought that over. "Make your point."

"Is that what you claim motivated you?"

Her eyes closed. Her expression smoothed over. She was looking deep inside for the answer. After twenty seconds she half opened her eyes. "Yes, partly," she said slowly. "More than half. I wanted to be personally sure he was happy and well—to make him happy myself, to be there and know that it was so."

"By giving him something he doesn't want."

"Damn it, he needs it—he must!"

"Ah, the old standby of the teenage male: 'Continence is unhealthy.' Anne, in your experience, do priests and monks tend to die young?"

"But why would *he* want to be celibate?"

"Did it ever occur to you that he might not have any choice? Let me tell you a story that is none of your—"

She shook her head. "Now you're doing what you said a moment ago—lying, giving me a plausible excuse. Some story about a war wound, or a tragic accident, or a wasting disease. Save it, please. Philip Rose's work could *not* have been produced by any kind of a eunuch. Furthermore, I *know* better. He had to be *very* rude to get rid of me. I got close enough to be sure that all his equipment was in place and functioning." She smiled bitterly. "I don't care much for puns, but I assure you: Philip rose."

So did his eyebrows. "My respect for you has jumped another notch. I'm impressed. And, frankly intrigued. And mildly annoyed at the low respect in which you seem to hold me. I have not lied to you yet, and I wasn't going to start. The story I was—"

"Why not?"

"Do you want to hear this story or not?"

His volume made her start. She must have spent a lot of time on the road; the small involuntary movements of her feet, brake, clutch, accelerator, made the chair pivot back and forth spasmodically, so that as her head nodded yes, her body said no.

Neither of them could help giggling at that; it broke some of the tension, leaving both with half smiles. She waited in silence, determined not to interrupt again, while he chose his words.

This took him longer than it should have. He found that he was staring at her eyelashes. They were so long and perfectly formed that he had assumed them false. Now he saw that they were real. He tore his gaze from them, fixed it on his own hands, whereupon he discovered that they were fidgeting, caressing each other. He forced them to be still—and his foot started tapping on the floor.

"You are certainly under twenty-five," he said, "so you cannot have been born earlier than 1970. Which does not," he added, "mean that you're ignorant of prior times. I know you are something of a historian. But you're not likely to have an intuitive feel for an era you haven't lived through."

He saw the ever-so-slight tightening of those muscles used to keep the mouth shut. Her mouth was as distracting as her eyes.

"Philip Rose," he went on doggedly, "was born in 1934. He didn't marry until he was twenty-five—that made it 1959. Marriage then was something different from marriage today. Which actually may not be all that relevant—Mr. Rose has never been a slave to convention. He has always, I think, made his own rules.

"Maybe that's the point I'm trying to make. If you are the kind of man who makes his own rules, in 1959, you *keep* the rules you make for yourself. That's the dilemma that Situational Ethics blundered into—if you can change them situationally, they're not rules; if you can't they're a straitjacket. What I mean is, Mr. Rose might change his own personal rules—but once he's made a promise, he'll keep it. No matter how much he might—or might not—regret making it.

"So in 1959 he married Regina Walton. There were several unconventional things about the marriage, and one very conventional thing.

"The first unconventional thing was the age difference. She was nearly ten years older than he, already well established in her field. The second unconventional thing—for the time—was that she kept her own last name. At his urging. A Rose by any other name, and so forth. The final unconventional thing was that they wrote their own wedding vows—and that was the thing that hurt.

"Can you see that? How that would make a difference to him? The conventional marriage ceremony of that time was an utterly standardized legal contract with ritual trappings. Everyone took the same vows, with minor variation, and as you took them you knew they could be dissolved in thirty days in Reno. If you must mouth a certain formula in order to cohabit legally, then, if you should ever change your mind, you can rationalize that it wasn't a 'real' promise. But the two of them wrote their own vows, thinking them through very carefully first—so they left themselves no loopholes at all.

"Which is a shame, because of the one conventional part I mentioned. Their contract is quite specific: lifetime sexual fidelity is spelled out. Old fashioned death-do-us-part monogamy.

"Conventional for the time: even though divorce was common then, term marriage was emphatically not. Oh, people got married knowing that 'forever' might translate, 'until we change our minds'—but they didn't get married at all unless they at least *hoped* for forever.

"But Philip and Regina *meant* it. They were practical romantics: they did not want a deal they could quit when the going got tough. They left themselves no escape clauses."

Involuntarily, she interrupted for the first time. "Foolish."

"Shut your stupid mouth," he said quietly. "It is not for you to criticize them."

She bit her lip.

"I read just the other week, the average term marriage runs three years, and the average 'lifetime' marriage now last about nine or ten years. The Rose-Walton union has lasted forty years so far."

He might just as well have kicked her in the belly. Her breath left her explosively, her hands and feet flew up from their resting places, snapped back. She drew air convulsively in through both nose and mouth, slumped down again in her chair and cried, "No!" She jumped up and began pacing around the room, turning to face him as she paced. "No. It's not possible! I would have *heard, some*thing—and there was no trace of a woman's hand in that apartment, I'm *certain* of that, damn it, the first thing I *thought* of was someone else." As she convinced herself, she began to get mad at him. "You lying son of a—"

"You don't listen very well," he said, enough edge on his voice to get through to her. "I said they were practical romantics. I said they thought it through. Her profession sometimes made long trips necessary, and his work-habits made him a homebody. They agreed to be faithful forever—but they did *not* promise to live together always."

She stopped pacing. She blinked those marvelous eyelashes so rapidly that he fancied he could feel the breeze. Then she shut her eyes and frowned.

"For more than twenty-five years," he continued, "all went well and more than well and better than that. I don't know why they never had children—I never will unless he chooses to tell me—but they don't seem to have suffered from the lack of children. They were never apart for more than three or four months at a time, and when they were together they were more together than most people ever get to be. He says that they supplied each other's missing parts, that between

them they made up one good and sane human being.
You said yourself he's a telepath. Anyone may have a
taste of telepathy, but it takes a really good marriage
to develop it to anything like his level."

He paused, and was silent in thought for a time,
and she waited patiently.

"Then the hammer fell on them.

"Her field was immunology, and she was one of
its leaders. It was a natural interest for her—she was
loaded with serious allergies herself, the kind that
have to be wrestled with permanently and can kill
you if you get careless. When the European Space
Station went up, it was a natural for her. What better place could there be to do medical research than
a totally and permanently sterile environment? So she
bullied and squeezed her way into a tour as the ESS's
first resident physician. She and her husband thought
it would be a pleasant vacation from her own allergies. I assume you know what happened to most of
the first-year ESS personnel."

She was gaping, perhaps for the first time in her
life. "You are telling me that 'Dr. R.V. Walton' is
Regina Wal . . . is *Philip Roses's wife?*"

"Trapped in space by free-fall adaptation—one of
the unlucky fourteen pioneers. She can never come
home again."

"Oh my God." Her eyes were open so wide that
the lashes now appeared normal size. She swayed
where she stood, and her hands made little seeking
gestures for something to clutch. They settled on the
robe she wore, and if he needed any further proof
of the extent of the impact on her, he had it, for as
she clenched at the pockets of the robe it parted,
baring her up to the belt, and she failed to notice.
"Oh filthy *God*," she cried. "Oh, couldn't he—"

"Not unless the fucking Space Taxi ever gets off the drawing boards," he said bitterly. "Ten years overdue already. The Shuttles are space trucks, big rough brutes. All his life Philip Rose has had a bad heart valve. He's in great shape for a man of sixty-five. He'll probably live another ten or fifteen years, here on Earth. But there's never been a day in his life when he could have survived a Shuttle blastoff."

She looked up at the ceiling. She looked down at the floor, and absently pulled the robe closed. She looked from side to side. She sat on the floor and stuck out her lower lip and burst into tears.

He went on his knees beside her, holding her in one strong arm and stroking her hair. She cried thoroughly and easily and for a long time, and when she was done she stopped. "And they still . . . how could . . .?"

"You know," he told her, "you did him a hell of a big favor, helping him get famous. The money came along just in time, Anne—his phone bill was getting to be a bonecrusher."

"You mean—"

"Every night they spend at least an hour on the phone together, talking, sharing their respective days, sometimes just looking at each other. With a three-quarter-second time lag." He shook her gently. "Anne, listen to me: It's sad, but it's not *that* sad. They live. They work. They have time together every day, more than some doctors' spouses—or writers' spouses—get by on. They just can't touch. They are, incredible as it may seem to you and me, both quite happy. In all the years I have known them, I've never heard either of them complain about the situation, not ever. Maybe there aren't many people who could maintain and enjoy a relationship like that. But they were already each other's other leg when she first went up into orbit. When one of them dies, the other will go within a month—but meanwhile what they have is enough for them."

She sat with her head bowed. Slowly, stiffly she got to her feet. He helped her and stood himself. He began gathering up dirty cups and dishes.

"Where's your laundry?"

"Down the hall there," he said, "just past the coat closet. Your clothes will be ready to wear by now. I'll call you a cab."

She was back, dressed and face repaired, by the time the cab showed on the door-screen. "Paul," she said formally, heading for the door, "I want to thank—"

He held up his hand. "Wait just one minute, please."

She paused, clearly already gone in her mind but trying to be politely attentive.

"Back when I first met Mr. Rose, before I knew his situation, I made my own pass. Tentatively, because I knew he was old-fashioned in some ways. But I made it clear that as his personal secretary and his fan I would do *anything* he wanted. He was flattered. Turned me down, of course, but it has made for a kind of intimacy between us, that we might never have shared otherwise. So I'm in a position to tell you something you have no business knowing. He won't mind, and I think I know you well enough now to believe that it may be a comfort of a kind to you. Do you know what he is doing now? Seventy percent certainty?"

She shook her head.

"He's on the phone with Regina. It's that time of night. He's telling her about your encounter, embellishing in spots, perhaps, and they are masturbating together."

She stood stock still, expressionless, for perhaps ten seconds. And then she smiled. "Thank you, Paul. It is a comfort."

And she left. He watched the door monitor until he was certain she had entered the cab safely.

A week later his phone blinked. He looked over the caller—and accepted at once. "Anne! Hello!"

"One question," she said briskly. "When the robe came open, you didn't look. Not even a glance. Are you gay-only?"

He caught the robe reference at once; the question took him a second. "Eh? Oh . . . I see. Emphatically no. It's just that I only look at skin that's being shown to me."

She nodded. "Thought so. Wanted to be sure." She smiled. "I know why you didn't lie to me. I'm going to be very busy for a long time. Be patient."

And the screen went dark, leaving him mystified.

Two years later he was talking to one of the dozens of reporters who crammed the pressroom at Edwards Air Force Base.

"—takes off just like a conventional plane," he was saying, "no more takeoff stress than a 797—so Mr. Rose should have no trouble at all. I think it's going to add twenty years to his life."

"What I can't figure," the reporter said, "is how incredibly *fast* the thing got pushed through. Two years from a standing start, wham, the damned thing is out of R & D, into production, and up in the air." He turned his head to watch the big monitor screen which showed the new Space Taxi climbing, endlessly climbing. "Two years ago it was too expensive and impractical. Now it's halfway to ESS and your boss has a firm reservation for the fourth flight in a couple of months. *Some*body in congress made a big muscle . . . but why wouldn't he cash in on the PR? I go back to the Shuttle days, Mr. Curry, and that was like pulling teeth. This went so quick it almost scares me."

Paul nodded. "Yep, it's a wonder, all right," he said, and then he said, "Excuse me, Phil," very abruptly, and seemed to teleport across the crowded pressroom.

She was waiting for him, exquisite in white and blue.

"Hello, Paul."

"Hello, Anne."

"Two years is a long time."

"Yes." He gestured at the huge monitor. "Short time for a project like that, though. You did a good job."

She smiled. "Today, for the first time in two years, my father is off the hook."

He smiled back. "I pity your enemies."

"You didn't lie to me, two years ago, because you were in love with me." The way she said it was somewhere between a question and an accusation.

"That's right."

"Are you sexually or romantically encumbered now?"

"No."

"Then there is some skin I'd like to show you."

"Yes."

"Should we have dinner before or after, do you think?"

An observer might have said she read her answer on his face, but it was really nothing of the sort.

COMMON SENSE

The blind man was watching a videotape when the phone chirped. Bemused, he put the tape deck on *pause* and hold, fed the phone circuit to the screen. He frowned at what he saw.

"Good day, Captain," he began formally. "What can I—"

"Ranny will you come to the bridge?" the caller interrupted.

The blind man closed his eyes, but nothing went away. He stiffened in his chair, and then slumped.

"That hurt, Jax," he said at last.

"Damn it, would I *ask* if I didn't need to?"

Ran's face changed. "I suppose not. Milk and sugar in mine." He shut off phone and deck and left, handling himself economically in free-fall.

Ran Mushomi concentrated on the people; the

bridge itself hurt too much to look at. He already
knew Captain Jaxwen Kartr and Executive Officer
Thorm Exton. But he was startled to see another
passenger on the bridge, and profoundly startled to
recognize him: Old Man Groombridge himself, president and owner of Intersystem Transport Incorpo-
rated. Ran's hackles rose.

"What's *he* doing here?"

"It's my starship," Groombridge said.

"Traveling to Koerner's world," the Captain said,
"like you and two hundred other people, Ranny."

"And a damned good thing, too," Groombridge
added.

"All right, what's this all about?"

"We need your help," the Captain said, tossing him
a bulb of coffee with milk and sugar.

Ran laughed. It was an ugly sound.

Groombridge snorted. "I told you it was a waste
of time."

"Ranny, *listen*," Captain Kartr said, her voice urgent.
"This is important, damn it."

"To a groundhog?" he asked bitterly.

"Look." She activated a screen. It showed
a . . . thing, apparently at rest in space.

"Looks like a lumpy testicle."

"Ran—"

"Or a planet with pimples. Wow, they move. How
big is it?"

"About two meters in diameter. It's alive. We think
it's sentient. And we think it's hurt."

Ran made no visible reaction; the widening of his
eyes was of course unseen beneath his goggles.

"We dropped into normal space for mid-course
corrections, as usual," Groombridge said, "and it
blundered right into our screens."

"How do you know it's alive?"

"It's trying to pull free of the tractor beam right now," the Captain said.

Ran nodded. "And it must be hurt, because it's not succeeding."

"More than that. Kreel tried to make contact with it." Like most ships' medicos, Kreel was a Domanti empath. "He's down in his own sickbay now, sedated, and you know what it takes to sedate a Domanti. That thing *hurts*."

"How do you know it's sentient?"

"We don't, for sure," the Exec said. "Kreel thought so, but . . ."

"So what do you want me for?"

"Advice," the Captain said. "I respect your brains, Ranny."

"Advice on what?"

"How to communicate with the damned thing."

"What's the problem? A ship's computer can translate *anything*."

"Given enough input, sure. That's the kicker. Ranny, *we don't know what it uses for senses*."

"Oh."

"Maybe we could cure whatever's wrong with it. Maybe not; maybe we could just talk to it until it dies, find out where and how to find its kin. It's a *new species*, Ranny, and interstellar space seems to be its natural habitat. We don't know what fires its metabolism, how it moves, we don't know *anything*."

"'The problem,'" Ran quoted to himself softly, "'is to get the mule's attention . . .'" He smiled. "I begin to see. A new species could make Intersystem even richer. But every minute you sit here in normal space, you lose millions in schedule penalties—and you dasn't move the thing."

"Correct," Groombridge said unhappily. "We can't take it into n-space with us without bringing it inboard, and we have no way of knowing whether it can survive inside a radiation-opaque hull."

"Let alone whether it can survive n-space," Ranny agreed. "A pretty problem."

"Hell, yes," Groombridge growled. "Every other sentient race we've ever encountered has been planet-dwellers, with sensory equipment more or less analogous to our own. I never imagined we'd find a space-dweller."

"And if we lose this one, the odds approach zero that I'll ever find another," Exton put in.

Ran was thinking hard. "Let's see—even a space-dweller would have *some* use for light, visible or otherwise."

"Sure," the Captain agreed. "On a cosmic scale. All we have to do to 'talk' with it is turn a couple of stars on and off. But how does it *reply*?"

"Doesn't it put out *any*thing?"

"Yeah. Constant body temperature about eight degrees Absolute. Electrical potential fluctuates around its surface in what might very well be meaningful patterns. If so, how do we reply? *My* electrical potential varies across my surface—but not at will. The computer has to have *dialogue*, even on the 'Me Tarzan—you Jane' level, before it can begin extrapolating language."

Ran locked his hands behind his head, the free-fall equivalent of chin-on-fist. "Hmm. I'd bet my socks it perceives gravity gradients, but that's no use. You must have tried radio frequencies by now." He squeezed coffee. "What's it made of?"

"Beats us."

"Damnation," Groombridge said. "We assume that

others of its race exist. They must have some means
of interspecies communication."

"Perhaps," Ran said. "But there's no reason to
assume it's anything we've ever encountered. Maybe
they communicate through n-space."

"How about—" the multibillionaire began, and then
caught himself.

"Mr. Groombridge," Captain Kartr said diplomati-
cally, "believe me, we've tried everything in the elec-
tromagnetic spectrum. As far as I know, the damned
things converse by witchcraft. We need something
else. A breakthrough."

"I've got it," Ran said with absolute confidence,
and sipped coffee.

Involuntary muscle reactions sent the other three
spinning around the bridge. Groombridge recovered
first. "Well? Out with it!"

"Will you meet my price?"

Groombridge began to sputter, then regained
control. "Name it."

"I want my ticket back."

"Out of the question."

Captain Kartr decided to stick her neck out. "Sir,
with all due respect, Ranny's the best skipper you ever
had. I was his exec when he lost his optic nerves
saving the *Heimdall*. He spent the last eighty-five
years getting rich enough to afford a Visual Analog
System, and now he's got better vision than I have.
Nobody deserves a master's ticket more."

Groombridge studied Ran's VAS goggles. The
computer built into them, which processed the sig-
nals for their camera lenses into a form his visual
cortex could accept, was as expensive as a good
starship computer. They did not provide sight as Ran
had once known it—it took about ten years to learn

to interpret the new data—but that accomplished, they provided a very satisfactory substitute. "I'm familiar with Mr. Mushomi's record and history. I followed his case, and I'm afraid I agree with what the Board decided last week. It simply isn't sensible to have all the command functions of an n-space vessel funneled through a single, potentially fallible system."

"I repeat," Ran said quietly, although there was murder in his heart. He had once been a *starship pilot*. "Meet my price and I can solve your problem. Payment on delivery."

Interstellar executives *hate* to reverse themselves— but Groombridge was not a fool, and the clock was ticking. "All right, damn you," he snarled. "You'll get your ticket and the command of your choice— witnessed, recorded and binding. Now *give*."

"Get me a pressure suit, Jax," Ran said instantly, and laughed, because his superior peripheral vision allowed him to see all three stunned faces at once.

Many hours later the ship was once again under way in n-space, and Ran and Jax were celebrating in the Captain's quarters.

"Who would ever have guessed that what the God damned thing needed was water ice?" she said, taking fresh bulbs of Scotch from the cooler and tossing one to Ran.

"Certainly not me. With a metabolism evolved in space, it must take a long time to get thirsty."

"And even longer to die of it," Jax agreed. "You *earned* your ticket back, Ranny. Nobody else in the Universe could have done it."

"Nonsense," he said cheerfully, and sucked Scotch. "I spent those eighty-five years earning my eyes on

Darkside, because my handicap didn't exist there. It's got a permanent, opaque, planet-wide cloud cover. The natives call it 'God's Rectum,' because it's the only place in the Universe where the sun never shines." The Captain giggled. "Quite a few optic-nerve cases go there—they're not different anymore. *Everybody* knows hand-talk on Darkside."

"S'not what I mean. Oh, that speeded things up, sure, which is penalty saved. But we couldn't have done *anything* without your original insight. I still don't see how you could have been so *sure* the thing had *tactile* sense."

"I wasn't," Ran said complacently. "I was bluffing Groombridge. What did I have to lose if I was wrong?"

Jax stared openmouthed, then roared with laughter. "You son of a bitch, you were *guessing*?"

"Well, it just seemed reasonable to me. I pictured a race of beings evolved in interstellar space, and I just . . . pictured them *touching* a lot. It's lonely out there." He drained his Scotch. "And after that, of course, all we had to do was use our . . . uh . . . common sense."

CHRONIC OFFENDER

In respectful memory of Damon Runyon,
Who knows no other tense than the present,
And sometimes the future.

You will think that when a guy sees eighty summers on Broadway, he sees it all, and until recently so will I. It is a long time since I see something that surprises me very much, and in fact the last time I remember being surprised is when the Giants take the wind for L.A. But when I come home a couple of nights after my eightieth birthday, along about four bells in the morning, and find a ghost watching my TV, I am surprised no little, and in fact more than somewhat.

At first I do not figure him for a ghost. What I figure him for is a hophead, what they call nowadays

263

a junkie, and most guys will figure this proposition
for a cinch, at that. I decide that my play is to go
out again, and have a cup of coffee, and come back
when he is finished, or maybe even ask the gendarmes
to come back *before* he is finished. But Astaire will
never hoof again and neither will I, because I have
not even managed to get her into reverse when this
character hauls out a short John Roscoe and says like
this:

"Stand and deliver."

This is when I figure him for a ghost, because I
recognize the words he uses, and then his voice, and
finally his face, and who is it but Harry the Horse.

Now, Harry the Horse is never a guy I am apt to
hang around with, as he is a very tough guy, who will
shoot you as soon as look at you, and maybe even
sooner. Furthermore he is many years dead at this
time, and I figure the chances are good that the
climate where he is lately is hot enough to make him
irritable. In fact, I am wishing more with every
passing moment to go have this cup of coffee, but
I cannot see any price at all on arguing with a John
Roscoe, especially such a John Roscoe as is being
piloted by Harry the Horse, or even his ghost. So I
up with my mitts and say as follows:

"Don't shoot, Harry."

Well, it turns out that nobody is more surprised
than Harry when *he* recognizes *me*. I cannot figure
this, since I always understand that ghosts know who
they are haunting, but then again I never hear of a
ghost packing a John Roscoe, at that. In fact, I start
to wonder if maybe Harry the Horse is not a hallu-
cination, and I am gone daffy.

You have to understand that Harry the Horse looks
not a day older than when I see him last, which is

going back about fifty years. Furthermore his suit is the kind they do not make for fifty years, except it looks no older than is customary on Harry when I know him, and likewise his hair is greased up like only some of the spics and smokes still do anymore, and in fact he looks in every respect like he does when I last see him, except that he is not smiling and not laying down and does not seem to have several .45 caliber holes in him. In fact, he looks pretty good, except for his forehead being wrinkled up a little like something is on his mind.

"Well," he says, "it is certainly good to see you, even if you do become an ugly old geezer. I will never think to guzzle your joint if I know it is you. If fact, I will not guzzle your joint, even though this causes me some inconvenience, because," he says, "you have always been aces with me. So now you must help me pick some other joint to guzzle."

Now, I hear of ghosts that like to scare a guy out of his pants, although personally I never meet one, but I never hear that they are interested in the contents of the pants pockets. Even if they are the ghost of Harry the Horse. "Harry," I say, "what would a guy such as yourself be doing working the second storey?"

"Well," Harry the Horse says, "that is a long story. But if I do not tell the story to someone soon I think I will go crazy, and in fact you are just the guy to tell it to, because you remember the way things used to be in 1930."

"Harry," I say, "I have nothing better to do than to hear your story."

And Harry the Horse nods, and says to me like this:

❖　　　❖　　　❖

One day me and Spanish John and Little Isadore all happen to be in the sneezer together, on account of a small misunderstanding about the color of some money we are spending, and I wish to say in passing that this beef is a total crock, as we steal that money fair and square from a bank on Third Avenue, and can we help it if things are so bad that banks are starting to pass out funny money? But anyway there we are in the sneezer, so naturally we call Judge Goldfobber to get us out. As you probably know, Judge Goldfobber is by no means a judge, and never is a judge, and in my line it is a hundred-to-one against him ever being a judge, but he is a lawyer by trade, and he is better than Houdini at getting citizens out of the sneezer, and in fact when it comes to getting out of the sneezer Goldfobber is usually cheaper than buying a real judge, at that.

So we call him and he comes right down and springs us, and then he takes us back uptown to his office and pours us a couple of shots of scotch, and furthermore it is scotch he gets from Dave the Dude, and you know that Dave the Dude handles only the very best merchandise. So we knock them back and then Goldfobber says like this: "Boys, when I spring a guy for bad paper it is my firm policy never to accept my fee in cash. None of you has any gold or securities, so I propose to take it out in trade."

"Judge," I say, "you have always been a good employer, and in fact it seems to me that every time you put a little job our way, we come away with a few bobs for our trouble. Furthermore you are a right gee, because you put down several potatoes to bail us out, and you must know that you have no more chance of seeing us show up in court than Hoover has of seeing another vote. So we are happy to entertain your proposition."

"Well," he says, "it is not exactly a job you can be proud of."

"How do you mean?" Little Isadore asks.

"For one thing, it involves chilling a guy, and an old guy besides, and furthermore he is one of those guys who is so brilliant that he is like a baby. It is not exactly sporting."

"Judge," Spanish John says to him, "I and my friends are suffering greatly from the unemployment situation, because if nobody is working and making money, there is nobody for us to rob, and if there is nobody for us to rob, we are reduced to robbing banks, and you see how that works out. I do not speak for my friends, but I myself will be happy to chill somebody just on general principles, and if it is an old guy that does not shoot back, why, so much the better."

"It involves work," Judge Goldfobber says.

"How do you mean 'work'?"

"Physical exertion. Manual labor. You will have to carry something very much like a phone booth, and which weighs maybe twice as much as a phone booth, down three flights of stairs and deliver it to my place out on the Island."

"Judge," I say, greatly horrified, "we are eternally grateful for what you do for us. But to do manual labor in satisfaction of a debt is perilously close to honest work, and that is more grateful than I, for one, wish to be. However," I say as he starts to frown, "not only am I grateful, but I just remember that you know where Isadore and me bury Boat-Race Benny three years ago, so we will accept your job."

So he gives us an address up in Harlem, and that

night we borrow a truck somebody is not using to go up there.

The job goes down as easy as a doll's drawers, or maybe even easier. The building is a big fancy joint, with a doorman and everything, but the lock on the back door does not give Little Isadore any difficulty, and neither does the lock on the apartment door of the old geezer. The name on his door is "Doctor Philbert Twitchell," so we figure him for a sawbones, except it turns out he is not that kind of doctor, but the professor kind.

Anyway, we stick him up in his bed, and we scare him so bad we nearly save ourselves the trouble of croaking him. We tell him to show us the phone booth, and toots wheat, and he just blinks at us. This Doc Twitchell is about a million years old and bald as an eight ball, and I wish to say I never see another guy like him for blinking. In fact I remember thinking that he will be a handy guy to have around on a hot day, since he keeps a pretty good breeze going, except of course that by the time the next hot day comes around he will not be blinking so good, and is apt to smell bad, besides.

About the time I haul the hammer back on my Roscoe he gives up blinking and gets up and puts on a bathrobe that looks like it belongs to Jack Johnson, and he takes us to the phone booth. It is in a big room way in back of his apartment, and the room is a kind of a lavatory, like in this movie I see when I am ten years old called *Frankenstein,* which I hear they are going to remake as a talkie. Anyway there is all kinds of machines and gadgets and gizmos, and a wire the size of a shotgun barrel taped along the floor from the wall to the bottom of this phone booth. It is the size and shape of a phone booth, but it does not really look much like one, and in fact it makes me think of a stand-up coffin, except for all the wires and things hanging off of it. There is no door in it, so I can see the thing is empty, and it occurs to me that it will make a fair coffin, at that, since we can carry the Doc downstairs in it and save an extra trip.

"Okay," I say. "This is a cinch. Spanish John, you go down and get the dolly out of the back of the truck. Little Isadore, you go along and wait for him at the door, keep lookout whilst I croak the Doc here." At this the Doc starts in blinking a mile a minute. He starts to say something, and then he thinks better of it and waits until Spanish John and Little Isadore are gone, and then he starts talking even faster than he is blinking, which is pretty fast talking indeed. He talks kind of tony, with lots of big fancy words, but I give you the gist:

"Goldfobber the mouthpiece sends you guys to see me, am I right?"

I admit this, and starting putting the silencer on my John Roscoe.

"Would you consider double-crossing Goldfobber?"

"Certainly. What is your proposition?"

"You mean Goldfobber does not tell you?" he says, very surprised.

"Tell me what?"

"This thing you call a phone booth is a time machine."

"You mean like a big clock? Where is the hands?"

"No, no," he says, real excited. "A machine for travelling in time.

"In time for what?"

"No, *through* time! My machine can take you into next week, or next year, or the year after that. It is the only one in the world."

"Well, I never hear of such a machine, at that."

"Of course not," he says. "You and me and that thief Goldfobber are the only three people in the world that know about it."

"Okay," I tell him. "So get to the part about why I should double-cross Goldfobber."

"Don't you see?" he says, blinking away. "You can travel to tomorrow night, read the stock market quotations, and then come back to today and buy everything that is going to go up."

"I do not know too many guys in the stock racket," I tell him, "and furthermore I hear it is a chancy proposition. But if I understand you, I can go to tomorrow night and read the racing results, and then come back and bet on all the winning ponies?" I am commencing to get excited.

"Exactly," he says, jumping up and down a little. "Likewise the World Series, and the football, and the elections, and—the sky is the limit."

By now I am figuring the angles, and I am more excited than somewhat. This is a machine such as a guy could get very rich with, and I am a guy such as likes the idea of being very rich. "Does it work backwards? Can I go back to yesterday, or last week?"

"Hell, no!" he says, or anyway that is what the things he says come down to. "Oh, it can be done," he says, "but I never have the guts to do it, and in fact only a dope will try it. Why—" His voice gets real quiet and solemn, like a funeral. "—you might make a pair of ducks."

I can make no sense of this, but he says it like it is something to be very, very afraid of, and I figure he ought to know. But I decide it does not matter, because I figure going to tomorrow is plenty good enough for me. I point my Roscoe at the Doc. "Prove to me that this machine does like you say."

"Give me your watch," he says, and I do so. "See?" he says. "It is just now exactly five minutes to midnight, am I right?" I look at the watch and he is perfectly right. He puts the watch on the floor of the phone booth. "How long do you figure it is before your associate comes back with the dolly?"

"Well," I tell him, "figuring he has a pint in his pants pocket, and he knows we are in no special hurry, maybe it takes him another five minutes."

"Okay," he says. "So I set the machine for two minutes." He fiddles with some dials and things on the outside of the phone booth, and pushes a button. The light goes way down, like when a guy gets it at Sing Sing, and even before it comes back up I see that the phone booth isn't there anymore. The big wire ends in a plug; the socket for it is gone. It scares me so much I almost scrag the Doc by accident—and now that I think of it, it is a better thing all the way around if I do, at that—but the slug misses him clean. Since I have the silencer on, it is six-to-one that Little Isadore never even hears the shot.

Then I just watch the Doc blink for two minutes, and finally—pop!—the phone booth is back again. My watch is still in it, and the watch is still ticking, but it says that it is still five minutes of midnight. The machine works.

"Say," I tell the Doc, "this is okay. Can you set this thing to go and then come right back again?"

"Certainly," he says. "Watch." He fiddles with it again, and this time when he pushes the button the light and the phone booth both kind of . . . flicker, like a movie. "See?" he says. "It just goes into tomorrow, stays there an hour, and comes right back to the instant it leaves."

My head hurts when I try to think about this. "Okay," I said, "here is what you do. You set that thing to take me into the future. I want to see what the world looks like when the Depression is over, so you better send me a long way. Say, fifty years—they ought to have the country back on its feet by then. Have the phone booth go to 1980, stay there for a whole day, and then come right back to here. You can do this?"

"It's a cinch," he says, blinking up a storm, and he does like I say. "There. Just push that button and off she goes."

"Can't I make it work from inside?"

"Certainly," he says, and shows me another button on the inside. "I am planning to experiment with people," he says, "instead of just objects and wop pigs, when you boys guzzle my joint. In fact I will do it already, except I decide I should patent the phone booth first, and I bring the idea to that gonif Goldfobber, which I now regret."

(Actually he does not call it a phone booth, any more than he uses any of the regular words I am putting in his mouth. What he calls it is—give me a minute—a Chronic Lodge Misplacer, I think he says.)

"What happens to the wop pigs?" I ask him, beginning to get a little nervous.

"Not a thing," he says. "They come back perfectly copacetic and in the pink, and in fact there they are now." And he points, and sure enough over in the corner is a bunch of cages full of little wop pigs, and I am relieved to see that they look happy, and there are no empty cages. "Well," he says, "what do you say? I make you rich and you do not make me dead; you cannot get a better deal than that."

"Sure I can," I say, and his eyelids commence to flutter so fast I can feel the breeze a clear six feet away. The right eye seems to blink faster than the left, so that is the eye I shoot him in. Then I go out and scrag Little Isadore, and I meet Spanish John on the landing where he is communing with his pint and scrag him too, and then I put him on the dolly and carry him upstairs and stretch him out next to Little Isadore. It make me no little sad to see them lying there, because they are my friends a long time, but I cannot help but think how fortunate it is that it is me Doc Twitchell tells his secret to, because otherwise I will be laying there stiff and one of my friends will be standing around feeling sad, and I do not wish a friend of mine to have this sorrow.

Then I go back to the phone booth.

I figure the deal for a cinch. I will go to 1980, and I will go to the Public Library. They got books in there that are records of all the pony-races ever run, and naturally I know where they keep these books since I often have recourse to them in the course of business. I will burgle the joint and heist such books as relate to races from 1930 to 1980, which certainly cannot take me more than a day, and then I will come back to 1930 and find out what it is like to be a millionaire.

So I step into the phone booth and push the button.

All of a sudden it is very dark, and the lights do not come back up, so I figure I maybe blow a fuse, or some such. I step out of the phone booth and light a match, and I almost drop it. The whole room is completely different. Mostly what it is, is empty. The

Doc's body is gone, and so are all the gizmos and gadgets and such, and even the cages full of little wop pigs.

The match goes out, and I think about it, and now I think about it, of course it figures that a joint does not look the same after fifty years, and especially not if you croak the guy who owns it. It does not seem like *any*body owns this joint for a long time, and I figure that for a piece of luck, all things considered.

Until I light the second match and notice the other thing that is missing.

The big wire.

Well, hell, I say to myself, of course it will not still be around after fifty years. So while I am out guzzling the track records I will guzzle a bunch of big wire from a wire place, and a plug as well . . .

Except the light switch does not work when I try it, and it looks like there is no electric in the apartment now, because I keep finding little home-made candles in all the rooms, all burned down. There is nothing else in the joint but junk, and there is no water in the crapper or the faucets, and I commence to get the idea that this building is abandoned. So now I must get the electric turned back on, as well as heist the track records and the wire. Except I do not see how I will get the electric turned on, as I do not happen to be holding any potatoes at the moment, and in fact what I am is broke. To heist potatoes and track records and wire and get the electric turned on, all in one day, is a pretty full day, even for a tough guy such as myself.

But if this is what I must do to be the richest guy in the world, then I will take a crack at it. So I leave, and you know what? Harlem is all full of smokes these days. Oh, you hear about this? Yeah, I guess you will at that. Anyways, not only is Harlem all over smokes, but these are very hostile smokes, such as I never see before. I run into one on the landing, and I show him the equalizer to clear him out of my way, and what does he do but say something about my ma and then haul out an equalizer of his own. It is only good fortune that I escape the shame of being croaked by a smoke, and this shakes me up no little. I pass some other smokes in the street outside, and they all act unfriendly too. One of them tries to tell me I am a Hunkie, which I cannot figure until I see he wears black cheaters and probably is blind. Except he is by no means blind, because he outs with a shiv as long as my foot and tries to put a couple new vents in my suit, and I am forced to break his face.

This brings a whole bunch of smokes, all hollering and carrying on in smoke, and some in spic, and I decide I will leave Harlem for the time being. I run pretty good and build up a good lead, but then I blow it when I decide to steal a heap. I get it hot-wired okay but the shift is all funny and I cannot find the clutch anyplace. So I leave the heap just before these ten dozen yelling smokes catch up, and a few blocks later I find a taxi waiting at a red light and jump in. The jockey starts to give me a hard time, but I show him the Roscoe and tell him to take me where the white people live, and toots wheat, so he shuts up and drives, without putting on the motor even. I try to see how he drives with no clutch, but I cannot see his feet, and besides he never seems to use the shift at all.

While he drives the short I look around. Harlem does not seem to be a class neighborhood anymore, naturally, what with all the smokes living in it, and in fact it is nothing but a dump. Doc Twitchell's

building is by no means the only one abandoned. But
when we get downtown I see that things are not
much better there. Oh, there are some awful fancy
big new buildings here and there, but there are also
a great many buildings just as broken down as the
ones up in Harlem. I see many more winos and
rumdums and hopheads on the street than I remember, and furthermore there is garbage all over the
place in big piles. So I tell the jockey to pull up and
buy a paper, and what do you know? I do not go far
enough forward in time, because it seems the
Depression is still going on, and nobody is looking
to see it get any better. I cannot figure this, because
I ask the jockey and he tells me the president after
Hoover is a Democrat, and furthermore who is it but
the governor of New York, Frank Roosevelt. So I
guess you never know.

It just keeps getting worse. I have the jockey take
me to the Library, only the Library is not where I
left it, and in fact it is a whole new building altogether. I can see that even if I get into this joint, I
cannot find where they now keep the track records
in the dark, and I have no flashlight, so there is
nothing for it but to do a daylight heist in the morning. And it figures I cannot get the electric turned
on or the wire until sun-up, either. So I figure all I
can do now is scare up some potatoes for operating
expenses. Only I decide to scare up a drink first, as
I am all of a sudden very very thirsty. So I take the
jockey's potatoes and tell him to take me to Lindy's.
Only he never hears of Lindy's or of Good-Time
Charlie's, or the Bohemian Club, or any other deadfall
I name, not even the Stork Club. So I tell him I wish
a drink, and he hauls me off and brings me to this
place all full of bright lights and guys wearing dolls'

clothes, and where they wish two bobs for a drink of scotch which is nothing but a shot. In fact, it is in my mind to shoot the jockey for this, except for some reason he is gone when I come out, even though I tell him to wait.

I walk a couple of blocks, figuring to guzzle a few pedestrians, but my luck is terrible, as half of them are broke and the other half shoot back, and one of them actually has the brass to pick my pocket while I am shaking him down and take the rest of the jockey's potatoes, so now I am broke again.

It goes like that all night. I can tell you all manner of stories, like what happens when I go over to Central Park to get a little shut-eye, and what a dump Times Square turns into, but you probably hear all this already and besides I see that you are tired, so I will make a long story short.

So when the Library opens up the next day, I go in and ask this old doll about the track records, and she says they do not have these books anymore. She says they have the information I wish but it is not in books anymore. I know this will sound nutty, but I make her say it twice, very slow: the information is on her crow film. So I ask her to give me some of her crow film, and she does, and what is it but a little tiny thing like a roll of caps, or maybe like a little reel for a movie that is two minutes long, and for all I know nowadays crows do watch such films in this town. She puts it in a machine and it makes words on a screen, like a newsreel, only it does not move unless you make it. I have her get the crow film with the right horse records on it, and I watch how she works it until I figure I can do it myself. So now I must steal not only the drawer full of crow film but the machine to read it; and I am not sure it will fit in the phone booth with me.

But I figure I will cross that bridge when I get to Brooklyn, and I thank the old doll and watch where she puts the drawer full of crow film back, and I go try to price the wire I need. You will not think there can be more than one kind of wire as big around as a shotgun barrel, but it turns out there are several dozen such kinds, and I do not know which kind I want. But I figure I will come back that night after closing and borrow a dozen kinds and try them all.

Then I shake down a necktie salesman for some change and call the electrics, and they tell me that to turn on the electric in that building, for even one night, they have to have a security deposit of no less than two hundred potatoes. This two yards must be in cash, and furthermore there are fire inspectors to be greased, and so forth, and it will take at least a week.

By this time I am commencing to get somewhat discouraged, and in fact I am downright unhappy. That night I go back up to Harlem, with some trivial difficulty, and I sit in that phone booth from eleven-thirty to twelve-thirty, just in case it will still go home without the electric, and it does not. I figure the Doc slips it to me pretty good, and in fact it is a dirty shame I cannot croak him twice, or even three times.

So I figure I am stuck here, and am not apt to become a rich guy after all, and in fact it is time to do a little second-storey work and build up my poke. So I bust your joint, and I wish to know how come, if the Depression is still around, movies get so cheap that you can show talkies in your own joint, with colors yet, and furthermore you can leave them running while you take the air. Also where is the projector?

When Harry the Horse finishes telling me this story, and I finish telling him about television, I get out the old nosepaint and we have a few, and in fact we have more than a few, although Harry the Horse says he once makes better booze in a trash can, and as a matter of fact I know this to be true. A little while after the bottle is empty an idea comes to me, and I say to Harry the Horse like this:

"Harry, you are welcome to stay at my joint as long as you wish, naturally, because you are always aces with me. But if you still wish to go back to 1930 and be a rich guy, I think I can fix it."

"It is too late," he says. "The Doc sets the phone booth to go home after twenty-four hours, and it does not, so I am stuck here even if I get the electric and the wire and the crow film machine, which I figure is about a twenty-to-one shot."

"Harry," I tell him, "you will naturally not know this, but nowadays almost all the clocks in this man's town are on electric, and if you pull out the plug, the clock *stops*. So I figure if we plug the phone booth back in, twenty-four hours after *that* it goes home, with you inside, and maybe also this crow film machine."

Harry thinks this over, and starts to cheer up. "This appeals to me no little," he says, "with or without the crow film machine. I like 1930 better."

I decide maybe Harry the Horse is not so dumb, at that.

"But can you fix the rest?" he asks.

"I think I can."

So I call up my friend Toomey the electrician, who

everybody calls Socket. He is a little agitated at being
woke up at five bells in the morning, but I tell him
there is a couple of guys here that wish to sell a dozen
lids of Hawaiian pot for thirty bobs a lid, and he says,
"On my way," and hangs up.

Harry the Horse wishes this translated. "Well," I
explain, "Prohibition is over since a little after I see
you last—"

Harry is greatly surprised to hear this. "What do
the coppers do for a living?"

"Well, there is this pot, which is nothing but
muggles, only it is now as illegal as booze used to
be. And right now in this man's town there are maybe
six million citizens as are apt to pay sixty bobs for
an ounce of this muggles, and thirty is a very good
price."

Harry the Horse shakes his head at this, and just
then the bell rings and it is none other than Socket,
all out of breath. He is a young guy, but a very good
electrician, and in fact he wires my joint for me when
I get the air condition, and for a young guy he knows
the way things are. He is very aggravated when he
finds that there is no Hawaiian muggles, and in fact
he turns and starts to leave. But when he puts his
hand out to the doorknob he finds a shiv pinning his
sleeve to the door so that he cannot reach the knob,
and when he looks around he sees Harry the Horse
deciding where to put the next one, so Socket decides
he does not wish to reach the knob after all, and says
as much.

So we explain the story to Socket, which uses up
my last bottle of sauce, and he says he is willing to
look the proposition over. When we hit the street I
wonder how we are going to get up to Harlem,
because I am not anxious to take the subway. But

right off we find a hack who is so thoughtless as to park where he cannot make a quick getaway, so when Harry the Horse sticks his John Roscoe in the window of the short there is nothing the jockey can do except get out and give us his short. A few blocks away we change plates, and then we pick up Socket's tools and electric stuff from his joint and head up Broadway at a hell of a clip, and we are in Harlem in no time, or maybe less.

We get into the building with no trouble, and Socket even manages to cop a lid of Mexican muggles from a little skinny smoke we find in the lobby, before we chase the smoke out. Socket puffs up on this muggles while he checks out the electric room in the basement, and likes what he sees in the electric room. "I can power this building for a few days," he tells us. "Alarms will go off downtown, and sooner or later an inspector comes to see what the hell, but with the red tape and all, it has to be a good two or three days before he gets here." He goes ahead and does this, and then he takes a light bulb out of his pouch and puts it in the wall, and it works. He puts away his flashlight and pokes around the basement, and what does he find but a real old hunk of wire, as big around as a shotgun barrel and in every respect such as Harry the Horse describes it, except for the cobwebs. In fact, Socket says he figures it is the original wire, which is tossed down in the basement and forgotten by whoever rents Doc Twitchell's apartment after he croaks. This is water on the wheel of Harry the Horse, who now begins to think maybe his luck is back with him, and to like Socket besides. Harry is very anxious for this to work, because a few minutes before he is obliged to plug a rat the size of a Doberman, and Harry the Horse is thoroughly disgusted with 1980 for letting rats into a class neighborhood like Harlem, smokes or no smokes.

So we go up to the third floor and there is the phone booth, just like Harry the Horse describes it except that there is a hophead sleeping in it. We chase the hophead out and Socket sets the wire back up the way it is supposed to be, and plugs it in. Right away the phone booth starts to hum, and Harry the Horse gets a great big smile on his pan.

Socket puts a light bulb in the ceiling and turns it on, and then he looks the phone booth over. "I cannot figure much of this," he says, "but this part here has to be the delay timer. If you want to go back right now you just twist this back to zero—"

"Not yet," Harry the Horse says. "It is nice to know I do not have to wait twenty-four hours, but I am not yet ready. I must go guzzle the crow film and the machine."

All of a sudden Harry the Horse frowns, like he sees a fly in the ointment. I begin to see the same fly too, and so does Socket, because he speaks up and says like this:

"Harry, I know what you are thinking. You do not wish to leave us here while you go rob my crow film—"

"What do you mean, your crow film?" Harry asks angrily. "It is my crow film."

"Of course," Socket says real quick. "The point is, you are afraid if you leave us behind with the machine, it may not be here when you get back, or us either for that matter, and I am honest enough to admit that this is at least a ten-to-one shot. If you are as honest, you will admit that what you think you will do about this is scrag us both. Is this not so?"

"I like your style, kid," Harry the Horse says to

him, "but I will admit that this seems like the good thing to do."

"I thank you for your honesty," Socket says. "You will understand that I am altogether opposed to this proposition, on general principles. So here is my thought: how about if I come with you while you swipe the crow film machine, and generally be of assistance (for it is sure to be heavy), and meanwhile our mutual friend here," meaning me, "will keep watch over the phone booth and keep the junkies out of it. He is not apt to take the lam with it, on account of he is an old geezer who cannot cut it in 1930 without a joint or a job, and besides if he does you will surely scrag me and I am his friend."

"This sounds jake to me," Harry the Horse decides, so off they go together, hurrying a bit because it is a little past six bells in the morning and the sun will be up soon. They come back in about an hour with a drawer full of crow film and the machine for it, and while Harry the Horse checks to make sure the machine fits in the phone booth, Socket looks over the phone booth some more. "I think I begin to figure this out," he says.

"Frankly," Harry the Horse says, "and I hope you will not be offended, I am not so sure. You say if I twist this little dingus here I go right back where I start, right?"

"Right to the moment you leave," Socket agrees.

"I am reluctant," Harry the Horse says, "to tamper with the way Doc Twitchell leaves the machine, and then test the result with my personal body. It is more than half a day until the phone booth is supposed to go back—suppose I get there a half day early?"

"That is impossible," Socket tells him. "That would be a pair of ducks."

Harry the Horse frowns. "That is exactly what I mean. I wish to have no truck whatsoever with these ducks, as Doc Twitchell tells me they are bad medicine."

By this time I am tired of hanging around in Harlem with Harry the Horse, and I do not care a fig if he does get a pair of ducks, or even a pair of goats or chickens. "Harry," I say, "my good friend Socket knows all about this science jazz. He reads all the rocket ship stuff and you can rely on him. It is a piece of cake."

Maybe I say it too enthusiastic, because Harry frowns even more. "If it is so safe," he says to me, "why do you not be the one who tries it out? In fact," he says, "I think this is a terrific idea."

Now, this horrifies me no little, and in fact more than somewhat, but I am not about to let on to Harry the Horse that I am horrified, or he is apt to figure I care more about myself than him, and become insulted. So I swallow and head for the phone booth.

"As soon as you get there and see that everything is copacetic," Harry tells me, "you push the button again. It is still set the same way, so it should bring you right back here. Do not monkey with it."

"Wait!" Socket yells, and this seems like a terrific idea to me. "Listen, Harry," he says, "I figure this gizmo will take him back to the very instant he leaves, or maybe a split second after. But if he then pushes the button again right away, it brings him forward the same amount of time as before—and he arrives a second after you do, a day and a half ago. Except that there is already a phone booth here, and nowhere for his to *go*, so there is a big explosion."

My blood pressure now goes up into the paint

cards. Harry thinks about this, and I can see it is a strain for him. "So how do we do this?"

"Well," Socket says, "I think I get the hang of this phone booth, and if I am right this dial here is for years, and this one is for days, and this one is hours, and so on. See, the years one is on fifty, and the rest are in neutral."

"So?"

"So all he has to do when he gets back to 1930 is move the days dial forward one notch, and the hours dial ahead seven notches, and the minutes, say thirty to be on the safe side, and he arrives here about fifteen minutes from now."

Harry the Horse looks at me. "Do you get that?" he says.

"Yeah," I tell him, a little distracted because something just occurs to me.

"Listen," Socket says to me, "for the love of Pete do not fail to set the delay timer again before you push the button to come back here. Anything over five minutes is probably fine. Otherwise as soon as you get here you slingshot right back to 1930 again."

"Got you," I say, and he turns the delay gizmo back to zero.

All of a sudden the lights get dim like a brown-out, and when they come back up again Harry the Horse and Socket are nowhere to be seen. What is to be seen is a lot of gadgets and gizmos and little wop pigs and an old dead guy I know is Doc Twitchell.

I will be damned, I say to myself, it works.

Perhaps I should do like I promise Harry the Horse and go right back. If I do not arrive back at the right time he is apt to get angry and scrag my young friend Socket. But I figure I can reset the dials to any time I want, and if it does not work out right it is Socket's fault for giving me the bum steer.

And besides, I cannot help myself.

I go into the livingroom and get some subway tokens and a couple of bobs from Little Isadore's pants pocket, and I take the A train down to Broadway.

Broadway is just beginning to jump when I get there, on account of it is just past midnight, and I wish to tell you it looks *swell*. The guys and dolls are all out taking the air, and I see faces I do not see for a long long time. I see Lance McGowan, and Dream Street Rose, and Bookie Bob, and Miss Missouri Martin, and Dave the Dude with Miss Billy Perry on his arm, and Regret the Horseplayer, and Nicely-Nicely Jones, and the Lemon Drop Kid, and Waldo Winchester the newspaper scribe, and all kinds of people. I see Joe the Joker give Frankie Ferocious a hotfoot while Frankie is taking a shine from a little smoke. I see Rusty Charlie punch a draft horse square in the kisser and stretch it in the street. I buy an apple from Madame La Gimp. I find the current location of Nathan Detroit's permanent floating crap game, and lose a few bobs. I stick my noodle into Lindy's, and I watch a couple of dolls take it off at the Stork Club, the way dolls used to take it off, and I even have a drink at Good-Time Charlie's, even though Good-Time Charlie naturally does not recognize me and serves me the same liquor he serves his customers. You know something? It is the best booze I taste in fifty years.

I see people and places and things that I say good-bye to a long time ago, and it feels so good that after a while I haul off and bust out crying.

Somehow I never seem to bump into myself—my thirty-year-old self—while I am walking around, and I guess this is just as well, at that. After a while I decide that I am awake a long time for a guy my age, so I walk over to Central Park and take a snooze near the pond. When I wake up it is just coming on daylight, and I am hungry and there is very little of Little Isadore's dough left, so I take the A train back up to Harlem and sneak in the back door of Doc Twitchell's building again. When I get back to the phone booth it is just about half past seven bells, so I set the dial ahead one day and no hours and no minutes, and then I set the delay thing and push the button.

The lights go down and up and there are Harry the Horse and Socket again. Socket looks very glad to see me, and for that matter so does Harry the Horse. "It works great," I tell them, and step out.

"This is good news," Harry says, "because I am commencing to get impatient. Socket, I am sorry I do not trust you. Both of you are right gees, and you both assist me more than somewhat, and I tell you what I will do. When I get back home and become a rich guy, I will put half of the first million I make into a suitcase, and I will bring the suitcase to the First National Bank downtown and tell them to surrender it to you guys in fifty years, and you can go right down there today and get it. How is that for gratitude?"

Socket's face gets all twisted up funny for a minute, like he wants to say something and does not want to say it, all at the same time. "Harry," I say, "do you ever come back yourself?"

"Naw," he says. "This stuff gives me the willies, and 1980 you can keep. As soon as I get back home I shoot up this phone booth until it does not work anymore. I have all I need to be a rich guy, and if anybody else gets ahold of the phone booth, maybe it gets around and they start not having horse races anymore or something. So this is good-bye." He puts the crow film machine and the drawer full of crow films in the booth, and steps in with them.

"Well, Harry," I say, "I wish to thank you for your generosity. Half a million bobs is pretty good wages for a electric guy and a dago pig. Enjoy your riches and good-bye."

He has Socket move the delay gizmo back to zero, and the lights go down and up again, and that is the last I ever see of Harry the Horse, any way you look at it.

"Socket," I start to say, "I hope you do not think for a minute that there is any half a million clams waiting at the bank for us—"

"I *know* there is not," he says, and he shows me a little teeny light bulb the size of a peanut. "I do not like the way this mug talks about plugging people such as yourself and me, so while he and I are guzzling the crow film machine I decide it will be a great gag if I take this bulb out when he is not looking, and sure enough he never knows any different. I regret this later when he speaks of a million iron men, but I cannot think of a tactful way to bring the matter up, and he still has the gat, so I let it ride. Without this bulb," he says, "Harry the Horse cannot read the crow film, and they do not make this bulb fifty years ago."

Well, at this I am so surprised that I never get around to telling Socket Toomey why it is that *I* am so certain that are no half a million potatoes waiting for us at the First National Bank. And perhaps

I even feel a little guilty, too, considering that Harry the Horse gives me the seven happiest hours of my life.

Because before I get on the A train to go back up to Harlem, fifty years ago, I call up Judge Goldfobber at his place out on the Island; and I tell him that the reason Harry the Horse and Spanish John and Little Isadore are late bringing the phone booth is because they are planning to double-cross him and keep it for themselves. Who Judge Goldfobber thinks I am, and why I am calling him, is anybody's guess—but I know he believes me, and furthermore makes very good time in from the Island, because I can remember back almost fifty years ago to when I am in the bleachers the day a real judge gives Judge Goldfobber the hot squat, on account of his personal revolver matches up with six slugs they dig out of Harry the Horse.

HIGH INFIDELITY

Ruby hung at the teetering edge of orgasm for as long as she could bear it, mewing with pleasure and with joy. Then control and consciousness spun away together: she clenched his hair with both hands, yanked in opposite directions, and went thundering over the edge. Her triumphant cry drowned out his triumphant growl; she heard neither. When the sweet explosion had subsided, she lay marinating in the afterglow, faintly surprised as always to be still alive. Her fingers toyed aimlessly with the curly hair they had just been yanking. The tongue at her clitoris gave one last, lazy lick, and a shudder rippled up her body. I am, she thought vaguely, a very lucky woman.

After a suitable time her husband lifted his head and smiled fondly up at her. "Who was I this time?" he asked.

"Sam Hamill," she said happily. "And you were terrific."

"My dear, your taste is as good as your taste is good," Paul Meade said.

She smiled. "Damn right. I married you, didn't I?"

"Was I in this one?"

"Watching from the doorway. Even bigger and harder than usual."

He climbed up her body. "Really?" She reached down to guide him into her, and he was even bigger and harder than usual. They both grinned at that, and gasped together as he slid inside. "I'll bet my eyes were the size of floppy discs."

"The old-fashioned big ones," she agreed. "Who can I be for you now?"

"Anonymous grateful groupie," he murmured in her ear, beginning to move his hips. "The Process saved your child's life, and you're thanking me as emphatically as you can."

If Ruby Meade had an insecurity, this was it. She knew that Paul got such offers—his work and his achievement made it inevitable—and she supposed that they must be uniquely hard to turn down. But she had trusted her husband utterly and implicitly for more than two decades now. "Oh, *doctor,*" she said in an altered voice, and locked her legs around his familiar back. "Anything you want, doctor, any way you want me." She suggested some ways in which he might want her, and his tempo increased with each suggestion, and soon she no longer had the breath to speak. Automatically he covered both her ears, the way she liked him to, with his left cheek and his left hand, and dropped into third gear. When he was very close, he lifted his head up as he always did, replacing his cheek with his right hand, and murmured "Give

me your tongue," and as always she gave him all the
tongue she had, and he sucked it into his mouth with
something just short of too much force as he galloped
to completion. He roared as his sperm sprayed into
her, and with the ease of long practice she brought
her legs down under his and pointed her toes so that
his last strokes could bring her off too.

I am, Ruby thought vaguely sometime later, an
especially lucky woman.

Paul rolled off with his usual care and reached for
his cigarettes. "'They say,'" he sang softly, puffing one
alight, "'Ruby you're like a dream, not always what
you seem . . .'"

"I love you too, baby."

They shared a warm smile, and then he pulled his
eyes away. "I have to go to Zurich tomorrow," he said.
"Be gone about a week, maybe a week and a half.
They called while you were working."

"A *week*—?" she began, and caught herself.

"I know," he said, misunderstanding. "It's a long
time. But it can't be helped. It seems they tried The
Process over there with a donor *of the opposite sex*.
Rather important official, and they didn't dare wait
for another donor. I want to check it out—I expect
it to be fascinating."

I am, Ruby thought, going to kill him.

"Besides," he said, "think how thirsty I'll be for you
when I get home. And how thirsty you'll be for me."

"Yes," she said, her voice convincing, "that'll be
nice."

"I'll be moving around a lot," he said, "but if you
need to get hold of me in an emergency, just get in
touch with Sam. He'll know where I am day to day."

"Okay," she said, thinking briefly that it would serve
him right if she did. Get in touch with Sam. Paul's

tendency toward automatic punning had, over the
years, rubbed off on her. She was ashamed of the
rogue thought at once, but her disappointment
remained.

She examined that disappointment the next morning, over a cup of caff, after she had kissed him good-
bye and sent him on his way.

It was not the trip itself she minded. He had been
away for longer periods before, and would be again;
the biophysicist whose work had made brain-transplant
a simple and convenient procedure would always be
in demand, and he refused as many invitations as he
possibly could. Nor did she envy him the trip; one
of the reasons she had become a writer was that she
liked squatting in her own cave, alone with her
thoughts; most strange places and strange people
made her uneasy. She was not truly jealous of his
groupies either, not seriously—she knew that she
would get the full benefit of whatever erotic charge
he got from them. (Oh, anyone could be tempted
beyond their ability to withstand . . . but she knew
from long experience that Paul was wise enough and
honest enough with himself not to get into such
situations. He was much more likely to be mugged
than seduced, and he had never been mugged.)
Besides, she got propositions of her own in her fan
mail.

No, it was the timing of the trip that gave her this
terrible hollow-stomach feeling.

He had forgotten.

How *could* he forget? Next Monday, the eighteenth
of July, 1999, was not only her forty-fifth birthday,
but their twentieth anniversary.

To be sure, he had been busier this last year, since

the news of his brain-stem matching process had become public knowledge, than ever before in their lives. His grasp on minutiae had begun to slip; he tended to be absentminded at times now. Nonetheless, *he should have remembered.*

She finished her caff and looked at his going-away present. As was their custom when he went on a trip, they had given each other erotic videotapes; "a little something to keep you company," was the ritual phrase. The one she had given him was a homemade job, featuring her in a nurse's uniform (at least at the outset), since she knew that nurses figured prominently in his fantasy life. Paul and Ruby had made a few erotic tapes together—most couples did nowadays—but somehow, from a vestige of old-fashioned shyness, perhaps, she had never made a solo tape for him until now. She had intended it for an anniversary present, one of several she had hidden away, and she resented a little not getting to see his reactions as he premiered it. But there had been no time to slip out to the store and pick up something else before his semiballistic had lifted for Zurich.

In fact, she had secretly hoped that he would express surprise at her having a present on hand for an unexpected trip, thereby forcing her to explain. But he truly was getting absentminded, for he had simply thanked her for the gift and put it into his luggage.

She unwrapped his gift now. It was a thoughtful selection; from the still on the box-cover she could see that it starred an actress she liked, a woman who had the same general build, coloration, and hairstyle as Ruby, and generally seemed to share an interest in multiple partners. She would probably enjoy the tape—would probably *have* enjoyed it, rather, if it had

been given to her on July eighteenth. Somehow that
made it worse.

She tossed the tape into the back of a drawer,
poured more caff, and went into her office to forget her resentment in work. Working on a novel
always cheered her when she was down; her characters' problems always seemed so much more
immediate and urgent than her own.

He'll remember, she thought just before sinking
entirely into the warm glow of creation. Sometime
between now and next Monday he'll see a calendar,
or something will jog his memory, and boy will he
be contrite when he calls! Why, he might even can-
cel and come right home.

But he did not call that night, or Friday night, or
Saturday night, and by Sunday she had stopped
believing that he would.

So she thought of calling him. But if she told him,
reminded him of the date, she would spoil his trip.
And if she didn't, she would hurt even more when
she hung up. Besides, to contact Paul she would have
to go through Sam Hamill, and if she called Sam he
would want to come over and chat—Sam was a lonely
divorcé—and a wise instinct told her not to spend
time with a single man, about whom she had frequently fantasized, at a time when she was mad as
hell at her absent husband. It was wisdom of the kind
that had kept Paul and Ruby's marriage alive for
twenty years.

So she took refuge in logic. My husband is a good
and kind and considerate man who has dedicated
himself to making me happy since 1979. He is as good
and as successful in his profession as I am in mine.
He is trustworthy and responsible. He is a gifted lover

and a valued friend, and surely I cannot be so irrational as to stack up against all that something as
trivial as a single memory-lapse, and I'm going to kill
the son of a bitch if he hasn't called me in ten seconds, I swear I will.

Unfortunately, she finished her novel that afternoon.

Late that night she selected one of her favorite
tapes, an "old reliable" that starred the actress who
vaguely resembled her, and popped it into the deck.
But halfway to her orgasm the tape reminded her of
Paul's going-away gift, which reminded her of her gift
to him and the warm glow in which it had been
recorded, the happy expectation of sharing it with him
on their anniversary. Suddenly, and for Ruby unusually, orgasm was unattainable. Shortly she gave up,
popped the tape, and cried herself to sleep.

And of course the next day was Monday. She woke
sad and stiff and horny in equal proportions, and her
house had never seemed emptier. Three times before
lunch she was strongly tempted to call him, once
coming so close as to put on make-up preparatory
to getting his number from Sam. But she could not.
She thought of rereading the new book to see if it
was any good, but knew she should give it a week
to seep out of her short-term memory before tack-
ling it. At four in the afternoon the phone rang and
she ran the length of the house . . . to find that the
call was from their son Tom in Luna City. He wanted
to wish them both a happy anniversary and her a
happy birthday, and he expressed great tactless surprise that Paul was away from home on this day of
days. She loved Tom dearly, but he was no diplomat,
and although she kept a cheerful mien through the
conversation, she hung up in black depression. It had

occurred to her briefly to have *Tom* call Paul, but it was not fair to involve the boy, and besides, he could not really afford a second interplanetary call. But an opportunity just out of reach is even worse than no opportunity at all.

Finally she decided that horniness was churning up her emotions unnecessarily. What she wanted, of course, was Paul, his lips and fingers and penis. She reckoned that the closest available substitute was to masturbate to the new tape he had given her. But her subconscious recalled her failure of the night before; she found herself taking the slidewalk to a pharmacy for a tube of Jumpstarts. It was a particularly hot day; the sun baked thoughts and feelings from her brain, and she was grateful to get back indoors again.

Ruby had never taken libido-enhancers in her life before, had never expected to need to. But she was in a go-to-hell mood, she was forty-five and alone on her anniversary, and she was determined to have herself a good time if it killed her. She took two Jumpstarts from the tube and washed them down with vodka. Then she got the new tape and took it into the bedroom, whistling softly. She stripped quickly. As she broke open the seal on the tape box, the drug smacked her, suddenly and hard: the *hollow* feeling in her stomach moved downward about a third of a meter, and she felt herself smiling a smile that Paul was going to regret having missed. She slid the tape home into the slot, acutely conscious of the sexual metaphor therein, and rummaged in her nighttable for her favorite vibrator, the one that strapped to her pubis and left both hands free. As she finished putting it on, she started to the window to polarize it. But when she was halfway there the TV screen lit

up with the tape's teaser, and she stopped in her
tracks. Her first impulse was to laugh—when Paul
heard about this, he would just die!—which sparked
her second impulse, to burst into tears, but both of
these were washed away in an elapsed time of about
half a second by her third impulse, which was to
switch on the vibrator and jump into bed. No, she
corrected just in time, the other way round!

The actor who shared the screen with her
doppelganger was an unknown. Not only had she
never seen him before, the tape's producers had not
seen fit to use his face on the cover. Paul could not
have known. But the resemblance that the star bore
to Ruby was nothing compared to the resemblance
that this rookie bore to Sam Hamill.

Jumpstart is a time-release drug. It keeps the user
on a rising crest of excitement for anywhere from a
half hour to an hour before it permits climax. The
tape was perhaps twenty minutes along, in the midst
of an especially delicious scenario, when Ruby thought
she heard a noise outside her bedroom window. She
cried out and tore her eyes from the screen, and was
not sure whether or not she caught a flicker of a head
pulling away from view. At once she put the tape on
pause and darkened the screen, her pulse hammering in her ears, and decided she should grab a robe
and then phone the police. No, dammit, the other
way round! Occasionally the MD plates on the car
in the garage attracted a junkie. She shut down the
vibrator to hear better.

The front door chimed.

Awash in adrenaline, she grabbed her robe, got the
family pistol and went to the door. She activated the
camera—and this time she did burst out laughing.
Standing on her doorstep, looking not in the least like

a junkie or a man who had just been peering in a lady's bedroom window, was Sam.

Either the drug is making me hear things, she decided, or Sam scared him away. She safetied the pistol and put it aside, and activated the door mike. "Hi, Sam. What's up?"

"Hi, Ruby. Nothing much. Paul asked me to look in on you while he was away."

He did, did he? she thought, and without thinking about what she was doing she shrugged on the robe and let him in.

She had forgotten what she must look and smell like. As he cleared the door he raised his eyebrows and said, "Oh, I—uh, I hope I'm not . . . disturbing you."

She blushed and then recovered. "Not at all, Sam, really. What are you drinking?"

"Anything cold would be wonderful," he said gratefully. "I've been walking for hours. God, it's hot out there. Look, do you suppose I could use your shower before we get talking?"

"Of course. You know where it is. Wups—half a minute."

She went quickly to the bedroom, shut the door behind her, popped the tape and put it and its box under the bed. After a second's hesitation she took off the vibrator and put that under the bed too. Then she adjusted the air unit to sweep the musk from the room, opened the door, and told him to come ahead. She was dimly aware that she was on dangerous ground. But she heard herself say, "I'll bring you that drink," as he disappeared into the master bathroom.

She was back with the drink nearly at once. She saw her hand reach for the bathroom doorknob, and forced it to knock instead. "Here's a knock for you," she punned, and he reached out for the drink. "Thanks, Ruby." She glimpsed a third of his bare upper torso and kept her face straight with a great effort until the door had closed again. Then she stood there, wrestling with her thoughts, until she heard the shower start up. The urge to go through that door was nearly overwhelming.

Well, she thought, there's only one way to defuse this. She went to her bed and stretched out on it. She switched the TV to the movie channel with the sound suppressed. I'm perfectly safe until the water stops, she thought, and when it does I just turn the sound up and pull the robe over me. Between my hair-trigger and this damned drug, there should be plenty of time. Reassured, she parted the robe and began to masturbate furiously. Just a door away, she thought wildly, that's the closest I've been to really cheating since I wrecked my first marriage.

The bathroom door opened and he emerged, dripping wet, the shower still roaring behind him.

They both froze in shock. She could see each individual water droplet on his body with total clarity, could see her tiny reflection in half a hundred of them, dancing with reflected TV light. His hair was still mostly dry. His erection was rampant. There was a mole just below his left ribs. She knew she would never forget the sight of him as long as she lived. "Was there something you wanted?" she heard herself say.

It took him two tries to get his voice working. "I won't lie to you, Ruby. I was looking for your laundry hamper."

Her weirdness quotient had been exceeded long since. "My laundry hamper."

"I was jerking off in the shower, and suddenly I

wanted something that smelled like you. I've wanted you for a long time, Ruby—you know that."

His penis twitched with his pulse. It had a different curve than Paul's. She spread her legs wide, and framed her vagina with her fingers. "Do you think this will smell enough like me, Sam?"

He came to her at once.

In the midst of it all, she momentarily regained enough rationality to be stunned at how good it was. One of the things that had helped her overcome the infrequent temptations of the last twenty years had been the awareness that on a purely physical level, no brief encounter with a stranger could ever be as satisfying as what she got from a husband who had devoted himself to a study of her body, of her likes and dislikes and her unique personal erogenous zones. Why, the logic went, risk all that for a seven-second spasm that was bound to be inferior? As Paul liked to say, familiarity breeds content.

She had failed, she now saw, to allow for the possibility of telepathy. Or rather, for the possibility that telepathy might come to pass between two people who had not spent years working on it. Sam seemed to sense her desires almost before she did, or else miraculously had precisely dovetailing desires of his own. Nor was he catering to her; there was a delicious selfishness in the way he plundered her.

She revelled in the *newness* of him, glorified in the discovery of hair where she was not accustomed to finding any, of bones and muscles knit together in unfamiliar ways, of an unmistakeably differently shaped penis, a mouth that tasted different. She had always known that variety was sweet, but in the more than two decades since she had foresworn it she had not thought she missed it. Now it enraptured her. And there was an extra fillip to her joy, for she had only had two other Caucasians in her life, and one of those a woman, and the straight hair snarled in her fingers now was a sweet mystery. For the first time in her life she came with her legs up in the air, and clawed deep tracks in his back without knowing it.

When she could see and hear and think again, she realized that he was still in her, still hard, still thrusting. All at once she was horrified at herself and what she had done. It was in her mind to expel him and roll away, to stop short at least of that one final symbolic infidelity, the acceptance of someone else's sperm. She wanted to do so very much. But she could not do it to Sam—poor, dear Sam, who had not asked to be involved in her problems, and had gone too far to stop now. She saw that she must, for her honor, do her very best to bring him off, and then send him home and never never never be alone with him again.

Which gave it all a sort of bittersweet poignance that, after a short time, was startlingly erotic—she felt herself being caught up again in the passion she was dutifully trying to fake. His knowing hands caressed her flanks, came up to knead her breasts against his chest, slid up her throat to her hair. Her breath came in noisy gulps, and she knew she was getting close again. His hands left her hair then and curled over both her ears, a split second after he murmured "Give me your tongue," and automatically she did and as he sucked it hard between his lips and came like gangbusters her eyes opened wide as they could go and looked into his from a distance of a few centimeters. His eyes were sparkling. She clutched at the top of his head and felt where the scalp flap had been resutured, and as his hands came away from her ears and went down to push her legs out straight beneath

him she heard him whisper in her open mouth,
"Happy Anniversary darling—Sam said to give you his
best," and her heart—there is no other way to say
it—came.

RUBBER SOUL

But I don't believe in this stuff, he thought, enjoying himself hugely. *I said I didn't, weren't you listening?*

He sensed amusement in those around him—Mum, Dad, Stuart, Brian, Mal, and the rest—but not in response to his attempt at irony. It was more like the amusement of a group of elders at a young man about to lose his virginity, amusement at his too-well-understood bravado. It was too benevolent to anger him, but it did succeed in irritating him. He determined to do this thing as well as it had ever been done.

Dead easy, he punned. *New and scary and wonderful, that's what I'm good at. Let's go!*

Then the source of the bright green light came that one increment nearer, and he was transfixed.

Oh!

Time stopped, and he began to understand.

And was grabbed by the scruff of the neck and yanked backwards. Foot of the line for you, my lad! He howled his protest, but the light began to recede; he felt himself moving backwards through the tunnel, slowly at first but with constant acceleration. He clutched at Dad and Mum, but for the second time they slipped through his fingers and were gone. The walls of the tunnel roared past him, the light grew faint, and then all at once he was in interstellar space, and the light was lost among a million billion other pinpoints. A planet was below him, rushing up fast, a familiar blue-green world.

Bloody hell, he thought. *Not again!*

Clouds whipped up past him. He was decelerating, somehow without stress. Landscape came up at him, an immense sprawling farm. He was aimed like a bomb at a large three-storey house, but he was decelerating so sharply now that he was not afraid. Sure enough, he reached the roof at the speed of a falling leaf—and sank gracefully through the roof, and the attic, finding himself at rest just below the ceiling of a third-floor room.

Given its rural setting, the room could hardly have been more incongruous. It looked like a very good Intensive Care Unit, with a single client. Two doctors garbed in traditional white gathered around the figure on the bed, adjusting wires and tubes, monitoring terminal readouts, moving with controlled haste.

The room was high-ceilinged; he floated about six feet above the body on the bed. He had always been nearsighted. He squinted down, and recognition came with a shock.

Christ! You're joking! I done *that bit.*

He began to sink downward. He tried to resist, could not. The shaven skull came closer, enveloped him. He gave up and invested the motor centers, intending to use this unwanted body to kick and punch and scream. Too late he saw the trap: the body was full of morphine. He had time to laugh with genuine appreciation at this last joke on him, and then consciousness faded.

After a measureless time he woke. Nothing hurt; he felt wonderful and lethargic. Nonetheless he knew from experience that he was no longer drugged, at least not heavily. Someone was standing over him, an old man he thought he knew.

"Mister Mac," he said, mildly surprised.

The other shook his head. "Nope. He's dead."

"So am I."

Another deadpan headshake from the old man. "Dirty rumor. We get 'em all the time, you and I."

His eyes widened. The voice was changed, but unmistakable. "Oh my God—it's *you!*"

"I often wonder."

"But you're *old.*"

"So are you, son. Oh, you don't look it, I'll grant you that, but if I told you how old you are you'd laugh yourself spastic, honest. Here, let me lift your bed."

The bed raised him to a half-sitting position, deliciously comfortable. "So you froze me carcass and then brought me back to life?"

The old man nodded. "Me and him." He gestured behind him.

The light was poor, but he could make out a figure seated in the darkness on the far side of the room. "Who—?"

The other stood and came forward slowly.

My God, was his first thought. *It's me!* Then he

squinted—and chuckled. "What do you know? The family Jules. Hello, son."

"Hello, Dad."

"You're a man grown, I see. It's good to see you. You look good." He ran out of words.

The man addressed began to smile, and burst into tears and fled the room.

He turned back to his older visitor. "Bit of a shock, I expect."

They looked at each other for an awkward moment. There were things that both wanted to say. Neither was quite ready yet.

"Where's Mother?" he asked finally.

"Not here," the old man said. "She didn't want any part of it."

"Really?" He was surprised, not sure whether or not to be hurt.

"She's into reincarnation, I think. This is all blasphemy and witchcraft to her. She cooperated—she gave us permission, and helped us cover up and all. But she doesn't want to hear about it. I don't know if she'll want to see you, even."

He thought about it. "I can understand that. I promised Mother once I'd never haunt her. Only fair. She still makin' music?"

"I don't think so."

There was another awkward silence.

"How's the wife?" he asked.

The old man winced slightly. "Gone."

"I'm sorry."

"Sorriest thing I've seen all day, son. You comfy?"

"Yeah. *How about Sean?*"

"He doesn't know about this yet. His mother decided not to burden him with it while he was growing up. But you can see him if you want, in a few days. You'll like him, he's turned out well. He loves you."

A surge of happiness suffused him, settled into a warm glow. To cover it he looked around the room, squinting at the bewildering array of machines and instruments. "This must have set you back a packet."

The old man smiled for the first time. "What's the good of being a multimillionaire if you can't resurrect the dead once in a while?"

"Aye, I've thought that a few times meself." He was still not ready to speak his heart. "What about the guy that got me?"

"Copped it in the nick. Seems a lot of your best fans were behind bars."

"Why'd he do it?"

"Who knows? Some say he thought he was you, and you were an impostor. Some say he just wanted to be somebody. He said God told him to do it, 'coz you were down on churches and that."

"Oh, Jesus. The silly fucker." He thought for a time. "You know that one I wrote about bein' scared, when I was alone that time?"

"I remember."

"Truest words I ever wrote. God, what a fuckin' prophet! 'Hatred and jealousy, gonna be the death of me.'"

"You had it backwards, you know."

"How do you mean?"

"Nobody ever had a better reason to hate you than Jules."

He made no reply.

"And nobody ever had better reason to be jealous of you than me."

Again he was speechless.

"But it was him thought it up in time, and me

pulled it off. His idea and enthusiasm. My money. Maybe nobody else on Earth could have made that much nicker drop off the books. So you got that backwards, about them bein' the *death* of you." He smiled suddenly. "Old Jules. Just doin' what I told him to do, really."

"Makin' it better."

The old man nodded. "He let you under his skin, you see."

"Am I the first one they brought back, then?"

"One of the first half-dozen. That Wilson feller in California got his daughter back. It's not exactly on the National Health."

"And nobody knows but you and Jules? And Mother?"

"Three doctors. My solicitor. A cop in New York used to know, a Captain, but he died. And George and Ringo know, they send their best."

He winced. "I was rough on George."

"That you were, son. He forgives you, of course. Nobody else knows in all the wide world."

"Christ, that's a relief. I thought I was due for another turn on the flaming cupcake. Can you imagine if they fuckin' *knew*? It'd be like the last time was *nothing*."

It was the old man's first real grin, and it melted twenty years or more from his face. "Sometimes when I'm lying awake I get the giggles just thinking about it."

He laughed aloud, noting that it did not hurt to laugh. "Talk about upstaging Jesus!"

They laughed together, the old man and the middle-aged man. When the laugh ended, they discovered to their mutual surprise that they were holding hands. The irony of that struck them both

simultaneously. But they were both of them used to
irony that might have stunned a normal man, and
used to sharing such irony with each other; they did
not let go. And so now there was only the last question to be asked.

"Why did you do it, then? Spend all that money
and all that time to bring me back?"

"Selfish reasons."

"Right. Did it ever occur to you that you might
be calling me back from something important?"

"I reckoned that if I could pull it off, then it was
okay for me to do it."

He thought wistfully of the green light . . . but he
was, for better or worse, truly alive now. Which was
to say that he wanted to stay alive. "Your instincts
were always good. Even back in the old scufflin' days."

"I didn't much care, if you want to know the truth
of it. You left me in the lurch, you know. It was the
end of the dream, you dying, and everybody reckoned I was the one broke us up so it was my fault
somehow. I copped it all. My music turned to shit
and they stopped comin' to hear it, I don't remember which happened first. It all went sour when you
snuffed it, lad. You had to go and break my balls in
that last interview . . ."

"That *was* bad karma," he agreed. "Did you call
me back to haunt me, then? Do you want me to go
on telly and set the record straight or something?"

The grip on his hand tightened.

"I called you back because you're a better
songwriter than I am. Because I miss you." The old
man did not cry easily. "Because I love you." He
broke, and wept unashamedly. "I've always loved you,
Johnny. It's shitty without you around."

"Oh Christ, I love you too, Paulie." They

embraced, clung to each other and wept together for some time.

At last the old man released him and stepped back. "It's a rotten shame we're not gay. We always did make such beautiful music together."

"Only the best fuckin' music in the history of the world."

"We will again. The others are willing. Nobody else would ever know. No tapes, nothing. Just sit around and play."

"You're incorrigible." But he was interested. "Are you serious? How could you possibly keep a thing like that secret? No bloody way—"

"It's been a *long* time," the old man interrupted. "You taught me, you taught all three of us, a long time ago, how to drop off the face of the earth. Just stop making records and giving interviews. They don't even come 'round on anniversaries any more. It'll be dead easy."

He was feeling somewhat weary. "How . . . how long has it been?"

"Since you snuffed it? Get this—I told you it'd give you a laugh. It's been two dozen years."

He worked it out, suddenly beginning to giggle. "You mean, I'm—?"

The old man was giggling too. "Yep."

He roared with laughter. "Will you still feed me, then?"

"Aye," the old man said, "And I'll always need you, too."

Slowly he sobered. The laugh had cost him the last of his strength. He felt sleep coming. "Do you really think it'll be good, old friend? Is it gonna be *fun?*"

"As much fun as whatever you've been doing for the last twenty-four years? I dunno. What was it like?"

"I dunno any more. I can't remember. Oh—Stu was there, and Brian." His voice slurred. "I think it was okay."

"This is going to be okay, too. You'll see. I've given you the middle eight. Last verse was always your specialty."

He nodded, almost asleep now. "You always did believe in yesterday."

The old man watched his sleeping friend for a time. Then he sighed deeply and went to comfort Julian and phone the others.

THE CRAZY YEARS

A Mission Statement

In 1939, the greatest science fiction writer who ever lived, Robert Anson Heinlein, produced one of the first of the many stunning innovations he was to bring to his field: he sat down and drew up a chart of the history of the future, for the next thousand years.

The device was intended as a simple memory aid, to assist him in keeping straight the details of a single, self-consistent imaginary future, which he could then mine as often as he liked for story ideas. But because Heinlein was who he was, his famous Future History came, over the next six decades, to have an uncanny—if nonspecific—predictive function. That is, no specific event he wrote of came to pass exactly as he invented it . . . but he was simply so smart and so well educated that, more often than not, he correctly nailed the general *shape* of things to come. He was, for instance, just about the only thinker in 1939 to seriously predict a moon landing before the 21st century—and he *invented* the water bed.

And in Heinlein's Future History chart, the last decades of the 20th century—the ones he wrote about and discussed as seldom as possible—were clearly and ominously marked: "THE CRAZY YEARS."

I discussed this with him several times, before his death in 1987. He had decided—half a century in advance—that a combination of information overload, overpopulation and Millennial Madness was going to drive our whole culture slug-nutty by the Eighties. One of his characters summed it up by describing The Crazy Years as ". . . a period when a man with all his gaskets tight would have been locked up."

I intend to test that proposition. This column will be dedicated to the notion that Heinlein was right: that future generations will look back on us as the silliest, goofiest, flat-out craziest crew of loonies that ever took part in the historical race from womb to tomb; that never before in human history has average human intelligence been anything like so low as it is today; and that no culture on record has ever behaved as insanely as this one now does routinely. I will seek out—I do not expect it to be much of a chore—outstanding examples of widespread brain damage, and discuss them in the light of reason. I intend to speak plain horse sense, on as many different societal psychoses as I can . . . and if Heinlein is right, before long I'll be comfortably ensconced in a padded cell, my frayed nerves soothed by powerful calming drugs.

Having summarized my mission, I have space left only to offer the most immediate and egregious specific contemporary example of the kind of thing I mean: The Terrorist Panic of '96. Every single commentator in/on every possible medium is babbling insane nonsense about terrorists; our own Minister of Foreign Affairs has begun to mutter warnings that we will have to toss all that Rights & Freedoms silliness now that There's a War On and we're beset by terrorists . . .

Whatever turns out to have been behind the destruction of Flight 800, *it cannot have been terrorists.* This was reasonably certain within an hour of the explosion, and became more utterly certain with every minute that passed thereafter; by dawn of the next day it was clear fact.

A terrorist blows up stuff *to make you do what he wants.* "Do what I say or I will blow up more stuff." *There is no point in blowing up stuff if you fail to tell people who you are and what you want them to do.*

Every single pundit, commentator, analyst and expert ("expert": an ordinary person, a long way from home) on the planet wants you to believe in terrorists smart enough to take a *huge* airplane out of the sky in a single instant . . . and too stupid to operate a payphone or a fax machine.

Feh. We may never know whether those people were the innocent bystander victims of a Mafia hit, CIA "wetwork," some pathetic cretin's suicidal selfishness, simple psychosis . . . or, just possibly, the thing you only see mentioned in the last paragraph of news stories continued on page D28: a 747 model identical to Flight 800 exploded in Iran about a decade ago, *apparently from a fuel leak that built up in one wing and blew off an entire engine* (sound familiar?).

But the one thing we know for certain is that it

had nothing to do with terrorists. Which does not mean some poor swarthy political crackpot won't eventually be identified, hunted down and paraded before the media as The Mad Terrorist of Flight 800 . . . just that he'll be innocent.

Ask me, there's a clear *shortage* of terrorists, lately. The media all but *dared* terrorists to come to Atlanta, hyping Olympic "security" for months . . . and all they could dredge up was some yahoo with a fizzle-yield pipe-bomb, one fatality. In 1949, hundreds more people than that were beaten unconscious with pipes while leaving a Paul Robeson concert in Peekskill, as the cops watched, if you want to talk about real terrorism.

Is all this a sign of some vast media conspiracy to foment war?

Oh, no. You're not going to get me doing it, too! Basic principle of The Crazy Years: never attribute to evil genius what can be satisfactorily explained by stupidity.

My 21-year-old daughter refuses to watch videos with her mother and me, because she says it drives her crazy when we sit there and pick apart the gaping holes in the plot logic. We spoil the fun. I now live in a world where every single reporter, shaper and explainer of current events and public affairs would, in his or her heart of hearts, really much rather be writing an Arnold Schwarzenegger script. Because that's what the public wants. Simple, clear—LOUD— hallucinations. Because the public is stupider and more insane at the moment than it has been for millennia—*just* as we reach the thinnest and most slippery part of the tightrope of history. We're living in The Crazy Years.

Watch this space for further bulletins, on such

symptoms of declining societal mental health as antismoking psychosis, anti-"nucular" neurosis, "environmental" brigandage, sexual hysteria and gender gibberish, galloping innumeracy, illiterate newscasters, the tragic general decline in public manners, and the general growing *refusal* of loud ignorant nitwits to mind their own damn business and quit telling their betters how to live.

Futures We Never Dreamed

Futures that science fiction never dreamed of have come to pass.

Sf has never claimed to predict the future, mind you. That's not its job. What most sf writers do is try to create *plausible* futures, which will generate compelling stories. Even our implausible futures are plausible, sometimes. That is, even when we create a satirical future, one we don't expect you to really believe—say, a world in which politicians are selected for intelligence—nonetheless once we've set the original, wild-card ground rules, we tend to proceed with rigorous logic and internal consistency. We can't help it; that's our training. (I speak here only of *written* sf; Hollywood sci fi is quite a different thing.)

Part of the theory is that a reader comfortable at adapting to unlikely-but-possible futures—for recreation—will be less disoriented by Future Shock in real life, and thus be a more intelligent voter and a happier citizen. But this only works if the imaginary futures *make sense*. Spending time in a cartoon universe, with rules that change as the author finds convenient, accomplishes little of use. So sf writers generally expend immense (and almost completely invisible) effort on making even our most improbable future worlds work logically.

One would think that after a century or so of this, we would—quite incidentally—have produced quite a few startlingly accurate predictions by now. This turns out to be the case . . . and the case has been made elsewhere, and I do not propose to make it here. Successful "prediction" by throwing darts is a *trivial* aspect of sf, one which can easily get in the way of understanding its true strengths and virtues.

What I'd like to talk about instead are some of the futures we sf writers could never have imagined . . . that have come true.

The recent fuss about evidences of life on ancient Mars brings up the most obvious and appalling: in eighty-some years of commercial sf, not one writer ever predicted, even as a joke, that humanity would achieve the means to conquer space—and then throw it away. None of us guessed there might be raised up a generation so dull and dreamless they would not realize (or listen when they were told) that incalculable wealth, inexhaustible energy and unlimited adventure are hanging in the sky right over their heads, a mere two hundred miles away. We could never have conceived of a society that, faced with an imminent rain of soup, would throw away its pails.

A few years ago in Florida I saw and photographed perhaps the most transcendently sad, baffling, infuriating sight I have ever seen: an Apollo Program booster, one of two or three left in the world, one of the most stupendous devices ever built by free men . . . lying on its side on the ground, rusting in the rain. I wept along with the sky. It is as if

Ferdinand, informed of the discovery of the New World, were to have forbidden any more of his ships to sail beyond sight of land—"We've got urgent problems right here in Spain: we can't go throwing money away in the ocean."—and no more sensible monarch could be found anywhere in Europe. Even in retrospect, I have trouble believing in a society that doesn't know it needs a frontier.

With the technology we already *know* how to build, Mars is ten weeks away: the same length of time it took the Pilgrims to reach Plymouth Rock. Why are we squinting at Antarctic rocks, for heaven's sake?

The next most obvious example: I don't think one sf writer predicted the quiet collapse of the Soviet Union. Even the most liberal of us accepted without question the seeming truism that a slave state could never collapse until the last kulak was expended. Apparently with all our vaunted exploration of the behavior of alien cultures, we failed to do enough homework on one of the most prominent ones available for study on *this* planet. In our defense, nearly every scrap of data permitted to leave the USSR was as suspect as they could make it—and even the spooks, privy to much more and better data than we were, and paid to specialize in it, were caught just as much by surprise. But it's still embarrassing.

Many sf writers have hopefully predicted the eventual conquest of all diseases. But none of us could have dreamed that one day mankind's oldest and deadliest scourge, the taker of more human lives than any other single cause—smallpox—would be eradicated from the planet, utterly and forever . . . and the event would arouse no notice at all. Did they have a party on *your* block when the last smallpox vaccines were destroyed awhile back? Was there a parade in *your* town, honoring the heros and heroines who avenged millions of our tortured, disfigured and slain ancestors? Are you familiar with their current efforts to do the same for polio, chickenpox, diphtheria and other diseases?

Several sf writers foresaw the VCR. Not one of us ever guessed that by the time it arrived, a sizable fraction of the populace would feel incompetent to operate one. We still have trouble grasping that there are people with shoes on who find it a challenge to set a watch, twice, and specify a channel number. Even harder is understanding why some of them seem proud of it.

I haven't checked, but I'm sure at least some sf writer predicted the disposable lighter—and that none ever envisioned a feature mandated by law which would make them virtually useless for senior citizens, musicians and invalids, while perfectly accessible to toddlers.

Nor could any of the thousands of us who foresaw computers, or even the dozens who foresaw personal computers, have guessed that in the end an operating system that Spoke Human would be supplanted by one that required you to learn to Speak Computer.

Being logical folks, perhaps we tend to be interested in and think about and write about other logical folks—so all of us, save Robert Heinlein himself, failed to see The Crazy Years coming.

And Now The News . . .

In the early '50s, the great sf writer Theodore Sturgeon wrote to his friend Robert Heinlein that he was both broke and blocked, literally could not think of a story to save his life. Robert's reply was typical of him: a check . . . and several pages of story ideas. All of them made money for Ted—but one in particular inspired a very prescient and powerful story.

Heinlein had said, "Write about the neurosis that derives from wallowing daily in the troubles of several billion strangers you can't help . . ."

From this seed, Sturgeon created "And Now The News—" (available in several collections and anthologies). His protagonist is a simple, good man with an obsessive addiction to the news—he takes every paper sold, subscribes to current affairs magazines, keeps news on the radio and TV at all times. When asked why, he quotes John Donne: "Every man's death diminishes me/for I am part of mankind." Over time, his obsession deepens, he makes a desperate attempt to go cold turkey . . . and events ensue so astonishing I honestly don't think it'll spoil the story for you if I give away the kicker here (SPOILER WARNING):

In the end, the guy tells his shrink he's finally found a viable solution to his problem: he's going to go out there and *diminish mankind right back*. The last line is, "He got twelve people before they cut him down."

This was forty years before the Unabomber.

If Earth is one big starship, the news media constitute its intercom. And almost nothing comes over the intercom but *damage reports*. Tragedies way over on the other side of the vessel, malfunctions in inaccessible compartments, tales of distant madness and mutiny, conflicting rumors of collision hazards in our path . . . and constant reminders that, first, our acceleration is increasing beyond design expectations, and second, *there is no Captain*, and the wheel is being fought over by vicious ignoramuses. Is it any wonder morale is so rotten on this starship?

Pessimism has become the very hallmark of sophistication. Only a dullard would go see a movie known to have a happy ending, these days. Every Hollywood sci fi future is either a nightmare . . . or dismissed as a fairy tale. We, the richest and luckiest humans who ever got to gripe for 70 or 80 years, are coming to subconsciously expect—in some perverse way, to crave—the imminent End of All Things. And so we find ourselves obsessed with damage reports, like a man staring in fascination at the slow progression of gangrene up his leg.

No rational person can blame the media for this: we demand it of them. We won't *pay* for good news. We insist on knowing the worst, even when we're helpless to do anything about it. God knows why. Attempts have been made to establish *cheerful* media, which would scour the planet to tell you everything that went *right* today, every averted tragedy, miraculous serendipity or realized dream that might give you hope, lighten your load . . . and they all went belly-up. There is no media conspiracy to depress people. I think most of us in the media realize we live in the same starship. But there *is* a media conspiracy to feed ourselves and our families, and that means we must sell you what you want to buy.

I don't propose that the media lie, or suppress facts, or strain for Panglossian slants—but if we're going to convey the truth and nothing but the truth, we ought to shoot for the *whole* truth. Every news outlet needs a regular feature, given equal weight with the day's lead story, titled "Silver Lining." The massive resources of the newsgathering industry could—and should, as both public- and self-service—manage to come up with one story a day that made us feel a little *less* like diminishing mankind right back. And it wouldn't hurt to quadruple the comics section, while we're at it.

I've experienced nearly five decades. With all its plagues, wars, disasters and injustices, the one just past (in which computers got friendly, the Berlin Wall came down, the Soviet Union peacefully folded its cards, nuclear apocalypse receded for the first time in my life, smallpox was annihilated, Mr. Mandela walked free, *perfect* music reproduction became trivially cheap, Geraldo's nose was broken on camera, and the Beatles put out two new singles) has been hands down the best. Yet it was back in 1965–75, a decade when just about everything that could possibly go wrong did, that a significant fraction of us last seemed to believe we could change the world.

Hope—belief in the possibility of beneficial change—is a scarce and precious resource. It has been throughout history; every society that ever ran out of it *died*. Our hope is battered daily by the barrage of bad news, and by the defeatist attitude it engenders: the cynical compulsion to deconstruct every comforting myth, to find (or if necessary invent) feet of clay for every hero, to explain away every hopeful event as a cursing in disguise.

Granted: we can't hide our heads in the sand. It is my obligation as a crewman of Starship Earth to listen to the intercom regularly. But it's also my obligation to *turn the damn thing off* when it starts to impair my morale. That means triaging my newspaper, and removing CNN and Newsworld from my remote-menu, and zapping the network news fungus whenever it appears. (You'd be surprised how little you miss that way: after a dogged, relentless effort to ignore the O.J. Simpson story, I find I know far more about it than the jury was allowed to.) It's possible to have *too much* information to do your job.

Fear is a subtle and potent drug, and it has its uses. Daily news is civilized man's analog for the exhilaration of facing the sabertooth: a daily hit of bracing fear. But dosage is crucial: at high concentrations (particularly if mainlined: taken by television), evil side effects start to set in. *You cannot kill the sabertooth.* There is nothing one can *do* about any of the horrors in the news (purely local bunfights excepted), except fret . . . and at some point panic, yield to despair. And when there are enough panicked, despairing people on the starship, The Crazy Years come.

Time we all turned to the funny pages. It's important to remember something else Robert Heinlein once said: "The last thing to come out of Pandora's Box was Hope . . ."

Says Who?

> *What are the facts? Again and again and again—what are the facts? Shun wishful thinking, ignore divine revelation, forget what "the stars foretell," avoid opinion, care not what the neighbors think, never mind the unguessable "verdict of history"—what are the facts, and to how many decimal places? You pilot always into an unknown future; facts are your only clue.*
>
> —Robert Heinlein,
> Time Enough For Love

✧   ✧   ✧

The first and most obvious problem is, it's getting harder to tell a fact from a factoid—let alone a factoid from pure mahooha.

Witness the public humiliation of poor old Pierre Salinger, unwary enough to trust data he'd gotten from the Internet, and publicly proclaim that Flight 800 had been shot down by the US Navy. (A theory which, at a minimum, requires one to believe not one sailor on the hypothetical offending vessel harbors the slightest desire to be rich and famous, and the captain has no enemies.) It has always surprised me to meet people who believed "It must be true: I read it somewhere," and in my lifetime it became surprising to find people who believed "It must be true: it was on TV." And *still* I find myself astonished again, now that I'm meeting people who tell me, "It must be true: I downloaded it."

The Internet, as presently constituted, is anarchy. Information ka-ka. Garbage in, garbage out. There are no fact-checkers. There is no peer review. Any fool who fancies him or herself an information guerilla can publish any gibberish he or she likes. Therefore all Internet "facts" not supported by checkable references have the same value: zero.

Our culture appears packed with people desperately eager to lay down a kilobuck or two, fill their desktops with large cranky gear, and devote hundreds of hours of skullsweat—to gain access to an endless cornucopia of suspect data. And, since it arrives via the highest of high tech, treat all of it as revealed truth. We're piloting on the basis of the most up-to-the-minute rumors. This strikes me as a recipe for the first global riot.

But the Internet is not the problem; only its latest

avatar. No matter how information comes to us, it takes hard work and careful analysis to decide how much it's worth. Okay, we can automatically discount anything on government stationery, or paid for by any political party or interest group. Sure, we can be suspicious of any announcement from anything calling itself an institute. Sooner or later *Time* or *Newsweek* will report on something of which we have personal experience, and we'll get a sense of how much faith can be placed in them. When I receive (and I swear I did) a junkmail from some psychic advisors that begins, "We hope this did not reach you too late," I can tell at once that it has reached me about 45 *years* too late.

But what are we to do when, for example, we read the flat assertion that "Children born to women who smoked dope while pregnant cannot make decisions. They cannot learn," in a November 20 *Vancouver Sun* Op-Ed column by one Connie Kuhns? Let's even suppose for argument that some shred of documentation had been offered, some study cited, some scientist named—suppose we'd been given facts, rather than a claim they exist. How are we to *check* the facts? Required: at least an hour in a good library (or navigating cyberspace) just to *find* the cited study and read it. (How many of us possess the necessary intellectual training to tell a good study from a statistical massage?) Another half hour to assess the professional competence of the author(s). An hour, minimum, wading through fat indexes of technical journals, to learn whether the claimed result is *reproducible*, or unique to the claimant. More work will be required to trace who *funded* the study, and where they got *their* money. Then, for context, you have to step back and derive for yourself the ratio of antito pro-marijuana studies that receive funding—and a dozen other threads. It was kind of Ms. Kuhns to spare us all that tedious work—but in consequence only those of us who chance to actually *know* any children of mothers who smoked pot while pregnant can tell she is speaking pernicious nonsense.

Bad data are dangerous, whether cybernetic or semantic. We all know that some downloaded programs contain viruses, bits of bad programming that instruct the host computer to do self-destructive things, and that the wise hacker practices safe surfing. But Richard Dawkins pointed out that ideas are very like viruses. If I think up a good idea and tell it to you, it takes over a little of your brain's processing power, forces it to make a copy of itself, and encourages you to pass it on to others. The stronger the idea, the faster and farther it replicates itself, until—if it be vigorous enough—it saturates the whole infoculture. An early hacker named K'ung Fu Tse, for instance, wrote some viruses that have survived for millennia. Such protonerds as Muhammad, Buddha and Jesus programmed infobots so powerful that they continue to crash operating systems and reformat whole hard drives to this day. A really good idea can spread like chicken pox through a daycare center.

So can a really bad one. As Heinlein said, "The truth of a proposition has nothing to do with its credibility—and vice versa."

We need some real-life equivalent of Disinfectant, the clever little program written by John Norstad of Northwestern University which constantly guards my Mac against infection by corrupting ideas. Information hygiene requires a cultural Crap-Detector, that will allow us to practice safe sentience.

And so we come at last to the second, less obvious and more serious problem, which I will have to leave for another column:

Nobody wants one. Not enough to pay for it. Deep down, we don't really *care* if the stories we download from the Net are true, as long as they're good stories, and support our preconceived prejudices. These are, after all, The Crazy Years.

Fat City

A previous column discussed the pernicious effects of the daily bath of Bad News we all receive, and ended by paraphrasing a Robert Heinlein quote I here reproduce accurately:

"Last to come out of Pandora's Box was a gleaming, beautiful thing—eternal Hope." At least one reader has since challenged me to *specify* at least one or two realistic Hopes, for that future which most other pundits assure him will be grim beyond imagining. Glad to oblige. For openers:

1) How would you—personally—like a hundred billion dollars? (U.S.)

Ever seen mining done? Metals cost so much because It's so hard to *get* them—immense amounts of energy are needed to rip them up out of the ground and haul them to where they're needed. Well, God obligingly took a large ore-rich planet, crushed it up into bite-sized chunks, and hung it in the sky, just past Mars. It's called the asteroid belt. Iron, nickel, platinum, cobalt, gold, silver, copper, titanium, uranium—gigatons of it.

Once you reach High Earth Orbit—which we

achieved 30 years ago—you're halfway there (You're halfway to *anywhere:* the same rocket blast that will send you to the Moon can, if differently aimed, send you to Mars, or Pluto, or Alpha Centauri . . . eventually. All it takes is more time.) In orbit you build a robot probe with a solar sail capable of a thousandth/g constant boost—which we already know how to do. It reaches the asteroid belt in (very) roughly a hundred days, picks out a likely rock and installs a rocket on it. Some time later (how much later depending on how big a rocket you sprang for) the rock arrives in Earth orbit for processing. And there are more in the pipeline behind it; they'll be arriving regularly, now . . .

What do you care? Well, if the entire asteroid belt could be sold, and the money divided equally among every man, woman and child presently alive on earth . . . your personal share would be US $100 billion. If you worked 40 hours a week counting $100 bills at a rate of one per second, you'd die before you could finish counting your take—even if you lived another 70 years. (These figures from John S. Lewis's *Mining the Sky*.)

Let's say something goes wrong, and somehow you *don't* get your fair share. Don't you think the trickle-down from that much wealth might at least help ease your mortgage some?

All this, of course, is over and above the hundreds of billions that are *already there* in High Orbit, right now, waiting for us to come and get them any time we're bright enough: zero g for convenient manufacture of priceless alloys and pharmaceuticals, infinite free solar power (not the 0.35% that strikes Toronto on (half of) the sunniest day, mind you: ALL of it), free vacuum, that sort of thing.

And that's just using existing, proven technology.

2) *How about INFINITE wealth—with immortality thrown in?*

There is a new and utterly astounding prospect on the horizon, called nanotechnology. It may change *everything*. It involves Very Tiny Machines, that move individual atoms around, in order to build things the same way nature does: molecule by molecule. At viral speeds. If it can be done, the implications are . . . well, totally unprecedented.

Picture a molecule-sized computerized probe, injected in your arm: programmed to make X copies of itself from available atoms, which will then cruise your bloodstream looking for (say) arterial plaque cells, disassemble any found, and build (for example) bourbon molecules from the parts. Now extrapolate to any other metabolic condition you'd like to correct: cancer cells, tobacco tar, glandular deficiency, organic damage. There's no reason to tolerate ill health—no reason to die until it suits you. Muscles of steel seem literally possible . . . though impractical.

Want to take the family to Venus for vacation? Buy an invisibly tiny spaceship-seed, drop it into a vat of chemicals, and close the lid. Your self-piloting fully fueled space yacht builds itself. If you like, turn it back into the vat of chemicals when you and the family get home from Venus.

For a much fuller discussion of this technology's staggering possibilities, see K. Eric Drexler's seminal *Engines of Creation* (or its slightly more accessible followup, *Unbounding the Future*). It includes sober discussion of the possible downside—the dread "gray goo problem," for instance—along with rational solutions and safeguards. But in summary, nano-technology's enthusiasts say its full utilization may well make us all immortal and infinitely rich—eventually. (By the way, I claim credit for coining the first shorthand term for "nanotechnology's enthusiasts." If cyberneticists are "computer weenies," and astronomers are "star weenies," then it seems to me nanotechnologists must be . . . teeny weenies.)

How *soon?* Best guestimate, nanotechnology should begin coming on line somewhere between 20 and 50 years: within the projected lifespan of most of my readers. At least one prominent teeny weeny—Keith Henson, one of the founders of Alcor, the cryonics outfit—is so sure he personally is going to live to be immortal and infinitely wealthy that he's already painstakingly worked the math to reassure himself that, even if it turns out the speed of light IS an absolute speed limit, there will in fact be just enough time for him and a few friends to *tour the entire universe, in person,* before it expires in heat death. There'll even be time, he calculates, for one Grand Memory Merge. Last I heard Keith was, with great seriousness and in exhaustive detail, planning the Party At The End Of Time. (He describes it as a "non-trivial problem." He expects, for instance, that he'll need to disassemble an entire solar system or two just to build enough beer cans.)

I find it enormously comforting that someone is thinking in these terms. I don't know about you, but I'd hate to arrive at the Last Party and find that somebody forgot to stock the beer nuts.

3) *How about a warm dry place to spend your money?*

There seems every reason to hope that the dreaded horror, Global Warming, will continue to stave off the latest in a long and startlingly regular series of Ice

Ages—which, by an interesting coincidence, has been theoretically overdue since . . . about the time the evil Industrial Revolution got underway.

Despite all the above reasons for hope, most of the bright, educated people I know are expecting Apocalypse any time now. These must be The Crazy Years.

The Fall-Guy Shortage

I don't know whether civilians have begun to consciously notice the problem yet . . . but I can tell you that we writers are in a state approaching panic. It is our function to be the canaries in society's coal mine, identifying problems before they affect anyone important . . . and what we are beginning to sense in the air is not just the end of civilization, or even the end of fiction, but the potential end of the only thing that could possibly compensate us for either: humor itself.

See if you can work it out for yourself. It's right under your nose, really. What do civilization, fiction and humor all require to exist?

That's right: a fall-guy.

There can be no civilization without scapegoats. Unspeakable things must be done to make a civilization flourish, unforgivable things . . . and somebody has to carry the can. In fiction the need is even more pressing: no matter how endearing you make your characters or settings, in every single story someone must be punished—the protagonist, if it's Serious Literature, or the villain, if it's Trash. And as for humor . . . well, it is not exaggeration to say that humor *is* the fall-guy, and vice-versa.

Picture that most enduring evergreen of the field: a man slipping on a banana peel. Funny? Eternally so. But now imagine the slippee is your favorite grandmother. Still funny, to be sure . . . but noticeably less so. Imagine it's you. Hmmm—not very funny at all, is it? Now imagine the victim is your boss. See what I mean? Now it's twice as funny. The more deserving the fall-guy, the riper the joke.

For us to endure as a society, we desperately need people that we all agree it is alright to hate. And these days the cupboard is damn near bare.

In a vain and reckless attempt to make ourselves more likeable, we no longer permit ourselves to hate people who speak a different tongue—or those with a different complexion, or politics, or superstitions, or habits, or *any* of the old stand-bys. Hell, half of us have even stopped insulting the other gender (in public)! The only large groups still fair game are fat people and white males. (Oh, bosses are still good, and politicians—but both of those still tend to come under the heading of "white males," don't they? Besides, it's not so much fun laughing at someone you know is probably going to have the last laugh.)

Society requires fall-guys—untouchables, on whom we can all unload our own random rage and contempt. These days witches and Jews and cripples and Gypsies and native people and people of color all have apologists and good attorneys. We *need* whores (how dare they sell what is most desperately sought, at a fair price?) and queers (how dare they offer to give it away?) and welfare mothers (how dare they get stiffed for it?) and junkies (how dare they avoid the problem?) and the homeless (how dare they not die when their credit fell to zero?). This civil rights nonsense has to end *somewhere*.

In fiction, the problem is even worse—since so many of us writers have at one time or another *been* whores, queers, supported by the NEA or Canada Council, junkies, or homeless. Screenwriters, teleplay writers, novelists, dramatists, political speech-writers— all of us are crying out for acceptable villains. It's worst in the adventure field, where they need someone so universally agreed to be vile that any conceivable brutality inflicted on him by the hero will elicit applause—people we *want* to see Arnold blow into chopped meat. And the supply is dwindling. Gooks won't do, any more.

It began back in the '50s, when the TV show *The Untouchables* was forced to stop giving its *mafiosi* Italian names—and that opened the floodgates. We're almost down to terrorists, serial killers and drug dealers, these days. And sadly, they're all beginning to wear a little thin as literary devices. Despite our best efforts at publicizing them, there just *aren't* many actual terrorists or serial killers—since both gigs require so much effort and risk, and pay so poorly. And drug dealers tend to turn up on many writers' own Rolodexes, so it has to be crack or heroin.

But society, as always, has shown us artists the way, and brought us the ideal villains, just as we needed them most:

Thank God for child molesters.

Apparently society wants them so badly it's decided to focus an immense, glaring spotlight of attention on them, to inspire others—and we writers are delighted to help. Child molesters are perfect: they sanctify total rage. Nothing Arnold could do to one is bad enough. There's no possible excuse or mitigation, no annoying shades of gray. Even a rape-murderer in prison can feel morally superior to a short-eyes. Even that damn ACLU might hesitate to defend one. Betraying the trust of a child is so self-evidently evil that not even a Senator or O.J. Simpson could get away with it, and you have to draw the line *somewhere,* don't you?

Best of all, it's like Commies in the State Department—you can find as many as you're willing to look for. People will believe in day-care sex rings and wide-scale commercial kiddyporn even when every single prosecution comes up empty. It's a *secret,* see?

So if you've been wondering why every single damn movie, TV show, novel, play, short story and country-western song you can locate this season features a child-molester theme or subplot, there's your answer. We may be traumatizing every child in the land, and every adult who is reckless enough to smile at (or, God forbid, touch) one, and glamorizing what must after all be a fairly lame and pathetic pleasure at best, and giving demagogues and lynch mobs something to work with, and we may even be making the problem itself substantially worse, and hampering efforts to deal with it—

—but hey, that's a small price to pay for drama. Or so it seems, in The Crazy Years.

Seduction of the Innocent

Paul Simon once said " . . . the words of the prophets are written on the subway walls/and tenement halls . . ." I have myself seen the future writ large upon my own sidewalk.

A few years ago, that sidewalk became so damaged

as to require repair. The freshly poured concrete naturally attracted *graffitisti* with popsicle sticks, determined to immortalize themselves. How few opportunities there are these days for a writer to have his or her work literally graven in stone! Inevitably, one of these was a young swain who wished to proclaim his undying love to the ages. His chilling masterpiece of . . . er . . . concrete poetry is located right at the foot of my walkway, where I must look at it every time I leave my home. It reads:

Tood + Janey

Now, I don't know about you, but I decline to believe that even in this day and age, any set of parents elected to name their son "Tood." I am forced to conclude that *young Todd is unable to spell his own flippin' name*. . . despite having reached an age sufficiently advanced for him to find Janey intriguing. (Assuming her name is not, in fact, Jeannie or Joanie.) As I make my living from literacy, I find this sign of the times demoralizing.

I was going to argue the case that illiteracy is on the increase, next—but on reflection, I don't think that's necessary. I don't suppose there's a literate human alive who doubts it. Let's move on to the more pressing questions: why is this happening, and what if anything can be done about it?

The late great John D. MacDonald, in an essay he wrote for the Library of Congress, put his finger on the problem: the complex code-system we call literacy—indeed, the very neural wiring that allows it—has existed for only the latest few heartbeats in the long history of human evolution. Literacy is a very hard skill to acquire, and once acquired it brings endless heartache—for the more one reads, the more one learns of life's intimidating complexity and confusion. But anyone who can learn to grunt is bright enough to watch TV . . . which teaches that life is simple, and happy endings come, at 30- and 60-minute intervals, to those whose hearts are in the right place.

Literacy made its greatest inroads when it was the best escape possible from a world defined by the narrow parameters of a family farm or a small village, the only opening onto a larger and more interesting world. But the "mind's eye" has only been evolving for thousands of years, whereas the body's eye has been perfected for millions of them. The mind's eye can show you things that no Hollywood special effects department can simulate—but only at the cost of years of effort spent learning to decode ink stains on paper. Writing still remains the unchallenged best way—indeed, nearly the only way except for mathematics—to express a complicated thought . . . and it seems clear that this is precisely one of its *disadvantages* from the consumers' point of view. Modern humans have begun to declare, voting with their eyes, that literacy is not worth the bother.

It is tempting to blame the whole thing on the educational system. But that answer is too easy, and the only solution it suggests—shoot all the English teachers—is perhaps hasty. By and large they are probably doing the best they can with the budgets we give them.

Nor can we look to government for help. Even if a more literate electorate were something politicians *wanted,* they are simply not up to the job. I've given up trying to get anyone to believe this, but I swear I once saw a U.S. government subway ad that read, "Illiterate? Write for help . . ." and gave a box number.

Those of us who are parents, however, can do some useful work. We can *con* our children into reading.

I offer two stratagems.

My mother's was, I think, artistically superior in that it required diabolical cleverness and fundamental dishonesty; it was however time- and labor-intensive. She would begin reading me a comic book—then, JUST as the Lone Ranger was hanging by his fingertips from the cliff, endangered-species stampede approaching, angry native peoples below . . . Mom would suddenly remember that she had to go sew the dishes or vacuum the cat.

By the age of 6, I had taught myself to read, out of pure frustration. So Mom sent me to the library with instructions to bring home a book. The librarian, God bless her, gave me a copy of Robert A. Heinlein's novel for children, *Rocket Ship Galileo* . . . and from that day on there was never any serious danger that I would be forced to work for a living. Mr. Heinlein wrote stories so intrinsically interesting that it was worth the trouble to stop and look up the odd word I didn't know. By age 7, I was tested as reading at college Junior level.

The only problem is, you cannot simply hand the child the comic book: you must read 80% of it to her, and then *stop* reading with pinpoint timing. With the best of intentions, you may not have that much time or energy to devote to the task of seducing your child.

If not, try the scheme my wife and I devised. From the day our daughter was old enough to have a defined "bed-time," we made it our firm policy that bed-time was bed-time, no excuses or exceptions— *unless* she were reading, in which case she could stay up as late as she pleased. The most precious prize any child can attain is a few minutes' awareness past bedtime. She went for the bait like a hungry trout . . . and was invariably chosen as The Narrator in school plays because of her fluency in reading. Today she is one of those rare 22-year-olds who owns as many books as she does CDs.

Doubtless there are other schemes. But one thing I promise: if we leave the problem to government, or the educational system, or a mythical animal called society—to anyone but ourselves—we will effectively be surrendering the battle, and giving our children over into the hands of Geraldo Rivera. As Mr. Heinlein said in his immortal *Stranger in a Strange Land*, "Thou art God—and cannot decline the nomination." Our only options are to do a good job, or not.

And the consequences of a bad job will make The Crazy Years look good . . .

Bloomin' Yoomins

Join me now as we beam down to a strange new planet. Our five-minute mission: to determine whether intelligent life exists here. And since we've only five minutes, there is no time for a proper study of the large-scale organization or behavior of the planet's dominant species—we must simply drop in, take one quick technology sample at random, assume it is representative, and draw the best conclusions we can. Ready? CUE THE SPECIAL EFFECTS—

God, that always tickles.

Okay. We're in a typical dwelling of this race—

Yoomins, they're called. We've tried to bias the test in their favor as much as possible, by choosing our sample from one of the most affluent regions of the planet; surely here will be found their most intelligent technology. Tricorders ready? Let's look around.

The room we're presently in—the name sounds like a sneeze—is the one in which yoomins store and prepare their food. The largest two items in the room are a heat-making machine and a heat-losing machine. They sit side by side . . . yet careful sensor readings indicate they are not connected in any way. Hmmm.

Let's look closer. The heat-loser is—bafflingly—designed to stand on its end, so that you *must* spill money on the floor every time you open it to access or even inspect its contents. And they put the coldest part *on top*.

The heat-maker is complementarily designed to spill money on the ceiling. Not just the four elements on top (one of which is *always* defective): the central module, called an *uvvin*, has a door which—inexplicably—opens *from the top*, so that you cannot touch the contents during cooking, even momentarily, without wasting *all* the heat. The whole unit is utterly unprogrammable, and lacks even the simplest temperature readouts: everything is done by guess.

Perhaps some sort of cultural blind-spot is at work here. Let's examine the water-recycling facilities.

Uh . . . there are none. Yoomins throw potable water away. They throw *hot* water away. And look at the temperature control system: there is none. No sensors, no thermocouples, taps completely uncalibrated—though all these technologies are trivially cheap here. They keep a large, almost-uninsulated tank full of water heated at all times to skin-scalding temperature (using none of the waste heat to warm the pipe, so that hot water will always be slow in arriving when needed), and then mix it with cold water to a safe temperature, by hand, adjusting the result *by testing it with their own skin*. With every use.

Well, perhaps yoomins customarily eat in restaurants, and this room is only intended as a fallback— in case, let us say, a wave of psychosis passes through the restaurant industry, and they all start turning away a quarter of their customers rather than run a fan. Let's try another room.

And let's make it as fundamental and essential a room as we can. A yoomin need not necessarily sleep in its bedroom, nor relax in its livingroom, nor work in its study—but there is one room in which every yoomin *must* spend some time, at least twice a day. Surely there, if anywhere, we will find the most thoughtful applications of intelligence.

The first and largest thing we find is a combination shower and bath. It cannot be used comfortably to bathe, and cannot be used safely to shower. Its principal purpose appears to be to kill the elderly, unfit and unlucky, which it does with ruthless efficiency. The shower head is generally fixed, impossible to train on the areas where it is most needed. It has *worse* temperature control than the sink in the other room, and is tested with the whole body. No provision is made for hair accumulation in the drain—or, usually, for venting of steam or gradual equalization of ambient temperature after a shower.

Let's move on to the central fixture: the commode. It enforces an unnatural, inefficient and uncomfortable posture, presents about the most uncomfortable sitting surface possible, has absolutely no facilities for cleansing or disinfecting either the user or itself—and after use, it takes the precious irreplaceable fertilizer and *throws it away*, using *gallons* of potable water to do so with no attempt at recycling. The obvious one-way valve, to prevent it backing up, is not present. And for a full 25% of its purported purpose—as a male urinal—it is completely and manifestly worthless, a constant source of domestic strife.

But if you think that's odd, keep going. There *is* a perfect, rationally designed male urinal, right here in this room—less than a meter away—but for some reason, no male human will admit to ever having used it for that purpose. That would somehow desecrate it, soil it. Officially it is reserved for saliva, nasal mucus, toothpaste spit-up, beard-hairs, blood, assorted skin-paints worn by females, and the truly disgusting things humans seem to have to rinse off their hands all the time. Needless to say, it too must have its water-temperature laboriously reset by guess with each use.

Above it, on the wall, hangs another curious thing: a cabinet designed to spill its contents. The spice-rack in the last room, meant to hold items of uniform size and shape, has retaining walls for them—but these shelves, intended to hold items of varied size and shape, do not. And they are always too small and shallow to hold what is required; the overflow goes under the sink where it can grow mold faster.

Let's go back to the commode. Does it come with a reading lamp? No? Not even a magazine rack? Good God, Spock, are these creatures *savages*?

There are stereo speakers built in, surely? Power and datafeeds for a laptop? *At least* tell me there's a built-in deodorizer . . .

Let's stop. It's time to beam back up. These

hominids may have developed some clever technology—but they are obviously not bright enough to have given the slightest thought to applying it to their own most basic personal comfort, and so they cannot possibly be regarded as sentient.

We'll check back in another century or so. It's possible yoomins are going through some sort of temporary cyclical madness—every adolescent species has its Crazy Years.

Yoomins Reconsidered

To: Kames T. Jerk, Commander,
            Starship *Exitprize*
From: Academician Npolfz Tuvefou,
            University of Aldeberan
Subject: Your Report on Sol III

Dear Captain:

I don't think you're being entirely fair to the yoomins of Sol III. I've read your recent assessment of their intelligence, as exemplified by the personal-comfort technology found in their fuel-intake and -exhaust chambers, and I cannot fault your data. But I think you've missed a subtle point, which colors your conclusion.

There is about yoomins a quality so profoundly strange that it renders questions of intelligence or stupidity simply irrelevant. I have spent some time in that sector of the Lesser Magellanic Cloud—not by *choice*, of course; a breakdown—and ask you to believe that this is true, however improbable it may seem:

Yoomins believe at their core that LIFE IS NOT TOUGH ENOUGH.

A primary example: like any sentient species, they recognized a need to transmit information nonverbally with high reliability over distance. Like most, they developed a symbol system: in their case, dark stains on leaves of whitened plant matter. (An unstable medium—but then their lives are short.) They called theirs an "alphabet."

So far so good. But yoomins believe life is not hard enough; they could not stop there. The most advanced tribe of them developed not two but *three* alphabets, almost but not quite identical—called "upper case," "lower case," and "script"—*for absolutely no reason at all.* These yoomins require their young to master all three, and an endless series of self-contradictory rules for when each may/must be used. The *largest* tribe of yoomins, on the other hand, uses an alphabet that has endured, essentially unchanged, for millennia . . . which contains *hundreds* of characters, of surpassing complexity, and is nearly impossible for most yoomins (even of that tribe) to learn, write, type, or translate.

Consider language itself. The purpose of language is to encode reality and communicate useful observations regarding it. Obviously, the more languages you construct, the more ways you have of looking at reality; integrate enough of them, and the noise should filter out, leaving a refined approximation. Yoomins have a reassuring plethora of languages— and much urgent reason to want to communicate with one another. BUT ALMOST NO YOOMIN LEARNS MORE THAN ONE LANGUAGE. Bitter emotional debates often rage on whether it should be permissible for the young to be schooled in as many as two.

This requires that *every message* between different tribes be laboriously translated by a single freak-expert, whose work can not practically be checked. Attempts at establishing a planetary pidgin—the very first sign of a civilization—have been made, but never seriously; yet yoomins maintain a planetary civilization. They do not believe life is hard enough.

The yoomin ecosystem *teems* with substances containing neurochemicals which induce pleasure in them. Nearly all yoomins show clear need for at least some such pleasure, above that provided by simple successful survival. Most of these chemicals have societally-damaging side effects, some great, some small. Dealing with those would be a large but entirely manageable problem.

But yoomins don't think life is tough enough. Their response is to absolutely forbid use of any such substance, punishing violators with death, torture, imprisonment and disgrace. I swear. Excepted, of course, are substances that do not make a yoomin feel good *enough* to arouse anyone else's envy (E.g., "sugar," "chocolate," "caffeine"). But the *only other* exception—one made almost universally around the planet—is for the single substance which demonstrably and unmistakably *has the most destructive effects* (ethanol). All substances in between tend to be demonized in direct proportion to their relative harmlessness, and the strength of the user's need for them.

This clearly does not work: produces a daily spectacle of slaughter, waste, corruption and degradation which has continued for several centuries. They simply do not see it—acquire a blank look when you point it out.

Yoomins reproduce sexually, and at high efficiency.

At present, they are confined to a single planet (for no explicable reason; apparently by choice), and thus suffer an overpopulation problem so intense it must be immediately apparent to the meanest intelligence among them. They are extremely blessed by nature in that a) contraception itself is trivially simple for them, and b) there are a number of alternative sexual recreations that offer no possibility of impregnation and are even more pleasurable than the procreative act itself. So what do yoomins do? *They deify ignorance.* They do their level best—knowing in advance that they cannot possibly succeed—to ensure that their young learn *nothing* about sex (not even simple hygiene) for as long as possible. Indeed, sexual ignorance in children is given the special name "innocence," and considered not only a virtue, but the ultimate virtue. Yoomins deliberately go to enormous trouble to guarantee that their own young will begin their sex lives incompetently, with maximum possible emotional trauma, JUST as they are most fertile.

Recently yoomins developed technology which makes unintended conception a correctable mistake, long before a developing fetus could possibly possess a single functioning nerve cell or pain receptor—and so now, inevitably, the most revered and popular religious leader in the history of their planet tells them such technology is evil. He himself is a celibate. Life is nowhere NEAR tough enough for the inhabitants of Sol III.

Yoomins made a terrible historical mistake. They destroyed or tamed every single predator that threatened them, from sabretooth to smallpox, and gained control over most natural catastrophes—long before they were emotionally prepared to do without them. They have become too accustomed to the regular sound of ringing alarm bells in their heads, and so will manufacture emergency if none arises naturally. In between emergencies, they fantasize about them. They are addicted to fear, and for some reason cannot admit it. They are neurologically wired up to deal with a more hostile environment than presently presents itself . . . and are undone by the lack of competition. They turn their own intelligence to making life difficult enough for their comfort, for their innate sense of the rightness of things.

Thus, the brighter they are, the stupider they appear to be.

It is what makes them happy. We can judge it only as art. And they are clearly great artists . . . currently shaping their greatest collaborative creation yet together, a masterpiece known as The Crazy Years.

BY ANY OTHER NAME

There's winds out on the ocean
Blowin' where they choose.
The winds got no emotion:
They don't know the blues.

—*traditional*

CHAPTER ONE

Excerpt from the Journal of Isham Stone

I hadn't meant to shoot the cat.

I hadn't meant to shoot anything, for that matter—
the pistol at my hip was strictly defensive armament
at the moment. But my adrenals were on overtime

and my peripheral vision was straining to meet itself
behind my head—when something appeared before
me with no warning at all my subconscious sentries
opted for the Best Defense. I was down and rolling
before I knew I'd fired, through a doorway I hadn't
known was there.

I fetched up with a heart-stopping crash against
the foot of a staircase just inside the door. The impact
dislodged something on the first-floor landing; it rolled
heavily down the steps and sprawled across me: the
upper portion of a skeleton, largely intact from the
sixth vertebra up. As I lurched in horror to my feet,
long-dead muscle and cartilage crumbled at last, and
random bones skittered across the dusty floor. Three
inches above my left elbow, someone was playing a
drum-roll with knives.

Cautiously I hooked an eye around the doorframe,
at about knee-level. The smashed remains of what had
recently been gray-and-white Persian tom lay against
a shattered fire hydrant whose faded red surface was
spattered with brighter red and less appealing colors. Overworked imagination produced the odor of
singed meat.

I'm as much cat-people as the One-Sleeved Man-
darin, and three shocks in quick succession, in the
condition I was in, were enough to override all the
iron discipline of Collaci's training. Eyes stinging, I
stumbled out onto the sidewalk, uttered an
unspellable sound, and pumped three slugs into a
wrecked '82 Buick lying on its right side across the
street.

I was pretty badly rattled—only the third slug hit
the exposed gas tank. But it was magnesium, not lead:
the car went up with a very satisfactory roar and the
prettiest fireball you ever saw. The left rear wheel

was blown high in the air: it soared gracefully over my head, bounced off a fourth-floor fire escape and came down flat and hard an inch behind me. Concrete buckled.

When my ears had stopped ringing and my eyes uncrossed, I became aware that I was rigid as a statue. *So much for catharsis,* I thought vaguely, and relaxed with an effort that hurt all over.

The cat was still dead.

I saw almost at once why he had startled me so badly. The tobacconist's display window from which he had leaped was completely shattered, so my subconscious sentries had incorrectly tagged it as one of the rare unbroken ones. Therefore, they reasoned, the hurtling object must be in fact emerging from the open door just beyond the window. Anything coming out a doorway that high from the ground just had to be a Musky, and my hand is *much* quicker than my eye.

Now that my eye had caught up, of course, I realized that I couldn't possibly track a Musky by eye. Which was exactly why I'd been keyed up enough to waste irreplaceable ammo and give away my position in the first place. Carlson had certainly made life complicated for me. I hoped I could manage to kill him slowly.

This was no consolation to the cat. I looked down at my Musky-gun, and found myself thinking of the day I got it, just three months past. The first gun I had ever owned myself, symbol of man's estate, *mine* for as long as it took me to kill Carlson, and for as long afterwards as I lived. After my father had presented it to me publicly, and formally charged me with the avenging of the human race, the friends and neighbors—and dark-eyed Alia—had scurried safely

inside for the ceremonial banquet. But my father took
me aside. We walked in silence through the West
Forest to Mama's grave, and through the trees the
setting sun over West Mountain looked like a knot-
hole in the wall of Hell. Dad turned to me at last,
pride and paternal concern fighting for control of his
ebony features, and said, "Isham. . . . Isham, I wasn't
much older than you when I got my first gun. That
was long ago and far away, in a place called
Montgomery—things were different then. But some
things never change." He tugged an earlobe reflectively, and continued, "Phil Collaci has taught you
well, but sometimes he'd rather shoot first and ask
directions later. Isham, you just can't go blazing away
indiscriminately. Not *ever*. You hear me?"

The crackling of the fire around the ruined Buick
brought me back to the present. Damn, you called
it again Dad, I thought as I shivered there on the
sidewalk. You *can't* go blazing away indiscriminately.

Not even here in New York City.

It was getting late, and my left arm ached abomi-
nably where Grey Brother had marked me—I reminded
myself sharply that I was here on business. I had no
wish to pass a night in any city, let alone this one, so
I continued on up the street, examining every building I passed with extreme care. If Carlson had ears,
he now knew someone was in New York, and he might
figure out why. I was on his home territory—every
alleyway and manhole was a potential ambush.

There were stores and shops of every conceivable
kind, commerce more fragmented and specialized
than I had ever seen before. Some shops dealt only
in a *single item*. Some I could make no sense of at
all. What the hell is an "rko"?

I kept to the sidewalk where I could. I told myself

I was being foolish, that I was no less conspicuous to Carlson or a Musky than if I'd stood on second base at the legendary Shea Stadium, and that the street held no surprise tomcats. But I kept to the sidewalk where I could. I remember Mama—a *long* time ago—telling me not to go in the street or the monsters would get me.

They got her.

Twice I was forced off the curb, once by a subway entrance and once by a supermarket. Dad had seen to it that I had the best plugs Fresh Start had to offer, but they weren't *that* good. Both times I hurried back to the sidewalk and was thoroughly disgusted with my pulse rate. But I never looked over my shoulder. Collaci says there's no sense being scared when it can't help you—and the fiasco with the cat proved him right.

It was early afternoon, and the same sunshine that was warming the forests and fields and work-zones of Fresh Start, my home, seemed to chill the air here, accentuating the barren emptiness of the ruined city. Silence and desolation were all around me as I walked, bleached bones and crumbling brick. Carlson had been efficient, all right, nearly as efficient as the atomic bomb folks used to be so scared of once. It seemed as though I were in some immense Devil's Autoclavo, that ignored filth and grime but grimly scrubbed out life of any kind.

Wishful thinking, I decided, and shook my head to banish the fantasy. If the city had been truly lifeless, I'd be approaching Carlson from uptown—I would never have had to detour as far south as the Lincoln Tunnel, and my left arm would not have ached so terribly. Grey Brother is extremely touchy about his territorial rights.

I decided to replace the makeshift dressing over

the torn biceps. I didn't like the drumming insistence of the pain: it kept me awake but interfered with my concentration. I ducked into the nearest store that looked defensible, and found myself sprawled on the floor behind an overturned table, wishing mightily that it weren't so flimsy.

Something had moved.

Then I rose sheepishly to my feet, holstering my heater and rapping my subconscious sentries sharply across the knuckles for the second time in half an hour. My own face looked back at me from the grimy mirror that ran along one whole wall, curly black hair in tangles, wide lips stretched back in what looked just like a grin. It was a grin. I hadn't realized how bad I looked.

Dad had told me a lot about Civilization, before the Exodus, but I don't suppose I'll ever understand it. A glance around this room raised more questions than it answered. On my left, opposite the long mirror, were a series of smaller mirrors that paralleled it for three-quarters of its length, with odd-looking chairs before them. Something like armchairs made of metal, padded where necessary, with levers to raise and lower them. On my right, below the longer mirror, were a lot of smaller, much plainer wooden chairs, in a tight row broken occasionally by strange frameworks from which lengths of rotting fabric dangled. I could only surmise that this was some sort of arcane narcissist's paradise, where men of large ego would come, remove their clothing, recline in luxuriously upholstered seats, and contemplate their own magnificence. The smaller, shabbier seats, too low to afford a decent view, no doubt represented the cut-rate or second-class accomodations.

But what was the significance of the cabinets

between the larger chairs and the wall, laden with bottles and plastic containers and heathen appliances? And why were all the skeletons in the room huddled together in the middle of the floor, as though their last seconds of life had been spent frantically fighting over something?

Something gleamed in the bone-heap, and I saw what the poor bastards had died fighting for, and knew what kind of place this had been. The contested prize was a straight razor.

My father had spent eighteen of my twenty years telling me why I ought to hate Wendell Carlson, and in the past few days I'd acquired nearly as many reasons of my own. I intended to put them in Carlson's obituary.

A wave of weariness passed over me. I moved to one of the big chairs, pressed gingerly down on the seat to make sure no cunning mechanism awaited my mass to trigger it (Collaci's training again—if Teach' ever gets to Heaven, he'll check it for booby traps), took off my rucksack and sat down. As I unrolled the bandage around my arm I glanced at myself in the mirror and froze, struck with wonder. An infinite series of *mes* stretched out into eternity, endless thousands of Isham Stones caught in that frozen second of time that holds endless thousands of possible futures, on the point of some unimaginable cusp. I knew it was simply the opposed mirrors, the one before me slightly askew, and could have predicted the phenomenon had I thought about it—but I was not expecting it and had never seen anything like it in my life. All at once I was enormously tempted to sit back, light a joint from the first-aid kit in my rucksack, and meditate awhile. I wondered what Alia was doing right now, right at this moment. Hell, I

could kill Carlson at twilight, and sleep in his bed—
or hole up here and get him tomorrow, or the next
day. When I was feeling better.

Then I saw the first image in line. Me. A black
man just doesn't bruise spectacularly as a rule, but
there was something colorful over my right eye that
would do until a bruise came along. I was filthy, I
needed a shave, and the long slash running from my
left eye to my upper lip looked angry. My black
turtleneck was torn in three places that I could see,
dirty where it wasn't torn, and bloodstained where
it wasn't dirty. It might be a long time before I felt
any better than I did right now.

Then I looked down at what was underneath the
gauze I'd just peeled off, saw the black streaks on
the chocolate brown of my arm, and the temptation
to set a spell vanished like an overheated Musky.

I looked closer, and began whistling "Good Morning Heartache" through my teeth very softly. I had
no more neosulfa, damned little bandage for that
matter, and it looked like I should save what analgesics I had to smoke on the way home. The best
thing I could do for myself was to finish up in the
city and get gone, find a Healer before my arm
rotted.

And all at once that was fine with me. I remembered the two sacred duties that had brought me to
New York: one to my father and my people, and one
to myself. I had nearly died proving to my satisfaction that the latter was impossible; the other would
keep me no great long time. New York and I were,
as Bierce would say, incompossible.

One way or another, it would all be over soon.

I carefully rebandaged the gangrenous arm, hoisted
the rucksack and went back outside, popping a

foodtab and a very small dosage of speed as I walked. There's no point in bringing real food to New York— you can't taste it anyway and it masses so damned much.

The sun was perceptibly lower in the sky—the day was in catabolism. I shifted my shoulders to settle the pack and continued on up the street, my eyes straining to decipher faded signs.

Two blocks up I found a shop that had specialized in psychedelia. A '69 Ford shared the display window with several smashed hookahs and a narghile or two. I paused there, sorely tempted again. A load of pipes and papers would be worth a good bit at home; Techno and Agro alike would pay dearly for fine-tooled smoking goods—more evidence that, as Dad is always saying, technology's usefulness has outlasted it.

But that reminded me of my mission again, and I shook my head savagely to drive away the daydreaming that sought to delay me. I was—what was the phrase Dad had used at my arming ceremony?—"The Hand of Man Incarnate," that was it, the product of two years personal combat training and eighteen years of racial hatred. After I finished the job I could rummage around in crumbling deathtraps for hash pipes and roach clips—my last detour had nearly killed me, miles to the north.

But I'd *had* to try. I was only two at the time of the Exodus, too young to retain much but a confused impression of universal terror, of random horror and awful revulsion everywhere. But I remember one incident very clearly. I remember my brother Israfel, all of eight years old, kneeling down in the middle of 116th Street and methodically smashing his head against the pavement. Long after Izzy's eight-year-old brains had splashed the concrete, his little body continued to slam the shattered skull down again and again in a literally mindless spasm of escape. I saw this over my mother's shoulder as she ran, screaming her fear, though the chaotically twisting nightmare that for as long as she could remember had been only a quietly throbbing nightmare; as she ran through Harlem.

Once when I was twelve I watched an Agro slaughter a chicken, and when the headless carcass got up and ran about I heard my mother's scream again. It was coming from my throat. Dad tells me I was unconscious for four days and woke up screaming.

Even here, even downtown, where the bones sprawled everywhere were those of strangers, I was wound up tight enough to burst, and ancient reflex fought with modern wisdom as I felt the irrational impulse to lift my head and cast about for an enemy's scent. I had failed to recover Izzy's small bones; Grey Brother, who had always lived in Harlem, now ruled it, and sharp indeed were his teeth. I had managed to hold off the chittering pack with incendiaries until I reached the Hudson, and they would not cross the bridge to pursue me. And so I lived—at least until gangrene got me.

And the only thing between me and Fresh Start was Carlson. I saw again in my mind's eye the familiar Carlson Poster, the first thing my father ran off when he got access to a mimeograph machine: a remarkably detailed sketch of thin, academic features surrounded by a mass of graying hair, with the legend, "WANTED: FOR THE MURDER OF HUMAN CIVILIZATION—WENDELL MORGAN CARLSON. An unlimited lifetime supply of hot-shot shells will be given to anyone bringing the head to The Council of Fresh Start."

No one ever took Dad up on it—at least, no one who survived to collect. And so it looked like it was up to me to settle the score for a shattered era and a planetful of corpses. The speed was taking hold now; I felt an exalted sense of destiny and a fever to be about it. I was the duly chosen instrument for mankind's revenge, and that reckoning was long overdue.

I unclipped one of the remaining incendiary grenades from my belt—it comforted me to hold that much raw power in my hand—and kept on walking uptown, feeling infinitely more than twenty years old. And as I stalked my prey through concrete canyons and brownstone foothills, I found myself thinking of his crime, of the twisted motives that had produced this barren jungle and countless hundreds like it. I remembered my father's eyewitness account of Carlson's actions, repeated so many times during my youth that I could almost recite it verbatim, heard again the Genesis of the world I knew from its first historian—my father, Jacob Stone. Yes, *that* Stone, the one man Carlson never expected to survive, to shout across a smashed planet the name of its unknown assassin. Jacob Stone, who first cried the name that became a curse, a blasphemy and a scream of rage in the throats of all humankind. Jacob Stone, who named our betrayer: Wendell Morgan Carlson!

And as I reviewed that grim story, I kept my hand near the rifle with which I hoped to write its happy ending. . . .

CHAPTER TWO

Excerpts from I WORKED WITH CARLSON,
by Jacob Stone, Ph.D., authorized version:
Fresh Start Press 1986 (Mimeo).

. . . The sense of smell is a curious phenomenon,
oddly resistant to measurement or rigorous analysis.
Each life form on Earth appears to have as much of
it as they need to survive, plus a little. The natural
human sense of smell, for instance, was always more
efficient than most people realized, so much so that
in the 1880s the delightfully eccentric Sir Francis
Galton had actually succeeded, by associating numbers with certain scents, in *training himself to add
and subtract by smell*, apparently just for the intellectual exercise.

But through a sort of neurological suppressor circuit of which next to nothing is known, most people
contrived to ignore all but the most pleasing or disturbing of the messages their noses brought them,
perhaps by way of reaction to a changing world in
which a finely-tuned olfactory apparatus became a
nuisance rather than a survival aid. The level of
sensitivity which a wolf requires to find food would
be a hindrance to a civilized human packed into a
city of his fellows.

By 1983, Professor Wendell Morgan Carlson had
raised olfactometry to the level of a precise science.
In the course of testing the theories of Beck and
Miles, Carlson almost absently-mindedly perfected the
classic "blast-injection" technique of measuring dif-
ferential sensitivity in olfaction, *without regard for the*

subjective impressions of the test subject. This not only refined his data, but also enabled him to work with life forms other than human, a singular advantage when one considers how much of the human brain is terra incognita.

His first subsequent experiments indicated that the average wolf utilized his sense of smell on the order of a thousand times more efficiently than a human. Carlson perceived that wolves lived in a world of scents, as rich and intricate as our human worlds of sight and word. To his surprise, however, he discovered that the *potential* sensitivity of the human olfactory apparatus far outstripped that of any known species.

This intrigued him. . . .

. . . Wendell Morgan Carlson, the greatest biochemist Columbia—and perhaps the world—had ever seen, was living proof of the truism that a genius can be a damned fool outside his own specialty.

Genius he unquestionably was; it was *not* serendipity that brought him the Nobel Prize for isolating a cure for the entire spectrum of virus infections called "the common cold." Rather it was the sort of inspired accident that comes only to those brilliant enough to perceive it, fanatic seekers like Pasteur.

But Pasteur was a boor and a braggart, who frittered away valuable time in childish feuds with men unfit to wash out his test tubes. Genius is seldom a good character reference.

Carlson was a left-wing radical.

Worse, he was the type of radical who dreams of romantic exploits in a celluloid underground: grim-eyed rebels planting homemade bombs, assassinating the bloated oppressors in their very strongholds and (although he certainly knew what hydrogen sulfide was) escaping through the city sewers.

It never occurred to him that it takes a very special kind of man to be a guerilla. He was convinced that the moral indignation he had acquired at Washington in '71 (during his undergraduate days) would see him through hardships and privation, and he would have been horrified if someone had pointed out to him that Che Guevara seldom had access to toilet paper. Never having experienced hunger, he thought it a glamorous state. He lived a compartmentalized life, and his wild talent for biochemistry had the thickest walls: only within them was he capable of logic or true intuition. He had spent a disastrous adolescent year in a seminary, enlisted as a "storm trooper of Mary," and had come out of it apostate but still saddled with a relentless need to Serve A Cause—and it chanced that the cry in 1982 was, once again, "Revolution Now!"

He left the cloistered halls of Columbia in July of that year, and applied to the smaller branch—the so-called "Action-Faction"—of the New Weathermen for a position as assassin. Fortunately he was taken for crazy and thrown out. The African Liberation Front was somewhat less discerning—they broke his leg in three places. In the Emergency Room of Jacobi Hospital Carlson came to the conclusion that the trouble with Serving A Cause was that it involved associating with unperceptive and dangerously unpredictable people. What he needed was a One-Man Cause.

And then, at the age of thirty-two, his emotions noticed his intellect for the first time.

When the two parts of him came together, they achieved critical mass—and that was a sad day for the world. I myself bear part of the blame for that coming-together—unwittingly I provided one of the final sparks, put forward the idea which sent Carlson on the most dangerous intuitive leap of his life. My own feelings of guilt for this will plague me to my dying day—and yet it might have been anyone. Or no one.

Fresh from a three-year stint doing biowar research for the Defense Department, I was a very minor colleague of Carlson's, but quickly found myself becoming a close friend. Frankly I was flattered that a man of his stature would speak to me, and I suspect Carlson was overjoyed to find a black man who would treat him as an equal.

But for reasons which are very difficult to explain to anyone who did not live through that period—and which need no explanation for those who did—I was reluctant to discuss the ALF with a honky, however "enlightened." And so when I went to visit Carlson in Jacobi Hospital and the conversation turned to the self-defeating nature of uncontrollable rage, I attempted to distract the patient with a hasty change of subject.

"The Movement's turning rancid, Jake," Carlson had just muttered, and an excellent digression occurred to me.

"Wendell," I said heedlessly, "do you realize that you personally are in a position to make this a better world?"

His eyes lit up. "How's that?"

"You are probably the world's greatest authority on olfactometry and the human olfactory apparatus, among other things—right?"

"As far as there is one, I suppose so. What of it?"

He shifted uneasily within his traction gear: wearing his radical *persona*, he was made uncomfortable by reference to his scientist-mode. He felt it had little to do with the Realities of Life—like nightsticks and grand juries.

"Has it ever occurred to you," I persisted to my everlasting regret, "that nearly all the undesirable by-products of twentieth-century living, Technological Man's most unlovable aspects, quite literally *stink*? The whole *world*'s going rancid, Wendell, not just the Movement. Automobiles, factory pollution, crowded cities—Wendell, why couldn't you develop a selective suppressant for the sense of smell—controlled anosmia? Oh, I know a snort of formaldehyde will do the trick, and having your adenoids removed sometimes works. But a man oughtn't to have to give up the smell of frying bacon just to survive in New York. And you know we're reaching that pass—in the past few years it hasn't been necessary to leave the city and then return to be aware of how evil it smells. The natural suppressor-mechanism in the brain—whatever it is—has gone about as far as it can go. Why don't you devise a small-spectrum filter to aid it? It would be welcomed by sanitation workers, engineers—why, it would be a godsend to the man on the street!"

Carlson was mildly interested. Such an anosmic filter would be both a mordant political statement and a genuine boon to Mankind. He had been vaguely pleased by the success of his cold-cure, and I believe he sincerely wished to make the world a happier place—however perverted his methods tended to be. We discussed the idea at some length, and I left.

Had Carlson not been bored silly in the hospital, he would never have rented a television set. It was extremely unfortunate that the Late Show (ed. note: a television show of the period) on that particular evening featured the film version of Alistair MacLean's *The Satan Bug*. Watching this absurd production, Carlson was intellectually repelled by the notion that a virus could be isolated so hellishly virulent that "a teaspoon of it would sweep the earth of life in a few days."

But it gave him a wild idea—a fancy, a fantasy, and a tasty one.

He checked with me by phone the next day, very casually, and I assured him from my experiences with advances in virus-vectoring that MacLean had *not* been whistling in the dark. In fact, I said, modern so-called "bacterial warfare" made the Satan Bug look like child's play. Carlson thanked me and changed the subject.

On his release from the hospital, he came to my office and asked me to work with him for a full year, to the exclusion of all else, on a project whose nature he was reluctant to discuss. "Why do you need me?" I asked, puzzled.

"Because," he finally told me, "you know how to make a Satan Bug. I intend to make a God Bug. And you could help me."

"Eh?"

"Listen, Jake," he said with that delightful informality of his. "I've licked the common cold—and there are still herds of people with the sniffles. All I could think of to do with the cure was to turn it over to the pharmaceuticals people, and I did all I could to make sure they didn't milk it, but there are still suffering folks who can't afford the damned stuff. Well, there's no need for that. Jake, a cold will kill someone sufficiently weakened by hunger—I can't help the hunger, but I could eliminate colds from the planet in forty-eight hours . . . with your help."

"A benevolent virus-vector . . ." I was flabbergasted, as much by the notion of decommercializing medicine as by the specific nostrum involved.

"It'd be a lot of work," Carlson went on. "In its present form my stuff isn't compatible with such a delivery system—I simply wasn't thinking along those lines. But I'll bet it could be made so, with your help. Jake, I haven't got time to learn your field—throw in with me. Those pharmaceuticals goniffs have made me rich enough to pay you twice what Columbia does, and we're both due for sabbatical anyway. What do you say?"

I thought it over, but not enough. The notion of collaborating with a Nobel Prize winner was simply too tempting. "All right, Wendell."

We set up operations in Carlson's laboratory-home on Long Island, he in the basement and myself on the main floor. There we worked like men possessed for the better part of a year, cherishing private dreams and slaughtering guinea pigs by the tens of thousands. Carlson was a stern if somewhat slapdash taskmaster, and as our work progressed he began "looking over my shoulder," learning my field while discouraging inquiries about his own progress. I assumed that he simply knew his field too well to converse intelligently about it with anyone but himself. And yet he absorbed all my own expertise with fluid rapidity, until eventually it seemed that he knew as much about virology as I did myself. One day he disappeared with no explanation, and returned a week or two later with what seemed to me a more nasal voice.

And near the end of the year there came a day

when he called me on the telephone. I was spending the weekend, as always, with my wife and two sons in Harlem. Chrismas was approaching, and Barbara and I were discussing the relative merits of plastic and natural trees when the phone rang. I was not at all surprised to hear Carlson's reedy voice, so reminiscent of an oboe lately—the only wonder was that he had called during conventional waking hours.

"Jake," he began without preamble, "I haven't the time or inclination to argue, so shut up and listen, right? Right. I advise and strongly urge you to take your family and leave New York *at once*—steal a car if you have to, or hijack a Greyhound (ed. note: a public transportation conveyance) for all of me, but be at least twenty miles away by midnight."

"But . . ."

". . . head north if you want my advice, and for God's sake stay away from all cities, towns, and people in any number. If you possibly can, get upwind of all nearby industry, and bring along all the formaldehyde you can—a gun too, if you own one. Goodbye, my friend, and remember I do this for the greater good of mankind. I don't know if you'll understand that, but I hope so."

"Wendell, what in the name of *God* are you . . . ?" I was talking to a dead phone.

Barbara was beside me, a worried look on her face, my son Isham in her arms. "What is it?"

"I'm not sure," I said unsteadily, "but I think Wendell has come unhinged. I must go to him. Stay with the children; I'll be back as quickly as I can. And Barbara . . ."

"Yes?"

"I know this sounds insane, but pack a bag and

be ready to leave town *at once* if I call and tell you
to."

"Leave town? Without you?"

"Yes, just that. Leave New York and never return.
I'm fairly certain you won't have to, but it's just possible that Wendell knows what he's talking about. If
he does, I'll meet you at the cabin by the lake, as
soon as I can." I put off her questions then and left,
heading for Long Island.

When I reached Carlson's home in Old Westbury
I let myself in with my key and made my way toward
his laboratory. But I found him upstairs in mine,
perched on a stool, gazing intently at a flask in his right
hand. Its interior swirled, changing color as I watched.

Carlson looked up. "You're a damned fool, Jake,"
he said quietly before I could speak. "I gave you a
chance."

"Wendell, what on earth is this all about? My wife
is scared half to—"

"Remember that controlled anosmia you told me
about when I was in the hospital?" he went on conversationally. "You said the trouble with the world is
that it stinks, right?"

I stared at him, vaguely recalling my words.

"Well," he said, "I've got a solution."

And Carlson told me what he held in his hand. A
single word.

I snapped, just completely snapped. I charged him,
clawing wildly for his throat, and he struck me with
his left hand, his faceted ring giving me the scar I
bear to this day, knocking me unconscious. When I
came to my senses I was alone, alone with a helpless guilt and terror. A note lay on the floor beside
me, in Wendell's sprawling hand, telling me that I
had—by my watch—another hour's grace. At once I

ran to the phone and wasted ten minutes trying to
call Barbara. I could not get through—trunk failure,
the operator said. Gibbering, I took all the formaldehyde I could find in both labs and a self-contained
breathing rig from Carlson's, stepped out into the
streetlit night and set about stealing a car.

It took me twenty minutes, not bad for a first
attempt but still cutting it fine—I barely made it to
Manhattan, with superb traffic conditions to help me,
before the highway became a butcher shop.

At precisely nine o'clock, Wendell Morgan Carlson
stood on the roof of Columbia's enormous Butler
Library, held high in the air by fake Greek columns
and centuries of human thought, gazing north across
a quadrangle within which grass and trees had nearly
given up trying to grow, toward the vast domed
Lowe Library and beyond toward the ghetto in
which my wife and children were waiting, oblivious.
In his hands he held the flask I had failed to wrest
from him, and within it were approximately two
teaspoons of an infinitely refined and concentrated
virus culture. It was the end result of our year's
work, and it duplicated what the military had spent
years and billions to obtain: a strain of virus that
could blanket the globe in about forty-eight hours.
There was no antidote for it, no vaccine, no defense
of any kind for virtually all of humanity. It was
diabolical, immoral and quite efficient. On the other
hand, it was not lethal.

Not that is, in and of itself. But Carlson had concluded, like so many before him, that a few million
lives was an acceptable price for saving the world,
and so at 9:00 P.M. on December 17, 1984 he leaned
over the parapet of Butler Hall and dropped his flask
six long stories to the concrete below. It shattered on

impact and sprayed its contents into what dismal breeze still blew through the campus.

Carlson had said one word to me that afternoon, and the word was "Hyperosmia."

Within forty-eight hours every man, woman and child left alive on earth possessed a sense of smell approximately a hundred times more efficient than that of any wolf that ever howled.

During those forty-eight hours, a little less than a fifth of the planet's population perished, by whatever means they could devise, and every city in the world spilled its remaining life into the surrounding countryside. The ancient smell-suppressing system of the human brain collapsed under unbearable demand, overloaded and burned out in an instant.

The great complex behemoth called Modern Civilization ground to a halt in a little less than two days. In the last hours, those pitiably few city-dwellers on the far side of the globe who were rigorous enough of thought to heed and believe the brief bewildered death-cries of the great mass media strove valiantly— and hopelessly—to effect emergency measures. The wiser attempted, as I had, to deaden their senses of smell with things like formaldehyde, but there is a limit to the amount of formaldehyde that even desperate men can lay hands on in a day or less, and its effects are generally temporary. Others with less vision opted for airtight environments if they could get them, and there they soon died, either by asphyxiation when their air supply ran out or by suicide when, fervently hoping they had outlived the virus, they cracked their airlocks at last. It was discovered that human technology had produced no commonly-available nose plug worth a damn, nor any air-purification system capable of filtering out Carlson's virus. Although the rest of the animal kingdom was not measurably affected by it, mankind failed utterly to check the effects of the ghastly Hyperosmic Plague, and the Exodus began . . .

. . . I don't believe Carlson rejoiced over the carnage that ensued, though a strict Malthusian might have considered it as a long-overdue pruning. But it is easy to understand why he thought it was necessary, to visualize the "better world" for which he spent so many lives: Cities fallen to ruin. Automobiles rotting where they stood. Heavy industry gone to join the dinosaurs. The synthetic-food industry utterly undone. Perfume what it had always been—a memory—as well as tobacco. A wave of cleanliness sweeping the globe, and public flatulation at last a criminal offense, punishable by death. Secaucus, New Jersey abandoned to the buzzards. The back-to-nature communalists achieving their apotheosis, helping to feed and instruct bewildered urban survivors (projected catch-phrase: "If you don't like hippies, next time you're hungry, call a cop"). The impetus of desperation forcing new developments in production of power by sun, wind and water rather than inefficient combustion of more precious resources. The long-delayed perfection of plumbing. And a profoundly interesting and far-reaching change in human mating customs as feigned interest or disinterest became unviable pretenses (as any wolf could have told us, the scent of desire can be neither faked nor masked).

All in all an observer as impartial as Carlson imagined himself to be might have predicted that an ultimate cost of perhaps thirty to forty percent of its population (no great loss), the world ten or twenty years after Carlson would be a much nicer place to live in.

Instead and in fact, there are four billion less people living in it, and this year Two AC we have achieved only a bare possibility of survival at a cost of eighty to ninety percent of our number.

The first thing Carlson could not have expected claimed over a billion and a half lives within the first month of the Brave New World. His compartmentalized mind had not been monitoring current developments in the field of psychology, a discipline he found frustrating. And so he was not aware of the work of Lynch and others, conclusively demonstrating that autism was the result of sensory overload. Autistic children, Lynch had proved, were victims of a physiochemical imbalance which disabled their suppressor-circuitry for sight, hearing, touch, smell, or any combination thereof, flooding their brains with an intolerable avalanche of useless data and shocking them into retreat. Lysergic acid diethylamide is said to produce a similar effect, on a smaller scale.

The Hyperosmic Virus produced a similar effect, on a larger scale. Within weeks, millions of near-catatonic adults and children perished from malnutrition, exposure, or accidental injury. Why some survived the shock and adapted, while some did not, remains a mystery, although there exists scattered data suggesting that those whose sense of smell was already relatively acute suffered most.

The second thing Carlson could not have expected was The War.

The War had been ordained by the plummeting fall of his flask, but he may perhaps be excused for not foreseeing it. It was not such a war as has ever been seen on earth before in all recorded history, humans versus each other or subordinate life forms. There was nothing for the confused, scattered survivors of the Hyperosmic Plague to fight over, few unbusy enough to fight over it; and with lesser life forms we are now *better* equipped to compete. No, war broke out between us bewildered refugees—and the Muskies.

It is difficult for us to imagine today how it was possible for the human race to know of the Muskies for so long without ever believing in them. Countless humans reported contact with Muskies—who at various times were called "ghosts," "poltergeists," "leprechauns," "fairies," "gremlins," and a host of other misleading labels—and not *one* of these thousands of witnesses was believed by humanity at large. Some of us saw our cats stare, transfixed, at nothing at all, and wondered—but did not believe—what they saw. In its arrogance the race assumed that the peculiar perversion of entropy called "life" was the exclusive property of solids and liquids.

Even today we know very little about the Muskies, save that they are gaseous in nature and perceptible only by smell. The interested reader may wish to examine Dr. Michael Gowan's ground-breaking attempt at a psychological analysis of these entirely alien creatures, *Riders of the Wind* (Fresh Start Press, 1986).

One thing we do know is that they are capable of an incredible and disturbing playfulness. While not true telepaths, Muskies can project and often impose mood patterns over short distances, and for centuries they seem to have delighted in scaring the daylights out of random humans. Perhaps they laughed like innocent children as women to whom their pranks were attributed were hung in Salem. Dr. Gowan suggests that this aspect of their racial psyche is truly infantile—he feels their race is still in its infancy. As, perhaps, is our own.

But in their childishness, Muskies can be dangerous both deliberately and involuntarily. Years ago, before the Exodus, people used to wonder why a race that could plan a space station couldn't design a safe airliner—the silly things used to fall out of the sky with appalling regularity. Often it was simply sheer bad engineering, but I suspect that at least as often a careless, drifting Musky, riding the trades lost in God knows what wildly *alien* thoughts, was sucked into the air intake of a hurtling jetliner and burst the engine asunder as it died. It was this guess which led me to theorize that extreme heat might disrupt and kill Muskies, and this gave us our first and so far only weapon in the bitter war that still rages between us and the windriders.

For, like many children, Muskies are dangerously paranoid. Almost at the instant they realized that men could somehow now perceive them directly, they attacked, with a ferocity that bespoke blind panic. They learned quickly how best to kill us: by clamping itself somehow to a man's face and forcing him to breathe it in, a Musky can lay waste to his respiratory system. The only solution under combat conditions is a weapon which fires a projectile hot enough to explode a Musky—and that is a flawed solution. If you fail to burn a Musky in time, before it reaches you, you may be faced with the unpleasant choice of wrecking your lungs or blowing off your face. All too many Faceless Ones roam the land, objects of horror and pity, supported by fellow men uncomfortably aware that it could happen to them tomorrow.

Further, we Technos here at Fresh Start, dedicated to rebuilding at least a minimum technology, must naturally wear our recently-developed nose plugs for long intervals while doing Civilized work. We therefore toil in constant fear that at any moment we may feel alien projections of terror and dread, catch even through our plugs the characteristic odor that gives Muskies their name, and gasp our lungs out in the final spasms of death.

God knows how Muskies communicate—or even if they do. Perhaps they simply have some sort of group-mind or hive-mentality. What would evolution select for a race of gas-clouds spinning across the earth on the howling mistral? Someday we may devise a way to take one prisoner and study it; for the present we are content to know that they can be killed. A good Musky is a dead Musky.

Some day we may climb back up the ladder of technological evolution enough to carry the battle to the Muskies' home ground; for the present we are at least becoming formidable defenders.

Some day we may have the time to seek out Wendell Morgan Carlson and present him with a bill; for the present we are satisfied that he dares not show himself outside New York City, where legend has him hiding from the consequences of his actions.

CHAPTER THREE

From the Journal of Isham Stone

. . . but my gestalt of the eighteen years that had brought me on an intersecting course with my father's betrayer was nowhere near as pedantically phrased as the historical accounts Dad had written. In fact, I had refined it down to four words.

God damn you, Carlson!

Nearly mid-afternoon, now. The speed was wearing off; time was short. Broadway got more depressing as I went. Have you ever seen a *bus-full* of skeletons—with pigeons living in it? My arm ached like hell, and a muscle in my thigh had just announced it was sprained—I acquired a slight but increasing limp. The rucksack gained an ounce with every step, and I fancied that my right plug was leaking the barest trifle around the flange.

I kept walking north.

I came to Columbus Circle, turned on a whim into Central Park. It was an enclave of life in this concrete land of death, and I could not pass it by—even though my intellect warned that I might encounter a Doberman who hadn't seen a can of dog food in twenty years.

The Exodus had been good to this place at least—it was lush with vegetation now that swarming humans no longer smothered its natural urge to be alive. Elms and oaks reached for the clouds with the same optimism of the maples and birches around Fresh Start, and the overgrown grasses were the greenest things I had seen in New York. And yet—in places the grass was dead, and there were dead bushes and shrubs scattered here and there. Perhaps first impressions were deceiving—perhaps a small parcel of land surrounded by an enormous concrete crypt was not a viable ecology after all. Then again, perhaps neither was Fresh Start.

I was getting depressed again.

I pocketed the grenade I still held and sat down on a park bench, telling myself that a rest would do wonders for my limp. After a time static bits of scenery moved—the place was alive. There were cats, and gaunt starved dogs of various breeds, apparently none old enough to know what a man was. I found their confidence refreshing—like I say, I'm a peaceful type assassin. Gregarious as hell.

I glanced about, wondering why so many of the comparatively few human skeletons here had been carrying weapons on the night of the Exodus—why go armed in a park? Then I heard a cough and looked around, and for a crazy second I thought I knew.

A leopard.

I recognized it from pictures in Dad's books, and I knew what it was and what it could do. But my adrenaline system was tired of putting my gun in my fist—I sat perfectly still and concentrated on smelling friendly. My hand-weapon was designed for high temperature, not stopping-power; grenades are ineffective against a moving target; and I was leaning back against my rifle—but that isn't why I sat still. I had learned that day that lashing out is not an optimum response to fear.

And so I took enough of a second look to realize that this leopard was incredibly ancient, hollow-bellied and claw-scarred, more noble than formidable. If wild game had been permitted to roam in Central Park, Dad would have told me—he knew my planned route. Yet this cat seemed old enough to predate the Exodus. I was certain he knew me for a man. I suppose he had escaped from a zoo in the confusion of the time, or perhaps he was some rich person's pet. I understand they had such things in the Old Days. Seems to me a leopard'd be more trouble than an eagle—Dad kept one for four years and I never had so much grief over livestock before or since. Dad used to say it was the symbol of something great that had died, but I thought it was ornery.

This old cat seemed friendly enough, though, now that I noticed. He looked patriarchal and wise, and he looked awful hungry if it came to that. I made a gambler's decision for no reason that I can name. Slipping off my rucksack slowly and deliberately, I got out a few foodtabs, took four steps toward the leopard and sat on my heels, holding out the tablets.

Instinct, memory or intuition, the big cat recognized my intent and loped my way without haste. Somehow the closer he got the less scared I got, until he was nuzzling my hand with a maw that could have amputated it. I *know* the foodtabs didn't smell like anything, let alone food, but he understood in some empathic way what I was offering—or perhaps he felt the symbolic irony of two ancient antagonists, black man and leopard, meeting in New York City to share food. He ate them all, without nipping my fingers. His tongue was startlingly rough and rasping, but I didn't flinch, or need to. When he was done he made a noise that was a cross between a cough and a snore and butted my leg with his head.

He was old, but powerful; I rocked backward and fell off my heels. I landed correctly, of course, but I didn't get back up again. My strength left me and I lay there gazing at the underside of the park bench.

For the first time since I entered New York, I had communicated with a living thing and been answered in kind, and somehow that knowledge took my strength from me. I sprawled on the turf and waited for the ground to stop heaving, astonished to discover how weak I was and in how many places I hurt unbearably. I said some words that Collaci had taught me, and they helped some but not enough. The speed had worn off faster than it should have, and there was no more.

It looked like it was time for a smoke. I argued with myself as I reached overhead to get the first-aid kit from the rucksack, but I saw no alternative. Carlson was not a trained fighter, had never had a teacher like Collaci: I could take him buzzed. And I might not get to my feet any other way.

The joint I selected was needle-slender—more than a little cannabis would do me more harm than good. I had no mind to get wrecked in *this* city. I lit up with my coil lighter and took a deep lungful, held it as long as I could. Halfway through the second toke the leaves dancing overhead began to sparkle, and my weariness got harder to locate. By the third I knew of it only by hearsay, and the last hit began melting the pains of my body as warm water melts snow. Nature's own analgesic, gift of the earth.

I started thinking about the leopard, who was lying down himself now, washing his haunches. He was magnificent in decay—something about his eyes said that he intended to live forever or die trying. He was the only one of his kind in his universe, and I could certainly identify with that—I'd always felt different from the other cats myself.

And yet—I was kin to those who had trapped him, caged him, exhibited him to the curious and then abandoned him to die half a world away from his home. Why wasn't he trying to kill me? In his place I might have acted differently . . .

With the clarity of smoke-logic I followed the thought through. At one time the leopard's ancestors had tried to kill mine, and *eat* them, and yet there was no reason for me to hate *him*. Killing him wouldn't help my ancestors. Killing me would

accomplish nothing for the leopard, make his existence no easier . . . except by a day's meal, and I had
given him that.

What then, I thought uneasily, *will my killing
Carlson accomplish?* It could not put the Hyperosmic Virus back in the flask, nor save the life of any
now living. Why come all this way to kill?

It was not, of course, a new thought. The question had arisen several times during my training in
survival and combat. Collaci insisted on debating
philosophy while he was working you over, and expected
reply; he maintained that a man who couldn't hold
up his end of the conversation while fighting for his
life would never make a really effective killer. You
could pause for thought, but if he decided you were
just hoarding your wind he stopped pulling his
punches.

One day we had no special topic, and I voiced my
self-doubts about the mission I was training for. What
good, I asked Collaci, would killing Carlson do?
Teach' disengaged and stood back, breathing a little
hard, and grinned his infrequent wolf's grin.

"Survival has strange permutations, Isham. Revenge
is a uniquely human attribute—somehow we find it
easier to bury our dead when we have avenged them.
We have many dead." He selected a toothpick, stuck
it into his grin. "And for your father's sake it has to
be you who does it—only if his son provides his
expiation can Dr. Stone grant himself absolution.
Otherwise I'd go kill that silly bastard myself." And
without warning, he had tried, unsuccessfully, to break
my collarbone.

And so now I sat tired, hungry, wounded and a
little stoned in the middle of an enormous island
mausoleum, asking myself the question I had next

asked Collaci, while trying—unsuccessfully—to cave in his rib cage: is it moral or ethical to kill a man?

Across the months, his answer came back: *Perhaps not, but it is sometimes necessary.*

And with that thought my strength came to me and I got to my feet. My thoughts were as slick as wet soap, within reach but skittering out of my grasp. I grabbed one from the tangle and welded it to me savagely: *I will kill Wendell Morgan Carlson.* It was enough.

And saying good-bye to the luckier leopard, who could never be hagridden by ancient ghosts, I left the park and continued on up Broadway, as alert and deadly as I knew how to be.

When I reached 114th Street, I looked above the rooftops, and there it was: a thin column of smoke north and a little east, toward Amsterdam Avenue. Legend and my father's intuition had been right. Carlson was holed up where he had always felt most secure—the academic womb-bag of Columbia. I felt a grin pry my face open. It would all be over soon now, and I could go back to being me—whoever that was.

I left the rucksack under a station wagon and considered my situation. I had three tracers left in my Musky-killing handgun, three incendiary grenades clipped to my belt, and the scope-sighted sniper-rifle with which I planned to kill Carlson. The latter held a full clip of eight man-killing slugs—seven more than I needed. I checked the action and jacked a slug into the chamber.

There was a detailed map of the Morningside Campus in my pack but I didn't bother to get it out— I had its twin brother in my head. Although neither Teach' nor I had entirely shared Dad's certainty that

Carlson would be at Columbia, I had spent hours studying the campus maps he gave me as thoroughly as the New York City street maps that Collaci had provided. It seemed the only direct contribution Dad could make to my mission.

It looked as though his effort had paid off.

I wondered whether Carlson was expecting me. I wasn't sure if the sound of the car I'd shot downtown could have traveled this far, nor whether an explosion in a city full of untended gas mains was unusual enough to put Carlson on his guard. Therefore I had to assume that it could have and it was. Other men had come to New York to deal with Carlson, as independents, and none had returned.

My mind was clicking efficiently now, all confusion gone. I was eager. A car-swiped lamppost leaned drunkenly against a building, and I briefly considered taking to the rooftops for maximum surprise factor. But rooftops are prime Musky territory, and besides I didn't have strength for climbing.

I entered the campus at the southwest, though the 115th Street gate. As my father had predicted, it was locked—only the main gates at 116th had been left open at night in those days, and it was late at night when Carlson dropped his flask. But the lock was a simple Series 10 American that might have made Teach' laugh out loud. I didn't laugh out loud. It yielded to the second pick I tried, and I slipped through the barred iron gate without a sound—having thought to oil the hinges first.

A flight of steps led to a short flagstone walkway, gray speckled hexagons in mosaic, a waist-high wall on either side. The walkway ran between Furnald and Ferris Booth Halls and, I knew, opened onto the great inner quadrangle of Columbia. Leaves lay scattered all about, and trees of all kinds thrashed in the lusty afternoon breeze, their leaves a million green pin-wheels.

I hugged the right wall until it abutted a taller perpendicular wall. Easing around that, I found myself before the great smashed glass and stone façade of Ferris Booth Hall, the student activities center, staring past it toward Butler Library, which I was seeing from the west side. There was a good deal of heavy construction equipment in the way one of the many student groups that had occupied space in Booth had managed to blow up itself and a sizable portion of the building in 1983, and rebuilding had still been in progress on Exodus Day. A massive crane stood before the ruined structure, surrounded by stacks of brick and pipe, a bulldozer, storage shacks, a few trucks, a two-hundred-gallon gasoline tank and a pair of construction trailers.

But my eyes looked past all the conventional hardware to a curious device beyond them, directly in front of Butler Library and nearly hidden by overgrown hedges. I couldn't have named it—it looked like an octopus making love to a console stereo—but it obviously didn't come with the landscaping. Dad's second intuition was also correct: Carlson was using Butler for his base of operations. God knew what the device was for, but a man without his adenoids in a city full of Muskies and hungry German shepherds would not have built it further from home than could be helped. This was the place.

I drew in a great chest- and belly-full of air, and my grin hurt my cheeks. I held up my rifle and watched my hands. Rock steady.

Carlson, you murdering bastard, I thought, *this is it. The human race has found you, and its Hand is near. A few more breaths and you die violently, old man, like a harmless cat in a smokeshop window, like an eight-year-old boy on a Harlem sidewalk, like a planetwide civilization you thought you could improve on. Get you ready.*

I moved forward.

Wendell Morgan Carlson stepped out between the big shattered lamps that bracketed Butler Hall's front entrance. I saw him plainly in profile, features memorized from the Carlson Poster and my father's sketches, recognizable in the afternoon light even through white beard and tangled hair. He glanced my way, flinched, and ducked back inside a split second ahead of my first shot.

Determined to nail him before he could reach a weapon and dig in, I put my head down and ran, flat out, for the greatest killer of all time.

And the first Musky struck.

Terror sleeted through my brain, driving out the rage, as something warm and intangible plastered itself across my face. I think I screamed then, but somehow I kept from inhaling as I fell and rolled, dropping the rifle and tearing uselessly at the thing on my face. The last thing I saw before invisible gases seared my vision was the huge crane beside me on the right, its long arm flung at the sky like a signpost to Heaven. Then the world shimmered and faded, and I clawed my pistol from its holster. I aimed without seeing, my finger spasmed, and the gun bucked in my hand.

The massive gasoline drum between me and the crane went up with a *whoom*, and I sobbed in relief as I heaved to my feet and dove headlong through the flames. The Musky's dying projections tore at my mind and I rolled clear, searing my lungs with a convulsive inhalation as the Musky exploded behind me. Even as I smashed into the fender of the crane, my hindbrain screamed *Muskies never travel alone!* and before I knew what I was doing I tore loose my plugs to locate my enemy.

Foul stenches smashed my sanity, noxious odors wrenched at my reason, I was torn, blasted, overwhelmed in abominable ordure. The universe was offal, and the world I saw was remote and unreal. My eyes saw the campus, but told me nothing of the rank flavor of putrefaction that lay upon it. They saw sky, but spoke nothing of the reeking layers of indescribable decay of which it was made. Even allowing for a greenhouse effect it was much worse than it should have been after twenty years, just as legend had said. I tasted excrement, I tasted metal, I tasted the flavor of the world's largest charnel house, population seven millions, and I writhed on the concrete. Forgotten childhood memories of the Exodus burst in my brain and reduced me to a screaming, whimpering child. I couldn't *stand* it, it was unbearable, *how had I walked, arrogant and unknowing, through this stinking hell all day?*

And with that I thought I remembered why I had come here, and knew I could not join Izzy in the peaceful, fragrant dark. I could not let go—I had to kill Carlson before I let the blackness claim me. Courage flowed from God knows where, feeding on black hatred and the terrible fear that I would let my people down, let my father down. I stood up and inhaled sharply, through my nose.

The nightmare world sprang into focus and time came to a halt.

There were six Muskies, skittering about before Butler as they sought to bend the breezes to their will.

I had three hot-shot shells and three grenades.

One steadied, banked my way. I fired from the hip and he flared out of existence.

A second caught hold of a prevailing current and came in like an express train. Panic tore through my mind, and I laughed and aimed and the Musky went incandescent.

Two came in at once then, like balloons in slow motion. I extrapolated their courses, pulled two grenades and armed them with opposing thumbs, counted to four and hurled them together as Collaci had taught me, aiming for a spot just short of my target. They kissed at that spot and rebounded, each toward an oncoming Musky. But one grenade went up before the other, killing its Musky but knocking the other one safely clear. It shot past my ear as I threw myself sideways.

Three Muskies. One slug, one grenade.

The one that had been spared sailed around the crane in a wide, graceful arc and came in low and fast, rising for my face as one of its brothers attacked from my left. Cursing, I burned the latter and flipped backwards through a great trail of burning gas from the tank I'd spoiled. The Musky failed to check in time, shot suddenly skyward and burst spectacularly. I slammed against a stack of twelve-inch pipe and heard ribs crack.

One Musky. One grenade.

As I staggered erect, beating at my smouldering turtleneck, Carlson re-emerged from Butler, a curious helmet over his flowing white hair.

I no longer cared about the remaining Musky. Almost absentmindedly I tossed my last grenade in its direction to keep it occupied, but I knew I would have all the time I needed. Imminent death was now a side issue. I lunged and rolled, came up with the rifle in my hands and aimed for the O in Carlson's scraggly white beard. Dimly I saw him plugging a wire from his helmet into the strange console-device, but it didn't matter at all. My finger tightened on the trigger.

And then something smashed me on the side of the neck behind the ear, and my finger clenched, and the blackness that had been waiting patiently for oh! so long swarmed in and washed away the pain and the hate and the weariness and oh Cod the awful smell. . . .

CHAPTER FOUR

Excerpts from the BUILDING OF FRESH START,
by Jacob Stone, Ph.D., authorized version,
Fresh Start Press, 2001.

Although Fresh Start grew slowly and apparently randomly as personnel and materials became available, its development followed the basic outline of a master plan conceived within a year of the Exodus. Of course, I had not the training or experience to visualize specifics of my dream at that early stage—but the basic layout was inherent in the shape and the landscape and in the nature of the new world Carlson had made for us all.

Five years prior to the Exodus, a man named Gallipolis had acquired title, by devious means, to a logged out area some distance northwest of New York City. It was an isolated two-hundred-acre parcel of an extremely odd shape. Seen from the air it must have resembled an enormous pair of sunglasses: two valleys choking with new growth, separated physically by a great perpendicular extrusion of the eastern mountain range, almost to the western slopes, leaving the north and south valleys joined only by a narow channel. The perpendicular "nose" between the valley "lenses" was a tall, rocky ridge, sharply sloped on both sides, forming a perfect natural division. The land dropped gently away from the foot of this ridge in either direction, and dirt roads left by the loggers cut great loops through both valleys. The land was utterly unsuited for farming, and too many miles from nowhere for suburban development—it was what real estate brokers called "an investment in the future."

Gallipolis was a mad Greek. Mad Greeks in literature are invariably swarthy, undereducated, poor and drunk. Gallipolis was florid, superbly educated, moderately well-off and a teetotaler. He looked upon his valleys and he smiled a mad smile and decided to hell with the future. He had a serviceable road cut through the north forest past the lake, to a lonely stretch of state highway which fed into the nearby interstate. He brought bulldozers down this road and had six widely-spaced acres cleared west of the logging road loop in the north valley, and a seventh acre on the lakeshore for himself. On these sites he built large and extremely comfortable homes, masterpieces of design which combined an appearance of "roughing it" with every imaginable modern convenience. He piped in water from spring-fed streams high on the slopes of The Nose (as he had come to call the central ridge). He built beach houses along the lakeshore. It was his plan to lease the homes to wealthy men as weekend or summer homes at an exorbitant fee, and use the proceeds to develop three similar sites in both valleys. He envisioned an ultimate two or three dozen homes and an early retirement, but the only two things he ultimately achieved were to go broke before a single home had been leased and to drop dead.

A nephew inherited the land—and the staggering tax bill. He chanced to be a student of mine, and was aware that I was in the market for a weekend haven from the rigors of the city; he approached me. Although the place was an absurdly long drive from New York, I went up with him one Saturday, looked over the house nearest the lake, made him a firm offer of a quarter of his asking price, and closed the deal on the spot. It was a beautiful place. My wife and I became quite fond of it, and never missed an opportunity to steal a weekend there. Before long we had neighbors, but we seldom saw them, save occasionally at the lake. We had all come there for a bit of solitude, and it was quite a big lake—none of us were socially inclined.

It was for this wooded retreat that my family and I made in the horrible hours of the Exodus, and only by the grace of God did we make it. Certainly none of the other tenants did, then or ever, and it must be assumed that they perished. Sarwar Krishnamurti, a chemist at Columbia who had been an occasional weekend guest at Stone Manor, remembered the place in his time of need and showed up almost at once, with his family. He was followed a few days later by George Dalhousie, a friend of mine from the Engineering Department to whom I had once given directions to the place.

We made them as welcome as we could under the circumstances—my wife was in a virtual state of shock from the loss of our eldest son, and none of us were in much better shape. I know we three men found enormous comfort in each other's presence, in having other men of science with whom to share our horror, our astonishment, our guesses and our grim extrapolations. It kept us sane, kept our minds on practical matters, on survival; for had we been alone, we might have succumbed, as did so many, to a numb, traumatized disinterest in living.

Instead, we survived the winter that came, the one that killed so many, and by spring we had laid our plans.

We made occasional abortive forays into the outside world, gathering information from wandering survivors. All media save rumor had perished; even my international-band radio was silent. On these expeditions we were always careful to conceal the existence and location of our home base, pretending to be as disorganized and homeless as the aimless drifters we continually encountered. We came to know every surviving farmer in the surrounding area, and established friendly relations with them by working for them in exchange for food. Like all men, we avoided areas of previous urbanization, for nose plugs were inferior in those days, and Muskies were omnipresent and terrifying. In fact, rumor claimed, they tended to cluster in cities and towns.

But that first spring, we conquered our fear and revulsion with great difficulty and began raiding small towns and industrial parks with a borrowed wagon. We found that rumor had been correct: urban areas were crawling with Muskies. But we needed tools and equipment of all kinds and descriptions, badly enough to risk our lives repeatedly for them. It went slowly, but Dalhousie had his priorities right, and soon we were ready.

We opened our first factory that spring, on a hand-cleared site in the south valley (which we christened "Southtown"). Our first product had been given careful thought, and we chose well—if for the wrong reasons. We anticipated difficulty in convincing people to buy goods from us with barter, when they could just as easily have scavenged from the abandoned urban areas. In fact, one of our central reasons for founding Fresh Start had been the conviction that the lice on a corpse are not a going concern: we did not want our brother survivors to remain dependent on a finite supply of tools, equipment and processed food. If we could risk Musky attack, so could others.

Consequently we selected as our first product an item unobtainable anywhere else, and utterly necessary in the changed world: effective nose plugs. I suggested them; Krishnamurti designed them and the primitive assembly line on which they were first turned out, and Dalhousie directed us all in their construction. All of us, men and women, worked on the line. It took us several months to achieve success, and by that time we were our own best customers—our factory smelled most abominable. Which we had expected, and planned for: the whole concept of Fresh Start rested on the single crucial fact that prevailing winds were virtually always from the north. On the rare occasions when the wind backed, the Nose formed a satisfactory natural barrier.

Once we were ready to offer our plugs for sale, we began advertising and recruiting on a large scale. Word of our plans was circulated by word of mouth, mimeographed flyer and shortwave broadcast. The only person who responded by the onset of winter was Helen Phinny, but her arrival was providential, freeing us almost overnight from dependence on stinking gasoline-powered generators for power. She was then and is now Fresh Start's only resident world-class genius, a recognized expert on what were then called "alternative" power sources—the only ones Carlson had left us. She quite naturally became a part of the planning process, as well as a warm friend of us all. Within a short time the malodorous generators had been replaced by water power from the streams that cascade like copious tears from the "bridge" of The Nose, and ultimately by methane gas and wind power from a series of "eggbeater" type windmills strung along The Nose itself. In recent years the generators have been put back on the line, largely for industrial use—but they no longer burn gasoline, nor does the single truck we have restored to service. Thanks to Phinney, they burn pure grain alcohol which we distill ourselves from field corn and rye, which works *more* efficiently than gasoline and produces only water and carbon dioxide as exhaust. (Pre-Exodus man could have used the same fuel in most of his internal combustion engines—but once Henry Ford made his choice, the industry he incidentally created tended of course to perpetuate itself.)

This then was the Council of Fresh Start, assembled by fate; myself, a dreamer, racked with guilt and seeking a truly worthwhile penance, trying to salvage some of the world I'd helped ruin. Krishnamurti, utterly practical wizard at both requirements analysis and design engineering, translator of ideas into plans. Dalhousie, the ultimate foreman, gifted at reducing any project to its component parts and accomplishing them with minimum time and effort. Phinney, the energy provider, devoted to drawing free power from the natural processes of the universe. Our personalities blended as well as our skills, and by that second spring we were a unit: the Council. I would suggest a thing, Krishnamurti would design the black box, Dalhousie would build it and Phinney would throw power to it. We fit. Together we felt *useful* again, more than scavenging survivors.

No other recruits arrived during the winter, which like the one before was unusually harsh for that part of the world (perhaps owing to the sudden drastic decline in the worldwide production of waste heat), but by spring volunteers began arriving in droves. We got all kinds: scientists, technicians, students, mechanics, handymen, construction workers, factory hands, a random assortment of men seeking civilized work. A colony of canvas tents grew in Northtown, in cleared areas we hoped would one day hold great dormitories. Our initial efforts that summer were aimed at providing water, power and sewage systems for our growing community, and enlarging our nose plug factory. A combination smithy-repair-shop-motor-pool grew of its own accord next to the factory in Southtown, and we began bartering repair work for food with local farmers to the east and northwest.

By common consent, all food, tools and other resources were shared equally by all members of the community, with the single exception of mad Gallipolis's summer homes. We the council members retained these homes, and have never been begrudged them by our followers (two of the homes were incomplete at the time of the Exodus, and remained so for another few years). That aside, all the inhabitants of Fresh Start stand or fall, eat or starve together. The Council's authority as governing committee has never in all the ensuing years been either confirmed or seriously challenged. The nearly one hundred technicians who have by now assembled to our call continue to follow our advice because it works: because it gives their lives direction and meaning, because it makes their hard-won skills useful again, because it pays them well to do what they do best, and thought they might never do again.

During that second summer we were frequently attacked by Muskies, invariably (of course) from the north, and suffered significant losses. For instance, Samuel Pegorski, the young hydraulic engineering major who with Phinney designed and perfected our plumbing and sewage systems, was cut down by the windriders before he lived to hear the first toilet flush in Northtown.

But with the timely arrival of Phillip Collaci, an ex-marine and former police chief from Pennsylvania, our security problems disappeared. A preternaturally effective fighting man, Collaci undertook to recruit, organize and train The Guard, comprising enough armed men to keep the northern perimeter of Fresh Start patrolled at all times. At first, these Guards did no more than sound an alarm if they smelled Muskies coming across the lake, whereupon all hands made for the nearest shelter and tried to blank their minds to the semitelepathic creatures.

But Collaci was not satisfied. He wanted an offensive weapon—or, failing that, a defense better than flight. He told me as much several times, and finally I put aside administrative worries and went to work on the problem from a biochecmical standpoint.

It seemed to me that extreme heat should work, but the problem was to devise a delivery system. Early experiments with a salvaged flamethrower were unsatisfactory—the cone of the fire tended to brush Muskies out of its path instead of consuming them.

Collaci suggested a line of alcohol-burning jets along the north perimeter, ready to guard Fresh Start with a wall of flame, an idea which has since been implemented—but at the time we could not spare the corn or rye to make the alcohol to power the jets. Finally, weeks of research led to the successful development of "hot-shot"—ammunition which could be fired from any existing heavy-caliber weapon after its barrel had been replaced, that would ignite as it cleared the modified barrel and generate enormous heat as it flew, punching through any Musky it encountered and destroying it instantly. An early mixture of magnesium and perchlorate of potash has since given way to an even slower-burning mix of aluminum powder and potassium permanganate which will probably remain standard until the last Musky has been slain (long-range plans for long-range artillery shot will have to wait until we can find a good cheap source of cerium, zirconium or thorium—unlikely in the near future). Hot-shot's effective range approximates that of a man's nose on a still day—good enough for personal combat. This turned out to be the single most important advance since the Exodus, not only for mankind, but for the fledging community of Fresh Start.

Because our only major misjudgement had been the climate of social opinion in which we expected to find ourselves. I said earlier that we feared people would scavenge from cities rather than buy from us, even in the face of terrible danger from the Muskies who prowled the urban skies. This turned out not to be the case.

Mostly, people preferred to do without.

Secure in our retreat, we had misjudged the *zeit-geist*, the mind of the common man. It was Collaci, fresh from over a year of wandering up and down the desolate eastern seaboard, who showed us our error. He made us realize that Lot was probably more eager to return to Gomorrah than the average human was to return to his cities and suburbs. Cities had been the scenes of the greatest racial trauma since The Flood, the places where friends and loved ones had died horribly and the skies had filled with Muskies. The Exodus and the subsequent weeks of horror were universally seen as the Hammer of God falling on the *idea of city* itself, and hard-core urban-ites who might have debated the point were mostly too dead to do so. The back-to-nature movement, already in full swing at the moment when Carlson dropped the flask, took on the stature and fervor of a Dionysian religion.

Fortunately, Collaci made us see in time that we would inevitably share in the superstition and hatred accorded to cities, become associated in the common mind with the evil-smelling steel-and-glass behemoth from which men had been so conclusively vomited. He made us realize something of the extent of the suspicion and intolerance we would incur—not ignored for our redundance, but loathed for our repugnance.

At Collaci's suggestion Krishnamurti enlisted the aid of some of the more substantial farmers in neighboring regions to the east, northeast and north-west. He negotiated agreements by which farmers who supported us with food received preferential access to Musky-killing ammunition, equipment maintenance and, one day (he promised), commercial power. I could never have sold the idea myself—while I have always understood public relations well from the theoretical standpoint, I have never been very successful in interpersonal diplomacy—at least, with non-technicals. The dour Krishnamurti might have seemed an even more unlikely choice—but his utter practicality convinced many a skeptical farmer where charm might have failed.

Krishnamurti's negotiations not only assured us a dependable supply of food (and incidentally, milled lumber), it had the invaluable secondary effect of gaining us psychological allies, non-Technos who were economically and emotionally committed to us.

Work progressed rapidly once our recruiting efforts began to pay off, and by our fifth year the Fresh Start of today was visible, at least in skeleton form. We had cut interior roads to supplement the northern and southern loops left by gyppo loggers two decades before; three dormitories were up and a fourth a-building; our "General Store" was a growing commercial concern; a line of windmills was taking shape along the central ridge of The Nose; our sewage plant/methane converter was nearly completed; plans were underway to establish a hospital and to blast a tunnel through The Nose to link North- and South-towns; "The Tool Shed," the depot which housed irreplaceable equipment and tools, was nearly full; and Southtown was more malodorous than ever, with a large fuel distillery, a chemistry lab, a primitive foundry, and glass blowing, match-making and weaving operations adjoining the hot-shot and nose-plug factories.

Despite these outward signs of prosperity, we led a precarious existence—there was strong public sentiment in favor of burning us to the ground, at least among the surviving humans who remained landless nomads. To combat this we were running and distributing a small mimeographed newspaper, *Got News*, and maintaining radio station WFS (then and now the only one in the world). In addition Krishnamurti and I made endless public relations trips for miles in every direction to explain our existence and purpose to groups and individuals.

But there were many who had no land, no homes, no families, nothing but a vast heritage of bitterness. These were the precursors of today's so-called Agro Party. Surviving where and as they could, socialized for an environment that no longer existed, they hated us for reminding them of the technological womb which had unforgivably thrust them out. They raided us, singly and in loosely-organized groups, often with unreasonable, suicidal fury. From humanitarian concerns as much as from public relations considerations, I sharply restrained Guard Chief Collaci, whose own inclination was to shoot any saboteur he apprehended— wherever possible they were captured and turned loose outside city limits. Collaci argued strongly for deterrent violence, but I was determined to show our neighbors that Fresh Start bore ill will to no man, and overruled him.

In that fifth year, however, I was myself overruled.

CHAPTER FIVE

". . . and when I came to, Carlson was dead with a slug through the head and the last Musky was nowhere in smell. So I reset my plugs, found the campfire behind the hedges and ate his supper, and then left the next morning. I found a Healer in Jersey. That's all there is, Dad."

My father chewed the pipe he had not smoked in

eighteen years and stared into the fire. Dry poplar and green birch together produced a steady blaze that warmed the spacious living room and peopled it with leaping shadows.

"Then it's over," he said at last, and heaved a great sigh.

"Yes, Dad. It's over."

He was silent, his coal-black features impassive, for a long time. Firelight danced among the valleys and crevices of his patriarch's face, and across the sharp scar on his left cheek (so like the one I now bore). His eyes glittered like rainy midnight. I wondered what he was thinking, after all these years and all that he had seen.

"Isham," he said at last, "you have done well."

"Have I, Dad?"

"Eh?"

"I just can't seem to get it straight in my mind. I guess I expected tangling with Carlson to be a kind of solution, to some things that have been bugging me all my life. Somehow I expected pulling that trigger to bring me peace. Instead I'm more confused than ever. Surely you can smell unease, Dad? Or are your plugs still in again?" Dad used the best plugs in Fresh Start, entirely internal, and he perpetually forgot to remove them after work. Even those who loved him agreed he was the picture of the absent-minded professor.

"No," he said hesitantly. "I can smell that you are uneasy, but I can't smell *why*. You must tell me, Isham."

"It's not easy to explain, Dad. I can't seem to find the words. Look, I wrote out a kind of journal of events in Jersey, while the Healer was working on me, and afterwards while I rested up. It's the same story

I just told you, but somehow on paper I think it conveys more of what's bothering me. Will you read it?"

He nodded. "If you wish."

I gave my father all the preceding manuscript, right up to the moment I pulled the trigger and blacked out, and brought him his glasses. He read it slowly and carefully, pausing now and again to gaze distantly into the flames. While he read, I unobtrusively fed the fire and immersed myself in the familiar smells of woodsmoke and ink and chemicals and the pines outside, all the thousand indefinable scents that tried to tell me I was home.

When Dad was done reading, he closed his eyes and nodded slowly for a time. Then he turned to me and regarded me with troubled eyes. "You've left out the ending," he said.

"Because I'm not sure how I feel about it."

He steepled his fingers. "What is it that troubles you, Isham?"

"Dad," I said earnestly, "Carlson is the first man I ever killed. That's . . . not a small thing. As it happens I didn't actually see my bullet blow off the back of his skull, and sometimes it's hard to believe in my gut that I really did it—I know it seemed unreal when I saw him afterward. But in fact I have killed a man. And as you just read, that may be necessary sometimes, but I'm not sure it's right. I *know* all that Carlson did, to us Stones and to the world, I know the guilt he bore. But I must ask you: Dad, was I *right* to kill him? Did he deserve to die?"

He came to me then and gripped my shoulder, and we stood like black iron statues before the raving fire. He locked eyes with me. "Perhaps you should ask your mother, Isham. Or your brother Israfel. Perhaps

you should have asked the people whose remains you
stepped over to kill Carlson. I do not know what is
'right' and 'wrong'; they are slippery terms to define.
I only know what is. And revenge, as Collaci told you,
is a uniquely human atribute.

"Superstitious Agro guerillas used to raid us from
time to time, and because we were reluctant to fire
on them they got away with it. Then one day in our
fifth year they captured Collaci's wife, not knowing
she was diabetic. By the time he caught up with them
she was dead of lack of insulin. Within seven days,
every guerilla in that raiding party had died, and
Fresh Start has not been raided in all the years since,
for all Jordan's rhetoric. Ask Collaci about vengeance."

"But Jordan's Agros hate us more than ever."

"But they buy our axheads and wheels, our sulfa
and our cloth, just like their more sensible neighbors,
and they leave us alone. Carlson's death will be an
eternal warning to any who would impose their val-
ues on the world at large, and an eternal comfort to
those who were robbed by him of the best of their
lives—of their homes and their loved ones.

"Isham, you . . . did . . . *right*. Don't ever think
differently, son. You did right, and I am deeply proud
of you. Your mother and Israfel are resting easier now,
and millions more too. I know that I will sleep easier
tonight than I have in eighteen years."

That's right, Dad, you will. I relaxed. "All right,
Dad. I guess you're right. I just wanted to hear
someone tell me besides myself. I wanted *you* to tell
me." He smiled and nodded and sat down again, and
I left him there, an old man lost in his thoughts.

I went to the bathroom and closed the door behind
me, glad that restored plumbing had been one of
Fresh Start's first priorities to be realized. I spent a

few minutes assembling some items I had brought
back from New York City, and removing the back of
the septic tank behind the toilet bowl. Then I flushed
the toilet.

Reaching into the tank I grabbed the gravity ball
and flexed it horizontal so that the tank would not
refill with water. Holding it in place awkwardly, I
made a long arm and picked up the large bottle of
chlorine bleach I had fetched from the city. As an
irreplaceable relic of Civilization it was priceless—
and utterly useless to modern man. I slipped my plugs
into place and filled the tank with bleach, replacing
the porcelain cover silently but leaving it slightly ajar.
I bent again and grabbed a large canister—also a
valuable but useless antique—of bathroom bowl
cleaner. It was labeled "Vanish," and I hoped the label
was prophetic. I poured the entire canister into the
bowl.

Hang the expense, I thought, and giggled insanely.

Then I put the cover down on the seat, hid the
bleach and bowl cleaner and left, whistling softly
through my teeth.

I felt good, better than I had since I left New York.

I walked through inky dark to the lake, and I sat
among the pines by the shore, flinging stones at the
water, trying to make them skip. I couldn't seem to
get it right. I was used to the balancing effect of a
left arm. I rubbed my stump ruefully and lay back
and just thought for awhile. I had lied to my father—
it was not over. But it would be soon.

Right or wrong, I thought, removing my plugs and
lighting a joint, *it sure can be necessary.*

Moonlight shattered on the branches overhead and
lay in shards on the ground. I breathed deep of the
cool darkness, tasted pot and woods and distant

animals and the good crisp scents of a balanced ecology, heard the faraway hum of wind-generators storing power for the work yet to be done. And I thought of a man gone mad with a dream of a better, simpler world; a man who, Heaven help him, meant well. And I thought of the tape recording I planned to leave behind me, explaining what I had done to The Council and the world.

CHAPTER SIX

Transcript of a Tape Recording Made by Isham Stone (Fresh Start Judicial Archives)

I might as well address this tape to you, Collaci—I'll bet my Musky-gun that you're the first one to notice and play it. I hope you'll listen to it as well, but that might be too much to ask, the first time around. Just keep playing it.

The story goes back a couple of months, to when I was in the city. By now you've no doubt found my journal, with its account of my day in New York, and you've probably noticed the missing ending. Well, there are two endings to that story. There's the ending I told my father, and then there's the one you're about to hear. The true one.

I drifted in the darkness for a thousand years, helpless as a Musky in a hurricane, caroming off the inside of my skull. Memories swept by like drifting blimps, and I clutched at them as I sailed past, but the ones tangible enough to grasp burned my fingers.

Vaguely, I sensed distant daylight on either side, decided those must be my ears and tried to steer for the right one, which seemed a bit closer. I singed my arm banking off an adolescent trauma, but it did the trick—I sailed out into daylight and landed on my face with a hell of a crash. I thought about getting up, but I couldn't remember whether I'd brought my legs with me, and they weren't talking. My arm hurt even more than my face, and something stank.

"Help?" I suggested faintly, and a pair of hands got me by the armpits. I rose in the air and closed my eyes against a sudden wave of vertigo. When it passed, I decided I was on my back in the bed I had just contrived to fall out of. High in my chest, a dull but insistent pain advised me to breathe shallowly.

I'll be damned, I thought weakly. *Collaci must have come along to back me up without telling me. Canny old son of a bitch, I should have thought to pick him up some toothpicks.*

"Hey, Teach'." I croaked, and opened my eyes.

Wendell Morgan Carlson leaned over me, concern in his gaze.

Curiously enough, I didn't try to reach up and crush his larynx. I closed my eyes, relaxed all over, counted to ten very slowly, shook my head to clear it and opened my eyes again. Carlson was still there.

Then I tried to reach up and crush his larynx. I failed, of course, not so much because I was too weak to *reach* his larynx as because only one arm even acknowledged the command. My brain said that my left arm was straining upwards for Carlson's throat, and complaining like hell about it too, but I didn't see the arm anywhere. I looked down and saw the neatly bandaged stump and lifted it up absently to see if my arm was underneath it and it wasn't. It dawned on me then that the stump was all the left arm I was ever going to find, and whacko: I was back inside my skull, safe in the friendly dark, ricocheting off smouldering recollections again.

The second time I woke up was completely different. One minute I was wrestling with a phantom, and then a switch was thrown and I was lucid. *Play for time* was my first thought, *the tactical situation sucks.* I opened my eyes.

Carlson was nowhere in sight. Or smell—but then my plugs were back in place.

I looked around the room. It was a room. Four walls, ceiling, floor, the bed I was in and assorted ugly furniture. Not a weapon in sight, nor anything I could make one from. A look out the window in the opposite wall confirmed my guess that I was in Butler Hall, apparently on the ground floor, not far from the main entrance. The great curved dome of Low "Library" was nearly centered in the windowframe, its great stone steps partly obscured by overgrown shrubbery in front of Butler. The shadows said it was morning, getting on toward noon. I closed my eyes, firmly.

Next I took stock of myself. My head throbbed a good deal, but it was easily drowned out by the ache in my chest. Unquestionably some ribs had broken, and it felt as through the ends were mismatched. But as near as I could tell the lung was intact—it didn't hurt more when I inhaled. Not much more, anyway. My legs both moved when I asked them to, with a minimum of backtalk, and the ankles appeared sound. No need to open my eyes again, was there?

I stopped the inventory for a moment. In the back of my skull a clawed lizard yammered for release, and I devoted a few minutes to reinforcing the walls of

its prison. When I could no longer hear the shriek-
ing, I switched on my eyes again and quite dispas-
sionately considered the stump on my left arm.

It looked like a good, clean job. The placement
of the cut said it was a surgical procedure—it seemed
as though the gangrene had been beaten. *Oh fine*,
I thought, *a benevolent madman I have to kill*. Then
I was ashamed. My mother had been benevolent, as
I remembered her; and Israfel never got much chance
to be anything. All men knew Carlson's intentions had
been good. I could kill him with one hand.

I wondered where he was.

A fly buzzed mournfully around the room. Hedges
rustled outside the window, and somewhere birds sang,
breathless trills that hung sparkling on the morning air.
It was a beautiful day, just warm enough to be comfortable, no clouds evident, just enough breeze and the
best part of the day was yet to come. It made me want
to do go down by the stream and poke frogs with a
stick, or go pick strawberries for Mr. Fletcher, red-
stained hands and a bellyful of sweet and the trots next
morning. It was a great day for an assassination.

I thought about it, considered the possibilities.
Carlson was . . . somewhere. I was weaker than a
Musky in a pressure cooker and my most basic armament was down by twenty-five percent. I was on unfamiliar territory, and the only objects in the room meaty
enough to constitute weaponry were too heavy for me
to lift. Break the windowpane and acquire a knife?
How would I hold it? My sneakers were in sight across
the room, under a chair holding the rest of my clothes,
and I wondered if I could hide behind the door until
Carlson entered, then strangle him with the laces.

I brought up short. How was I going to strangle
Carlson with one hand?

Things swam then for a bit, as I got the first of an endless series of flashes of just how drastically my life was altered now by the loss of my arm. *You'll never use a chainsaw again, or a shovel, or a catcher's mitt, or* . . .

I buried the lizard again and forced myself to concentrate. Perhaps I could fashion a noose from my sneaker laces. With one hand? *Could* I? Maybe if I fastened one end of the lace to something, then looped the other end around his neck and pulled? I needn't be strong, it could be arranged so that my weight did the killing. . . .

Just in that one little instant I think I decided not to die, decided to keep on living with one arm, and the question never really arose in my mind again. I was too busy to despair, and by the time I could afford to—much later—the urge was gone.

All of my tentative plans, therapeutic as they were, hinged on one important question: could I stand up? It seemed essential to find out.

Until then I had moved only my eyes—now I tried to sit up. It was no harder than juggling bulldozers, and I managed to cut the scream down to an explosive, "Uh *huh*!" My ribs felt like glass, broken glass ripping through the muscle sheathing and pleural tissue. Sweat broke out on my forehead and I fought down dizziness and nausea, savagely commanding my body to obey me like a desperate rider digging spurs into a dying horse. I locked my right arm behind me and leaned on it, swaying but upright, and waited for the room to stop spinning. I spent the time counting to one thousand by eighths. Finally it stopped, leaving me with the feeling that a stiff breeze could start it spinning again.

All right then. *Let's get this show on the road, Stone.* I swung a leg over the side of the bed, discovered with relief that my foot reached the floor. That would make it easier to balance upright on the edge of the bed before attempting to stand. Before I could lose my nerve I swung the other leg over, pushed off with my arm, and was sitting upright. The floor was an incredible distance below—had I really fallen that far and lived? Perhaps I should just wait for Carlson to return, get him to come close and sink my teeth into his jugular.

I stood up.

A staggering crescendo in the symphony of pain, ribs still carrying the melody. I locked my knees and tottered, moaning piteously like a kitten trapped on a cornice. It was the closest I could come to stealthy silence, and all things considered it was pretty damn close. My right shoulder was discernibly heavier than the left one, and it played hob with my balance. The floor, which had been steadily receding, was now so far away I stopped worrying about it—surely there would be time for the 'chute to open.

Well then, why not try a step or two?

My left leg was as light as a helium balloon—once peeled off the floor it tried to head for the ceiling, and it took an enormous effort to force it down again. The right leg fared no better. Then the room started spinning again, just as I'd feared, and it was suddenly impossible to keep either leg beneath my body, which began losing altitude rapidly. The 'chute didn't open. There was a jarring crash, and a ghastly *bounce*. Many pretty lights appeared, and one of the screams fenced in behind closed teeth managed to break loose. The pretty lights gave way to flaking ceiling, and the ceiling gave way to blackness. I remembered a line from an old song Doctor Mike used to sing, something about ". . . roadmaps in a well-cracked ceiling . . ." and wished I'd had time to read the map. . . .

I came out of it almost at once, I think. It *felt* as though the room was still spinning, but I was now spinning with it at the same velocity. By great good fortune I had toppled backward, across the bed. I took a tentative breath, and it still felt like my lung was intact. I was drenched with sweat, and I seemed to be lying on someone's rock collection.

Okay, I decided, *if you're too weak to kill Carlson now, pretend you're even weaker. Get back under the sheets and play dead, until your position improves.* Isham Machiavelli, that's me. You'd've been proud of me, Teach'.

The rock collection turned out to be wrinkled sheets. Getting turned around and back to where I'd started was easier than rolling a whale into a rowboat, and I had enough strength to arrange the sheets plausibly before all my muscles turned into peanut butter. Then I just lay there breathing as shallowly as I could manage, wondering why my left . . . why my stump didn't seem to hurt enough. I hated to look a gift horse in the mouth; the psychological burden was quite heavy enough, thanks. But it made me uneasy.

I began composing a square-dance tune in time to the throbbing of my ribs. The room reeled to it, slightly out of synch at first but then so rhythmically that it actually seemed to stumble when the snare-drummer out in the hall muffed a paradiddle. The music stopped, but the drummer staggered on off-rhythm, faint at first but getting louder. Footsteps.

It had to be Carlson.

He was making a hell of a racket. Feverishly I

envisioned him dragging a bazooka into the room and
lining it up on me. Crazy. A flyswatter would have
more than sufficed. But what the hell *was* he carrying then?

The answer came through the doorway: a large
carton filled with things that clanked and rattled.
Close behind it came Wendell Morgan Carlson himself, and it was as well that the square-dance music
had stopped—the acceleration of my pulse would have
made the tune undanceable. My nostrils tried to flare
around the plugs, and the hair on the back of my
neck might have bristled in atavistic reflex if there
hadn't been a thousand pounds of head lying on it.

The Enemy!

He had no weapons visible. He looked much
older than his picture on the Carlson Poster—but
the craggy brow, thin pinched nose and high cheeks
were unmistakable, even if the lantern jaw was
obscured by an inordinate amount of gray beard. He
was a bit taller than I had pictured him, with more
hair and narrower shoulders. I hadn't expected the
pot belly. He wore baggy jeans and a plaid flannel
shirt, both ineptly patched here and there, and a
pair of black sandals.

His face held more intelligence than I like in an
antagonist—he would not be easy to fool. *Wendell
who? Never heard of him. Just got back from
Pellucidar myself, and I was wondering if you could
tell me where all the people went? Sorry I took a shot
at you, and oh, yeah, thanks for cutting off my arm;
you're a brick.*

He put the carton down on an ancient brown desk,
crushing a faded photograph of someone's children,
turned at once to meet my gaze and said an incredible
thing.

"I'm sorry I woke you."

I don't know what I'd expected. But in the few fevered moments I'd had to prepare myself for this moment, my first exchange of words with Wendell Morgan Carlson, I had never imagined such an opening gambit. I had no riposte prepared.

"You're welcome," I croaked insanely, and tried to smile. Whatever it was I actually did seemed to upset him; his face took on that look of concern I had glimpsed once before—when? Yesterday? *How long had I been here?*

"I'm glad you are awake," he went on obligingly. "You've been unconscious for nearly a week." No wonder I felt constructed-of-inferior-materials. I decided I must be a pretty tough mothafucka. It was nice to know I wasn't copping out.

"What's in the box?" I asked, with a little less fuzz-tone.

"Box?" He looked down. "Oh yes, I thought . . . you see, it's intravenous feeding equipment. I studied the literature, and I . . ." he trailed off. His voice was a reedy but pleasant alto, with rustling brass edges. He appeared unfamiliar with its use.

"You were going to . . ." An ice cube formed in my bowels. Needle into sleeping arm, suck my life from a tube; have a hit of old Isham. *Steady boy, steady.*

"Perhaps it might still be a good idea," he mused. "All I have to offer you at the moment is bread and milk. Not real milk of course . . . but then you could have honey with the bread. I suppose that's as good as glucose."

"Fine with me, Doctor," I said hastily. "I have a thing about needles." And other sharp instruments. "But where do you get your honey?"

He frowned quizzically. "How did you know I have a Ph.D.?"

Think quick. "I didn't. I assumed you were a Healer. It was you who amputated my arm?" I kept my voice even.

His frown deepened, a striking expression on that craggy face. "Young man," he said reluctantly, "I have no formal medical training of any sort. Perhaps your arm could have stayed on—but it seemed to me . . ." He was, to my astonishment, mortally embarrassed.

"Doctor, it needed extensive cutting the last time I saw it, and I'm sure it got worse while I was under. Don't . . . worry about it. I'm sure you did the best you could." If he was inclined to forget my attempt to blow his head off, who was *I* to hold a grudge? Let bygones be bygones—I didn't need a new reason to kill him.

"I read all I could find on field amputation," he went on, still apologetic, "but of course I'd never done one before." On anything smaller than a race. I assured him that it looked to me like a textbook job. It was inexpressibly weird to have this man seek my pardon for saving my life when I planned to take his at the earliest possible opportunity. It upset me, made me irritable. My wounds provided a convenient distraction, and I moved enough to justify a moan.

Carlson was instantly solicitous. From his cardboard carton he produced a paper package which, torn open, revealed a plastic syringe. Taking a stoppered jar from the carton, he drew off a small amount of clear fluid.

"What's that?" I said, trying to keep the suspicion from my voice.

"Demerol."

I shook my head. "No, thanks, Doc. I told you I don't like needles."

He nodded, put down the spike and took another object from the carton. "Here's oral Demerol, then. I'll leave it where you can reach it." He put it on a bed-side table. I picked up the jar, gave it a quick glance. It said it was Demerol. I could not break the seal around the cap with one hand—Carlson had to open it for me. *Thank you, my enemy.* Weird, weird, weird! I palmed a pill, pretending to swallow it. He looked satisfied.

"Thanks, Doc."

"Please don't call me 'Doc,'" he asked. "My name is Wendell Carlson."

If he was expecting a reaction, he was disappointed. "Sure thing, Wendell. I'm Tony Latimer. Pleased to meet you." It was the first name that entered my head.

There was a lull in the conversation. We studied each other with the frank curiosity of men who have not known human company for a while. At last he looked embarrassed again and tore his gaze from mine. "I'd better see about that food. You must be terribly hungry."

I thought about it. It seemed to me that I could put away a quarter-horse. Raw. With my fingers. "I could eat."

Carlson left the room, looking at his sandals.

I thought of loading the hypo with an overdose and ambushing him when he returned, but it was just a thought. That hypo was mighty far away. I returned my attention to the jar on the table. It still said it was Demerol—and it *had* been sealed, with white plastic. But Carlson could have soaked off and replaced a skull-and-crossbones label—I decided to live with the pain awhile longer.

It seemed like a long time before he returned, but

my time-sense was not too reliable. He fetched a half-loaf of brown bread, a mason jar of soymilk and some thick, crystallized honey. They say that smell is essential to taste, and I couldn't unplug, but it tasted better than food ever had before.

"You never told me where you get honey, Wendell."

"I have a small hive down in Central Park. Only a few supers, but adequate for my needs. Wintering the bees is quite a trick, but I manage."

"I'll bet it is." Small talk in the slaughterhouse. I ate what he gave me and drank soymilk until I was full. My body still hurt, but not as much.

We talked for about half an hour, mostly inconsequentialities, and it seemed that a tension grew up between us, because of the very inconsequentiality of our words. There were things of which we did not speak, of which innocent men should have spoken. In my dazed condition I could concoct no plausible explanation for my presence in New York, nor for the shot I had fired at him. Somehow he accepted this, but in return I was not to ask him how he came to be living in New York City. I was not supposed to have any idea who Wendell Morgan Carlson was. It was an absurd bargain, a truth-level impossible to maintain, but it suited both of us. I couldn't imagine what he thought of my own conversational omissions, but I was convinced that his silence was an admission of guilt, and my resolve was firmed. He left me at last, advising me to sleep if I could and promising to return the next day.

I didn't sleep. Not at first. I lay there looking at the Demerol bottle for a hundred years, explaining to myself how unlikely it was that the bottle wasn't

genuine. I could not help it—hatred and distrust of
Carlson were ingrained in me.

But enough pain will break through the strongest
conditioning. About sundown I ate the pill I'd palmed,
and in a very short time I was unconscious.

The next few days passed slowly.

Whoops—I'm out of tape. Time to flip over the
re—

CHAPTER SEVEN

Stone Tape Transcript, Side Two

The days passed slowly, but not so slowly as the
pain. Lucidity returned slowly, but no faster than
physical strength.

You've got to understand how it was, Teach'.

The Demerol helped—but not by killing the
pain. What it did was keep me so stoned that I
often forgot the pain was there. In a warm, creative glow I would devise a splendidly subtle and
poetic means of Killing Carlson—then half an hour
later the same plan would seem hopelessly
crackbrained. An imperfection of the glass in the
window across the room, warping the clean proud
line of Low Dome, held me fascinated for hours—
yet I could not seem to concentrate for five minutes on practical matters.

Carlson came and went, asking few questions and
answering fewer, and in my stupor I tried to fire my
hate to the killing point, and—Collaci, my instruc-
tor and mentor and (I hope) friend—I failed.

You must understand me—I spent hours trying to focus on the hatred my father had passed on to me, to live up to the geas that fate had laid on me, to do my duty. But it was damned hard work. Carlson was an absurd combination: so absentminded as to remind me of Dad—and as thoughtful, in his way, as you. He would forget his coat when he left at night—but be back on time with a hot breakfast, shivering and failing to notice. He would forget my name, but never my chamberpot. He would search, blinking, in all directions for the coffee cup that sat perched on his lap, but he never failed to put mine where I could reach it without strain on my ribs. I discovered quite by accident that I slept in the only bed Carlson had ever hauled into Butler, that he himself dossed on a makeshift bed out in the hall, so as to be near if I cried out in the night.

He offered no clue to his motivations, no insight into what had kept him entombed in New York City. He spoke of his life of exile as a simple fact, requiring no explanation. It seemed more and more obvious that his silence was an admission of guilt: that he could not explain his survival and continued presence in this smelly mausoleum without admitting his crime. I tried, how I tried, to hate him.

But it was damnably difficult. He supplied my needs before I could voice them, wants before I could form them. He sensed when I craved company and when to leave me be, when I needed to talk and when I needed to be talked to. He suffered my irritability and occasional rages in a way that somehow allowed me to keep my self-respect.

He was gone for long periods of time during the day and night, and never spoke of his activities. I never pressed him for information; as a recuperating assassin it behooved me to display no undue curiosity. I could not risk arousing his suspicions.

We never, for instance, chanced to speak of my weapons or their whereabouts.

And so the subconscious tension of our first conversation stayed with us, born of the things of which we did not speak. It was obvious to both of us—and yet it was a curious kind of kinship, too: both of us lived with something we could not share, and recognized the condition in the other. Even as I planned his death I felt a kind of empathy between Wendell Morgan Carlson and myself. It bothered the hell out of me. If Carlson was what I *knew* he was, what his guilty silence only proved him to be, then his death was necessary and just—for my father had taught me that debts are always paid. But I could not help but like the absentminded old man.

Yet that tension was there. We spoke only of neutral things: where he got gasoline to feed the generator that powered wallsockets in the ground-floor rooms (we did not discuss what he would store it in now that I'd ruined his 200-gallon tank). How far he had to walk these days to find scavengeable flour, beans and grains. The trouble he had encountered in maintaining the University's hydroponics cultures by himself. What he did with sewage and compost. The probability of tomatoes growing another year in the miserable sandy soil of Central Park. What a turkey he'd been to not think of using the pure-grain alky in Organic Chem for fuel. Never did we talk of why he undertook all the complex difficulty of living in New York, nor why I had sought him here. He . . . diverted the patient with light conversation; and the patient allowed him to do so.

I had the hate part all ready to go, but I couldn't

superimpose my lifetime picture of Carlson over this fuzzy, pleasant old academic and make it fit. And so the hate boiled in my skull and made convalescence an aimless, confused time. It got much worse when Carlson, explaining that few things on earth are more addictive than oral Demerol, cut me off cold turkey in my second week. Less potent analgesics, Talwin, aspirin, all had decayed years ago, and if I sent Carlson rummaging through the rucksack I had left under a station wagon on 114th Street for the remaining weed, he would in all likelihood come across the annotated map of New York given me by Collaci, and the mimeo'd Carlson Poster. Besides, my ribs hurt too much to smoke.

One night I woke in a sweat-soaked agony to find the room at a crazy angle, the candle flame slanting out of the dark like a questing tongue. I had half-fallen out of bed, and my right arm kept me from falling the rest of the way, but I could not get back up without another arm. I didn't seem to have one. Ribs began to throb as I considered the dilemma, and I cried out in pain.

From out in the hallway came a honking snore that broke off in a grunted "Whazzat? Wha?" and then a series of gasps as Carlson dutifully rolled from his bed to assist me. There came a crash, then a greater one attended by a splash, then a really tremendous crash that echoed and re-echoed. Carlson lurched into view, a pot-bellied old man in yellow pajamas, eyes three-quarters closed and unfocused, one foot trapped in a galvanized wastebasket, gallantly coming to my rescue. He hit the doorframe a glancing blow with his shoulder, overbalanced and went down on his face. I believe he came fully awake a second after he hit the floor; his eyes opened wide and he saw me staring at him in a dazed disbelief from a few inches away. And for one timeless moment the absurdity of our respective positions hit us, and we broke up, simultaneous whoops of laughter at ourselves that cut off at once, and a second later he was helping me back into bed with strong, gentle hands, and I was trying not to groan aloud.

Dammit, I liked him.

Then one day while he was away I rose from the bed all by myself, quite gratified to find that I could, and hobbled like an old, old man composed of glass to the window that looked out on the entrance area of Butler and the hedge-hidden quadrangle beyond. It was a chill, slightly off-white day, but to me even the meager colors of shrub and tree seemed unaccountably vivid. From the overfamiliar closeness of the sickroom, the decaying campus had a magnificent depth. Everything was so *far away*. It was a little overwhelming. Moving closer to the window, I looked to the right.

Carlson stood before the front doors, staring up at the sky over the quadrangle with his back to me. On his head was the same curious helmet I had seen once before, days ago, framed in the crosshairs of my rifle. The odd-looking machine was before him, wired to his helmet and his arms, I wondered again what it could be, and then I saw something that made me freeze, made me forget the pain and the dizziness and stare with full attention.

Carlson was staring down the row between two greatly overgrown hedges that ran parallel to each other and perpendicular to Butler, facing toward Low's mighty cascade of steps. But he stared as a man watching something *near* him, and its position followed that of the wind-tossed upper reaches of the hedges.

Intuitively I knew that he was using the strange machine to communicate with a Musky, and all the hatred and rage for which I had found no outlet boiled over, contorting my face with fury.

It seemed an enormous effort not to cry out some primal challenge; I believe I bared my teeth. *You bastard,* I thought savagely, *you set us up for them, made them our enemies, and now you're hand in glove with them.* I was stupefied by such incredible treachery, could not make any sense of it, did not care. As I watched from behind and to the left I saw his lips move silently, but I did not care what they said, what kind of deal Carlson had worked out with the murderous gas-clouds. He had one. He dealt with the creatures that had killed my mother, that he had virtually created. He would soon die.

I shuffled with infinite care back to bed, and planned.

I was ready to kill him within a week. My ribs were mostly healed now—I came to realize that my body's repair-process had been waiting only for me to decide to heal, to leave the safe haven of convalescence. My strength returned to me and soon I could walk easily, and even dress myself with care, letting the left sleeve dangle. Most of the pain was gone from the stump, leaving only the many annoying tactile phenomena of severed nerves, the classic "phantom arm" and the flood of sweat which seemed to pour from my left armpit but could not be found on my side. Thanks to Carlson's tendency toward sound sleep, I was familiar with the layout of the main floor—and had recovered the weapons he was too absentminded to destroy. He had "hidden" them in the broom closet.

I wanted to take him in a time and place where his Musky pals couldn't help him; it seemed to me certain that the ones I had destroyed were bodyguards. A blustery cold night obliged by occurring almost immediately, breezes too choppy to be effectively used by a windrider.

The kind of night which, in my childhood, we chose for a picnic or a hayride.

We ate together in my room, a bean and lentil dish with tamari and fresh bread, and as he was finishing his last sip of coffee I brought the rifle out from under the blanket and drew a bead on his face.

"End of the line, Wendell."

He sat absolutely still, cup still raised to his lips, gazing gravely over it at me, for a long moment. Then he put the cup down very slowly, and sighed. "I didn't think you'd do it so soon. You're not well enough, you know."

I grinned. "You were expecting this, huh?"

"Ever since you discovered your weapons the night before last, Tony."

My grin faded. "And you let me live? Wendell, have you a death wish?"

"I cannot kill," he said sadly, and I roared with sudden laughter.

"Maybe not any more, Wendell. Certainly not in another few minutes." *But you have killed before, killed more than anyone in history. Hell, Hitler, Attila, they're all punks beside you!*

He grimaced. "So you know who I am."

"The whole world knows. What's left of it."

Pain filled his eyes, and he nodded. "The last few times I tried to leave the city, to find others to help me in my work, they shot at me. Two years ago I found a man down in the Bowery who had been attacked by a dog-pack. He had a tooth missing. He said he had come to kill me, for the price on my head, and he died, cursing me, in my arms as I brought him here. The price he named was high, and I knew there would be others."

"And you nursed me back to health? You must know that you deserve to die." I sneered. "Musky-lover."

"You know even that, then?"

"I saw you talking with them, with that crazy helmet of yours. The ones who attacked me were your bodyguards, weren't they?"

"The windriders came to me almost twenty years ago," he said softly, eyes far away. "They did not harm me. Since then I have slowly learned to speak with them, after a fashion, using the undermind. We might yet have understood one another."

The gun was becoming heavy on my single arm, difficult to aim properly. I rested the barrel on my knee, and shifted my grip slightly. My hands were sweaty.

"Well?" he said gruffly. "Why haven't you killed me already?"

A good question. I swept it aside irritably. "Why did you do it?" I barked.

"Why did I create the Hyperosmic Virus?" His weathered face saddened even more, and he tugged at his beard. "Because I was a damned fool, I suppose. Because it was a pretty problem in biochemistry. Because no one else could have done it, and because I wasn't certain that I could. I never suspected when I began that it would be used as it was."

"Its release was a spur of the moment decision,

is that it?" I snarled, tightening my grip on the
trigger.

"I suppose so," he said quietly. "Only Jacob could
say, of course."

"*Who*?"

"Jacob Stone," he said, startled by my violence. "My
assistant. I thought you said you . . ."

"So you knew who I was all the time," I growled.

He blinked at me, plainly astounded. Then understanding flooded his craggy features. "Of course," he
murmured. "Of *course*. You're young Isham—I should
have recognized you. I smelled your hate, of course,
but I never . . ."

"You *what*?"

"Smelled the scent of hate upon you," he repeated,
puzzled. "Not much of a trick—you've been reeking
with it lately."

How could he? . . . impossible, sweep it aside.

"And now I imagine you'll want to discharge that
hate and avenge your father's death. That was his own
doing, but no matter: it was I who made it possible.
Go ahead, pull the trigger." He closed his eyes.

"My father is not dead," I said, drowning now in
confusion.

Carlson opened his eyes at once. "No? I assumed
he perished when he released the Virus."

My ears roared; the rifle was suddenly impossible
to aim. I wanted to cry out, to damn Carlson for a
liar, but I knew the fuzzy professor was no actor and
all at once I sprang up out of the bed and burst from
the room, through wrought-iron lobby doors and out
of the great empty hall, out into blackness and
howling wind and a great swirling kaleidoscope of
stars that reeled drunkenly overhead. Ribs pulsing,

I walked for a hundred years, clutching my idiot rifle, heedless of danger from Musky or hungry Doberman, pursued by a thousand howling demons. Dimly I heard Carlson calling out behind me for a time, but I lost him easily and continued, seeking oblivion. The city, finding its natural prey for the first time in two decades, obligingly swallowed me up.

More than a day later I had my next conscious thought. I became aware that I had been staring at my socks for at least an hour, trying to decide what color they were.

My second coherent thought was that my ass hurt.

I looked around: beyond smashed observation windows, the great steel and stone corpse of New York City was laid out below me like some incredible three-dimensional jigsaw. I was at the top of the Empire State Building.

I had no memory of the long climb, nor of the flight downtown from Columbia University, and it was only after I had worked out how tired I must be that I realized how tired I was. My ribs felt sandblasted and the winds that swept the observation tower were very very cold.

I was higher from the earth than I had ever been before in my life, facing south toward the empty World Trade Center, toward that part of the Atlantic into which this city had once dumped five hundred cubic feet of human shit every day; but I saw neither city nor sea. Instead I saw a frustrated, ambitious black man, obsessed with a scheme for quick-and-easy world salvation, conning a fuzzy-headed genius whose eminence he could never hope to attain. I saw that man, terrified by the ghastly results of his folly, fashioning a story to shift blame from himself and

repeating it until all men believed it—and perhaps
he himself as well. I saw at last the true face of that
story's villain: a tormented, guilt-driven old man, exiled
for the high crime of gullibility, befriended only by
his race's bitterest enemies, nursing his assassin back
to health. And I saw as though for the first time that
assassin, trained and schooled to complete a cover-
up, the embittered black man's last bucket of white-
wash.

My father had loaded me with all the hatred and
anger he felt for himself, aimed me toward a scape-
goat and fired me like a cannon.

But I would ricochet.

I became aware of noise below me, in the interior of the building. I waited incuriously, not even
troubling to lift my rifle from my lap. The noise
became weary footsteps on the floor below me. They
shuffled slowly up the iron stairway nearest me, and
paused at the top. I heard hoarse, wheezing breath,
struggling to slow itself, succeeding. I did not turn.

"Hell of a view," I said, squinting at it.

"View of a hell," Carlson wheezed behind me.

"How'd you find me, Wendell?"

"I followed your spoor."

I spun, stared at him, "You—"

"Followed your spoor."

I turned around again, and giggled. The giggle
became a chuckle, and then I sat on it. "Still got your
adenoids, eh, Doc? Sure. Twenty years in this rotten graveyard and I'll bet you've never owned a set
of nose plugs. Punishment to fit the crime—and then
some."

He did not reply. His breathing was easier now.

"My father, Wendell, now there's an absentminded
man for you," I went on conversationally. "Always

doing some sort of Civilized work, always forgetting to remove his plugs when he comes home—he surely does take a lot of kidding. Our security chief, Phil Collaci, quietly makes sure Dad has a Guard with him when he goes outdoors—just can't depend on Dad's sense of smell, Teach' says. Dad always was a terrible cook, you know? He always puts too much garlic in the soup. Am I boring you, Wendell? Would you like to hear a lovely death I just dreamed? I am the last assassin on earth, and I have just created a brand-new death, a unique one. It convicts as it kills—if you die, you deserve to." My voice was quite shrill now, and a part of me clinically diagnosed hysteria. Carlson said something I did not hear as I raved of toilet bowls and brains splashing on a sidewalk and impossible thousands of chittering gray rats and my eyes went nova and a carillon shattered in my skull and when the world came back I realized that the exhausted old man had slapped my head near off my shoulders. He crouched beside me, holding his hand and wincing.

"Why have no Muskies attacked me, here in the heights?" My voice was soft now, wind-tossed.

"The windriders project and receive emotions. Those who sorrow as you and I engender respect and fear in them. You are protected now, as I have been these twenty years. An expensive shield."

I blinked at him and burst into tears.

He held me then in his frail old arms, as my father had never done, and rocked me while I wept. I wept until I was exhausted, and when I had not cried for a time he said softly, "You will put away your new death, unused. You are his son, and you love him."

I shivered then, and he held me closer, and did not see me smile.

✧   ✧   ✧

So there you have it, Teach'. Stop thinking of Jacob Stone as the Father of Fresh Start, and see him as a man—and you will not only realize that his sense of smell was a hoax, but like me will wonder how you were ever taken in by so transparent a fiction. There are a dozen blameless explanations for Dad's anosmia—none of which would have required pretense.

So look at the method of his dying. The lid of the septic tank will be found ajar—the bathroom will surely smell of chlorine. Ask yourself how a chemist could possibly walk into such a trap—*if he had any sense of smell at all?*

Better yet, examine the corpse for adenoids.

When you've put it all together, come look me up. I'll be at Columbia University, with my good friend Wendell Morgan Carlson. We have a lot of work to do, and I suspect we'll need the help of you and the Council before long. We're learning to talk with Muskies, you see.

If you come at night, I've got a little place of my own set up in the lobby of the Waldorf-Astoria. You can't miss me. But be sure to knock: I'm Musky-proof these days, but I've still got those subconscious sentries you gave me.

And I'm scared of the dark.

DAVID WEBER

The Honor Harrington series: *(cont.)*

Flag in Exile

Hounded into retirement and disgrace by political enemies, Honor Harrington has retreated to planet Grayson, where powerful men plot to reverse the changes she has brought to their world. And for their plans to succeed, Honor Harrington must die!

Honor Among Enemies

Offered a chance to end her exile and again command a ship, Honor Harrington must use a crew drawn from the dregs of the service to stop pirates who are plundering commerce. Her enemies have chosen the mission carefully, thinking that either she will stop the raiders or they will kill her . . . and either way, her enemies will win. . . .

In Enemy Hands

After being ambushed, Honor finds herself aboard an enemy cruiser, bound for her scheduled execution. But one lesson Honor has never learned is how to give up!

Echoes of Honor

"Brilliant! Brilliant! Brilliant!"—*Anne McCaffrey*

Ashes of Victory

Honor has escaped from the prison planet called Hell and returned to the Manticoran Alliance, to the heart of a furnace of new weapons, new strategies, new tactics, spies, diplomacy, and assassination.

continued ☞

TIME SCOUTS CAN DO

the early part of the 21st century disaster struck—an experiment went wrong, bad wrong. The Accident almost destroyed the universe, and ripples in time washed over the Earth. Soon, the people of the depopulated post-disaster Earth learned that things were going to be a little different.... They'd be able to travel into the past, utilizing remnant time strings. It took brave pioneers to map the time gates: you can zap yourself out of existence with a careless jump, to say nothing of getting killed by some rowdy downtimer who doesn't like people who can't speak his language. So elaborate rules are evolved and Time Travel stations become big business.

But wild and wooly pioneers aren't the most likely people to follow rules... Which makes for great adventures as Time Scouts Kit Carson, Skeeter Jackson, and Margo Carson explore Jack the Ripper's London, the Wild West of the '49 Gold Rush, Edo Japan, the Roman Empire and more.

The Time Scout series
by Robert Asprin & Linda Evans

Time Scout	87698-8	$5.99	___
Wagers of Sin	87730-5	$5.99	___
Ripping Time	57867-7	$6.99	___
The House that Jack Built	31965-5	$6.99	___

PRAISE FOR
LOIS McMASTER BUJOLD

What the critics say:

The Warrior's Apprentice: "Now here's a fun romp through the spaceways—not so much a space opera as space ballet.... it has all the 'right stuff.' A lot of thought and thoughtfulness stand behind the all-too-human characters. Enjoy this one, and look forward to the next."   —Dean Lambe, *SF Reviews*

"The pace is breathless, the characterization thoughtful and emotionally powerful, and the author's narrative technique and command of language compelling. Highly recommended."
—Booklist

Brothers in Arms: " ...she gives it a genuine depth of character, while reveling in the wild turnings of her tale.... Bujold is as audacious as her favorite hero, and as brilliantly (if sneakily) successful."   *—Locus*

"Miles Vorkosigan is such a great character that I'll read anything Lois wants to write about him.... a book to re-read on cold rainy days." —Robert Coulson, *Comic Buyer's Guide*

Borders of Infinity: "Bujold's series hero Miles Vorkosigan may be a lord by birth and an admiral by rank, but a bone disease that has left him hobbled and in frequent pain has sensitized him to the suffering of outcasts in his very hierarchical era.... Playing off Miles's reserve and cleverness, Bujold draws outrageous and outlandish foils to color her high-minded adventures."   *—Publishers Weekly*

Falling Free: "In *Falling Free* Lois McMaster Bujold has written her fourth straight superb novel.... How to break down a talent like Bujold's into analyzable components? Best not to try. Best to say: 'Read, or you will be missing something extraordinary.' "   —Roland Green, *Chicago Sun-Times*

The Vor Game: "The chronicles of Miles Vorkosigan are far too witty to be literary junk food, but they rouse the kind of craving that makes popcorn magically vanish during a double feature."
—Faren Miller, *Locus*

MORE PRAISE FOR
LOIS McMASTER BUJOLD

What the readers say:

"My copy of *Shards of Honor* is falling apart I've reread it so often. . . . I'll read whatever you write. You've certainly proved yourself a grand storyteller."
—Lisa Kolbe, Colorado Springs, CO

"I experience the stories of Miles Vorkosigan as almost viscerally uplifting. . . . But certainly, even the weightiest theme would have less impact than a cinder on snow were it not for a rousing good story, and good story-telling with it. This is the second thing I want to thank you for. . . . I suppose if you boiled down all I've said to its simplest expression, it would be that I immensely enjoy and admire your work. I submit that, as literature, your work raises the overall level of the science fiction genre, and spiritually, your work cannot avoid positively influencing all who read it."
—Glen Stonebraker, Gaithersburg, MD

" 'The Mountains of Mourning' [in *Borders of Infinity*] was one of the best-crafted, and simply best, works I'd ever read. When I finished it, I immediately turned back to the beginning and read it again, and I can't remember the last time I did that."
—Betsy Bizot, Lisle, IL

"I can only hope that you will continue to write, so that I can continue to read (and of course buy) your books, for they make me laugh and cry and think . . . rare indeed."
—Steven Knott, Major, USAF

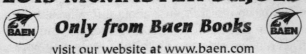